AF424944

The Northern Roseaarde Series, Book 1:

NEFARIOUS GIFT

R.E. Holding

NEFARIOUS GIFT
Book 1 of the Northern Roseaarde Series
Copyright © 2024 by R.E. Holding.

All rights reserved.

No portion of this book may be reproduced in any form without written permission from the publisher or author, except as permitted by U.S. copyright law.

This book is a work of fiction. Names, characters, businesses, organizations, places, events and incidents either are the product of the author's imagination or are used fictitiously. Any resemblance to actual persons, living or dead, events, or locales is entirely coincidental.

Certified Created not Generated © – all text was created by a real person with images crafted using licensed stock images and real art, with no use of artificial intelligence (AI).

For information contact:
https://www.cliffcavebooks.com

Edited by Sara Kelly
Cover art by Mighty Pejes Studio
Interior design and propaganda pages by R.E. Holding
Cover format by R.E. Holding
Map design using Inkarnate by R.E. Holding
Previous Title: Reaper's Gamble

ISBN (paperback): 978-1-963125-33-7
First Edition (under new title): January 2026
10 9 8 7 6 5 4 3 2 1

Contents

PART 3

EXTRAS

Other books by R.E. Holding:

Metaxysm
Hillbilly Vamp
Nefarious Gift
Despicable Boon
Existential Pest
Subcutaneous (coming 2026)

SIGN UP FOR THE NEWSLETTER by visiting https://www.reholdingauthor.com or scan the QRC below:

INDEX

Read as a reference to the main text - reading ahead may contain spoilers.

Anglia: a race of people marked by their paper-white skin and hair. Eyes are typically light-colored and can even manifest as pink or red.

Arts: a non-Guild sub-faction career path that includes crafters of all kinds, entertainers, guides, storytellers, and musicians.

Ascendia: the Engineering capital of Roseaarde. It lies in a cluster with the other seven cities on the western bank of the North continent.

Audioxine: an illicit street drug, claimed to be crafted by the Yeunish and circulated to the youth.

Audun: the capitol city of Roseaarde. Officials control the activities of the northern continent and the southern morass.

Beast Tamer: an enhanced version of a Shepherd, only present in the Yeunish.

Black eneris (obsenis forturum): life essence that comes from a failed pull. It can be used as ink or if corrupted, can become toxic.

Blood fish: Carnivorous fish that generally live in deeper parts of the sea.

Blue eneris (lapis piscus): the life essence that is pulled from aquatic creatures.

Breach: the festering rot at a root of Great Tree sealed shut by Maron Valoa'brenga.

Cap 1 and Cap 2: periods of time marking the beginning and end of each year.

Celerity: the Reader capital of Roseaarde. It lies in a cluster with the other seven cities on the western bank of the North continent.

Chitter Birds: Small, quick and dark colored birds that can swarm. They are known for being early risers and waking citizens in the desert with their calls.

Chromatis hominum: a special kind of essence pulled from a Weggevens skin walker midway between human and animal.

Cirv'e: the beast of the breach and tormentor.

Corl: small fishing town south of Kanckette on the coast where the border blends with the southern continent. The town is widely ignored by Audun, and its residents live off the land rather than ration blocks.

Danashi: a race of people marked by their dark skin and hair. They can have any color eyes, including hazel and dark brown.

Desert Maelstrom: the annual energy storm that occurs in the middle of the span that begins around day 140 (middle of period X) and ends around day 180 (beginning of Split 2).

Deygo Lilac: Multicolored flowers that bloom just before the maelstrom. Pleasant scent.

Draught: also known as a "pot," these are solutions crafted by Formulators.

E-disk: a communication device popular with the citizens of Roseaarde. Its functions vary from making calls to sending QuickChats, watching holofilms, and performing daily tasks, such as depositing plats.

Elementalist: a new type of Weggevens that manifests as the controlling of elements. Ayala is a fire-based elementalist and Quint is an ice-based elementalist. The power is strong and capable of rapidly draining the host if used for a prolonged period.

Eletonk: a species of large land mammal typically residing in the desert.

Eneris: the essence of life pulled from recently deceased (or living) organisms.

Engineer: a Guild member who can sense the potential of materials to craft technology.

Flash ink: a type of tech text meant to disappear once the intended reader takes in the message.

Formulator: a Guild member who can sense the potential of eneris and other formulations to craft draughts.

Foscan: a race of people marked by their grayish-tan skin, black hair, and white eyes. Foscans were accused of rebelling against Audun hundreds of years ago and have been forced to serve as slaves for various households and businesses.

Giltberries: A special gold-colored berry that's been extinct for ages.

Gold eneris (auris hominum): a special essence that comes from a Reaper who pulls their own. Extremely rare and widely not practiced.

Great Tree: an ancient tree that used to grow at the northeast tip of the North continent. It has since burned to ash.

Green eneris (verdigris plantum): the life essence that is pulled from plant material.

G-scan: a tech device that uses a touch of blood along with a fingerprint to determine genetic markers, as well as any hidden Guild talent. Eloria was subject to a G-scan when receiving her diagnosis, and Lor was given a G-scan when confirming his Yeunish identity (not explicitly stated in the text).

Guild (see Engineer, Formulator, Reader, Reaper, Shepherd): a special title given to individuals who attend the Heart Island program and leave with a special ability.

Guild Central: the Eastern branch of the Seven Cities, commonly abbreviated GC. Working at GC means living in the apartment halls, with all expenses paid. Working hours are, however, long.

Haerow: a small coastal area known to draw individuals seeking private, and oftentiems salacious vacations.

Hanso Fruit: A type of island fruit with a sweet smell and bitter flavor. The residents of Heart Island are fond of the aroma, and it is ever present at the resort.

Holoconfetti: a special virtual confetti used in celebrations to reduce litter.

Holofilm: a type of entertainment loved by everyone, starring non-Guild members of the Art faction of storytelling.

Holopic: an image viewable in 270 degrees.

Howie Rod: a popular construction piece meant for sturdy buildings. Made of metal.

Igni: an extinct race of people who were former guardians of the Great Tree.

Ivory Saltpeter: a white eneris-based formulation invented by Jack that acts as a mild poison and potential explosive, depending on use. Dill shoots Hammer with Ivory Saltpeter to weaken his strongman ability.

Jaune Spirit: a yellow phial invented by Jack that gives the user an intense burst of energy. Dill used the phial in the cavern tussle.

Jumper: a type of on and off-roading vehicle with large spherical tires that can rotate in all directions. Popular choice as a taxi vehicle.

Kanckette (a.k.a "tent city"): the only city in the desert zone known as the Span.

Kanckette is the last train stop, as the Desert Maelstrom always destroyed any further travel east. A band of people live under the tracks in a series of tents, usually collecting any discarded items from the station above to use.

Lapis Evening: a Yeunish sleep aid draught invented by Jack. Used by the team to keep Hare sedated.

Last Grudge: an offensive phial invented by Jack and using Fowler's chromatis, tossing the formulation creates a multi-colored windstorm intense enough to cut like razors. Anything caught in its path is obliterated. Crow was a victim of the draught.

Law: a non-Guild sub-faction career path that includes roundsmen, judges, officials, and barristers.

Leaper: a small amphibious creature inhabiting the Southern Morass. Not edible.

Medicine: a non-Guild sub-faction career path that includes medics, observers, apothecarians, and advisers. Mesaman: a race of people marked by their tanned and ruddy complexions. The most diverse race, their hair can range from light to dark, with eyes typically light and no darker than hazel.

Milaris: the Formulator capital of Roseaarde. It lies in a cluster with the other seven cities on the western bank of the North continent.

Mount Gehenna: the towering mountain on the northeastern tip of the North continent. It is known for its black sands and constant guard.

Nazagora: Dark alien creatures that inhabit the span. Predatory, but edible with body parts that grow back. Amphibious.

Newslite: an old-fashioned news delivery format requiring a subscription.

Non-Guild (see Arts, Law, Medicine): any profession that doesn't fall into the Seven Cities' definition of prestige.

Noxeine (a.k.a. "Klik"): a recreational substance mostly used by teens for a numbing high. Hare claimed his childhood crush, Tilly, traded sexual favors for the drug.

Oatcress: a ration block consisting of oats and protein.

Obsidia: the Reaper capital of Roseaarde. It lies in a cluster with the other seven cities on the western bank of the North continent.

Orange eneris (naranis corpum): the life essence that is pulled from a specific species of fruit.

Pandemonia: the Weggevens capital of Roseaarde. It lies in a cluster with the other seven cities on the western bank of the North continent.

Patch: crafted from ancient tech and a silver alternative, the patch is a device surgically attached to a Weggevens to prevent the drain. Invented by Verena and using Jack's alternative silver, the patch is proprietary and not shared with the Seven Cities.

Pau'tan virus: a type of infection that became a pandemic in Lor's early years, and took many lives. The cities now have a cure.

Peakwood: a mid-sized city just outside the peninsula of the Seven Cities. Lor's hometown.

Phial: a specialized glass vessel used to collect eneris for Reapers or to store draughts for Formulators.

Phillo bloom: a pink bloom in tropical areas with a light perfumy aroma that goes well with the scent of hanso. Flowers are not edible.

Plat: the system of cash, with the symbol of pL.

Pohay'an: a small tourist location north of the Seven Cities and nestled in the mountains. Location of the famous ivory forests and hot springs, and home to Val when not serving in the program.

Puck: a species of fish.

Purple eneris (purpuris porum): the life essence that is pulled from any purple-colored plant.

QuickChat: a message sent to another user via e-disk.

Reader: a Guild member who has the ability to read minds. Skilled members can even push ideas and thoughts. Gaining the ability naturally isn't as common as a Shepherd spending plat to earn special training.

Reaper: a Guild member with the ability to pull life force (eneris) from any recently deceased (or living) thing. Other abilities granted to a Reaper have been shrouded in mystery.

Reaper's gold: the gold eneris within a Reaper, extractable only by self, or by tough metal gloves employed by the cities made with enhanced tech.

Red eneris (roujis emporum): the life essence that is pulled from land creatures.

Red Mash: an offensive phial invented by Jack that absorbs through the skin and erodes in a series of large blisters. Used to attack Hammer in the cavern.

Roseaarde: the world.

Runner: a type of Weggevens ability that grants super speed to the user.

Sarga Fruit: a type of yellow fruit that is sometimes sent in rations. They're juicy, fitting in the palm of the hand, and are a favorite of Lor's.

Saxeroot: a root vegetable, blue in color, that's been thought to be extinct for centuries.

Second sun: a purple-colored sun that rises at the 24th hour and lasts a standard hour.

Seven Cities (see Ascendia, Audun, Celerity, Milaris, Obsidia, Pandemonia, and Wild Crag): the cluster of cities on the western bank of the Northern continent that serve as governmental rule for Roseaarde, consisting of representatives for each Guild house.

Shepherd: a Guild member with the ability to communicate with animals.

Silver eneris (argenis hominum): a special type of essence that comes from humans.

Skin walker, or skin changer: a type of Weggevens ability that grants the ability to transform into an animal to the user.

Southern Morass: a second continent loosely attached to the North by stretches of sand banks. The morass is a bog-like zone where the cities banish the Yeunish to die.

Span: the entire middle section of the Northern continent, covered in desert and mostly uninhabitable except for the city of Kanckette. Several encampments litter the sand underneath the trains, and the vast poverty of the zone has bred brigands.

Split 1 and Split 2: the periods of time in the middle sections of the year.

Storyteller: a non-Guild profession in Entertainment. Someone who acts in holofilms.

Strongman: a type of Weggevens ability that grants inhuman strength to the user.

Trega's Sky: a city on the West coast, just north of Peakwood, where most holofilms are made. A very affluent city.

Two-mind: a type of Weggevens ability that involves the attachment of another "mind" to the user. Known to possess secrets of the dead. Highly deadly affliction.

Valoan (see void brothers): a cult group of members who forsake bonding with the Maker in favor of worshipping the breach.

Vegemeal: a ration block consisting of a variety of vegetable and fruit matter compressed together.

Verdigris Biosore: a deadly phial that can degrade the flesh rapidly. Its intensity depends on the strength or weakness of its victim. Pigeon was killed with a needle of biosore, and Hare was threatened with it.

Verdigris Mend: a potent and almost instant healing draught invented by Jack, that uses a small drop of Reaper's gold to formulate. Used to mend Verena after her attack, Gale after his attack, Hare after getting punched, and Lor after being shot by Crow.

V-Note: a touch sensitive tablet that is widely used as a job-related recording system. Lor uses a V-Note to capture his visions when reaping, and medics use V-notes to record patient data.

Void brothers (see Valoan): a cult group of members who forsake bonding with the Maker in favor of worshipping the breach.

Volatile: a new type of Weggevens with random and serious outcomes. Each one has a unique second personality that can come out in violent ways, often resulting in the death of the host.

Waterbird: a species of bird that congregates around larger bodies of water.

Weggevens (see runner, strongman, skin walker/changer, two-mind, volatile, elementalist): a Guild member with an unpredictable outcome. Whatever the outcome, the ability is volatile and has consequences for the user.

White eneris (witis volatus): the life essence that is pulled from air creatures.

Witis Rejuvenate: an important drug invented by Jack to help treat a Weggevens suffering from life drain.

Wild Crag: the Shepherd capital of Roseaarde. It lies in a cluster with the other seven cities on the western bank of the North continent.

X: the period of time in the middle of the year, marking the beginning of the Desert Maelstrom.

Yeuni / Yeunish: a race of people born by the Anglia and Foscan. Their kind is hunted and banished to the southern morass for reasons lost to history.

Climate and standard annum

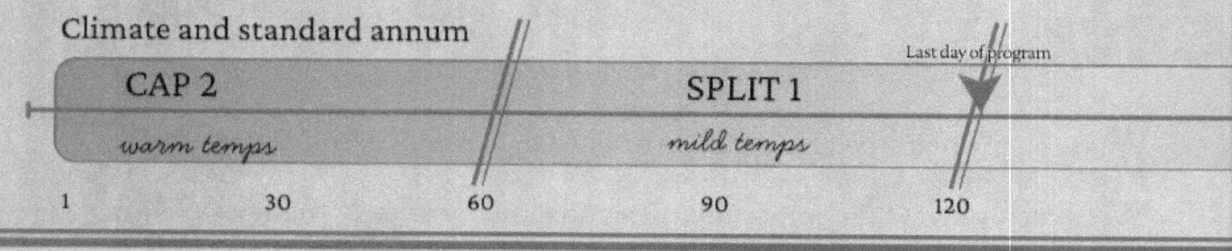

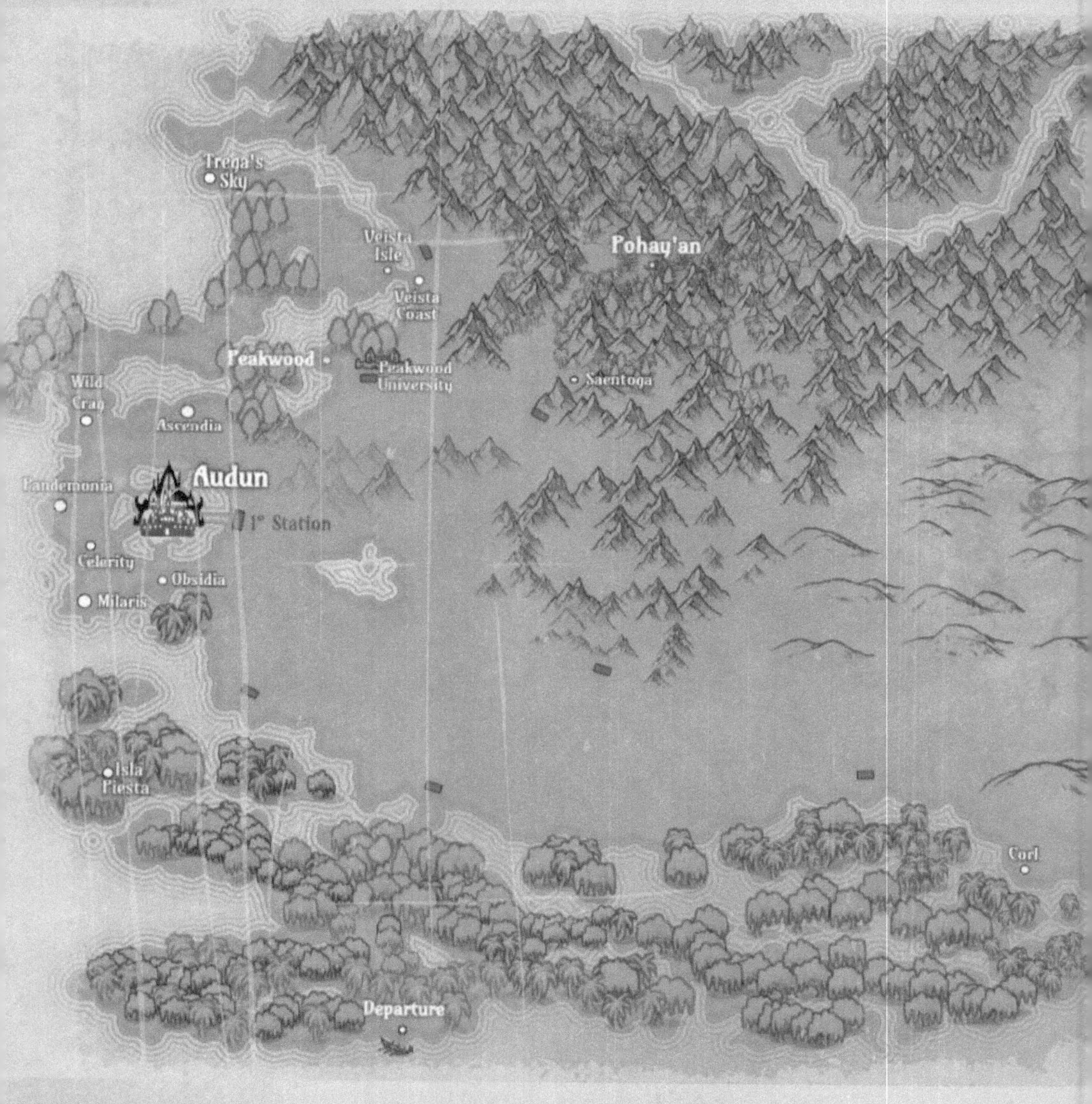

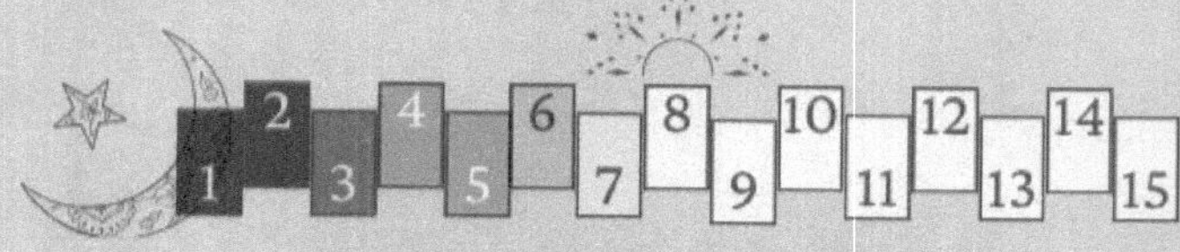

Daily sun rise & sun set

ONE DAY, 30 HOURS:
1st sun rise: 08:00
2nd sun rise: 24:00
Evening: 26:00-07:30

First day of program
X
desert maelstrom
SPLIT 2
CAP 1
cold temps
mild temps
warm temps
150
180
210
240
270
300
Moentaegar
Mt. Gehenna
Guild Central
Heart Island
Sevas
Kanckette
Final Station
16
17
18
19
20
21
22
23
24
25
26
27
28
29
30
N
W
E
S

PART 1

Prologue

Waves of desert heat pulsed over Loren's skin, but all he felt was cold. He strained to sense his surroundings, seeing wave after wave of yellow dust blowing over the dunes. A grinding static muffled his eardrums, drowning out the screams of his friend.

None of his books had ever taught him this. No book ever told him what it was like to die.

Chapter 1

Lor and His Dad
LOREN

"LOREN B. TURTINGAS! GET UP here, now!" Gale's voice found its way through the thick basement door, jumping down the steps two at a time and rolling into Lor's dreamy ears. He yawned and turned on a small techlight perched on his nightstand. Its white light painted the crude and splintered wooden surface.

A thick and dusty manual titled *Guide for the Non-Guild Faction of Law: Roundsmen* sat like a boring brick on the nightstand. Pages poked out from the sides as if desperate to escape their own binding, and a stained wet ring encircled the word *Law*.

Next to the book, his fingers flopped over a small black disk the size of his palm, and he drew a series of taps on the slick shell. A holopic of his QuickChat sprayed from the disk and hovered. No messages, no calls, no friends.

"Coming!" he shouted back up the stairs.

He had overslept again. Yawning once more, he swung his legs over the side of his hard mattress, throwing aside a padded woolen comforter inlaid with silver threads—a lavish gift his sister, Eva, had purchased from a Shepherd in Audun.

Loren dragged his feet to the base of the stairs and flipped on the main light. A golden hue bathed the area, transforming his ordinary bedroom into what his stepfather always told him resembled a dingy smoking den. He never agreed with that assessment. To him, it was cozy and quaint. He would never leave if he had a choice.

An oversized dark red chair and three tall bookcases crowded the far corner at the foot of the bed. The bookcases were filled with tomes of all shapes and sizes in a rainbow of colors tinted by the golden cast of the light.

He rummaged through the closet with white socks pulled over his calves and a loose left toe that folded over the tip of his foot. Loren chose a wrinkled, plain black shirt to pull down over his messy hair and a pair of stained tan pants and brown boots scuffed all over the toe. Gale always told him he had a laziness in his walk that he couldn't quite put his finger on, and that was why he wore his boots and socks out too fast.

He slid the black disk in his back pocket and checked the mirror. Light gray eyes set into a ruddy face, and a mess of ash blond hair stared back at him.

"Loren! Get up here!" Gale shouted again, as loud as the first time.

The blond mop on his head flopped over a sweaty brow, which he slicked back with a wet palm. The stairs protested under his boots in squeaks and fits as he lay leaden steps over them. Reluctantly, he made his way upstairs and into reality.

Light slapped his tired eyes when he opened the door leading to the main house. A stark white hall stretched before him toward the kitchen. Digital pictures decorated the walls, which cycled through images of the family, places they'd visited, and his stepfather's medic friends. Only one holopic of Loren and Gale together had been programmed into the cycle of images, and it wouldn't show when he walked through the hall.

The frames blinked and strobed through their cycles, which made him dizzy. He focused on his feet to drive him forward through the hall until he stepped onto the marble tile flecked with gold. A serious, middle-aged man with thick-rimmed glasses sat at a wide island counter with an assortment of many tools lying next to him. They were impeccably vertical, with an occasional tube-based tool wrapped in a spiral and fixed neatly in place. They were all pointing at Loren.

"How many times have I told you not to walk around in the house with your shoes on? Take them off."

"Yes, sir." Loren slid his droopy socks from the boots and shuffled toward Gale, who glanced up at Loren and shook his head.

Their small house servant stood in the corner of the kitchen, watching the pair still as stone. She was a Foscan, eerie and beautiful. Dag the Small, Gale called her, in the tradition of assigning bastard names to Foscan rebels. She was far from any rebel. Lor only knew her as meek and fragile, with ethereal beauty in unblemished pale gray skin, shiny black hair, and those indescribable eyes. Like a typical Foscan, her eyes were white, catching the light at angles that gave them the appearance of an inner glow. He swore he saw those reflections in the darkness of his room at times.

Gale rustled a newslite paper in his fist. His studied gaze peered over the top of the paper at Loren's wrinkled shirt and stained pants. "You look like a slob," he said.

"I need to do laundry," Loren responded, settling into the chair opposite Gale.

A trio of chirps emitted from the black disk sitting near the tools, identical to the one in Loren's pocket. Gale's dark brown eyes continued to study him over the glasses, then he held up a finger.

Yes, of course I'll wait. Lor sighed.

Gale pressed the center of the disk, and a holopic slung out in front of them.

"Go for Gale," he said.

"Hey, Gale, we are going to need you in about two standard hours." The holopic buzzed in a robotic, stilted voice.

"Right. Be there in one and a half."

"Heard. Donnelly out."

Gale pressed the center again, and the disk sucked the holopic into its core. He sighed and set his glasses on the counter, rubbing his face pink.

"Lor," he said, tapping the newslite paper resting on the counter, "have you given any more thought to the program?"

Gale called him by his nickname. Lor knew this game well—it was a manipulation tactic.

"I have," Lor said as he ran his hand across the smooth stone edge, activating the center of the countertop. A pair of sliding doors hissed open, revealing a maw in the middle of the counter, and a tray of the day's rations rose from the center.

Among the bland blocks of oatcress and vegemeal, there was a bowl of yellow sarga fruit, which he snatched the second he saw them. The plump fruit was soft in his hand, and he took a big, wet bite.

Lor smacked his lips. "But what would I do without these fine rations to start each glorious day?"

"Don't talk with your mouth full. And try to conserve those, yeah?"

He plucked a piece of toast from the neat stack sitting next to the bowl of fruit and flicked his hand across the sensor again. The food plinth descended into its refrigerated holding cell as the doors snapped shut.

"I'm serious, Lor. It's important that you at least try to join the program. The next class begins nine months from now, after the Desert Maelstrom, and it's not too late to register."

Lor swallowed the rest of his fruit. He stared at the toast in his hand, debating whether to stuff it in his mouth and delay his answer, but he knew it would be trouble for him. Then it would be back to being called Loren B. Turtingas.

"I-I just really think I'd be better suited in... Law. Sir."

Gale pushed his chair back and gaped at Lor.

"Law? Are you serious? What kind of *Law*?"

This wasn't what he wanted to discuss today. He didn't want to discuss it any day.

"Well, I was reading about roundsmen, and I—"

"Absolutely *not!*" Gale slammed a pencil down on the counter that Lor didn't see him holding. "Do you want to end up like that kid Gregory?"

"He wasn't a kid, Dad. I'm pretty sure he was your age."

"Whatever, he was just a kid when I was a kid." Gale jabbed a thumb at his chest. "My point stands. Do you want to end up like him?"

"No, but roundsmen work is *tricky*, and Gregory messed up, right? I've been researching the role, and I think that—"

"I said *no*."

Lor knew the conversation was over. He swiped the toast and crammed the whole piece in his mouth. Gale pretended Gregory's death didn't bother him, but it did. He rarely talked about the guy, but Lor knew he meant something to him at some point long ago. The name had come up for the first time shortly after his mother died while Lor was still young. He had wandered near the bedroom while Gale talked about the incident with someone over the phone. It was the first time he had seen the shimmer of a tear in his stepfather's eye... and the last.

"Look, Eva is happy in her city and she is thriving. I only want the same for you. You understand that, don't you?"

Dry toast seized his tongue, and he wriggled his jaw to position the partially soggy ball under his teeth. The wad of bread finally broke down enough to swallow a piece without choking.

"I guess so."

"Besides, if you don't develop a gift, you can still be a part of one of the many *other* non-Guild memberships out there."

"You mean like Law?"

"Stop it."

"Isn't it expensive? I don't want to fail and waste plats."

"Don't worry about plats."

Lor stared just beyond Gale's shoulder through the window. The Audun capitol tower stood in the far distance, barely visible against the clear horizon—such an innocent-looking thing to serve as the puppet master of all seven cities.

"I don't want to fail."

"You won't fail."

"Like you did?" He shouldn't have said that.

Why did I say that?

Gale glared at him. His mouth zipped up so tight he could crush a hunk of rock between those lips and pull out a diamond. He straightened his collar and ran a hand over the side of his balding head, blowing a puff of air from that tight mouth making an angry whistle.

"I didn't mean that," Lor said, tucking his hands in his lap. The words may as well have been a middle finger.

Dag the Small watched them while in her corner, waiting for the tea kettle in Gale's head to explode. He scared her. He always scared her. She shifted her weight, moving for the first time since Lor arrived in the kitchen.

Gale rose slowly, backing out from the counter and pushing his chair snugly against the stone.

"You had better watch your tone, Loren."

"S-Sorry, sir. I was just trying to tell you that I'm afraid to fail."

"Doesn't matter now." Gale clicked his tongue. "I'm signing you up for the program, so you find a way to deal with that and swallow your pride."

Lor's heart sank. Three words were all it took to course-correct his future. *Like you did? What were you thinking?*

"I have to go, they need me. Figure it out, Loren."

With a final huff, Gale stormed past the servant, who flinched when he left the kitchen. Lor noticed her watching him with her eerie white gaze.

"Stop it," he said.

Nine months to figure it out.

Lor slid down the stairs to his bedroom and plopped on his red reading chair. The passage of time between that moment and leaving for Heart Island would be an unmeasurable drag. He prayed for the Desert Maelstrom to blow away the island and take the program with it. He knew very little about the school and had no desire to find his "gift." It all seemed a little *woo-woo* to him, with all the channeling and meditations. There was also rumor of a commune cult on the same island.

One thing he knew for sure was that the program was not far from the black sands of Mount Gehenna. Eva's first letters to him while she was in the program obsessed over her fear of the mountain. Eventually, she stopped writing about that and focused on how misunderstood the area was. Her language morphed into an aloofness that gave Lor even more pause about the brainwashing program.

He leaned over to study the books on his shelf, searching for anything that might give him insight on what he was getting into.

Cycles and Tradition, Roundsmen Duties
Unusual Flora and Fauna of Northern Continent
The History of Guild Abilities: Formative Years, Tome 1

> *How to Relate to Others and Maintain Relationships*
> *Medical Marvels and the Salvation Behind Them*
> *Well-Rounded Rations and the Kurb Diet: What They Don't Tell You.*

Lor sighed. At least nothing on *this* small shelf was of any use.

The one thing that baked his mind was the sheer cost of the program, with no guarantee of success. The price of prestige was steep, and he didn't want it.

Why stick it near Mount Gehenna?

Why would Gale want to spend plats to put me through a program that might fail us both?

Eva was lucky to find a home with the Engineers in Ascendia. Gale was so proud of her when she discovered her gift, as it brought more social credit to the household. Lor always found it odd that something like Guild work was praised higher than what Gale did, which was saving lives as a medic.

Lor slumped back in the chair, pulling *Cycles and Tradition, Roundsman Duties* from the bookshelf. He flipped through the musty pages to a dog-eared corner that marked a chapter on dress. Law had his heart, and it was free to learn at Peakwood Academy just down the road. He could live at home, save money, and learn what he wanted, *when* he wanted.

He tried to remember his conversation with Eva when she came back from the program. She had an implant, and that didn't sit well with him.

Eva showed him the lump under her skin. "It's how they unlock your gift."

"It's kinda big." He poked it, watching it slither around under her skin.

"Yeah, it hurt at first, but I don't feel it anymore. They do it right on your second day, so you have plenty of time to heal."

"How long does it take for you to find out?"

"Find out what?"

"You know... whether you belong to a Guild?"

"Oh, it depends on the person. It took me about a month, which the guide said was on the longer side."

"Well, what do you do for the other five months that you are there if a month is a long time?"

"That is when we practice using our gift. Trust me, it takes some getting used to." She smiled at that, a wistful look in her eye she didn't explain further. Lor didn't ask—he didn't care.

It wasn't long after that she got the call from Ascendia with an offer from the Seven Cities. Her acceptance marked the moment her shadow cast long and dark over Lor.

CHAPTER 2

Silver and Secrets
LOREN

A SWEET AROMA HUNG IN THE air. Powdered black sand mixed with natural grains spilled into the cavern through a small crack in the wall. Blue luminescence coated the walls and the vegetation all around. A singularity of mustard-colored brightness poked through a subtle crack in the ceiling. The room softly quaked, allowing natural sand to slip in through the wall crack, making a translucent veil that hissed to the ground.

"Were you followed?" A coarse man in a long yellow duster with gray scruff and scarlet-brown eyes glared at the hooded figure strolling into the cavern. The figure swiped at the cloak's fabric, flicking sand from the fibers.

"No, I've got Book with me."

Another figure covering their head with their cloak moved from behind, taking a seat on one of the many rocks littered throughout the blue cave. She sat between an older woman in a linen duster and a jittery younger man.

The cavern shook again, more sand pouring through the crack.

"How much time do we have?" The boorish man flicked open a small, tear-shaped black device.

"Not long. The storm will end soon."

"Let's get on with it then." He motioned for the figure to sit.

"I'll stand," the figure said.

"Suit yourself."

"Is everyone here?"

"Just waitin' on you, luv." Another burly man came from the shadows, glinting black modifier tech from between his teeth.

"Very good, Crow," the figure said, flicking off the hood to reveal long hair underneath and a pair of ruby dust goggles over her face.

"The time is almost here, beloved," she addressed the group.

A low murmur spread through the cavern, echoing deep into the cold void. She peered upward to look for stray tawny bats. She was not in the mood to deal with the little bloodsuckers.

"Pigeon, what do we know so far?" she asked the woman.

The older woman with the linen duster leaned heavily to the left—a crooked back cursed by age but exacerbated by a kick to the side from an ornery cud-chewer as a child.

Pigeon made silent hand motions, parting her lips and wagging her tongue in the gap of the ghost of her front teeth. She made wet clicking noises while attempting to push words out of a broken mouth.

"She says ther's room for th' Locksmith," Crow translated Pigeon's silent language.

"Excellent. What about you, Crow? Are you prepared?"

"Aye, 'smith. Got a new gadge just waitin' to use. It's a snipin' splitter." The hairy man grinned with his mouthful of black teeth. He held out a tube with dials and buttons. Crow was not shy with his gift, replacing a new body part with increasing intensity. No one in the group could imagine a man of his size squeezing from Pigeon's womb.

"Can't wait," Locksmith said sarcastically, "try not to overdo it this time."

The Crow sniggered. "No such thing as too much'a good thing, luv."

"Where's Hare?" she asked.

"Here, here, I'm here." The attractive but jittery younger man sat up from the rock next to the girl called Book. "Don't squeeze me just yet."

"What makes you think I'd do that?" she asked.

He shrugged.

"Do you need a kick?"

"I'm good, I'm good. Cricket keeps me stocked. I can run wherever."

He plunked back down on the rock, shaking a leg. His shoulders twitched, and he scratched at his neck. Wild, curly hair crowned his head, permanently dusted yellow by sand. Blue goggles propped above his brow, framing a ruddy face with permanent tan lines encircling his eyes.

"Are you sure you're okay? You seem... twitchy," she said.

"Yeah, yeah, I'm good, don't worry about me."

"Okay then... Book?" She strolled to the girl she came in with.

"Yes, ma'am. How can I help?" A small, stout girl peered up at the Locksmith through thick-lensed glasses that amplified her eyes.

"My little prodigy. There's a chance I might need access. Can you do that?"

"I think so." Book's eyes flicked to a man sitting on the ground, then back at the Locksmith. "It might be hard if there are more than one at a time."

"Don't worry, I'll make sure of that."

"Thanks, ma'am."

Locksmith paced in front of the crew, shooting the occasional glare at the man sitting on the ground.

"It won't be long, everyone. My match is close, and we'll be able to peel that slime from the breach very soon. But it will have to be in a year's time."

The cavern groaned a discordant vibration upward, rousing a few tawny bats. They squeaked but stayed put.

"Quiet. You knew what this was."

"How do you know your match will even agree to the plan? Some punk kid won't even know their ass from the breach."

"Don't push it, Hammer."

Hammer raised hands in surrender.

"Hey, *Locksmith*." A spindly tall man stepped from the shadows, sidling up to Hare. "I don't know if these concoctions will stay fresh that long."

The man's spider-like fingers tapped the sides of skinny legs. He wore a white cloak with jaundiced patches of sand dust staining the surface and mingled with other colorful filth.

"Make more, Cricket," she said.

The slender man studied her under black goggles. A long, pale face and dark curtain of hair framed his cheeks. He pursed his small mouth.

"Do you have any idea what it takes to make some of these pots?" he said.

Locksmith pondered his dilemma, tapping her lip with a forefinger. "Okay. I can get your silver. Just let me figure that out."

Locksmith had found Cricket years ago, orphaned in a track camp under the Span. He was a child then—living in squalor under the trains carrying unwary passengers to and from the capitol. Someone loved him once. They loved him enough to give him a name. *I'm just Cricket*, he told her when they met. His face was just as pale and angular then, with slight fat from youth and a pair of black goggles, squeezed firmly against his eyes. *And why do they call you that?* She bent down to his level, and he shrugged. *Because I'm lucky!*

Ever since, he had been almost a son to her. Even now, with the cruelty of adulthood, her affection for him was a disease in her veins. She couldn't help but crack a smile at her boy. Her disturbing spider boy.

He bobbed his head, moving with an uncanny fluidity that could prickle the hair on the neck. He slinked back into the shadow, disappearing into its depths.

Locksmith peered back down at the man sitting cross-legged in the sand—the same man that Book had peered at earlier. The others followed her gaze, staring down at him as well. He wore a brown duster with an ornate glittering clasp at the chest. His goggles parked on top of his head with a fancy chromatic hue. His attention was on the ground, poking at glowing blue algae. Unaware of the attention, she finally cleared her throat.

"*Bat,*" she said.

His name echoed through the cavern, and he jolted upright, brushing the folds from his cloak.

"Y-yes, ma'am. H-how can I help?"

"That's quite an accessory you have there. And those goggles? Where are they from? Audun?"

"I, u-uh, I don't r-remember, ma'am."

She paced thoughtfully in front of him, not taking her eyes from his face.

"Very interesting. You see, I don't seem to remember you owning such delightful items at the start of our relationship."

"They a-ah were a g-gift, ma'am. Y-yes, a gift." His hands shook in his lap.

"A gift? From whom? Surely not from anyone here." She motioned to the group.

"A-ah, u-uhm." His eyes darted around the room.

"Are you aware, my fine friend, that your intel on the Island was in fact, *misleading?*" She drew out the last word.

"W-what do you m-mean by that, ma'am? I d-did what you asked with the man."

"Oh, Bat, Bat, Bat... you didn't follow instructions, and went to the wrong target. A Weggevens two-mind at that."

He gulped, sitting up straight and scooting back.

"I-I'm sorry, I didn't know."

"Yes, see, that's the rub, isn't it? You probably *would* have known if you hadn't been working behind our backs to line your own pockets. Wouldn't you agree?"

"I, well, I don't know what you mean, ma'am."

She paced through the sand, tipping a graceful toe one after the other as her cloak trailed behind her. She moved to an unheard beat inside her head, swishing her arms back and forth before her. She moved with the breeze, bobbing and swaying with graceful fluid movements. Hammer stood upright, watching her with renewed interest.

As a young child, she had suffered disappointment at the hands of her parents. Her former match abandoned her. Her mentor failed to explain the depths to which she could travel with her ability. So she stole his gold and fled as a wanderer until years passed and no one knew her name. She used the dance to recharge her soul.

She turned an ear to the depths of the cavern, cupping a hand around it. The tiniest squeak came from the darkness.

"Do you know what I think?" she said with all the calmness of an activated bomb.

"W-what's that, ma'am?" His eyes were rounded and wet.

More squeaks echoed in the depths.

"I think we have enough bats in this cave."

Bat opened his mouth to speak, but Locksmith leapt at him with a dancer's grace. He desperately clawed at the ground to back away, but he was no match. She grabbed the bare flesh of his arm, freezing him in place. He let out a staccato chirp, much like the animals clinging to the ceiling.

His left eye rolled upward to the back of his skull, and the whites glistened pale yellow. The other light hazel eye, flecked with bits of brown and beautiful any other day, glazed over and cracked. They sank into their sockets, giving rise to a shimmering liquid pool.

The room quaked as more sand poured inside. She ground her teeth, rage coloring her cheeks to a pink flush.

The violence excited Hammer. He panted at it, igniting his own anger. He lusted for her with a smile on his lips, cracking thick knuckles that popped to the beat of Bat's body breaking in her clutches.

She pulled her hand away from his arm, seeing a wash of the same shimmering liquid from his eye sockets smeared over his skin and collected in her hand.

She snatched an empty canteen from her hip, cupping her hand over the opening and funneling the fluid into it. She returned for seconds and thirds as Bat's body morphed into a dried husk, folding in on itself.

The glittering clasp holding his cloak thunked into the blue algae. Bat's head caved in, loosening the chromatic goggles over a pruned head. They tipped over his flattened nose, and the strap fell into a cracked open mouth, silently screaming into the void.

Crow bent over to pick up the fancy clasp and handed it to Pigeon. She accepted the gift with wrinkled fingers and pinned it to her duster. Her smile showcased the hollow gap at her son.

Hare stole the chromatic goggles and laughed. Hammer swiped at his collar, staring at Locksmith red-faced and hot.

Satisfied with the pull, Locksmith whipped her head back, wiping a slick of sweat from her brow as she took in several shallow breaths. Strands of hair clung to the sides of her pink cheeks. She corked the canteen and wagged it toward the group. Thick liquid sloshed up the sides. While gripping the neck, she pointed it toward Cricket.

"Hey, Cricket. Here's your silver."

The man crawled from the shadows and approached her. She shoved the canteen in Cricket's hands.

"Everyone get out! Except you, Hammer. Take care of me right *now*." She panted.

"Yes, ma'am!" He breathed heavily, throwing off his cloak.

CHAPTER 3

Traveling with Animals
LOREN

TODAY WAS THE DAY.

The Desert Maelstrom died down, and the program awaited Lor's tuition money.

"I'm not going to repeat myself, Loren. Get your bags and hurry up—our tickets have us departing in a standard hour!" Gale's voice carried down to the basement bedroom like always.

It was a shame he couldn't bring any of his books.

Lor took in the golden room resembling a smoking den. He had six months in the program to either succeed or fail. Failure was his desired outcome. That way, he could pursue what he actually wanted to do. He would deal with the guilt of wasted plats another day.

The woolen blanket from Eva hung at the corner of his bed and glistened at the silver filigree. Something so simple as a covering like this one probably cost a small fortune. If he didn't fail, he could at least look forward to earning a decent income as a Guilder.

He would miss that blanket. He thought maybe he could write to her too while he was away... but then he remembered he never took down her address.

Taking one last look at his cozy den, he sighed and slogged up the stairs to the white hallway covered in flashing picture frames. Any other time he would zero in on the floor and race through the hall to avoid the strobing effect, but today he procrastinated. Strolling through, he tried to catch some of the images. Gale with his med partner, Eva with her diploma, his mother with them at the beach... so many random photos flashed in succession. One particular frame grabbed his attention.

It was a simple black frame, but the pictures inside were of his childhood. An image of him and Eva at the park cycled to one of him sitting in Gale's lap. His stepfather was happier then, with a full head of hair and handsome features showing teeth in a wide grin. Before he got a good look at happier times with him, the image flashed over to one Lor never remembered seeing before.

It was him as a newborn in the lap of Dag the Small. A smile painted her face, giving her already stunning features a touch of magic. She gazed down at him in her lap, and he to her with the bottle propped between soft gums. The image hit him weird. He didn't realize she had been a part of the family since he was born. The picture suggested she'd been there even before, and the fact he had never seen this picture baffled him. He leaned in for a closer look, when the image melted into one of his mother holding hands with a young Eva at some park in Etherton.

"Loren?" Gale called out.

Lor jumped at the noise, grabbing his duffel and noticing he was wearing his shoes. Gale would kill him if he didn't take them off. Slipping out of them, he then hooked two fingers at the heel to carry them the rest of the way to the front door.

Gale stood at the door, arms folded tight across his chest with a deep scowl etched into his face. Seeing him like that was a jarring contrast to the images on the wall. Lor shuffled through the entryway, glancing at a dark corner to see Dag's shimmering eyes in the shadow. She traced him with those white eyes as he drifted past.

After seeing that photo, he couldn't help but run through memories of her in their home. As long as he knew her, she never smiled or spoke. What changed between then and now?

Gale windmilled his arm to beckon Lor forward faster. He slipped over the tile in socks, nearly twisting an ankle. The duffel slapped his leg as he ran, rocking his balance from the weight inside.

"About time," Gale said, stretching an arm outside for Lor to follow.

Lor stepped outside to slip his shoes back on and waited for Gale to lock up.

"We're taking a jumper to the station," Gale said, grabbing the duffel from Lor and hoisting it over a shoulder. Lor followed without a word.

Jumpers were a standard feature in the cities, but Lor had never been on the train, and that's what made him nervous. Most Guild members used the train to travel between the seven cities in a loop around and through Audun. Others rode it to the east side of the continent for business.

Lor took the long walk to the end of the street, when their jumper squealed around the corner. A fat spherical front tire screeched to a halt in front of them. In the driver's seat, a dirty Danashi man with thick black dreads made a checkered grin at the pair.

"I'll take that." He tugged the duffel from Gale, circling to the back of the jumper where a single cargo hold sat above a squat rear tire.

The Danashi led Lor to the back seat; a cozy two-seater guaranteed to make the ride uncomfortable with his legs pressed against his stepfather. The hot stench of metal and animal hide filled the cramped cabin, and Lor could only hope the ride wouldn't be long enough to cause his long legs to cramp.

"Station eight, right?" the Danashi asked.

"That's right. If you could please get us there within a half standard, that would be great."

"No problem, Captain," he replied, flicking various switches. The jumper rumbled, ready to zip to the station.

The ride remained quiet. Lor couldn't exchange any words with Gale without feeling resentment. He assumed his stepfather agreed, as he only uttered anything when he felt he had to teach Lor something. "This area over here is blah and blah, and that place is ran by what's his nuts...." Lor wished Gale would just keep his mouth shut—he wasn't learning anything and he didn't care.

When Gale showed signs of giving up with random small talk, Lor closed his eyes. As he did this, he would never see just blackness. It was a swirling light show of colors. Ever since he was young, he had seen these colors, and through fascination, he would visit often. Random patterns of colors bumped into each other, circled around each other, and sometimes slammed into each other, making a new color with electric sparks.

Before obsessing about Law, he had thought about Arts. He tried using paint to create a canvas of what he saw, but it never looked right, so he gave up on the idea.

It wasn't long before the jumper screamed to a stop, interrupting Lor's peace.

"Well done, well done, here we are! Station eight." The driver opened the hatch and let them out.

Lor unfolded from the cramped cabin, stretching to his full height, which happened to be exactly one head length taller than Gale. Gale slung Lor's duffel over a shoulder while slipping the driver a few plat and shooing him away.

Jumpers buzzed to and fro, dropping off an eclectic mix of passengers. One Mesaman girl bumped into his elbow, muttering "sorry" while speed-walking toward the gate. Filth stunk up the air, like a funk of garbage and ash. Festering bins overflowed onto the concrete, swarmed by a rainbow of insects.

The pair hustled to the window, where a petite redhead with wild curly hair sat behind the sales counter. Her little heart-shaped face peered up at them and she smiled.

"Reservation?" she asked. Her cute face was betrayed by her voice. It was awful.

"Yes, a-ah." Gale patted his pockets and withdrew two identical transparent tickets with bright blue text flashing their train reservation time. He handed them over to her, and she slid them in the counter slot, followed by a pleasant *click*. She pulled them out again, and the text had turned yellow.

"Thank you, Mr. Turtingas. Have an enjoyable trip!"

"Hurry, Loren." Gale tugged his arm, guiding him through the gate and toward their car.

The train was a slender black bullet, and people crawled in and out of it like bugs on a rotting sausage.

"We need to go to car fi—" Gale's voice was cut short by a woman's shrill scream. Lor jumped and spun around to see a cluster of roundsmen marching toward them. Gale grabbed Lor's wrist and yanked him closer.

The roundsmen didn't even look at Lor and Gale. They marched right past and made a line toward car seven. Lor glanced down at Gale—his face was relaxed, but his chest heaved up and down as if his heart would leap from his ribs.

More screams and shouts came from the car, and Lor heard the loud thumps of a beat stick connecting with a skull. He jumped at each hit, as more people shouted and jeered.

A Danashi man bellowed for the roundsmen to "leave him alone," while a pale-skinned Anglia cheered for them to "break his neck!"

Lor craned his neck for a better view of the commotion through the train window, when the roundsmen dragged a very underfed man from the car. His skin was grayish-pale like Dag's, with unkempt black hair tied in a knot at the top of his head, spilling loose hairs from their binding. He was a Yeuni.

Gale pulled Lor to the side to let them through. The roundsmen lifted the guy up until he was walking on his own. He seemed to have given up and didn't resist. The man had the marks of exile—threadbare clothing, rotting shoes, and the distinct burn scar in the middle of his forehead shaped like the seal of Audun. They had his hands bound in front of him and sealed in a clear box. His fingernails were dirty and chipped, as if he had clawed his way from somewhere.

The man glanced at the train as they moved past. His eyes were like Dag's—eerie and reflective—only yellow. He looked like any other man, but malnourished, with the skin and eyes of a Foscan blend.

Lor had only read about the Yeunish in one of his Law books. It was in a chapter on dealing with brigands, with only a brief description of what they look like and how the public should do their civic duty to turn them in. He never saw one before and was fascinated by the man as the roundsmen took him away.

"That was... something," Gale said, blowing out a terse puff of air.

"And what exactly did I just witness?" Lor scratched his head.

"That was a Yeunish arrest. It happens every once in a while. You should know... don't you study all there is to know about *Law*?" He mocked in a bitter slant.

"Yeah, but my book doesn't go into detail about the Yeunish."

"That's a shame." Gale beckoned Lor toward their car. "They're a part of our world too."

They reached car five, and a digital panel flashed names on the outside door.

"Turtingas, two passengers. Here we are." Gale stepped aside for Lor.

He climbed into the car and scanned the area. Plush black bench seats lined the edges in clusters. One bench, large enough for two, sat across from another bench with a simple table in between. He wasn't thrilled about sitting next to some stranger.

He slid into the seat next to the window while Gale worked on stuffing the duffel in an overhead compartment. He grunted and punched the bag while cursing. The car filled up quickly, and an odd-looking passenger took the bench across from Lor.

The man's eyes were solid black and glassy, reminding Lor of some hybrid animal. The edges of his eyelids tilted upwards and stretched near to his temples. A pointed nose and chin stuck out sharply, with hair pulling back like an opposing force. It was slicked back tight enough that individual hairs looked like they were trying to break free from his scalp.

"Good afternoon," he said to the pair in a voice deep enough to rumble Lor's rib cage.

"Ah, good afternoon." Gale stuck out a hand, deflecting the man's attention. He winced at the stranger's deceptively tight grip.

"Wow." He let go and shook out his hand. "Are you a Weggevens?"

The man laughed, emitting the strangest sound between a low tenor and a high-pitched wheeze. A group of girls from the opposite bench turned around and giggled.

"Why, how could you tell?" He unfurled his hands, revealing long, slender fingers and dark, pointed nails matching the man's eyes.

"Just a guess." Gale smiled at the stranger. It had been so long since Lor saw his stepfather smile that the image was surprising. He could be handsome if he tried.

"Wait, are you a skin walker? Do you have a picture of what you used to look like?" Lor asked.

"Loren! That's rude." Gale clicked his tongue.

The man laughed again in the deep wheeze, clicking his creepy fingernails over the surface of the shared table.

"How do you know this isn't my real face?" He wagged his pencil-thin eyebrows at Lor. Lor was shocked the man could even move the skin on his forehead.

"I didn't mean anything by it, sir."

"My name is Fowler, by the way." He grinned, showing a row of sharp, inhuman teeth.

"Excuse my *son*." Gale gave Lor the look that he knew too well. "I'm Gale, and this is Loren. We're heading to Heart Island so he can attend the program."

The train lurched forward, rocking everyone in car five. Metal wheels thumped in rhythm slowly at first, then picked up speed after a whistle blast. The passengers relaxed, and the conversation noises crescendoed.

"Is that right?" Fowler scratched his pointy chin with the tips of those cursed nails.

"Did you attend the program?" Gale asked.

"Indeed. Class of 989."

"Oh yeah? I was class of 990. Seems we just missed each other."

"So it seems."

Lor chuckled. "I actually wanted to do Law, but daddy-o said no." He leaned back in the seat.

"Hmmm... Wise man, your father." Fowler nodded at Gale.

Lor wasn't keen on giving Gale any more praise, so he didn't say anything. He scanned Fowler's arm, resting his eyes on that familiar lump just under the skin. It matched Eva's, except on Fowler there were blue veins under semi-transparent skin, stretched over the implant.

"He's a bright kid, he just doesn't apply himself well enough." Gale glared at Lor, clicking his tongue.

"Well, Lor, I have a bit of advice for you, if you don't mind." Fowler laced his fingers over the table as if he were sitting down to a fancy dinner.

"Yeah, sure."

"You should know that finding your Guild alone is just the start of a blessing. However, it is only when you truly understand it... I mean truly understand where it comes from and how it shapes you as a man, is when your gift becomes your skill."

A blessing? Who would call looking in the mirror every day to see that amalgam of man-creature a blessing?

Fowler's quip had a strange effect on Gale—Lor saw it in the subtle furrow of his brow.

"Let me explain...Yes, I am a Weggevens skin walker. The two are exclusive, yet not. It's a dangerous combination of animal and instability. No sane person would wish to become a Weggevens, let alone call it a blessing. It can have unintended catastrophic outcomes. Many skin walkers learn to harness the halfway existence."

"Halfway existence?" Lor interrupted. "So, you're saying you're basically straddling the line between human and creature?"

Fowler laughed. "You were right, Gale. He *is* a bright kid."

Gale huffed and cracked a small grin.

"My point here is that this is not simply a gift, it is a skill to master. The program gives you the blueprint, but you must build the structure... in here, and in here." Fowler pointed to his heart, then his head.

Lor chuffed. "Sounds like *work.*" He sank back into the seat. The idea of putting energy into learning anything other than Law curdled in his stomach.

"It is work, indeed." Fowler tittered. "Perhaps he doesn't apply himself as you said." He nodded at Gale, and they laughed.

This is going to be a long train ride.

Lor closed his eyes to watch the colors behind his eyelids for the rest of the ride.

⚗ ⚗ ⚗

"Well, it was a pleasure to meet you, young man." Fowler stuck out a sinewy hand.

Lor gripped the stick-like fingers and winced at the strength.

"Likewise," Lor said.

Gale hopped from the car with Lor's duffel.

"If you ever find yourself in the town of Secas during the program or after, you should look me up. I live in Guild Central."

"Oh really? I will, thanks." Lor had no idea if he would ever be in Secas during his time in the program. The idea of a Guild offshoot outside of the Seven Cities, however, sparked his interest.

"Remember what I said, and you will do great things."

"You mean, doing work?" Lor grinned.

Fowler laughed. "Yes, I mean as much. Laziness can open you up to restless forces. Take care not to let them get to you."

He picked up his bag and took a step back to leave.

"Hey, Fowler?" Lor called to him. He turned back around and cocked his head. "What is your spirit animal?"

Lor half joked but wanted to know what kind of creature would twist the man's face into such a hair-raising visage.

Fowler chuckled. "Why, a bird of course." He turned back and disappeared from the platform.

GOT A YEUNI?
GET CASH!

WANTED

CALL 01-7C-BOOK-EM (2775)

Get the scourge off our streets and
serve your country!

Subject to current going rate, call to find
out and get yourself some pLat!*

*False reports are punishable by law, and can incur a fee of 5,000 pLat, or 10 years imprisonment.

CHAPTER 4

A Smooth Ferry Ride
LOREN

GALE MARCHED TOWARD A BANK of jumpers lined up for fresh passengers. A demographic of Danashi drivers stood outside vehicles, peddling their services.

Lor hurried after him, listening to the cacophony of shouts, laughter, and buskers blowing into, banging, or strumming their instruments. Several locals had set up small stands, selling their grifts.

"This is Kanckette," Gale shouted over his shoulder. The noise throbbed over his ears.

Lor knew of Kanckette. It was the only city that existed among the sprawling desert known as the Span. He didn't realize it would be so... tribal. In retrospect, it made sense since the Desert Maelstrom ravaged this zone year after year, stifling any efforts at building it up. It was a pass-through city, desperate for attention.

The crowd was thick, and Lor studied his surroundings—people in rags, people in everyday clothes, some travelers in suits, a naked man running by... He could have slipped away in that moment, and Gale would never have found him again. Then he would be free from the future life that terrified him.

Instead, he followed his stepfather into the cabin of yet another cramped jumper cab. This time, good fortune assigned a driver with a better sense of hygiene.

Lor remembered when he was a kid, hearing about the Desert Maelstrom destroying the train tracks from Kanckette to Secas. Audun never saw fit to replace them, creating the opportunity for hundreds of jumper taxis to set up their businesses.

The hatch hummed closed and it made a squeaky kiss as it sealed them inside and left the noise outside. They pulled away from the station, gliding across the sand.

Kankette was a harsh shade of yellow. Smoky dust particles rose in the air, creating a hazy, putrid film over blue skies, coloring it green. Miles of sand stretched in all directions, dotted with silhouettes of residents in rippling cloaks. Tracks of all shapes and sizes peppered the terrain, smoothing out to nothing as the jumper traveled farther from the city into uninhabitable space.

Plumes of sand fog occasionally belched up into the horizon, making Lor think of dusty farts. Leftover energy from the maelstrom was all he could think of that would create these jet puffs of sand.

Tall dunes undulated in hypnotic waves through the thick window. Lor's stomach bubbled even though he hadn't eaten that morning, forcing him to close his eyes periodically, only to be met with his own dizzying color show.

He had to open his eyes again to keep from throwing up. Glancing forward, a copse of trees grew larger in the distance.

Gale cleared his throat again, and the sound was sharp as needles in the silence. "That's Secas up ahead through the trees," he said.

Lor's heart thumped. He longed for his home in Peakwood. He was comfortable there. The climate was cooler, cleaner, and more advanced. He had everything he needed in Peakwood and kicked himself for having been insufferably stubborn toward Gale.

The jumper zipped toward the trees, and the closer they got, the more Lor saw of the variety of colors within them.

Secas was enclosed by dense forest—tall and skinny trees with wiry branches poked out among short, squatty ones with fat knobby trunks. There were needly pines, trees with wide yellow canopies, and some with braided trunks and deep red leaves. The most beautiful of them all were the ones covered in a downy white haze that lifted from the branches into the sky. It reminded Lor of the snow in Peakwood.

The jumper slid into the small, two-lane road leading into town. A towering hand-carved wooden sign stood next to the arched entrance. Chiseled twirls weaved around the perimeter of the sign, with letters painted in white and green declaring: "Welcome to Secas, population 4500."

"This is a very small town with a proud culture. You'd better be on your best behavior when visiting," Gale said.

Lor didn't answer but took in a deep breath, smelling hints of seawater through the air vents. The tree-lined path allowed slender beams of light through, illuminating silvery pollen in the air that swirled violently as they buzzed past. He wished he could roll a window down, but jumpers were sealed for quick travel.

The path widened into an open and colorful venue. Traditional shops and tourist traps lined the entrance, decorated with winding vines and exotic plants. The jumper pulled around to a square orange building with scalloped roofing and a sign that said: "Visitor Center."

Lor and Gale slid from the jumper with the driver's help. Lor caught sight of a painted white ferry in the distance with a colored pennant string and twinkling lights decorating the rail.

The next vessel to usher me to this waste of time and plats. And it has to be cheerful while doing it.

"That's your ferry," Gale announced on cue, as if reading his mind. "We need to get your pass at the visitor center."

They strolled to the orange building, where Lor noticed an unusual number of cats lounging around. Tourists stopped to stroke their chins, and they rolled in the sun, unbothered by the strangers. He tittered at the sight of them.

"I wonder if any of those cats are actually perverted skin walkers wanting hapless passersby to rub their bellies," he said.

Gale *tsk*'ed and shook his head. "You and your imagination," he said. Lor might have been seeing things, but he thought he caught a small grin from his humorless stepfather.

Inside, the building was cool, with fans of older technology mounted to the ceiling and coated in dust. One of them squeaked as it ran, rocking back and forth and sprinkling motes of its filth into the air below. Lor covered his mouth as they made their way to the reception counter. Once there, Gale told Lor to go look around while he waited for the ferry pass.

He obeyed and meandered through the lobby, finding a rack of hundreds of colored brochures mounted to the far wall. He recognized some of the shops from outside on a few advertisements, as well as parks, water shows, rentals, and the huge open marketplace. Each brochure promised Lor the time of his life, only for the low, low cost of expensive.

A black brochure caught his eye, and he slid the slick paper from the holder. The front had gilded letters embossed over the surface that said: *Guild Central* in fancy script. He pocketed the ad without opening it, while thinking about taking Fowler up on his offer to look him up sometime.

He ran a finger over a pink and white brochure just below the Guild Central stack. It stood out from the others by its simplicity:

Visit the enchanting and mystical Heart Island, home of the Guild Program and rare pink sands! Book a ticket today—space is limited! You'll also get a great view of the black, stony peak of Mount Gehenna—a historical marvel full of mystery and intrigue!

Only 7299 pL for a one-week visit*, all expenses paid at

the sunny island resort overlooking the eastern deep!

*Tech is banned and will be confiscated at Secas port.

Lor flipped the brochure over, where a cartoonish map was drawn to represent the different buildings and attractions. The island itself was unironically shaped like a heart, but upside down, with the butt end facing Secas's peninsula. The ferry route was a dotted line on this map, tracing over the water from the tip of the peninsula, straight into the "crack" of the heart. He looked forward to watching his ferry nosedive into that crack on his ride there.

He had hoped the brochure would show him more about campus, but the crudely placed drawing was one large gray square with the word "campus" printed on it. He slid the brochure back into the rack.

Seventy-three hundred plat for a week's vacation… how much did Gale spend on six months of the program?

He glanced over his shoulder at Gale, who was arguing with the lobby attendant. He rubbed his face like he did when he was frustrated, and he could see his reddened skin from the brochure rack. When the attendant trotted away, Gale peered over at Lor and waved him over.

"They must've lost your reservation, but she says they're going to fix it," he said. He checked his e-disk for the time, then blew out a long breath of air. "I've got to get back before tomorrow morning."

Lor raised an eyebrow. "Are you not coming with me?"

"No, not on the ferry. It's a short enough ride, and we can say our goodbyes at the pier. Besides, if I'm going to save any money on this, I can skip a ticket to the island."

Lor knew it, and he felt bad. He frowned and stubbed his toe over the floor, making it squeak. If he were to guess, based on the number in the brochure for just a small vacation, Gale was probably spending somewhere in the six-figure range for the program. That was a lot of money to make your stepson disappear for a while.

"Am I… a *burden* to you?" Lor blurted. He didn't know why he cared, but something about the whole situation seemed forced, unnecessary, and pricey.

"Don't be ridiculous." Gale snorted.

"Sorry, I wasn't trying to be sarcastic, I just…"

The attendant bounced back to the counter with the ticket flopping in her grip. The material warbled, flashing his name in glowing blue along the edge. She put on her best customer service smile, and Lor could tell that it snuffed Gale's fuse.

"Here you are, sir!" She handed the ticket to him. "We are terribly sorry about the mix-up."

"No problem, thanks." Gale took the ticket and passed it to Lor. They turned to leave. Lor had a feeling the girl was cursing them under her breath.

"Thank you for visiting Secas, and I hope you have a colorful day!" Lor turned to give her a pathetic wave and banged his head into the doorframe.

Gale rolled his eyes and grabbed Lor's arm, stepping back into the bright outdoors.

Lor rubbed his brow. "Ow."

Gale chuffed. "Yes, very smooth, son. I'm sure you will woo all the ladies at the program."

"Bah, I only hope the rest of my day is...colorful." Lor sniggered.

"That's what they say around here. Remember to be respectful."

"Sorry."

Gale ushered him toward the dock and handed him his duffel. Lor's shoulder dipped and he wondered if he packed too much. That whole time, Gale was unfazed by its weight.

I need to work out or something.

As he glanced at his arm, marveling at the slender sinewy muscle, he felt Gale tug on the other. They marched down the pier, and the planks squealed from their footfalls, sprinkling crusted salt back into the water below. The white party ferry was anchored ahead, billowing puffs of blue-gray smoke in the air. Buoys with bulbs of techlight dotted the path out of town, creating a lane just for the boat, clear of the visitors and townies who were playing in the water.

Lor watched the groups of friends and families splash around, laughing and screaming in the water. It made him miss the Eva he knew before she became an Engineer.

They used to visit the cold beaches of West Cordan during the middle of the year at its chilliest. He and Eva loved wading into the shallow end with their pants hiked up to their thighs so they could jump over the low waves rolling into shore. His mother laughed and clapped every time, even after the thousandth jump.

One of the women in the water reminded Lor of his mother as she clapped for her daughter going down a slide over and over.

He sighed, remembering her long fight against the Pa'taun virus. The heartbreak came again when the cure was found only two standard months later. Dag took great care of his mom at the time, spending every moment with her. He thought maybe Gale blamed her for not doing enough, and that was why he had treated her badly ever since.

Gale cleared his throat, snapping Lor from his trance. "You better keep your eyes on girls your own age," he said, peering at the woman.

"Oh, I u-uh..." Lor tried to come up with something witty, but he choked. "You're right, sorry."

"Please try to control your daydreams during the program. You really need to focus your efforts on the material."

"Yes, sir."

"I'll see you again in six months at the end of the program, here in Secas. Got it?"

"Yes, sir."

Gale paused and eyed Lor. He rapped him twice on the shoulder. "Be good."

CHAPTER 5

In the Heart
LOREN

HEART ISLAND. AN ISOLATED PARADISE in the proximity of the black peak known as Mount Gehenna. Lor repositioned his heavy duffel and gazed to the north. The immense rocky shadow towered in the distance with a thin wisp of smoke rising from its tip. The drifting clouds cast circular shadows across the mountain, making it look like a festering log of open lesions. Lor sighed, spying the rear of the white ferry taking its colors and lights back to Secas for the next round of recruits.

So Gale wants me to find out whether or not I belong to a Guild. My bet is on not, although I'd never risk precious plats on a stupid gamble.

Lor flicked the light pink sand from the tip of his boot. It hissed over a stout cactus-like plant. He swiped a palm over the slick of sweat glazed over his brow.

"Hello!"

He jumped and spun around to see a striking girl standing in front of him, with her hand stuck out, waiting for a shake.

"Ooooh, scared you, did I? My name is Paerli. Do you come from the cities?" Her hand was still planked forward. She blinked at him with curling lashes over the most vibrant shade of turquoise he had ever seen.

"I, uhhhh..." *This one is closer to my age, Gale...* He slid his wet hand across her palm to return her greeting. Her grip was tight, and Lor firmed up to match her squeeze with a firm bob of fists. Still smiling, she withdrew her hand and watched him, discreetly wiping her palm on the back of her pants.

Very smooth, Lor.

"I, uh, n-no, I'm not from the cities, but my dad hopes I end up at one of them. He doesn't care which. Are you? From the cities, that is?"

Paerli tittered and smiled at the thought. "No way. I'm from the Span.

Can't you tell?" She turned around, craning her neck to look at him while showing off her skin and clothes. She had the general look of a desert Danashi, but much cleaner than his jumper drivers. Her arms were darkened by the sun of the desert, and her frame was slender and lithe—suitable for a life of foraging and long treks through the sand. Her long, steely-black hair was tied back into a chunky braid, with curled wisps poking out from the twists. Her pants were a light, strategic brand of fabric, ballooning out from her thighs and billowing in the light breeze. Her gauzy white top forked downward at the collar, showing off a shimmering golden pendant. He meant to work out what it was but didn't want to appear as if he was gawking at her chest.

She curled her slender fingers over the pendant and smiled at him with a row of perfectly white teeth that stood in contrast to the brown of her face. "It's just that you look like you grew up out west. So, where *did* you come from? And what's your name anyway, guy not from the cities?"

She jutted her hip to the side and rested her other fist on top, balancing it like a feather. A wavy black wisp of hair passed over one eye, and she batted it away. He found himself inexplicably drawn to her.

"Oh, I did grow up out west, just not in the cities. I'm Loren. Loren Turtingas. Friends call me Lor. I mean, if I had a lot of friends, they'd call me that. I think. Well, my sister does anyway."

Just shut up, Lor.

Paerli chuckled and let go of the pendant, cupping her hands behind her. "Well, *Lor*, I'm glad to meet you. And it's a good thing we are getting along, because we are stuck together for the next six months... and without any tech, can you believe that?"

His eyes widened. He didn't consider there would be a technology drought that came with the program. He remembered the small disclaimer at the bottom of the brochure from the visitor center: *Tech is prohibited and will be confiscated at Secas port...* He dropped his duffel down and whipped open the side pocket to fish around for his e-disk. He didn't know why he cared, since no one really reached out to him except Eva and Gale. He liked the games on it.

"Damn," he muttered when he pulled out an empty fist.

Gale must have taken it at some point when he had my duffel.

"Yeah, sucks, right? We're going to have to find other ways of entertaining ourselves other than watching holofilm." She paused. "So, we should become friends. Us against *them*." She nodded over to a cluster of students over by the edge of the water. "Them" looked like a bunch of lost shadows ambling in the distance, and he wondered if he would ever make friends with of any of them. Only Paerli seemed interested in him at the moment. He found it odd that a girl of her caliber was the first warm body to latch on to him.

She's out of your league, doof.

She turned her head toward the shore, distracted by the other recruits, and he took the opportunity to give his armpit a quick whiff.

She circled her attention back to Lor, and he stood at attention, feeling the sweat pooling under his arms. "What do you want to bet almost half of our class goes undiscovered?" she said, wagging her eyebrows up and down and slanting a puckish half smirk.

She's out of your league.

"Well, I don't know... I don't like to gamble. It's a waste of money."

She clicked her tongue. "We don't have to use plats to make *this* bet... This could be more of a *favor*-based bet."

"A ...favor?"

"Sure! I don't know what yet, but I can think of something. I'll make sure it's interesting. You in?"

Loren paused, peering at her through squinted lids. He wasn't sure if he squinted like that from the sunlight reflecting off the sand, or if his brain drifted off again. He was leery of any stranger, beautiful or not. In the world he read about, there was always someone willing to use someone else's back as a jump-off point.

You don't know her, Lor. What if the favor she comes up with is painful, deadly, or humiliating? That could be a gamble in itself! You know you don't gamble. Tell her no. Just smile and be cool about it. Just say no thank you, you're good.

"Okay, sure."

"Bet is on!" She grinned, sticking her hand out once again. He clutched her warm, dry hand with his cold and wet one. "This is going to be fun! Hey! Hey, over here!" She waved over a different group nearby. There was a large, over-tall guy with them who had a round, boyish face. Lor felt a pang of jealousy. "I'll see you around, Lor." Paerli sauntered away, meeting the cluster halfway.

Lor eyeballed his feet with the awkward scuff marks in the toe and frayed binding on the sole.

You're such a goofy bastard.

"Gather 'round, gather 'round, all ye hopefuls!" A flamboyant man stood several paces from the beach in front of a shaggy building, built of grass and mud.

No technology, Lor told himself under his breath and sighed. He dragged his feet toward the man at the hut, leaving uneven grooves in the sand. The silhouettes on the beach weren't far behind, and they formed a semi-circle in front of the hut. Paerli slid next to Lor as if they came there together.

"Welcome, welcome!" the man bellowed as the recruits inched closer. "I am your guide, Horace Wanner. I will be your teacher and your mentor during this fabulous journey for the next six months."

Lor couldn't help but immediately like the man. His hair was wild and blond like his, but fluffy and bobbing above his head like a wad of stretched cotton fluff. A pair of black reading glasses similar to Gale's sat in the nest, half buried in the strands.

"Before we get to learning, let's go over the fun stuff—your dorms!" He flapped a stack of papers in the air. "I have on these sheets of parchment your dorm assignments. You will also find on your paper your future best friend, or worst enemy, also known as your roommate. Please come forward and get your assignment."

The recruits murmured and giggled, crowding each other to get to Horace.

Lor waited, watching Paerli strut toward the wild-haired man from behind. Her hips swayed like a dancer, and the thin fabric clung to her backside in a pleasing way. She grabbed her paper and returned with a sly look in her eye. "I know you were looking at my butt."

Lor's throat seized and his cheeks flushed. "What? No, I didn't."

Yes, you did.

She smirked at him. Having made enough of a fool of himself, he darted over to Horace, attempting to stop the sweat from breaking out everywhere.

"Ah, you must be Loren Turtingas," Horace said, holding out the last slip of paper.

"Thank you." Lor took it and debated whether to face Paerli again.

"I do apologize in advance, everyone," Horace shouted to the class, "but I am rather terrible with names. I assure you, I will learn them all at least by the end of term. And by then, maybe you will forget mine."

Lor chuffed and read the wrinkled parchment already splotched with sweat spots. Bold letters in the header said, "Building 2C, Room 14," with the caption, "Roommate: Dill Storgut."

He trotted over to Paerli. "What dorm are you in?"

"Two B, room three."

"I'm in two C. I wonder if the buildings are next to each other?"

"So we can sneak out together in the middle of the night?"

"I... Uh... that's not what I meant." Lor's cheeks flushed.

"I'm kidding!" she said, laughing. "...or *am* I?"

What does she mean by that? Why do I like it?

"Everyone, please may I have your attention, now that you all have your assignments?" Horace called through cupped hands. "We won't be wasting any time in this program, so I expect to meet you all in this building behind me for our first session."

He opened an arm toward the mud and grass hut to a wave of audible groans.

"Leave your bags, please! Our helpers will bring them to your dorms while we are in session—provided you followed our instructions and put your names on them."

Several *piff-piff-piffs* struck the sand as bags dropped. One tawny girl with curled chestnut hair huffed, placing several tufted lavender and ivory bags studded with pearls strategically in the dust. She wore a pressed white linen blouse with a chain of the same pearls wrapped around her slender neck.

"I think that's my roommate," Paerli whispered to Lor.

"Looks high-maintenance to me." He shrugged, plunking his duffel next to Paerli's. Their name tags dangled from the handles.

"Ready for this?" she asked. Dimples dug into her cheeks with her smile. Lor nodded, making sure to "watch her back" up and through the entrance, trading the smell of the beach's salty air for the musty dirt of the shack.

CHAPTER 6

Day One of the Rest of His Life
LOREN

THE CLASSROOM WAS LARGER THAN Lor expected from the outside. There were rows of old style double-wide desks, ravaged by sand and salt. No tech meant a long blackboard mounted in the front of the class, between rows of bookshelves. Paerli led Lor to one of the double desks in the front, swinging the hinged seat from its post. Others wandered to desks, with repeating echoes of seats in dire need of an oiling.

Horace followed the crowd into the room with a limp Lor didn't notice at first impression. He was also barefoot.

"Formulator, Engineer, Shepherd, Reader, and Reaper." Guide Horace paced between the rows seated with wide-eyed hopefuls, each word in beat with his odd gait. "And if you're incredibly unlucky, maybe you'll still find a home with the Weggevens."

Nervous laughter bubbled from the group. Fowler was a Weggevens, and it didn't seem that bad. He was ugly for sure, but not a horrible person.

"I hope you are well rested," Horace continued, coming to a stop at the front of the room, "because six months is not a very long time to tap into your calling... or *lack* thereof." He scanned the room with fluffy ash blond hair bobbing above his head and those glasses threatening to fall.

Striding up to the primitive blackboard, he swiped a piece of chalk. The chalk scratched over the surface as he dug out the number 1009. He dusted his hands with dramatic claps.

"There have been more than a thousand classes before you. At least, since Audun started to count these classes." He grinned at the class with a crooked set of teeth. "So... what *exactly* does that mean?" He pointed to a mousy-looking Danashi kid near the back. "You, what is your name?"

He flinched and sat upright. "Dill Storgut, sir."

So that's my roommate...

Horace belly laughed. "Sir? Did you call me... sir?" He placed a hand over his chest in mock surprise. "I like that, Dill, but I am just a *humble* servant to the Guilds. Please... just call me Horace." He spread his arms wide in the showy gesture of a stage entertainer.

"Sorry, si...Horace." Little Dill cleared his throat. "What does that mean? Is it because there've been over a thousand years of Guild prep classes?"

"Ahhhh, my wise friend, Mister Storgut... you are correct! There have been over a thousand years of legacy to live up to! Guild prep is an ancient practice and must be shown the respect it deserves." Horace resumed his pacing.

"I will warn you, however... not all of you will have *the gift.*"

Horace kicked up small plumes of the pink sand coating the floor of the classroom. Lor envied the foot freedom, suddenly feeling the cramped toe box of his boot. He wiggled his toes, wishing for the cue that he could throw off his shoes and bury his feet deep into the grains.

"You." Horace pointed at Lor. "Which one are you?" He picked up a roster from the glossy wooden desk up front to study the names written on it. He squinted hard, not even trying to work out the readers from his fluff of hair.

"I'm, ah, Loren. Loren Turtingas, sir. I mean, Horace." He was used to addressing Gale more formally than that.

"Ah, yes, well, can you tell me what an *Engineer* does, Loren Turtingas?"

Lor relaxed, knowing the answer because of Eva.

"Yes, sir... I mean Horace. An Engineer is a mechanical master, a member of the Guild responsible for all of our technical advances. My sister practices Engineering in Ascendia."

"Oh ho! A very good textbook answer, Mister Turtingas." Horace grinned, but it wasn't in a way Lor liked. He wasn't ready to be humiliated in front of a bunch of strangers on his first day. "But can you tell me... *what* does an Engineer *do*?"

Lor sank an inch down in his seat. "I, uh, well." He gulped and licked his lower lip. "I-I guess I don't know?"

"Is that a question?"

Loren paused, studying the guide. "I'm not sure what you want me to say."

Horace stood upright, grinning at the class for an uncomfortably long pause. The breeze pushed through a hole in the wall that resembled a makeshift window, playing at Horace's billowy hair. The glasses teetered on the edge of his head, and Lor was invested in the drama unfolding of them holding on for dear life.

"You seem to be a bright class so far. But I fear we must gain a better understanding of the implications of Guild membership. It will come in time."

Horace turned his attention to the board once again, scratching out the word "Engineer." Chalk snow trickled from the nib, disappearing into the sand. Paerli jabbed her hand in the air, all fingers squeezed together in salute. Her presence seemed out of place among their peers. She sat upright, shoulders back, and full of adroit confidence. Horace caught her hand from the corner of his eye.

"Ah, yes, Miss...?

"Paerli Harea. It's spelled weird, but it's pronounced PAR-lee."

The disappointment Lor felt when Horace remembered the readers in his hair was like the end credits to an amazing holofilm. No more drama, no more distraction. It was time for him to focus, and that made him squirm.

"Ah, yes, I see you here. You are from Kanckette?"

As soon as Lor heard the city, he remembered the train station. He tried to picture her streaking through there like the man with no clothes. What a sight.

Paerli nodded with a small shrug, looking at Lor for some kind of approval. All he could see now was her naked at the station. He pushed his fists down into his lap.

"Well, what a beautiful Anglia name."

"Yeah, my mom was a fan of the language. Just call me Par, if it's easier."

"I see," Horace continued, "and what was your question then, Par?"

"It wasn't really a question, more of an expansion to Lor's original answer about Engineers."

"Ah! Well then, enlighten us, please!" Horace gave her an exaggerated bow. She flicked a swath of her black locks behind her shoulder.

"Well, they have the ability to witness the potential hidden inside of materials, and the material responds to the Engineer's input. They use the power of touch to meditate on its composition, offering the material suggestions for best possible outcomes."

"Very good, Miss Harea! You see, class, these abilities are special for a reason, and Guild membership is considered a high honor. You may have a basic understanding of the outcome of their craft, but to really understand it, to truly understand... you must nurture it."

It was the same advice Fowler gave him on the train. It didn't sound any less like work than when the bird man told him. Lor sighed.

"Now! In order to prevent any conflict of interest, you will not find any of an Engineer's wondrous projects here on Heart Island. In other words, no technology, if that wasn't already clear." Horace finally tired of limping around the room and chose to lean against the front desk.

The class murmured and groaned, looking around at each other, making pained faces. The wooden chairs creaked on their posts as they shifted around in them. An outgoing girl with shiny brown hair in the middle of the room shot an arm up, not waiting for her cue to speak.

"Excuse me, Horace? What Guild do *you* belong to?" Her question was purposefully rude. She carried the attitude of a girl from the west where Lor was from, which was why he didn't seek out friendships while growing up.

"Ah, friend. What is *your* name?" He ignored her question like an expert guide.

"My name is Nariah Blevens. My father is a Reader in the city Celerity. Surely you've heard of him? Melven Blevens?" Nariah's voice stabbed at Lor's ears. She sat next to a handsome Mesaman, who happened to look right at Lor. He rolled his eyes and shrugged, pointing at Nariah's back, cracking a dimpled grin.

"Oh, you're a westerner!" Horace said.

Lor smiled to himself. He knew it.

"Well, I am so sorry, Nariah, I have not heard of your father, Melven." Horace tapped on his lower lip. "You say he's a Reader? Did he *earn* his title, or was he a natural?"

"Excuse me? What do you mean by that exactly?" She huffed.

"Excellent! This is another lesson for the classroom!"

Horace took great pains to limp back to the blackboard, where he scratched the words "Reader" and "Shepherd." "If you didn't know already, these two Guilds are a little more complicated than the rest. Does anyone know why?"

The class was silent. Horace picked at his nails as if he forgot he had asked a question. Someone cleared their throat.

"To put it simply..." he said after two full turns of the second hand, "Shepherds can *become* Readers if they spend plats for specialized training. Not many students are natural Readers, and the training is quite expensive. So! How is it that a Shepherd can become a Reader to begin with?"

Paerli shot her hand up again.

"My star pupil, Miss Harea. Please tell us."

She giggled, and the music of her laughter hit Lor like a jumper. Jealousy nagged at him for a second when he had the fleeting thought of her flirting with the guide.

Don't be stupid, Lor, he could be her dad. Wait, what if she liked older men?

"Shepherds are beast masters, able to communicate with and control animals with their minds." She showed a peek of those perfect teeth—a vast difference from what he witnessed from the mass of drivers and peddlers at Kanckette station. "Readers can do the same thing, but... with people."

"And what is a person but another animal?" Horace said with a laugh, throwing his hands up in the air. "But yes, you're right Par. That's the problem, though, isn't it? It costs a pretty coin to learn the art of reading as a Shepherd. So, Miss Blevens from the west, with the famous Reader father..." He limped over to Nariah's table and bent down to meet her eyes. "Which is it? Natural, or paid for?"

Nariah's cheeks flushed crimson, making her dip down into her seat.

The room murmured again, and someone giggled. Desk mates whispered to each other, glancing over at a freshly shamed Nariah.

Did he go too far? Nah. She deserved it.

"Please understand this," Horace said. "We are not here to boast about the accomplishments of others. We are here to explore our *personal* greatness."

He murmured something directly to Nariah, and Lor caught only a couple words: *insult* and *harm*. Her accompanying smile told him that his words must have been kind.

"You are capable of great things, Guild or not," he announced to the class.

He must not be in a Guild. What a clever man.

Lor liked him even more.

"Excuse me, Horace." Lor raised a hand. The guide nodded at Lor. "Bought or not, isn't Reading a powerful skill? I've heard it can even be somewhat... scary."

"It *can* be!" Horace jabbed a finger in the air and marched toward one of the many ravaged bookshelves. The ancient wooden case was full of partially rotting books. He slid one from the shelf, loosing a plume of dust and fine sand.

"This," he said with an artistic flourish, "is the book of rules and regulations regarding Guild membership. It's called *The Ethics Counsel Rules for Guilds*, edition eleven. A fine read, that! If you find yourself troubled to fall asleep one night, I will let you borrow this for some light reading." He slapped the book down on the desk to murmurs and giggles.

He tapped the cover. "Once you find your calling, the seven cities will be in contact with you. They will most likely hand you this fine specimen here.

"But to answer your question more thoroughly, Mister Turtingas, there are rules in place for each Guild. If you shirk the rules, you risk either imprisonment or *banishment*."

The recruits chattered openly about fear of breaking the rules by accident, while others aired their doubts wanting to be in a Guild at all.

"I hear you, I hear you. Guild membership is not for the faint of heart. The roles of the Guild are of extreme importance. This is why these rules are in place to maintain harmony in the population.

"We will not get into great detail now, but does anyone know the story of the Foscans and why they are shamefully treated as servants?"

Lor immediately thought of Dag. He never wanted to treat her poorly, but sometimes he dismissed her because Gale usually did.

The class went silent at their mention. Only the sound of an occasional trickle of sand from the bookcase broke through the quiet. Horace stood at the front of the classroom, waiting for any answer from the group.

The whisper of Paerli's linen shirt cut the silence when she raised her hand.

"Yes, Miss Harea?" Horace said.

"Was it shameful when they rebelled and wiped out an entire town from existence?" She swallowed and licked her full lips. Black lashes pointed toward Horace, with light beaming through her aqua eyes. The high-maintenance girl with the pearls gawked at her.

Horace huffed and shook his head. "Yes, it's true, they rebelled. What's the story behind that, do you know?" Horace goaded her for more.

"They tried to overthrow Audun."

"And...?"

"... and they were punished for it?"

"Is that a question?" Horace smiled at her. "We can talk more on this topic another time. For now, friends, welcome to Heart Island. I think you've learned enough for your first day, so we'll reconvene tomorrow for the best part of the program. Class dismissed!"

Horace waved his hand toward the exit. The abrupt end confused Lor, but the way Horace limped around had him thinking pain and exhaustion could have been the reasons. The class sat for a moment, experiencing the same confusion until seats creaked on their poles and students rose from their desks.

The front door burst open to the outside beaches, and the recruits filtered from the opening, spreading out into the sand and wandering around the beach. Conversations circled around what Guilds were most desired.

"Oh, I do hope I'm a Reader!" The high-maintenance girl clutched her hands at her chest and walked with Nariah. The little one from the back of the room, and Lor's new roommate, Dill, barged through from between the two girls.

"I hope I'm a *Reaper*! Did you know they can live forever?" He skipped next to Lor and Paerli.

"That's just a rumor." Paerli rolled her eyes and chuckled. In one swift move, she snaked her arm around Lor's. It was nonchalant and comfortable, as if she always belonged there. Her fingers wrapped around his bicep, and he was embarrassed at how small they must feel. He had never been touched by a woman other than his mom or Eva, and it made the color rise in his pale cheeks. He couldn't be sure of what he looked like, but he knew it had to be obvious.

Don't think about her naked, don't think about her naked.

Her deep black hair smelled like sweet apples and cherries.

"No way, I read about Valoa'brenga in one of my brother's old crusty history books," Dill asserted himself, lifting his chin high. He looked like a miniature version of all the jumper drivers in Kanckette.

"Aw, you're so cute!" Nariah rubbed his head, and he glared at her. The high-maintenance girl giggled. "That's a fairy tale, not history."

Their banter broke the spell, helping Lor breathe again.

Valoa'brenga? The name wasn't familiar to Lor, but it sounded like old Foscan.

"You guys just wait... When I become a Reaper, I'll show you true power!" Dill pretended to squeeze an invisible ball between his palms.

"You sure do have a lot of... energy." The high-maintenance girl turned up her nose.

Dill ignored her. "So, Lor, right? We're roommates! What do you want to be?"

"Me? Oh, uh, I dunno really," Lor said. A drop of sweat tickled his brow. Was it the heat, or Paerli touching him?

"Well, I know for sure that if I become a Weggevens, I'll just kill myself," Nariah said, putting a hand to her throat.

"Don't be so dramatic," Paerli said.

"Well, If I got that, I'd be dead anyway, so may as well do it myself."

"Not necessarily," Lor said. "I met a pretty solid Weggevens on the train here."

"Ew, you took the *train*?" the high-maintenance girl said.

"Dude, what even is your name?" Dill asked, saving Lor the trouble.

She let out a small cry and turned her nose the other way. "My *name* is *Emilia*, not... *dude*."

Lor snorted, inviting a glare from Emilia.

"But the Weggevens power is completely random!" Nariah said, continuing her thoughts.

"Yeah, that sucks, but if you don't like it, you could defect. Go live your life as an entertainer."

"And go non-Guild? Are you *crazy*?"

"Better than offing yourself." Lor shrugged, thinking about his own father's need for acceptance despite his successes as a medic.

"You'd be a *great* storyteller," Paerli said, chuckling. "I mean, you're already dramatic."

Nariah huffed at them, scrunching her whole face inward.

"Look, I wouldn't want to be a Weggevens either, Nariah," Lor said. His response tempered her anger, relaxing the wrinkles in her face.

"What about a Shepherd?" Paerli suggested. "I mean, talking to animals is pretty cool."

Nariah chuffed. "I guess that would be better than Weggevens. But I still want to be like my dad."

Lor glanced toward the beach and saw an Anglia girl standing by the water. She was alone and had her hands cupped in prayer, away from the mountain. Her long white hair trailed behind her in the breeze, undulating with the delicate fabric of her pale blue dress. She lifted her gaze, looking right at him, and smiled. He smiled back at her, unable to peel his eyes away. Something about her standing alone on the shore, with her milk-pale skin under the hot sun, made him forget where he was.

"Helloooo, Lor!" Dill snapped his fingers in front of his face.

"Sorry... what?" Lor rubbed his face. Paerli's arm was still coiled around his, making him sweaty.

"I asked who that Weggevens was that you met on the train? What kind was he?"

"Fowler? He was a skin changer. Very ugly guy. Oh, that reminds me—he said he lives in Secas. Maybe we'll run into him sometime."

Dill burst out laughing. "Ugly? Like... how ugly we talking?"

"He's half *bird*."

Nariah reared back. "Okay, I'm back to killing myself again."

"Oh, come on, it's not that bad. He just lives halfway between. Says it works best for him."

"That sounds like the worst thing *ever*." Nariah threw her head back and groaned.

"There's always entertainment..." Paerli said in a singsong tone.

"Oh, Maker's limbo, not with that again."

Paerli grinned and shrugged, tugging on Lor's arm toward the dorm cluster. He went along with it, taking another look at the Anglia girl. She was praying again, eyes closed toward the water. He watched her as they walked by, causing him to stub a toe on something in the sand.

"What in Gehenna?" He stumbled and looked down to see the corner of an ivory piece of debris sticking out of the pink grains.

"Oh neat, it's a piece of ancient tech!" Dill knelt down and reached a hand out.

"Don't touch it," Paerli warned.

Dill recoiled, standing back up. "It's dead, though, isn't it?"

"It's hard to say, just don't touch it."

"Look, it's all *over* the place." Dill pointed forward at several ivory pieces dotted all along the beach. "I'm bound to accidentally touch one. Surely they wouldn't have this here if we aren't allowed real tech."

"Who knows." Lor tried to look over his shoulder, but the Anglia girl was gone.

CHAPTER 7

Nudge
Loren

THE AIR WAS STILL, AND the sound of water gently licking over packed sand produced a welcome calm in the air on day two of the program. Lor skipped down the steps from his dorm and landed with a *piff!* into the miniature pink dunes at the bottom. He kicked off his boots and socks to feel the warmth from the grains. North of his vantage point, the broken fragments of land between Heart Island and Mount Gehenna dotted the horizon like stepping stones.

After Eva had stopped worrying about the mountain, she regurgitated her mantra to him, assuring that the zone was harmless. Lor bit his lip as he surveyed the misty black giant. Waves of heat pulsed over his arms as he watched, making him wonder if it was some bizarre radiation drifting over his skin.

The mist was clear enough that he saw more details of the stone. It had an eerie quality to it that didn't quite look like the type of stone an ordinary mountain would have. He read in his book that there was always a patrol of roundsmen guarding the mountain. He assumed that they must switch shifts at some point during the second sun. That made the most sense to Lor, but the book, as thick as it was, didn't go into great detail about how the roundsmen managed shifts.

The dorm's front door swung open, slamming at the jamb. Lor recognized the recruit who came down the stairs, as he had sat next to Nariah the day before. Seeing him in the morning light only made Lor feel that much more insecure—bright crystalline eyes, a chiseled jaw with deep dimples, and thick dusty dark blond hair encircled his scalp like a curly golden crown. Jealously nagged at his insides. It was a feeling he wasn't used to, having spent his formative years in his bedroom hole, making friends with the wrong books. The handsome classmate stepped barefoot into the sand next to him.

"Hey," he said, "it's... Loren, right?" His deep baritone enhanced his perfect features.

"Hey, yeah. You can call me Lor. I'm sorry, I don't think I know your name, but I remember your face."

Who would ever forget that face?

He cracked a smile and stuck out a hand. "I'm Nico. It's not short for anything, and I just go by Nico."

Lor gripped his hand and gave him a much drier handshake than he had given Paerli the day before.

"Are you... Mesaman?" Lor asked. Gale always told him his conversational etiquette needed work. This was probably one of those moments.

"Actually I am... How could you tell?"

Nico exuded the traits of a Mesaman—skin the color of beechwood with ruddy cheeks and dusty blond hair like his own.

"I'm a Mesaman too. It just seemed like you were."

"Yeah, I grew up in Secas port area. I've spent my whole life close to that thing." Nico pointed at Gehenna. "It seems scarier from here, don't you think?"

"Yeah... I kinda want to see it someday." Lor didn't know why he said that.

"Seriously? Why?"

"To be honest... I don't know."

The dorm door swung open again, and Dill shuffled down the steps. He also stepped barefoot in the sand. Horace's naked feet the day before didn't seem lost on anyone.

"How's it goin', guys?" Dill said, swinging his arms in front of him and clapping his hands. He couldn't stay still for a moment. "I can't stop thinking about yesterday... I can't wait to see what Guild I'll be in!"

Nico laughed. "How do you know you'll get one? Are you sure you actually *want* one?"

"You know I do! I can just feel it, you know? I had a dream about it last night. I was the most bad-ass Reaper... *and* I was flying!"

Lor belly laughed. "I don't think Reapers can fly."

"This one will!" Dill jabbed a thumb at his chest.

Lor's spritely Danashi roommate brought an annoying levity to his situation on the island that he found charming, like the way he'd find clouds of gee flies charming. During cap-year camping trips with Eva, they would buzz around their faces when they boated on the lake. He always remembered his beloved trips, and the gee flies were a parasite on that memory.

"I didn't want to come here at all," Lor blurted out. "Guilds are overrated." In truth, Lor didn't know much about Guilds at all, let alone enough to make that assessment. He made it anyway. "My dad made me come here. He wasted a bunch of plat on this when all I wanted to be was a roundsman."

Dill clucked. "A roundsman? That's *boring* as puck dung! Your dad is smart—I bet you'll get some awesome Guild, better than a stuffy *Law* man."

Lor was warming up to the program. Particularly the hottest girl in class who had seemed to latch on to him, of all people. He glanced at dorm 2B, just across from his own building, wondering if he might catch a glimpse of Paerli's carefree hips swaying down the steps.

Waves of other girls trotted from the building, but no sign of Paerli. Emilia and Nariah caught him watching their dorm, but their attention shifted toward Nico. They giggled and hurried off.

"We'd better head toward class, I guess," Nico said as more recruits wandered toward the classroom.

The three of them followed the crowd toward the crude hut, passing handfuls of other giggling girls along the way.

"What's wrong with them?" Dill asked, raising an eyebrow.

Lor saw other girls staring at Nico and whispering to each other with thin smiles spread across their faces. One girl pointed with a hand over her mouth as she spoke to another girl next to her, not being particularly subtle. Nico scanned the beach, aloof and dodging ancient tech without noticing them.

"I think they're talking about Nico," Lor said, laughing.

"What, me?" Nico spun around toward the girls, making them freeze, their faces stuck with thin curling grins and wide eyes.

"They must think you're *keey-ute*," Dill said, rolling his eyes and flicking his wrist toward the girls, making them scatter.

Lor sighed, searching for Paerli again, wanting the same desire for himself.

He fixed his attention toward the school to see if she was waiting there for him. Nothing. But the Anglia girl stood there with her hands clasped in front of her and gazing off into the ocean depths. Behind her, there was an unnecessarily huge padlock dangling from the handle of the rotted wooden door.

"What the..." Dill jogged to the door, swinging around the Anglia girl and tugging at the padlock. He pulled out a folded note that was stuffed at the frame.

"We're supposed to wait here," he shouted back to the gathering crowd.

Lor moved toward the classroom, catching a pinky toe on a piece of ancient tech.

"Augh, *hell!*" He jumped up and down before examining the toe, already turning purple.

"Are you alright?" The voice was a twinkling chime that hung in the air. The Anglia girl approached him. She moved as if she were in water, flowing toward him like a trickling brook. She bent down to look at his toe.

Lor stood up and brushed the wrinkles carved in his shirt, unsuccessfully. Her white hair was pulled into two buns atop her head, with pieces falling from the binding and waving in the breeze. A golden hue sat at the core of each strand, giving her an aura of warmth as she studied his toe.

"I think you just might live," she said, standing up. She had a petite frame, with the top of her head Lor imagined was barely able to brush the scruff of his chin. She smiled at him. Her alabaster skin flushed with the perfect touch of peach in the cheeks with scattered freckles over her nose. She had the starkest white eyelashes that framed the most beautiful shade of light blue, almost violet eyes. Lor's voice caught in his throat, and he croaked.

"I'm Damaetra, by the way. I think I saw you stubbing your toe yesterday." She giggled, making him blush and finally remember to breathe.

"Yeah, that was probably me," he said, *knowing* it was him. "I'm Loren, but you can call me Lor."

Her smile widened and her eyes fluttered. "I like Loren," she said.

You can call me whatever you want...

"Loren it is." He grinned back at her. They locked eyes. Her white gold strands tickled her freckled cheeks as she gazed up at him in crystal violet.

A breeze coasted beside him, smelling of apple and cherry. The familiar warm arm wrapped through his. He flinched and saw Paerli there.

"Hey," she whispered.

"Hey! I, uh, this is Damaetra. We just met."

You awkward fool.

"Hello, Damaetra." Paerli took the girl's pale hand in her bronzed one.

"Where were you?" he asked Paerli.

"Oh, I just... took a morning walk up and down the beach."

"I love walking along the waterline." Damaetra offered, "We should walk together sometime."

Paerli's face relaxed and she smiled at the girl. "Yes, we should."

"There he is." Nico pointed back toward the dorms.

Horace came trotting down the beach, carrying a metal case, glinting in the morning sun. His hair flapped without the glasses buried in it, and he waved at the students. Every footfall threw sand bursts into the air, and he barely missed a chunk of dead tech. Lor's stomach turned at the memory, and he wriggled his pinky into the cool layers of sand. Horace met the group in quick, exhausted breaths.

"Whew, 'bout lost a toe there! Good morning!"

He moved to the front door of the mud hut with all the grace of a lame donkey and set the case down onto the crooked steps. The clasps flicked upward and the lid sprang open. A circle of students gathered so tightly around him, Lor could only catch glimpses of the case between slits in the crowd. He dreaded the day ahead, but Paerli's presence helped him relax. Damaetra stood next to her, with her small hands folded in front of her with all the etiquette of royalty.

Wispy blond hair swooped above the crowd when Horace jerked upright, holding a golden object.

"This, my friends, is your *nudge!*" he shouted, dragging the object through the air in a semi-circle for everyone to see. The horde of students crowding him took a coordinated step backwards.

"I bet this is the implant!" Dill whispered between Lor and Nico. Lor didn't realize Dill was standing right there.

Eva had shown him that lump under her skin. He pictured the golden beetle resting there, inside his sister's arm.

"I know I said there would be no tech on the island during the program, but I promise, this will be the only one you will need." Horace bobbed the device in front of the crowd. He beckoned at Nariah to come forward.

The girl trembled, taking small steps toward the trusted guide. She glanced at Nico and blushed.

"Here, take this," he said, stretching the golden implant toward her.

She plucked the object from his palm, holding it between two light fingers as if it were a piece of mold. The implant was around the size of the pad of a thumb. It glistened in her fingers.

"Now, this is very old technology, but very robust," Horace said. "It's been passed down from Engineer to Engineer from the inception of this program. This is your implant—it will help stimulate your nervous system to unveil your gift."

"Now, if you would, Nariah, please press the little button underneath... yes, right there."

Nariah gaped at him with her thumb hovering over the button.

"It'll be alright, it heals in no time! It might sting a little..." Horace pulled out another golden beetle to hand to a tall, skinny student with dark hair in the front.

Nariah fumbled the implant, nearly dropping it before catching it swiftly and jamming her thumb over the button. The tall student followed her example, and they both held the implant, waiting for their next instruction.

"Now," Horace said, "if you would just hover the bottom over your forearm... no, where the button is, hold that over—no, the button side..."

Paerli passed a gadget to Lor.

"Are these sterile?" he whispered.

"Probably not. But... they're gold, right? Maybe they're naturally sterile."

Lor pushed his button. Nariah shrieked, pulling everyone's attention.

"Holy crap!" Dill gasped and grinned as the implant sprouted slender black legs, jamming them into the flesh of her forearm. A pinprick of blood trickled down the side.

"This is what it's supposed to do!" Horace shouted, tamping his hands down to calm the crowd.

Several more gasps and groans bubbled from frightened lips as dozens of little black legs stuck the recruits. Nariah shuddered and groaned as the implant took on a life of its own and burrowed under a flap of her skin.

Lor hissed through his teeth as the spider poked his arm. Just like Nariah, a little trickle of blood pooled at the puncture site, then dribbled down the side. The golden insect settled its body onto his arm like a new pet, biting a slit over tender pale skin.

"Ow, this is weird as hell." He turned to Paerli.

She wasn't there. Cries and moans rose from the crowd as the spiders invaded each recruit.

"Par?" Lor scouted the area, with no sign of her long shiny black hair and deep swarthy skin.

The pinch of the implant wriggled into his forearm, making a blanket for itself out of his flesh. He sucked in a deep breath and held it until the golden parasite settled under the skin and stopped moving.

"Gnarly!" Dill held his forearm up, moving it back and forth to watch the light bend over the new lump.

"I'm glad *you're* having fun." Nico had his arm pointed down, gritting his teeth while the implant settled in.

Emilia held on to Nariah and wept in wheezing hiccups as the bug nuzzled under her skin.

Lor raised his arm to see the lump. He prodded it, wondering what it was like for Eva, and whether she had friends this early in the program to be there with her.

"That was unpleasant," Paerli said from behind him.

Lor spun around to see her standing there, holding her arm. "Where were you?"

"I was right here." She raised an eyebrow.

"I swear you weren't."

"Well, I was." She chuckled, gripping her arm tighter.

The groaning died down as the students acclimated to the implant. Nico observed his implant the way Dill did with no complaint.

Lor didn't realize Damaetra stood nearby. She suffered through the ordeal without uttering a sound, wandering up to Lor and picking up his arm. Her soft hands traced the skin, sending prickles down his spine.

She clicked her tongue. "I'm not sure if we'll survive this one." She winked at him.

"Aw, geez, what are we going to do?" he whispered.

"I guess we'll have to go to the Promised Land together," she whispered back.

Her eyes fluttered and she set his arm back down. The breeze rolled under the hair falling from her buns, touching him with the scent of violets. She exuded light, as if made of gold under a translucent white shell.

"See you around, Loren." She kept her voice low, turning to make her way to the shore again.

He watched her dress billow in the breeze.

"She seems like a nice girl," Paerli said, standing next to Lor, holding her arm with a wad of cloth.

"Can I see?" he asked, nodding at her arm.

"Not yet, it's still bleeding."

"Still?"

"Yeah. It'll be alright, don't worry about it."

"If you say so."

Horace stepped up on the classroom stair, shouting to the crowd again, "Yoo hoo! Everyone listen up! Now that you are all implanted, I order you to have a relaxing rest of your day. No classes today!"

Everyone cheered, and several recruits just ran off. Lor winced at the thought of them slicing feet on ancient tech.

CHAPTER 8

Damaetra
LOREN

"HEY, I'M GOING TO GO back to the dorm. I'll see you tomorrow, yeah?" Paerli held up her arm and nodded toward the dorm.

"Yeah, sure. Take care of that thing. I'm sure someone around here will help you if it doesn't stop bleeding."

Paerli smiled at him. "Thanks, Lor. I will."

"See you tomorrow then." He ran his hand down her arm, squeezing her hand. She blushed and spun around to make the walk back to her room.

"Are you guys, like, *together*?" Dill asked.

Lor jumped, forgetting about Dill and Nico. "What, together with Paerli? No, no... no."

"Are you sure? 'Cause you sure are red."

Lor rubbed at his face. "No, I'm not."

Nico chuckled. "It's alright, man, she's pretty hot."

"We're not together. She's *way* out of my league." Lor glanced over at Damaetra standing on the shore in prayer. He wondered what she always asked for.

"Nah, you're a good-looking dude, I think!" Dill said, nudging Lor's implant-free arm. "I mean, don't get me wrong, it's not like I want to be your girlfriend or anything."

Nico belly laughed. "You are hilarious."

"If you want to know what I think," Lor said, summoning them toward himself to a secret circle. They dipped their heads low, meeting him in whisper range. "I think I might be interested in *her*." Lor pointed at Damaetra, who remained planted at the shore with her eyes closed in silent prayer.

"The Anglia?" Dill said.

"Shh, yes, her. And her name is Damaetra."

"She's pretty cute too," Nico offered.

"Well, your god-like face can stay away from her," Lor said, laughing.

"He's got a point," Dill said, observing Nico.

"What? You guys are crazy." Nico blushed, showing off those deep dimples.

"No, seriously, in the definition tome, your picture is there next to 'handsome.'"

"Whatever." Nico waved his hand.

"Did you not see all those girls mopping up their drool earlier?" Dill made a motion of long strings of slobber dripping from his mouth.

Nico gave a small smile, waving off Dill. "I have no intention of going after your girl, Lor," he said.

"I know, I know, I was just messing with you. But you are handsome. I'm jealous."

"Me too," Dill said.

"Okay, stop it. This isn't about me—go talk to her." Nico pointed toward Damaetra.

Lor grinned. "Wish me luck," he said as he turned toward the shore.

The breeze ruffled her loose strands spilling from the buns, waving behind her with the train of her dress. She didn't look real.

"Oh, hey, Loren," Damaetra said, turning toward him. "Where did your girlfriend go?"

Her words struck him in the gut. "Oh, Paerli? She's just a friend."

Damaetra smiled, her cheeks flushed under the freckles. "Oh, I see. That's good to hear."

"It is?"

She tittered and rocked on her heels. "How's your toe?"

He glanced down to see a purple pinky hugging the rest of his foot. "I think I just might live."

"I knew you'd make it. What did you have planned today?" she asked.

"Nothing actually, I just thought I'd come over here and see what you were up to."

She turned over her arm, pointing at the lump. "It looks like it's already healed."

Lor glanced at his own implant, and sure enough, all that remained was a bulge, with only the ghost of a slit in his flesh. "The implant must have some kind of healing magic in it."

"Do you believe in magic?"

"What are Guilds but some kind of magic?"

"I suppose you have a point." She smiled with tiny freckles stretched across her face.

"What do you pray about?" Lor nodded toward the ocean.

She glanced out at the sea, and she relaxed her eyelids, giving her a look of desire to cross over the waters. "Oh, anything and everything," she said.

"Any*one*?"

"Always." She picked up his hand and held it in hers. His average-sized mitt barely fit between both hers. "Do you want to pray with me?"

"S-sure." He swallowed. "I'm not sure what to pray for."

She giggled. "Pray for anything and everything. The Maker always listens."

Lor wondered if Paerli believed in the Maker. Or Nico and Dill. Gale used to talk to the Maker a lot after Mom died, but he stopped doing that after a while. Lor never tried himself.

"Do I just... talk?"

Damaetra laughed. "You can if you want, but the Maker knows your heart. You can just say things in your head—that's what I like to do."

"How long do you do that for?"

"There's no rule. Here, come over this way." She led him over to the shore.

She strode behind him, putting her small white hands around his arms and turned him toward the vast openness beyond the sea, away from Mount Gehenna. Not one clump of land graced the horizon, and Lor wondered how far it went.

She stood next to him. "Now just close your eyes... like me."

"I, uh." Lor swallowed, not wanting to tell her that he saw things under his eyelids. She might think he was crazy.

"Go ahead, I'm right here with you," she said. Her eyes were already closed, and she reached out a smooth pinky finger to touch the top of his hand. His skin looked dirty against hers.

Lor closed his eyes. The colors swirled under his lids. They were a strong distraction.

"Just breathe and try to push everything out of your mind," she continued.

Her finger just barely touched his skin.

He let out a sigh and tried to push it all out.

"Just tell the Maker anything," she said.

"I want a million plat," he joked.

She giggled. "Well, He might give that to you, but I'd try something small first."

"Okay, okay, I'll focus."

The colors swirled, and he tried not to focus on them. It was hard. They begged for his attention.

Maker...

His own voice echoed inside his head, and the tide whooshed over the sand.

Um, hello. Hi.

The colors bounced around, batting his voice around in his hollow mind.

Is it weird that I think I like this girl?

Something happened that Lor had never seen before. The colors crystallized into fractal patterns, opening a hole in the middle that dilated like a lens.

Is that a yes or a no?

The lens pulsed, narrowing and widening in a fractal mouth.

What should I do?

It continued to pulse, waiting to devour anything that passed through the void.

Is this real?

The hole shrank a little, then snapped open. The cool touch of Damaetra's finger moved, and he was suddenly aware of everything.

So, can you tell me what to do?

The fractals spun in place around the geometric opening. While watching the show, each piece flipped around, snapping into place and reflecting white gold. After the last piece came to rest, the opening pulsed once again, under the glittering mirror of white gold.

Lor's eyes fluttered open. The deep blue ocean spanned before him, but the ghost of the lens lingered in the distance.

"Damaetra, do you see colors?" he asked.

Please don't think I'm crazy.

"Colors? What do you mean?" Her eyes were still closed, and he looked down to see her small finger remained stuck out, touching him.

"When you close your eyes. Do you see colors there?"

Damaetra hummed. "Not that I can tell. I just see white." She opened her eyes toward the sea.

"What did you pray for?" she asked.

"I can't tell you, or it won't come true."

"That's only for wishes."

Lor smiled. "What did *you* pray for?"

"I can't tell you." She grinned.

"That's cheating."

"Not if you're setting the rules."

She continued to look out at the water.

"How do you do it?" he asked.

She chuckled. "Do what?"

Lor couldn't put it into words. She calmed him, and he didn't know how to say it.

"You... seem unbothered by anything."

"Is that bad?"

"It's the best."

She spun to gaze up at him. "Life is too short to worry."

Lor chuffed. "That reminds me of an old thing my dad used to tell us as kids. He would say, 'worrying is like a rocking chair...'"

"'It gives you something to do but gets you nowhere.'" She finished his quote, grinning.

"So you know that already."

"I do."

He just met the girl. She was delicate and beautiful. She exuded tenderness and care. Her presence brought him a sense of calm, and he wondered if he did anything for her. After all, he'd heard chatter among his women classmates that a lot of them enroll not only for the chance to get a gift, but to meet a future husband. Maybe Damatra felt that way. He could be a husband.... He scanned her heart-shaped face, settling on her mouth, blushed by the sun. All the little rumors swirled in his mind, and his heart thumped erratically. He wanted to kiss her.

"Damaetra..." he said in the most casual way he could muster.

"Yes, Loren?" She met his nonchalance with her own charming brand of whisper. Her eyes reflected blue-violet, and he noticed specks of white in the irises.

It's just your cave-dwelling lizard brain talking, Lor. You meet two girls in the first week and can't even keep the blood in your head.

"Nevermind."

CHAPTER 9

Juicy Greens
LOREN

LOR LEFT THE DORM EARLY the next morning. The silhouettes of Paerli and Damaetra were walking down the beach, lit by the purple and pink hues of the first sun peeking up from the horizon. He wondered what they were talking about.

The air was thick that morning. Lor took in a deep breath, smelling salt and seaweed. Gentle waves rolled in from the shallows. He wanted to roll up his pants and jump over them like he used to with Eva. Only, this ocean was the same shade of turquoise he saw in Paerli's eyes, with pink sand Horace mentioned was due to microscopic ore particles and algae.

Dill's fairy tales suggested it was the taint of blood from the age of the Great Conflict. With the smattering of ancient tech littered throughout the beach, it didn't seem too far-fetched that blood was the actual reason. He stuck his toes into the sand, withdrawing clumps of the pink grains. They slid off his feet, and he imagined a sticky trail of blood in their wake.

"You got up early!" Dill smacked Lor's shoulder, making him jump and spin around.

"You scared the hell out of me," Lor said, putting a hand to his chest.

"Sorry, bud, but in all fairness you woke *me* up."

Lor tittered. "Hey, did you have that book with you here at the program?"

"What book?"

"You know, the one you said was your brother's crusty history book?"

"Oh, that one? I do, actually. I have a few books."

Lor stuck a toe in the sand, flicking it up and sending grains arcing through the air. "I wish I brought a book. Can I borrow yours?"

"I thought you thought they were just fairy tales?"

"That was Nariah. *I'm* interested, though."

"Yeah, I can give it to you later. It's got some pretty wild things in there."

"Like what?"

Dill sucked his teeth. "Well, for starters, the book is old. I don't know where bro got it from, but some things are just like history books today, but some things are changed... details, dates... that sort of thing."

"Yeah, give it to me after class."

"Sure thing," He said, rubbing his hands together. "What do you think today's class will be?"

"Who knows."

The first sun continued to climb, casting yellowish hues over the sand, making it look orange. The image of the white gold fractals nagged his brain. He wanted to see it again. Was it the Maker talking back to him through his visions?

Nico finally emerged, jogging up to the pair.

"Let's roll!" Dill waved them along.

Recruits wandered to tables with sand swishing and grinding under their feet. Each one settled into the creaky pole chairs armed with a simple bound book of parchment and a single pencil. Lor sighed as he pinched the pencil between his fingers and rocked it back and forth over the table. This was his life for the next six months. He hadn't used a pencil to write anything in years. Using voice command tablets was the new normal, offering a blessing and a curse. He didn't know anyone who had the ability to write legibly anymore. The hardened finger callous of his youth had gone soft—this was going to hurt.

Paerli settled into her chair, slapping her bound parchment on the table and pulling her pencil from behind her ear. She flexed her fingers and rotated her wrist a few times in preparation for the ache of manual note-taking.

"Don't forget to do your stretches," she joked, continuing to rotate her wrist.

Emilia passed through the door, choosing a seat next to Nariah. Dill sat with Nico at the next table. Lor turned around, catching Damaetra's gaze. The seat next to her was empty.

He glanced at Paerli, and she methodically wiggled the pencil between her fingers. He hoped they would stay friends after graduation, Guild or not.

"Hey," she said, catching him watching her play with the pencil.

"Hey. How was your day yesterday?"

"Eh, it was okay. I just hung around the dorm reading nonsense books about nonsense things."

"Oh? Like what kind of nonsense?"

"Just stupid theories about Roseaarde that take a touch of truth to craft fairy tales about our history."

Lor tilted his head. "What kind of book was *that?*"

"I don't remember what it was called. What did you do yesterday?"

"I spent the day with Nico, Dill, and Damaetra." Lor didn't really want to go into detail about it. He wondered if the book she was talking about was similar to Dill's. If so, why did she talk so dismissively about it?

"Is that so?"

Her attitude seemed off. She wasn't as pleasant as usual, making Lor wonder if something happened the night before that she wasn't willing to discuss.

"Hey, are you okay?"

She huffed out her nostrils and played with her pencil some more. "Yeah, I'm fine. Why do you ask?"

"I don't know, you seem... sad? Upset? I don't know."

"Totally fine." She put her pencil down and grinned at him, hooking her arm through his.

It felt like a ritual at that point. Paerli was hands down the most attractive girl in the program in the traditional sense, and she always came to him. That made him feel a little less awkward, and truthfully more desirable in a way. He couldn't help but notice some of the girls look at him differently with her around, laced in his arm. He relaxed in her grip, taking in the aroma of sweet apples in her hair.

Horace hobbled into the class, grabbing a piece of chalk and scratching over the board's surface. As students realized he was there, mouths closed in succession, bringing a hush to the room. He wrote the word "FORMULATOR" on the board, each stroke a painful jab to the board, piercing the air with staccato thumps and scratches. He finalized the word with a thick underline, catching the board with a fingernail and releasing a high-pitched squeal. Recruits cried out and covered their ears. Lor heard Damaetra giggle behind him, and that made him smile.

"Sorry about that," Horace said, slapping the chalk onto the table. "Welcome back! I do hope everyone's experience yesterday with the 'nudge' wasn't too traumatic," he said.

"I also hope you all brought your binders and pencils because today we are starting with one of the most underrated Guild memberships: the Formulator."

Sounds of parchment swishing filled the room as recruits opened their books. Dill folded his in half, running his fist across the binding, breaking it. Lor wrote the header, "Formulator," at the top of the page, feeling each grind of the nib in his softened writing finger. Paerli tottered her pencil between her index and middle finger, resting her chin on her palm and not writing.

She's pretty smart and probably already knows what he's going to say.

"The Formulator," Horace continued, "is a grade three Guild class that, despite its low grade, is quite a useful and life-saving skill. Does anyone know what they do?"

Lor didn't know anything about grades or levels, or the significance of anything. He kept his mouth pressed shut, turning away from Horace in hopes that he wouldn't randomly call on him.

Instead, Horace glanced over at Paerli, his *star pupil.* She smiled at him, not giving in to his look. He took the hint and looked around the room to be met with continued silence.

"Oh, seems like we have a long way to go." Horace sighed, limping to the bookshelf to pull out another dusty tome. He licked a finger to flip through pages, and Lor imagined doing that must taste like dirt.

"Ah, yes, okay, I will give you the 'textbook' description of the Formulator. Get your pencils ready."

Horace read the lines in the book:

The Formulator is granted holy insight into the potential of eneris, with the ability to craft living draughts to aid their fellow citizen in day-to-day activities.

"Sounds a bit dry, but to put it simply, a Formulator can taste eneris to see what it can become, much like the Engineers we talked about on your first day." Horace slapped the book shut, throwing particles in the air. "But the unique thing about both Formulators and Engineers is that the material is open to the crafter's suggestions, so they can have a little control over what it becomes."

A demure knock rapped at the door. Horace limped over to it, letting in a Foscan servant pushing a cart. He struggled against the sand with manual wheels. If tech were allowed, his job would have been easier with a hover cart. Its contents rattled and clanged with each lump in the sand. The servant was a man—small, slender, and otherworldly with perfect cool-toned skin and a shock of silvery black hair. The servant took a peek at the class, and Lor caught those white eyes, just like Dag's.

"Thank you, Valge'jor." Horace bowed low to the servant. "You can leave the cart here."

Valge'jor bowed to Horace, then to the class, then hurried out of the room.

"Valge'jor is a respected friend of the program, and a valuable asset to us."

Nariah stuck her hand in the air, wagging her fingers.

"Yes, Nariah?"

"Isn't he a Foscan? Doesn't that make him a *danger* to us?"

Horace barked a laugh from deep within his belly. "Oh ho! A danger? Oh no, girl. He is less a danger to you than you are to him."

Nervous laughter rose in the room. Paerli had her cheek pressed into her hand, wagging that pencil and looking bored.

The guide made his way to the cart, fussing with a few random manual tools lying on top. Most remarkable to Lor were the three boxes, clasped shut in three strategic locations. The surface of the boxes had a classic feel to them, with a quilted black covering under bronze clamps.

Horace moved to undo the closures on the boxes, drawing Lor's full attention.

"These are Formulator chests," Horace said, undoing the first box. He unfolded the partitions to reveal three sections, each one lined with rows of flasks.

"You will see most Formulators with one of these, or a variation of one." He pulled out a flask filled with green liquid, holding it up for the class.

"You all should know what this is, but in case you don't, this is a phial of green eneris."

Lor stared at the phial twinkling under the beam of sunlight pooling from the window. He had a mild understanding of eneris, knowing that it was essence squeezed from anything that was once alive. The thought always sickened him—it felt wrong for anyone to be using a former life force.

Horace slid one of the phials across Dill and Nico's table. "Mister Storgut," he said. Dill jumped and raised his eyes from the phial. "Would you mind terribly passing out some of these phials with your table mate, Mister Dicus?"

Lor chuckled at the formality. He could picture Nico being called "mister," but Dill?

"No problem-o," Dill said, scooting from his chair and going to the box. He stared at it, trying to figure out how he would handle passing out glass vessels. He shrugged at Nico, then threaded the necks between fingers, carrying four in each hand. Nico did the same.

Dill came to Lor and Paerli's desk and scratched a phial over his table with a wry smile. "Enjoy," he whispered.

They passed out all the phials, one per table, then returned to their own.

"What you have in front of you is a test. A test of the Formulator," Horace said. He peered at the class over those glasses and cracked a smile. "It's a *taste* test."

There was a low murmur in the room.

"So I gotta put my mouth on something that this guy put his jibs all over?" Dill asked, laughing at Nico. The class burst into laughter, and Nico put his arms on the table, burying his face in them.

Horace laughed. "You don't have to chug the phial, just put a little on your finger."

With that, there was a sound of several glass stoppers scraping from glass necks.

"Don't forget to document your experiences," Horace said.

Paerli popped the top of their phial and tipped it toward Lor. The green inside was syrupy and stank like mildew. She dripped a little on the pad of his index finger, and he grimaced at it.

"I hope it doesn't taste the way it smells," Lor said, holding the blob up to his nose as it threatened to dribble down his finger.

"I don't think it will taste like anything," Paerli said, serving herself a drop.

"Why do you say that?" A skin started to form on the surface of Lor's sample.

"You'd better taste that." She nodded at the drop as it started to dry.

"Oh shoot." He stuck the finger in his mouth, feeling the thick sap on his tongue.

"Well?" Paerli said, licking her lower lip.

Lor smacked his lips, using his tongue to spread the syrup around the roof of his mouth. He made a series of faces at Paerli—concentration, concern, disgust.

"It just feels... thick. And gross."

Paerli chuckled. "See, I told you it wouldn't taste like anything." She stuck the tip of her finger in her mouth again, giving him a sultry look.

Did she ever run around naked in Kanckette? Stop it, Lor.

He turned to watch Damaetra, who still hadn't opened her phial. It sat on her table glimmering, and she stared at it with her hands folded on the table.

"Does it scare you?" Lor joked.

Damaetra cracked a small grin, keeping her eye on the phial. "I don't think scared is the word, but maybe a close cousin of the word. Or a sister."

"It didn't taste like anything to me. It was just thick."

"Maybe I should wait to see what happens to you." She looked up at him. The light of the classroom reflected blue in her eyes.

Lor reached over the back of his chair and put his hand over hers.

"Horace wouldn't give us anything that would hurt you."

"Promise?"

"I promise. Look at us, we're doing alright so far." He pointed to himself and Paerli. Paerli turned around at the mention.

"You still haven't tried it yet?" she asked.

Damaetra shook her head.

Paerli leaned over and cupped her hand to the side of her mouth. "It doesn't taste like anything," she whispered.

Damaetra pursed her lips, then wrapped her fingers around the base of the phial. Paerli turned around, but Lor stayed with her. He pulled the stopper from the neck and took the phial.

"Just put a little on your finger," he said, tilting the phial toward her. The goop crawled down the neck, and Damaetra held out her index finger.

A blob plunked on it when air rushed through the phial, making *bloop, bloop, bloop!* sounds.

"Oh, crap, I'm sorry!" Lor pulled the phial back up as green syrup dribbled all over Damaetra's tiny finger. She flinched, letting the liquid pool on the table.

"I didn't know it would come out that fast, I'm so sorry."

"It smells awful," she said, wrinkling her nose.

"Like mildew, right?"

"That's a good way to put it." She stuck the finger in her mouth, and excess green fluid ran through the crack between her soft pink lips.

She perked her head up, eyes going wide.

"Tastes like nothing, right?" Lor smiled at her.

She pulled the finger from her mouth and ran a green tongue over her bottom lip, catching the excess.

"Actually," she said, moving her jaw back and forth and wrinkling her brow, "there's *something* there."

"Seriously?" Lor asked.

Paerli turned around again, watching the girl.

"Yeah," Damaetra said. She picked up the phial again, taking care not to let it sploosh over her finger. She held it to her nose and wrinkled her face in disgust. "It definitely doesn't taste like *that*. But... it doesn't taste like nothing."

She sucked on her finger, rolling her eyes back and forth, trying to search her brain for some kind of answer.

"Hey, Horace," Paerli summoned the guide.

He limped to their table.

"Are we witnessing something spectacular?" he asked, eyeballing the thick puddle of green on Damaetra's table.

"She's got something," Paerli said, pointing at Damaetra.

"Oh? Do tell." Horace gripped the table to lean over it.

"Well," Damaetra said, sucking on her tongue, "there's a hint of... palm grass maybe? Mixed with something floral."

"Yes? Is there anything else?" Horace grinned. At this point, the whole class was silent, watching her table.

Dill's eyes were wide with an open-mouthed grin, and he bobbed his head back and forth to get a better view.

"Um, there's a flavor to it, I'm not sure how to explain it." Damaetra spoke softly. "Like, if it just had a touch of something else, it could ease the stomach."

Horace jolted upright and clapped his hands. The students murmured and followed his claps with confused expressions. Dill was not confused; he slapped his hands together with straight arms in front of him.

"Well *done*, Miss Praes!"

Lor realized he never asked Damaetra's last name. It was fitting for her, as someone who always prayed. Her name was literally a simple sentence: Damaetra "prays." He chuckled to himself, planning to tell her about that.

Horace put a hand on Damaetra's shoulder. "You just began your journey as a beginner Formulator."

"What did I discover?" she asked.

Horace smiled at her and chuckled under his breath. "That is only for the Formulator to know," he said. He then turned to face the rest of the class.

"Everyone, please congratulate your program mate for officially being the first recruit in *my* tenure to find her ability in the first week of the program!" He clapped again, this time with a roar from the class.

Damaetra sank down in her seat, a flush sweeping over her pale cheeks.

Lor grinned wide at her and she smiled at him, with a touch of green still clinging to her lips. He felt Paerli watching him from the corner of his eye as she tugged at his shirt.

***

"Miss Praes, if you could please stay behind, I should like to discuss with you the implications of your new ability and your assignments going forward. For the rest of you, class dismissed." Horace beckoned her to him as the class slid from their squeaky chairs.

Lor stood up and rounded the table to Damaetra. She glanced up at him. "I'll see you around, Loren."

"Yes, you will."

He started his walk toward the exit and watched her as he went, nearly running into Nico's back.

"Whoa there," Nico said, jumping to the side. He put Lor in a headlock and knuckled his hair. "You about ran into me gawking at your woman."

Lor pretended to punch him in the ribs. "Quiet, she doesn't know that yet."

"Man, I'm so jealous already!" Dill shouted into the beachy air as they skipped down the stairs.

"Don't worry, I'm sure you'll be a Weggevens before too long," Nico joked.

Dill hissed at him like a cat. "Never!"

Lor belly laughed and slapped Nico on the shoulder.

"Hey, guys, I'm going to walk along the beach for a while and wait for her, if you don't mind."

Dill clicked his tongue. "I see how it is, once a girl comes along, the boys get the shaft."

"It's not like that, you'll always be my boys," Lor said, laughing.

"Go get her, you dog." Nico pushed Lor's arm and dragged Dill away.

Strongman
LOREN

RATHER THAN HEAD TO THE dorm after the lesson, Loren paced the coast alone to wait for Damaetra. His head started to hurt, and he partially attributed that to the lump in his arm. A part of him imagined a more sinister ploy behind its existence. He skipped past a jagged piece of tech in the sand. In the distance, a tall building stood glistening against a border of trees. Its construction was very unlike the mud and grass used to build the campus. He saw the shimmering building on his first day but didn't consider it until now.

That must be the resort from the brochure.

He was curious about the line in one of the brochures he read about the "void brothers." They weren't mentioned in any of his books, and he wanted to meet one and see if they were a part of the cult he heard about. He wasn't sure if Horace would let him near the resort while still a part of the program.

Pitter-patters in the sand jogged up next to him, and he saw Paerli there, her arm wrapping itself around his like usual. Lor didn't have anything to say, and she stayed quiet, just taking solace in the crook of his arm.

Other students passed in front of them, gabbing with each other about things that were meaningless in Lor's eyes. Who was their favorite storyteller, the drama with some famous family, new wave music... Lor heard someone mention paying a thousand plats to visit a tourist restaurant where a famous storyteller once pitched an idea.

What a waste of money.

A Mesaman about Dill's size walked with his opposite—a bulky, square Mesaman taller than even Lor. They examined each other's implants, poking, prodding, and squeezing them.

"Maybe this will make it work faster..." the bigger guy said.

Paerli clicked her tongue, breaking the silence between them.

"That's not how it works," she whispered.

Lor cleared his throat. "How does it work then?"

"Not like that," she said, giggling. Lor sighed, brushing his fingers through his hair. He rubbed at his scalp, attempting to stamp out the headache. Without realizing it, he ran his hand down his face the way Gale did so many times before in frustration. The last thing Lor wanted was to emulate Gale's bad habits.

"You know," he said to her, "I always wanted to be a roundsman."

She fluttered her eyelashes. "A roundsman? Why?"

Lor chewed his lip for a moment. Truth was, he didn't really have a reason. When he learned about Gale's old friend, Gregory, it was almost as if a deep seated desire to defy his stepfather roused him to choose that profession. Greg's death was gruesome and an unnecessary outcome to a domestic dispute involving rotator tech. Lor asked himself many times if he wanted the same for himself, and he always came up with empty reasons. The more he pondered Paerli's simple question, the more he asked himself the same thing: Why?

Did my rebelliousness against Gale run so deep? Why?

"I don't know," was all he could utter.

"You don't want to be in the program?"

"Well, I didn't. But"—he glanced at her, then back at the hut where Damaetra was finishing up—"I do now."

He wanted to know more about everything. Now that Damaetra was a Formulator, he wanted to learn everything with her.

She smiled. "I'm glad you're here."

She rested her head on his shoulder, and his heart fluttered. The beat had an echo, as if a second heart was jammed behind his own. It took his breath away.

"Are you okay?" She bolted upright.

Lor put a hand to his chest. "Yeah, I think so. That was weird."

It was another moment to carve suspicion within him about the implant. What if it was a kill switch?

"So, I think Damaetra likes you," she said, changing the subject.

His heart fluttered again, but only his own. "Did she tell you that?"

"In so many ways. We walked the beach this morning and she asked me about you."

Attention from beautiful women didn't exist on Lor's list of things that could happen to him during the program. While he liked the attention, it made him nervous.

"I've never had a girlfriend before," he muttered.

"Really?" Paerli grinned.

"Don't look at me like that," he joked. "I dunno, I just never tried."

"I see... the mom's basement type, is it?" she said.

Lor laughed. "Dad's basement actually."

Paerli chuckled and sighed, resting her head back on his arm.

"You really think she likes me?"

"Mm-hmm."

He was inexperienced with the judgment of girls, but he didn't think Paerli would lie to him about that.

"I've actually been meaning to ask you," Lor said, raising his arm with her hooked in it. "What does this mean?"

"What?"

"You know what."

"No, tell me. Did I do something wrong?"

"Why do you latch on to me all the time? Don't get me wrong, I'm not complaining, but I just want to know."

"Oh, well... I don't know, I just feel drawn to you. Don't you feel the same?"

"But you just told me you thought Damaetra liked me."

Women are weird.

"She does! And I like you too but... as a friend. A *close* friend."

"We just met like, three days ago."

Paerli giggled. "Do you not believe in friendship at first sight?"

Lor shrugged. There was something about her that he couldn't shake. Maybe there was such a thing as friendship at first sight. After all, he made fast friends with Dill and Nico, so why not Paerli too?

He opened his mouth to answer her when a hair-raising scream came from near the dorms.

They spun toward the buildings, seeing the shadow of a student lying on the ground, twitching and kicking up plumes of sand. The black silhouette of Horace sprinted from the classroom, running as fast as his limp would carry him. Damaetra stood at the base of the classroom stairs, watching the commotion from afar. Other recruits swarmed the scene, screaming and shouting at each other, making the situation infinitely worse.

A snap of electricity cut through the air, smelling of charged ozone. He gripped his arm in reflex, worried about the stability of his implant. Screams of *"help him!"* to *"don't let him die!"* called to Horace as he reached the student. Horace wiped his brow and knelt to the ground near the head of the thrashing recruit.

"Back up, everyone!" Horace shouted, waving his hand to brush the crowd away.

Lor craned his neck over the crowd.

"It's the kid that was squeezing his implant earlier, trying to make it work faster," he told Paerli.

She sucked air through her teeth.

Horace sat cross-legged in the sand, cradling the boy's head in his lap. His bulging arms pulsed under the skin and pounded the sand, sending tremors through the ground and sand flying upward in a thin curtain. Several of the students closest to him jumped back. Some fell over and scrambled away from him. Rocking with the violence, Horace kept a tight hold against the kid's temples, speaking calm affirmations to him.

"You will defeat the rage inside you... you will survive." Horace continued the assurances.

Survive?

While Horace talked with the kid, Lor noticed with each blow to the ground, a new cluster of boils appeared on his skin.

A deep, guttural groan that morphed into an animalistic scream vibrated in Lor's chest, and he shrank down, clasping his ears. The other recruits did the same.

"Valge'jor!" Horace shouted behind him, continuing to grip the kid's trembling head. "You will survive... you will survive... Valge'jor!"

The slender Foscan servant who had delivered the eneris during class sprang up the beach from the classroom. He was all muscle and sinew. A wispy rag of a shirt clung to his chest, rippling in the breeze.

The kid roared again, even louder than before. The recruits clapped their ears again in horror.

Valge'jor caught up to Horace, kneeling next to him and uttering his strange language. "Vles'tan jorech ma goethe'te?"

"Yes, yes, please... and hurry! Shh, shh, you will beat this, you will survive..."

Lor watched Valge'jor fly on muscled legs back to the hut, curious that Horace seemed to understand the language. Another cursed wail came from the student, except this time a chunky stream of vomit spewed from his throat, splattering over the front of his shirt. Horace bobbed and ducked out of the way.

All his muscles flexed, and the kid spread-eagled in the sand, each fiber going rigid. The biceps quivered with bundles of muscle groups rising like Emilia's pearls under the skin. Boils warbled over his forearms, threatening to pop. He heaved and rocked his head back and forth under Horace's mantra. The golden implant slithered under paper-thin skin as he lay there, supine and flexing.

Lor only closed his eyes for the sharpest moment when the implant burst from the kid's arm like a champagne cork, sending shards of gold and blood through the air, raining onto the sand and bouncing off ancient tech with a clang. Emilia screeched, grabbing on to Nariah, who stood slack-jawed, unable to move.

Horace covered the boy's forehead with his palm and pressed his brow on top. His lips moved in a soundless whisper as the poor kid shuddered and went still. His head rolled to the side, eyes open and mouth agape. Valge'jor returned too late with any meaningful help, but he held a white round-bottomed flask. Horace nodded at him.

"Foest opaecha'te? Ouv maes'te?" Valge'jor said in the same foreign tongue.

"Yes, they're not just kids anymore. It's okay." Horace used a trembling hand to wipe sweat from his forehead. He ran two fingers down the recruit's eyelids and pushed his jaw back into place. If Lor hadn't seen the spectacle, he would think the kid was taking a nap on the beach, only with a hole in his arm and puke on his shirt.

Valge'jor grunted as he perched on his knees next to the recruit's head. He ran slender alien fingers down the boy's cheek, then curled them around his neck. Valge'jor tensed, squeezing the sallow throat, and the kid's skin blanched under his grip.

Paerli pressed into Lor, watching the transaction in a trance, almost intrigued by it. Cold silence gripped them, save for the occasional squawking waterbird high above. Morbid spectators held their breath, watching the Foscan squeeze their dead classmate's jugular.

Valge'jor rolled his eyes back, quivering in place as the kid's head trembled under his grip. Paerli gasped when the kid's flesh rippled and sank. Veins and fibers shriveled into wads of dry paper. The length of his body shrank in on itself, bringing the wrinkled remains in to around the same height as his friend, who held his mouth nearby. A peek of silver rippled within the crater made by the exploding implant. It pooled and mingled with blood, creating a swirling scarlet liquid.

Is that eneris?

The kid's eyes glazed over, spilling silver from the sockets, which Valge'jor dutifully scooped up with the white round-bottomed flask. More silver oozed from pores, occasionally pulsing in bursts as if unblocked by microscopic plugs of filth. Valge'jor moved like a tender nurse, dipping the flask and collecting most of the shiny essence. He caught a small geyser in the flask, and Lor heard the liquid squirt to the bottom. It made him sick.

"You're a freaking Reaper! Oh my god, the *Foscan* is a *Reaper!*" Nariah squealed at Valge'jor, her face twisted in horror.

Her cry of disgust roused the others from their stupor, making another girl wail. More students screamed, but only Lor and his friends remained still, watching.

Valge'jor ignored the screaming to scrape the remaining silver from the strip of jerky that used to be a student. He stood and faced Horace, capping the flask.

"Tad Arons," Valge'jor said in Northern Common with a low bow. Horace nodded and sent him away.

Lor managed to burble out the smallest peep of protest. "What... what...?" Paerli squeezed his arm.

"Calm down, everyone, please!" Horace held his hands in the air.

"Why did you let that *monster* suck him dry? He killed him!" Nariah screamed. Tears ran over her flushed cheeks, falling in swollen drops from her chin.

"Valge'jor is *not* a monster, Miss Blevens, and you'd do right by taking that attitude elsewhere, as I will *not* tolerate it here." Horace's face turned red, contrasting with his light blond hairline. His eyes bulged with rage and frustration.

He jabbed a quaking finger at the dorms. "Everyone to your rooms! You're done for today!"

The guide's fingers shook when he slid his hand across his forehead.

The crowd scattered. Nariah sobbed with Emilia, taking in whooping breaths, trying to talk.

"I... can't... do... this... anymore!" she cried. Emilia hushed her, telling her how everything was going to be okay between sobs of her own.

Lor dragged his feet toward the dorm with Paerli, leaving Dill and Nico at the death site. He glanced back toward the classroom to see Damaetra still standing there as still as a statue. Workers scurried around her, tending to different areas around the class building.

Their hazy shapes moved around as a backdrop to Horace trying to carry the saggy remains of the boy away.

"They've probably seen this before. It probably doesn't shock them anymore." Paerli pinched the fabric of Lor's sleeve, tugging it to draw his attention.

"I don't get it. What even happened?"

"Have you never seen a pull before?" Her voice was soft, sultry.

"Is that what that was called?"

"Well, that's not what they call it in the texts, but essentially, yeah."

"How do you even know that?"

Paerli shrugged. "I've been around."

"So... *that* is what Dill wants to be?" He thought of his funny roommate pogo-ing around with the power of death in his palm. "And what, exactly, happened to that kid? Did the implant do that to him? It exploded!"

Paerli fidgeted. "No, I don't think it was the implant."

Lor ran his finger over the lump on his arm, blowing a tight puff of air through his lips, toward his wet forehead. "Well, what was that then? You seem to know everything."

Paerli clicked her tongue. "I don't know everything."

"Come on, Par. You know a lot of things."

"Maybe. Maybe I do know what happened."

"Stop teasing. What happened?"

She circled her toe in the sand, letting the breeze carry her apple-scented hair. "That's what happens to an uncontrolled Weggevens. A strongman, specifically," she mumbled.

"A strongman…" Lor drew out the word. "I still don't understand."

"We can talk more about the Wegs later. Just try not to think about it too much tonight." She spun on her heel to walk down the shore. She passed the dorm buildings, moving toward the resort.

Lor watched her, curious about where she was going. She didn't go far, settling in on one of the stones dotting the edge of the tree line and looking out at the water. He moved over to the side of the building, peering around the corner.

She crossed her legs on the stone, then turned her head to see if anyone was watching her. Lor dipped his head back to the side of the building and waited for a minute. He creeped his gaze back around the corner when Paerli let out a sharp whistle.

After a moment, a handful of waterbirds flew up to her, circling overhead in a strange, robotic pattern. One of the birds flew down next to her on the rock, and she gave it something from her hand.

Did she become a Shepherd overnight?

The waterbirds flew off, and she continued to gaze beyond the horizon.

NOW ACCEPTING APPLICANTS FOR CLASS OF 1010!

Join the Guild program and infuse your world with power and might, while using your abilities to create a better, more vibrant Roseaarde!

Explore the intellectual depths of *engineering*, the creativity of *formulation*, or the communication of *shepherding* and *reading*. The most special recruits might even discover they have the benevolence of *reaping*!*

Financial questions? Audun can help! The non-Guild Finance Faction offers a 2 standard annum, 0% financing agreement, with a 12% APR thereafter. Schedule an e-Disk holo-consultation at 27-F6-7789.

*Reaping is extremely rare and the program does not guarantee any gift of any kind. Recruits enter the program at their own risk, as side effects from such gifts may include insomnia, fatigue, muscle breakdown, disturbing thoughts, lucid dreaming, a Weggevens curse, and death.

CHAPTER 11

In Memorium
LOREN

A HEAVINESS HOVERED OVER THE ISLAND the morning after the death of a Strongman. The first sun was high and bright, betraying the mood of the campus. Lor added "death of a classmate" to the list of things he never imagined happening in the program next to "attention from two hot girls." Even if he had read anything about Guilds before coming to this place, texts were only good at waxing theoretical, with only wisps of truth buried in the hypotheses.

He was the last to leave the dorm. With feet clad in clunky boots, he wasn't in the mood to catch any dangling piggies on ancient tech. There was a weaving path he learned that was safe enough from the sharp corners, but he wouldn't be taking that today.

He ran sweaty fingers through messy hair, donning a white short-sleeved button-up shirt with tan pants too long for his legs. They dragged in the sand, pulling grains along with him as he walked. Why pack a suit for a hot island adventure?

How would I know someone would die? Did Eva see someone die?

The message from Horace stated the memorial would be held in Secas. He imagined his first trip back to Secas as an excursion through the outdoor market with his friends, trying foreign foods and hiking through the colorful wilds... not surrounded by grief-stricken relatives.

A hinge squeaked from dorm 2B. Paerli shuffled down the steps, and her eyes found Lor. She waved for his attention. It was impossible for him not to see her. She wandered toward him in a white flowy dress, perfect for beach weather. Chiffon trimming rippled in the gentle breeze as the long sleeves clung to her dark skin. She traded loose hair in a fat braid for a twisted updo, showing off her slender neck and golden chain. He had tried to figure out what the pendant was on their first day, but she covered it then. Now, it rocked over the divot in her throat, glinting red sparkles from a rounded stone. The smooth stone was black, which made a fascinating gem that Lor had never seen before.

"Hey you," she said.

"Hey you."

"When does the ferry leave?"

Lor scanned the east side of campus to see others dragging themselves toward the pier where they met.

"Probably soon."

They began the walk toward the pier when Dill shouted after them.

"Hey, Lor! Hey, wait up!"

He spun around to see him running toward them.

"Oh hey, I'm sorry, I thought you already left." Lor grimaced.

"S'okay," he huffed, taking in a deep breath. "I was the last one out, I think."

The faint bellow of Horace's voice called for the students to file in line.

Lor, Paerli, and Dill picked up to a trot toward the group. Dill lifted his knees high as he jogged, while Lor chose a low, shuffling trot. Paerli ran alongside the boys with the sides of her wispy skirt clenched in her fists at her thighs.

"Sorry, Horace," Dill gasped as they approached the end of the line.

Horace grunted at them, waving his hand forward to board the ferry.

All recruits crammed into the ferry for one trip.

Damaetra sat in a far corner, wearing a violet dress and gazing out of the small window with her chin in her hand. He kept his eyes on her as she watched the island fade from the little porthole. When the program ended, he hoped she could visit him in Peakwood. It wasn't beachy or warm, but relaxed all the same.

Did she like to read?

Lor pictured her in that violet dress sitting on his bed, cross-legged and reading *Tales of the Promised Land* as her gossamer hair draped along the sides of the pages. He would find a few of the strands tucked between pages, marking her journey through the tome. As any proper gentleman, he would offer Eva's blanket to her in the chilly den. He might get under it with her, because after all, body heat was the best type of heat.

The recruit's death forced Lor to reevaluate how he spent his moments on Roseaarde. He wanted to tell Damaetra how he felt about her. The boat bobbed, rocking Damaetra from her hand. Her eyes met Lor's.

He sent her a low, stunted wave, which she returned.

I'm glad she's not a Reader.

The rest of the ride was calm, with only one recruit making a dash to the tiny one-person toilet.

The painted town swelled into view with the marina full of boats bobbing listlessly against the pier while a mix of rentals darted around the water. A raucous blend of music styles blared from the rentals. When originally introduced to the town and this sight, it made Lor wistful. Now, it was grating.

"Don't touch anything," Horace warned the students as they filtered out of the shuttle onto the funeral grounds. "Secas still employs the use of tech, and I don't want it to corrupt your learning progress."

Dill leaned over to Lor and whispered, "Who even wants to be in a Guild now?" He scratched at the lump in his arm. Lor reached over to touch his own, feeling Paerli's fingers wrapped around his forearm.

"It was probably a fluke. I'm sure we'll all be fine." Nico slid next to the group, picking at his nails.

"But what about that Foscan taking his... stuff? I mean, I know it happens, but seeing it in person makes it seem kinda messed up... you know?"

"It *was* kinda jarring," Nico agreed, "but we have to grow up sometime."

"This is life," Paerli said. She let go of Lor and glided toward the cluster of chairs set up in traditional funeral rows. People filled the seats, and Horace marched to the front row where two larger than average Mesamen sat. Lor assumed they were the kid's mother and father, rushed to Secas overnight to attend the memorial.

A large image of him was propped on a makeshift frame as he smiled at the crowd, draped in dripping blue spike lily garlands studded with pearly orbs. The orbs matched his pearly teeth. A banner under the image had bold script letters that said: Tad Arons. In the chaos, Lor had forgotten to ask the kid's name.

The picture was the first time Lor had really gotten a good look at Tad's features. He was a large boy, with a square head, square shoulders, and a beefy chest—he was practically born to be a Strongman. The haunting look in his smiling eyes made Lor shiver.

Will they get the silver Vale'jor pulled from him?

Lor didn't know how these things worked. When his mother died, Gale hired a Reaper from the Seven Cities to "take care of things" when she was finally gone, but he was too young to know anything about what that meant.

Paerli took a seat in the back, crossing her legs and gazing forward at the mound of pink and white flowers piled on top of the bronze casket. Little pops of golden accents dotted the floral arrangement.

He glanced beyond the rows of chairs to see Damaetra standing alone next to an old canopy tree with her back to the coffin. The light filtered through the leaves, casting lobed shadows over her. She was a pastel ghost in the diffuse breeze.

"Go save me a seat next to you guys with Paerli," Lor said to Nico and Dill as he nodded at Damaetra. Dill wagged his eyebrows and smirked.

"Stop it." Nico tugged at Dill.

"Stay smooth, Lor," Dill called back as Nico dragged him away.

Lor chuckled to himself and made his way toward Damaetra. His feet shuffled through the grass, and he tried to pick them up a little higher to not disturb her with the noise. He stood next to her, gazing at her delicate features. His heart fluttered, and he parted his lips to speak, but she spoke first.

"Hey, Loren." Her eyes were still closed.

"How did you know it was me?"

"You have a smell about you." She smiled, eyes still closed.

"A smell? Is it bad?" He stuck a nose in each armpit, trying to assess the damage he'd already done.

"Not at all. I like it." She opened her eyes and gazed up at him. Her cheeks were flushed, making her freckles more prominent. "It's like the smell of ocean rain and hyacinth."

"Flowers and salt?"

She giggled. "No, silly. It's *very* manly." She winked at him.

"Were you talking to the Maker about Tad?" Lor peered off in the direction she was facing.

"You know me already," she whispered.

"What did He tell you?"

"Tad is in the Promised Land."

"That's a good answer."

"The Maker is good." She turned to him, and her hand brushed against his. He reached a finger out and felt her skin.

"Damaetra." Lor swallowed, licking his lip.

"Yes, Loren?"

"I—" Her eyes studied him, colored in lilac under the sun's light. "I think about you. A lot."

"You do?"

"I do."

"What would you like to do about that?"

"I wanted to ask you if..." Lor glanced off toward the rows of people filing in. Paerli had craned around, waving her hand to summon him. He put up a finger, and she shrugged, turning back around.

"...If?" Damaetra asked.

"I don't know if this is appropriate." Lor started to rethink his plan.

"If Tad and the rocking chair has taught us anything, it's that life is short." She tilted her head, her long hair trickling off her shoulder, showing bare skin with a smattering of freckles matching her cheeks.

"You're right. Life is short, no time to worry." He struggled to pull the words out.

"And so?"

"Will you, I mean, do you..." Lor sighed and steeled himself. "Damaetra, I would be honored if you thought about me too."

She tilted her head. "Thought about you?"

"Yeah."

You're still a damn goofy bastard.

She glanced off in the distance for a moment, her white eyelashes shimmered in the light, and she cracked a small relaxed smile.

"I think about you. A lot," she said.

"You do?"

"I do."

Lor grinned. "What would you like to do about that?"

"I wanted to ask you if you would be *my* salty flower."

"Is it manly?"

"You know it is." She laced her fingers between his.

Lor returned to sit with his friends. Damaetra asked to stay at the tree, saying that she struggled to look at Tad's picture up front. Lor didn't disagree, leaving her to continue her thoughts while gazing into the open field behind the memorial. He slid into the seat between Paerli and Dill.

"Well, don't you have the goofiest grin on your face," Dill whispered.

Nico reached out his fist, and Lor bumped it with his own.

Horace stepped up to the podium and cleared his throat. "We gather today to honor the class of one thousand nine's beloved student..." His voice faded from Lor's mind as he closed his eyes to try talking to the Maker again. The colors swished back and forth, waiting for instruction. Paerli nudged him with her knee, and he swung his eyes open.

"Tad was a meek, shy boy with a big heart..." Horace peered down at Tad's parents.

Lor sighed and nodded at Paerli with a smile. She patted his knee, looking back forward and shaking her foot. Dill caught the contagion and shook his foot on the other side, rocking Lor back and forth between them.

He turned his head back to Damaetra's tree, but she moved to the other side of the trunk, with only a peek of purple waving from behind. An occasional flash of her white gold hair flicked out from behind the woody sentinel.

"We are joined today by Mister and Missus Aron..."

The ceremony ended with the casket descending into the ground, along with the smiling image of Tad and his flowers. His bright eyes peeked from sprigs of grass before disappearing below the dirt. The bottom of the box hit the underground carrier with a metallic thud. The buried network of funeral tunnels now contained the wooden box, triggering it to whir to life. It pulled the casket deeper into the earth where Tad's remains would be laid to rest in his assigned vault. The sliding door sealed shut with a hiss. Lor imagined the casket with a king-sized piece of jerky resting on the pillowed interior.

The crowd meandered from the ceremony square, gathering near the cluster of pines toward the road. Once the square was clear, the funeral director hit a few commands on a different control panel by the parking circle. All the neatly organized chairs dropped into their own underground vault, replaced by a trapdoor covered in lush grass.

"Everyone please gather over here." Horace waved his hands above the crowd. "Please file into your shuttle in alphabetical order by last name. A through M is here, N through Z is here."

"Well, I'll see you in town," Paerli said to Lor.

"See you there."

She let go of him and walked with Nico to their shuttle.

"It's you and me, bud!" Dill clapped Lor's back.

Lor craned his neck to try and find his new girlfriend when he felt a tap on the shoulder. He spun around, and she had found him. He grabbed her hand, twining his fingers with hers.

"Aw, you guys are just so *precious*," Dill said.

"Shut up, Dill," Lor said, laughing.

"I think I might just burst with all the cuteness!"

"Just make sure you spray that way." Damaetra pointed toward the cemetery.

"Oh ho! Quippy!"

She giggled at him.

"So, where are we going for lunch?" Dill asked once they boarded the shuttle.

"I don't know anything about this town. Nico is from here, maybe he could make a suggestion?" Lor replied.

The shuttle lurched forward, rocking the students and belching acrid gray smoke.

The trip into town didn't take long, but Lor made the most of it by holding on to his girl and enduring googly looks from Dill.

When the wheels ground to a halt, Lor peered from the window, seeing the familiar orange visitor center he had stopped at with Gale. It had only been a week, but it felt like an eternity. So much had already changed in him, and he was grateful for it.

Once everyone clustered in front of the orange building, Horace pointed beyond it toward the marketplace.

"Alright, everyone, listen up!" Horace's voice carried through the lively splashing and music by the ferry.

"Considering the events of yesterday's tragedy and today's memorial," he continued, "I have decided that it's best if you are able to enjoy yourselves for the rest of the day in town. The town is small, so you won't get lost. Since you are all full adults, we are trusting that you will stay together and not run off.

"There are restaurants and shops, and just like campus, there is limited technology. I'm trusting you all to keep your hands off any tech if you come across it while you are here. I'm trusting you to be adults, understand?"

The class murmured.

"I said, understand?"

"Yes, Horace," came in waves from students, creating an echo.

"Great," Horace continued, "don't wander alone, and take care of each other. I'll be in the market with you, so find me if you need anything."

Horace turned to the side and stretched out his arm for the recruits to wander into the square. As they made their way beyond the orange building, Horace cupped his hands around his mouth to shout after them, "And don't fall for the grifters!"

Lor craned his neck to find Nico. His curly-headed friend had his hand planked over his brow, scanning the crowd next to Paerli. He spotted Lor and pointed at him, smiling, and then they strolled over.

Paerli peered at Damaetra's hand buried in Lor's. He noticed she opted not to hook herself to him. Lor's heart fluttered the way it had before, with the second beat squeezing out from behind his own, causing him to grip his chest.

"Are you alright?" Damaetra whispered, squeezing his hand.

"Yeah, it's nothing," Lor said.

"Wow, this is so cool!" Dill said, scanning the stalls and watching the vendors hawk their wares.

"Hey, guys, one of the better places to eat is right over there." Nico pointed to a small building stuffed between stalls with a green and yellow awning. "They have a great stew."

Horace disappeared into the same building.

"Looks like our esteemed guide agrees," Lor said.

The group made their way to the building, where Lor had to duck to get under the hem of the awning.

The aroma of broiled, grilled, and smoked meats hovered in the air.

"This seems cozy." Damaetra closed her eyes and took in a deep breath. Lor smiled to himself, wondering if his flowery smell was mingled in there somewhere.

"Check it out," Nico whispered to Lor. He subtly pointed to a booth in the corner next to a grimy window. Two men sat there—one with their back to the entrance. Lor recognized the lofty ash blond hair bobbing up and down. The other man was odd-looking and seemed out of place, with sand goggles over his eyes.

"Let's sit over here," Lor suggested, pointing at a table on the opposite side of the restaurant from Horace and his "friend."

"Agreed," Nico said.

Not long after sitting, a big-boned waitress approached their table. "Hey, luvs, what'll it be?"

The five of them looked around at each other and shrugged.

"Oh, sorry, kids, we usually only get regulars in here. It's a habit. Let me get you some menus." Her hips swayed with a jiggle as she hurried to the front to retrieve the menus.

"That's the kind of woman I want," Dill whispered to the group. He bit his lip and wagged his eyebrows.

"Maker's limbo, Dill. You like the older ones, do you?" Nico whispered back, laughing.

Damaetra giggled to herself, but Paerli sat there unamused.

"Make sure those menus aren't laced with tech," Paerli said as the waitress came back to the table.

Everyone except Damaetra raised their hands back when she placed the parchment slabs on the table. The waitress chuckled at them.

"Oh, honey, we don't have any tech in here. Just good old-fashioned manual tools." She tapped the paper, then made her way to the next table over.

A collective exhale circled around the group, and they all relaxed, examining the paper.

"I'm having the stew Nico is all hot and bothered for," Dill said, nudging Nico.

"That sounds nice," Damaetra agreed.

Lor peered back at Horace. The guide flapped his hands around, occasionally perching one on his forehead and shaking his head. The man sitting across from him sat rigidly still, resting his chin over the back of his spindly fingers. The stranger reminded him of Fowler, but less ugly and wearing goggles. He pulled out a small package wrapped in brown paper and twine, sliding it to Horace, who snatched it. Horace plunked a pile of plats in front of the man. The stranger turned his head toward Lor.

"Ah, uh, I'll have the stew also," Lor stuttered, jerking his gaze away from Horace's table and holding a hand at his brow to cover his face.

Paerli twisted around to see what Lor was spooked by. The stranger stared at her, but she didn't turn away. After a terribly long minute, the stranger turned his attention back to their guide.

"Who is that with Horace?" Damaetra whispered to Lor.

"I don't know. He gave Horace a package," Lor said.

"He did?" Paerli spun back around and narrowed her eyes. "What *kind* of package?"

"I don't know, it was small, wrapped in paper and twine."

Paerli bit her lip. She looked angry. "I'll have the stew too," she said.

The waitress strutted toward the table again, getting Dill excited. "Were you able to find somethin' you might like?" she asked.

"Stew!" Dill blurted. The waitress giggled. She had a lovely voice.

"Stew it is," she replied, giving Dill a small pinch on his cheek. She left the table and he blushed, putting a hand to his face.

"I think she likes you," Nico said.

"Oh, I hope so," Dill said.

Lor caught Horace peering at them from over his shoulder. He worked his way from the booth, summoning his friend to get up with him.

"Mister Turtingas, Storgut, Dicus, and Miss Harea and Praes, how lovely to see you," Horace said to the group. He leaned over to the stranger.

"This is my colleague, Jack. You know, Miss Praes is a new Formulator. Perhaps you two will run in the same circles."

"Are you a Formulator too?" Damaetra asked Jack.

The man nodded wordlessly.

"He's one of the best," Horace continued.

Paerli raised an eyebrow.

Something seemed off about Jack. He didn't look like a Danashi, Mesaman, or Anglia. He had a lot of Foscan traits, but Foscans were servants, so Jack had to be some sort of Mesaman from another zone.

Horace cleared his throat. "Well, carry on, friends! This is a fine little establishment, and you will enjoy the stew. Remember, be back at the ferry two hours before first sundown."

"Yes, Horace," they all said in unison.

"Excellent. Bye bye now." He hurried from the restaurant, turning left into the marketplace, while Jack veered right.

"That was weird." Nico craned his neck to watch the men walk away.

Lor wanted to say something, but a bloodcurdling scream came from the market.

The whole group shot out of their seats to see what was happening.

A naked man bolted through the aisles, with three roundsmen chasing after him.

"He made me touch him! I thought he was a cat!" a woman screamed.

Lor opened his mouth in a wide grin, thinking back to the cluster of cats hanging around the visitor center and telling Gale about his theory on the skin walkers.

"I *knew* it!" he said.

Chapter 12

In the Alley
LOREN

THE SILENCE OF THE CLASSROOM was palpable. Horace was not there yet, but the chairs were full with the occasional squeaking of wood shifting from recruits fidgeting and messing with their implant lumps. Many whispers circulated, expressing whether they would become the next catastrophe. Paerli picked at her fingernails with a vacant gaze. Lor felt he couldn't leave her alone at the table even though he was in a relationship. Damaetra told him she was okay with that.

Horace finally showed up looking sweaty and disheveled.

"I want you all to know that what happened to Tad is a one-in-a-million occurrence." He paced toward the front of the room, running his fingers through his wild hair.

The class watched him in silence while he limped back and forth, rubbing his face. It reminded Lor of Gale.

"Thank you for being here," he said, "but I'm in no state to be here."

The recruits whispered to each other.

"I haven't lost a student in over fifteen standards."

I guess Par was wrong about them being used to losing students.

"I need to take a personal day today. I hope everyone understands."

The class murmured again, talking a little louder with each other.

"However!" he shouted over the din. "We can't let you fall behind."

Horace bent down near the back of the front desk and dragged out a box full of textbooks.

"Mister Dicus, do you mind?"

Nico jumped from his chair, content with being the class mule. He pulled out a stack of texts, and Lor breathed a sigh of relief when he saw how thin they were. His friend placed one in front of Lor, and the title said: *Engineering and You: Life as a Technological Crafter.*

Dill hummed at the cover, entertained by the images of circuits and wires. Seemed dull to Lor.

"Miss Praes, I haven't forgotten you. Focus on your ability, and we will talk again soon. As for everyone else, please read through the book for the next class. For now, you are dismissed."

Not a soul was eager to spend another minute in the room. Recruits dashed out the door with their new books. Lor took his time, swinging around to Damaetra.

"Hey, Loren." She smiled, touching his hand. They left with the others, fanning out from the building.

Damaetra squeezed his hand and lifted it to her lips. "I think I will go to the dorms for now."

"Is everything okay?" he asked.

"Everything is perfect." She ran her cheek across the back of his hand. "I just want to spend some time learning a little more about formulation."

"Alright, but don't get too lost in your gift that you forget about us. About me." He smiled.

"Never." She kissed his hand again and let go, turning toward the dorms. She walked in tiny steps, one foot after the other as her dress twisted and waved behind her.

"Trouble in paradise already?" Dill bumped into Lor's shoulder.

Lor tittered. "Nah, she just wants to focus on her new ability. I don't blame her."

"Well, I'm going to go for a swim." Dill pointed at the beach where several recruits had already left their belongings on the shore to jump in with their clothes.

"Watch out for the parasites in the water," Paerli said, threading her arm through Lor's.

"Parasites?" Dill shivered and slapped at his skin.

"She's screwing with you," Nico said, laughing at Dill squirming.

Nariah and Emilia were in the water, and Lor found it funny that Emilia still had her pearls on. Dill noticed them too and sucked his teeth.

"I'm going to go make friends," he said, pointing.

"But you *hate* them," Paerli said.

"What? How could I hate Emilia? I bet her family's rich." Dill dropped his stuff and sprinted off to the water, splashing in next to them, making them squeal.

Lor laughed. "That guy..."

They walked along the beach toward the dorms. Lor glanced at the resort in the distance and rubbed at his implant.

"Are you afraid?" Paerli asked, nodding at the implant.

"Afraid isn't really the word for it."

"Why don't you cut it out?"

"I'm sorry, did I do something wrong? Cut what out?"

Paerli giggled. "No, no, I mean... cut *it* out." She poked the implant, making a slicing motion.

He sucked in a sharp breath and cupped his hand over it. "Are you joking?"

"I think it's a good idea," Paerli said. "What do you think, Nico?"

"What's a good idea?" Nico said.

"Lor and I were just talking about performing some surgery." She made the same slicing motion over Nico's arm.

Nico's face dropped. "What? No way. We can't do that... can we?"

"Why not?" Paerli shrugged.

"Couldn't that kill us or something?"

"Why do you think it would kill you?"

"Isn't it, like, tied to our neural network or something?" Nico rubbed at the spot at the same time as Lor.

Paerli laughed. "Neural network? Listen to yourself... Who told you that?"

"Hold on for a second. Has anyone ever *tried* to cut theirs out?" Lor asked.

Paerli rocked on her heels. "Well, not that I know of. But I do know that it doesn't do what you think it does."

"So what does it do?" Nico asked.

"Not what you think it does."

"Come on, Par, you're being evasive," Lor said.

"I am *not*. I don't know what it does exactly, but I know it doesn't give you your ability. I knew someone one time that got inducted into a Guild without one."

"Well, that sells it." Nico rolled his eyes.

"No, seriously"—she held her hands up—"honest to Maker."

Lor pinched the implant, imagining it exploding from his flesh and the raw pain of muscle and nerves exposed to salty air.

"I'm sold. For real," Lor said.

"Seriously?" Nico took a step back.

"For real."

Paerli grinned, raising her brow and holding her palms out to Nico for his answer.

"Let me ask Dill what he wants to do. If he's game, I'm game. In fact, I think we should only do it if we are *all* game."

"What about Damaetra?" Lor asked. "She has her ability. I don't want to risk hurting her if it does do something."

"I *told* you, it doesn't give you your ability," Paerli said.

"Even still, I don't want her cutting hers out."

"Just because she's your girlfriend doesn't mean you can tell her what to do," Paerli argued.

"I'm not telling her what to do..." Lor thought about it for a minute, biting his lower lip.

Nico bumped his arm. "Tell you what, just ask her what she wants, I'll ask Dill, and we'll figure it out."

"Well, I was going to head back to the dorm anyway... Do you want me to ask her?" Paerli suggested.

Lor wasn't sure when Damaetra would come back out. Maybe having Paerli ask her would make the decision come faster.

"Okay, you can ask her."

"Great—I'll go now. You guys work on Dill, and let's make a pact to sneak out and meet after second sun."

"Why sneak out?" Nico asked.

"Do you want Horace and everyone else to know that we are mutilating ourselves?"

"Point taken."

"Okay then, let's meet behind your dorm... Building two C. Right after second sun, no earlier, no later."

Paerli pointed to the back of the dorm. It faced the rest of the island, away from campus and away from Horace's hut.

Gale will kill me if he finds out.

"Okay, we'll see you then," Lor said.

Paerli squeezed his arm, giving him a sly smile, then left for building two B.

Nico furrowed his brow, rubbing over his implant.

"You seem unsure," Lor said.

"No, actually, I think I want to do it. I was just thinking, though..."

Nico paused and flexed his jaw.

"What were you thinking?"

"Well..." He blew out a sigh. "Don't take this the wrong way. We're friends, and I just want to act like one for you."

"Okay, what is it?"

"I thought that you might want to stop letting Paerli get so close to you."

Lor chuckled and took a step back. "What do you mean? Are you interested in her?" He watched Paerli flow up the steps to her building with her gauzy white top flapping behind her.

"No, I mean, I don't know her very well. It's just that she hangs all over you, and you have Damaetra now. Don't you think she'd get upset by that?"

"Par and I are just friends, she knows that."

"Friends that are always *snuggling*?"

Lor tittered. "We aren't snuggling."

Nico threaded his arm through Lor's and put on a high-pitched voice. "Oh, Lor, I think we should meet after dark, and tee hee!"

Lor couldn't help but laugh at his comely friend mocking Paerli like that. "She doesn't go *tee hee*." Lor sniggered.

"I said what I said." Nico pulled his arm away and punched Lor's shoulder.

"I'll think about it," Lor said, "but I can't control what Paerli does."

"No, but you can control what *you* do. She's not exactly ugly, you know."

"What are you saying?"

"You know exactly what I'm saying." Nico put the tips of his fingers together with his thumb.

"Ugh, nerd. Let's go find Dill."

The purple haze of the second sun dispersed, and Lor shook his knee at the edge of his bed.

"Ready?" he said to Dill, who sat across from him, also shaking his knee.

"No. But we're doing this." Dill sprang up and swiped a shirt from the side table.

"Alright, let's go."

They snuck through the hall, which was easy on the soft thatch but hard with the squeaky wood subfloor. They weaved barefoot around the extra cranky spots, praying not to wake anyone.

Lor carefully closed the latch of the outer door and landed in the sand.

"Looks clear," he whispered after taking a quick look around.

"How can you see anything?" Dill whispered.

The island was dark. No tech lights allowed on campus made the nights extra black. Only twinkling moonlight spread over the calm water, lighting their path behind the building.

Lor grabbed Dill's sleeve as they groped around the dorm hut, finding a way to the back.

Once they turned the corner for the back wall, there was a small orange glow illuminating Damaetra's face.

"She's here," Lor whispered.

Paerli sat on her knees in the sand next to Damaetra. Her eyes found them creeping around the corner and waved them over.

"I found a candle and flint," Damaetra whispered. Lor didn't think she could get any more alluring, but the orange glow cast an ethereal beauty onto her features.

"You came," Lor whispered.

"I came for you." She touched his arm.

"I'm worried for you."

"There are no rocking chairs here." She grinned.

"Are you going to do it?"

"I don't think I should." She bit her lip, looking down at the golden orb under her perfectly pale skin.

Lor exhaled, relieved that she felt the same as him.

He lifted her arm and kissed the delicate skin over the implant.

Paerli peered at them in the candlelight.

"Get a room." Dill pinched Lor.

"Am I late?" Nico huffed behind Dill.

"No, we just got here."

"Oh good. I didn't know if my roommate would ever stop talking to me."

"Maybe he thinks you're cute too."

"Shut up, Dill." Nico pushed his shoulder. "Did anyone bring something to cut with?"

"I pilfered this from the kitchens." Paerli pulled out a six-inch blade from a fold in her pants.

"Oh damn!" Dill hissed as a glint from the moon flashed over the blade. "I brought an old shirt we can use to wrap our arms."

"And I brought *this*," Damaetra whispered, holding up a small box with a red heart printed on the side. "I was worried about the bleeding, so I went to the medic and asked for a kit."

"You just asked for them? And they didn't ask you why?" Lor said.

"Health care is free during the program. No questions asked." She grinned at him.

"The Maker is good."

"Yes, He is."

"Are you guys ready to do this?" Nico asked.

The darkness couldn't mask the dread in their faces. Paerli spun the blade around, holding the faded wooden handle toward Lor.

He wrapped his fingers around the handle, feeling each splinter in the wood.

Gale is going to kill me.

"I'll go first," Lor said.

The silvery mirrored edge reflected the moon as he pressed the sharp tip at the edge of his implant.

Dill ripped a strip from his old shirt. Damaetra sat by him with the kit trembling in her hands. Lor pushed the tip harder into his skin when the first layer of flesh popped. A thin trickle of blood welled up at the point, dribbling over the curve of his forearm. A dark red drop clung to his elbow and shimmered orange in the candlelight.

"Oh Gehenna," Dill hissed, going pale. He wadded the shirt strip in his hand, shaking it toward Lor.

Lor's stomach dropped, and he felt the cursed second heart thumping behind his own. It was a weird feeling—a hint of excitement under the fear.

Can't stop now.

Lor drove the knife beneath the edge of the implant and sawed a small slit across his skin, sending more red liquid down his arm, spattering in the sand. Each fiber opening up was a zing of pain. Once enough of the flesh was freed, the skin slithered over the top of the implant, opening his arm like an eye. The golden beetle sat there, latched into his muscle.

Lor wriggled the knife under its belly, wrenching it upward. The pain surged in a sharp wave. More blood bubbled and oozed over his arm, and he gripped the thing between thumb and forefinger, sliding it out.

The group made a collective gasp, and after a brief pause, he felt a soft pressure against his arm. Damaetra was pushing a wad of medical cloth against his wound with one hand and held a bottle of antibac spray in the other. He held the implant up toward the light of the moon and saw the stinger slicked with blood. There was a small pinprick of light blinking at the tip that faded with each pulse until it finally went dark.

"Did you guys see that?" Lor whispered.

Paerli grabbed the knife from Lor.

"No, what was it?" Nico examined the red-slicked beetle.

"The stinger was *blinking,*" Lor said.

"I don't know if I can do it," Dill whispered. "Can someone else do it for me?"

"Damn it," Paerli hissed. The group shot glances at her to see blood smeared over her arm. Damaetra pulled out more first aid cloth for her.

"I dropped it," she said, looking around frantically while pressing the cloth to her arm. She swept her foot across the sand in search of it. Nothing. "There's too much of the cursed ancient tech buried over here. It's gone."

"I hope Horace doesn't find it," Lor said. He sucked his teeth when Damaetra sprayed his wound. She took strips of quickstitch and taped the flap of skin closed, finishing it off with a patch of bandage.

"Here, I'll take that." Paerli held her hand out for the med kit, then passed Lor the blade. She hurried to spray the antibac, slap on quickstitch, and bandage herself before passing the box back to Damaetra.

"Seriously, guys, can someone else do it for me?" Dill swayed.

"Here." Lor ripped a strip from Dill's old shirt and crammed it between his friend's teeth. He bit down hard.

"Do it," Dill muffled through the shirt. He held the broad side of his forearm out, squeezing his eyes shut. A twinge of gold stretched underneath thin skin as if his body had already started rejecting it.

Lor poked at the edge of Dill's implant, and his skin split easily, opening up another golden eye. Lor jammed thumb and forefinger into the opening to yank it out before Dill could wrench his arm free. He groaned, his dark face draining of color. Lor turned the implant stinger toward Nico.

"Look at this," he said. The tip of the stinger flashed and died as it did with Lor's implant.

"What is that? Some kind of... tracker?" Nico whispered.

Damaetra busied herself with Dill's wound as he wobbled, directing him to sit down. He plunked in the sand like a stone.

"I don't know *what* it is," Lor said.

"Okay, get this thing out of me." Nico swiped the knife from Lor and jabbed it into the skin at the bottom of the implant. The skin snapped open, and he didn't give it time to bleed before snatching it from his arm. Damaetra zipped out some quickstitch to patch him up, giving him a squirt of antibac.

"Damn, Nico. You took that like a boss," Dill whispered and swayed. He belched under his breath.

"Are you going to puke?" Paerli scooted over to Dill, putting a hand on his forehead. "You're all sweaty and cold."

"Nah, nah, I'm ...ugh... I'm goo—" Dill vomited.

"Thanks for turning the other way," Paerli remarked while rubbing his back. She shrugged at Lor.

"You going to survive, man?" Lor asked.

"Yeah." Dill wiped thick drool from the corner of his mouth.

Nico kicked sand over the pool of vomit on the ground. "Horace would definitely find *that*," he said.

Lor ripped more strips from the old shirt, tying one around Paerli's bandage. "We've got to hide these," he said, tearing off another.

"Do we have to wear these for six months?" Nico asked, ripping free another piece.

"Well, it's either that or long-sleeved shirts every day in the blazing heat," Lor said, tying the band over Nico's arm.

"It's going to get all wet and crusty after a while," Dill moaned, holding out his arm for a band.

"Just hand-wash it, but don't let anyone see your arm when you do," Nico said, tying Lor's band on.

"What about in public?" Paerli asked. "Won't people question that we don't have the lump in our arms?"

Lor chewed on his cheek.

She has a point. I didn't think about that.

"I guess we can cross that bridge when we get to it," Lor said.

"Yeah, I'm with Lor. I don't want to think about anything else other than lying in bed right now," Dill said, still green in the cheeks.

"Here, let's get you back to the dorm. Par, since you got it, can you take care of the knife?" Nico said while helping Dill up. He glanced at Lor and nodded at Damaetra, who was cleaning up the med kit supplies.

"Sure." Paerli pinched the knife at the handle and peered at Lor. "We'll catch up tomorrow."

She ran her hand down Lor's arm, squeezing his hand, and wandered back toward her dorm.

Nico shook his head.

"No, *we'll* catch up tomorrow," he said. "Come on, Dill." Nico shooed Lor toward Damaetra, who was still preoccupied with the med supplies. Nico and Dill hobbled off toward the dorm, leaving them alone in the candlelight. Damaetra finished packing up the box and securing the lid.

"Alone at last," she whispered with a smile, holding their only source of light.

"I've been waiting all day." He laced his fingers in her other hand. "Did you get some good studying in?"

"Some. I was a little... distracted." She peered up at him with eyes that morphed into crystal blue in the night.

"By what?" he breathed.

"My salt flower," she whispered, running her hand up his cheek. His heart relaxed, beating slow thumps and sending warm signals to his fingers.

He closed his eyes, kissing her palm. The fractal patterns under his lids pulsed in white gold. He could still smell violets underneath the sharp antibac residue on her hand. He walked his fingers across her small back, pulling her closer to him. Silken hair fluttered over her milky shoulder, glistening under the golden hue of the candle.

"I've been meaning to tell you," he said.

"You've decided to tell me what you prayed for after all?" She moved even closer to him, running her hand across the back of his neck. Her cool fingers sent hot shivers down his spine.

"Exactly."

He leaned over and blew out the candle.

PART 2

CHAPTER 13

Dill's Journal, Class of 1009
DILL

DILLY-O: CAP 2, STANDARD YEAR 2585, DAY 16

So, I'm not a Reaper, but Engineer is cool. I like gadgets and circuits. Maybe I can make something so cool that no one could live without it. Paerli was right about the tech in the sand. I don't feel any of it talking to me. At least not here.

That one girl, Nariah, is already a Shepherd, and it sucks that she kinda got what she wanted. She's such a snob! Blah! I'd still take her out, though. If she wanted. I wish I could do Engineering things here, but I can only meditate on random materials and take notes. I can't actually do the work. That's stupid.

DILL: CAP 2, 2585, DAY 28

I should write every week, but I don't. Whatever.

DILL DILL: C-2: S-2585, DAY 29

Okay, it's the next day. I had an interesting piece of flexible plastic today that was cool, but I couldn't really tell what it wanted to be. Horace says I need to meditate more to listen to it, but that's hard! I got a letter from Aunt Petra today and I just smushed it up and threw it in the trash. Lor found it and asked me about it, but no one needs to know about her. She sucks.

MR. STORGUT: C-2: S-2585, DAY 35

I'm trying to be better about writing things down, but the pencil still hurts my finger. I wish I had my V-Note. Then I could just tell it things.   Then again, maybe it's good that I can't just talk to it. The files would be way too long, and I'd never go back and read it. I probably won't read this either. Trash can, dunk! That Foscan devil keeps coming around while I'm trying to study in the library, and he creeps me out. He only talks in that weird clicky language to Horace. It actually sounds pretty cool. I wish I knew Foscan. But screw that guy.

Dill McGeeeee: C-2: S-2585, Day 38

I wish a girl liked me. Am I that bad? They're all over Nico, but he says they're too immature for him. I'm all like, "Guy, what do you want? Grandma?" He just laughs at me. He knows he looks good, and I'm just a stupid, shrimpy Danashi. Well, I don't think Nico thinks I am, but I think I am.

Dill the Danashi: C2/2585, Day 40

Every time I see Lor with Damaetra, I get jealous. I try not to be, but he's got it so good with her. Even though he still hasn't found his ability yet.   He might not ever. She has hers, though, so she can be the working chick taking home plats while he stays home with their millions of Anglia-Mesaman babies. I bet they'd be cute. Like peach skinned with white hair. That would be cool.

Dilly: C2/2585, Day 41

I don't get it. Why can't I hear plastic? Metal screams at me, but I'm too focused on girls to write down what it says. Some are musical instruments... I think. There are others that want to be ID plates. Like what? Who would want that? I guess metal wants weird things. Ugh, I need a *woman*. There's this bouncy chick with huge boobs that works the cafeteria counter. I could motor those allllll day. If only she'd notice me...

Mr. Dill Dawg: C2/2585, Day 42

Nico is a Formulator now! Damaetra's been showing him a lot of stuff. Sometimes while they're studying together, Lor is wandering the beach with Paerli drooling all over him. I don't get it. The dude is taken, but I'm available! She's so smart, it's kinda hot. She gave me a cool piece of ancient tech she found buried by the trees and told me that maybe someday it would talk again. She's always doing thoughtful things like that. Maybe she just tries to be thoughtful with Lor too and I don't understand. Can I take this off the island?

Dillllll: C2/2585, Day 46

So, Paerli is a Reaper. Of course she is. It's not fair! Nice, smart, hot... Reaper. Horace made a big deal about it because Reapers are super rare. She's gonna be so freakin' rich. Would she ever go for a guy like me? I bet the stuff she reaps would do some cool things in gadgets. Has anyone tried that? Surely...

Dee be Illin': C2/2585, Day 53

The weirdest thing happened today. Me and the girls were on the beach, and one of the "void brothers" from the resort came through campus passing out flyers. He was so freaking creepy. He kept talking about the light of the breach and the creator's magic. I told him to shut up and go away, but Paerli took a flyer, probably just to be nice. She's like that. I'd never seen Damaetra so like... pissed? That Foscan devil ran up to him and spit on his shoe, and the guy cursed him and ran off. The Foscan yanked the flyer from Paerli and crumpled it up. So weird.

Just call me Big D: C2/2585, Day 56

Horace made me try with wires today. They weren't cooperating. The funniest thing happened last night. I snuck out for fun and I caught Lor making out with Damaetra hard-core behind the dorm. Right where we cut out the implants! I puked there too. I hope Damaetra didn't get it in her hair! I don't think they heard me because they couldn't stop tonguing each other. He'd kill me if he knew I hung around for a little bit. We're all adults here, right?

Dilly Dill Pickle: S1/2585/84

I'm worried about Lor. Dude still hasn't gotten his Guild. Maybe he really truly never will. I just found out Damaetra has two sisters. I wonder if they're hot? Nico told us about Guild Central. It's like an extension of the Seven Cities on the outskirts of Secas. It would be so cool if we could all move there together for work. Lor said he knew someone there and would write to him about us.If only he would get his frackin' Guild already!!!

Dilly-D: S1/2585/86

The cafeteria chick with big boobies gave me extra chips today. That's love! Just kidding, I'm a shrimp.

Dee Dee: S1/2585/92

Okay, I need to stop thinking about girls! They're all over the place here. Emilia likes me as her fun tiny "friend," nothing more. ~~Boy what I wouldn't give to grab those pearls and ride her like a~~ Nariah called a herd of waterbirds at me to steal my lunch. I won't tell on her, though. It was kinda funny.

Dilz: S1/2585/113

Come on, Lor. There's only seven days left to get your Guild! I'm getting better at listening to metal. It just talks all at once. Kinda like me! Plastic still won't say much, though. Now wires, that's the good stuff. And contacts, and resistors. Anything electrical, hydraulic... maybe I can be a good Engineer after all. Then I'll be drippin' with the ladies.

CHAPTER 14

Nico's Journal, Class of 1009
NICO

NICO DICUS: C2/2585/38, WEEKLY ENTRY

This is my first entry. I became a Formulator today, which isn't too bad. It's better than a Weggevens, that's for sure. As a side thought, we did get a few Weggevens in class... two skin walkers, a runner, and another strongman. Thank the Maker she didn't explode like Tad. It's strange to see a woman able to fling boulders into the water like it's nothing. Anyway, I think a lot of things can be done with formulations. It's a shame we can't really perform our abilities on the island, but once we get out of here, it won't be long before we get to the Seven Cities. Horace said I need to catch up with verdigris platum (green eneris) and lapis piscus (blue eneris). Damaetra has been nice enough to volunteer to help me catch up.

NICO DICUS: C2/2585/48, WEEKLY ENTRY

Last week was rough. There was a lot to learn about green and blue. I think I'm caught up to Horace's standards, but there's more to learn. This week we focused on roujis emporum, otherwise known as "red" eneris. It comes from land animals. I won't lie, it smelled like a steak. The flavor was too complex for me. With practice, I might be able to pick out individual flavors. In other news, Paerli became a Reaper this week. I don't know how I feel about that. It's crazy rare, and why she would get it, of all people, is just weird. Now I'm more nervous for Lor. If she doesn't know how to control herself, well... I'll keep my eye on them.

NICO DICUS: C2/2585/58, WEEKLY ENTRY

There are ten of us now. I'm glad I'm not the last Formulator; they seem to keep trickling in. This week, Horace let us try witis volatus, otherwise known as "white" eneris. It smelled kinda nice... like a cooked bird. It was a much simpler flavor, and I could see a few things I could make with it. Damaetra's been struggling with them lately. To her credit, she's pretty good with green. I think she's distracted by Lor. I don't blame her... I'm pretty sure she's not blind to Paerli latching herself to him. She's pretty laid back, so I don't think she'd say anything, but how could she *not* see it? Everyone else does.

NICO DICUS: S1/2585/68, WEEKLY ENTRY

We got another Formulator. Class of 1009 seems to be the class of Formulators. Dill has a few Engineers with him, like that girl Emilia that he's so hot for. I was surprised of all things that was what she was. This week we had naranis corpum, or "orange" eneris. It apparently comes from a certain species of fruit, so it's not as common as the others so far. Horace made us share because there wasn't as much to go around. It was definitely my favorite of everything so far, but I do like fruit, after all. In other news, Dill is girl crazy. The guy has it so bad. I told him that Emilia might actually like him if he wasn't constantly flirting with everyone. He talks dirty about the kitchen girl a lot within earshot of Emilia.

NICO DICUS: S1/2585/78, WEEKLY ENTRY

There weren't any new Formulators this week. That's a good thing because I'd feel bad for someone to have to catch up with all the eneris we've already tested so far. This week was purpuris porum, or "violet" eneris. It's very pretty and comes from any purple-petaled flower. Reapers have to be careful not to pull the green with it, or it becomes almost unusable—only almost unusable because it turns into obsenis forturum, or "black" eneris. It's the most common type but goes widely to waste. Horace said a lot of Formulators just use it as ink, but there are some uses for it in phials. Nothing we would learn in the program, though.

NICO DICUS: S1/2585/88, WEEKLY ENTRY

I'm just going to start this entry by saying that, yes, maybe there are a lot of girls hanging all over me. I'm not interested in anyone here. Dill gets so worked up about it, but I keep trying to tell him that once he gets out of the program, there are millions of girls—*women*—on Roseaarde for him to choose from. If he doesn't focus now, he'll struggle as an Engineer.

As for me? This is totally private, but Lor talks to me sometimes about his sister, Eva. I think I'd like to meet her. From what he's said about her, she's got a good head on her shoulders. He says she's single... would he kill me if I made a pass at her? Maybe, but I hope not. He's my best friend.

My final thought on all matters of relationships: I'd rather Lor stay away from Paerli. When she thinks Damaetra isn't watching, she wraps herself around him, and he still lets her do it. I have no idea why. I've tried talking to him about it a couple of times, but he promised me it was nothing. I just don't believe that. There's something happening there, but I have no idea what. Truth be told, I don't even think it's love. I get a weird vibe from it, but I can't put my finger on it. Either way, it's out of my control.

Okay, now that's done, I told everyone about Guild Central a few days ago. I had forgotten about it because I was so concerned about the Seven Cities. The more I think about it, the more I think I might like staying near home for work. If everyone wants to come, that would be even better. Lor mentioned the Weggevens skin walker he met named Fowler and said he would write to him about us wanting to work there. I don't think it would be hard to get a spot as long as we operate under him as his "charges." Hopefully, Fowler writes back. We could always visit the Seven Cities, but there's nothing like the relaxed atmosphere of Secas.

Just watch out for the cats.

Nico Dicus: S1/2585/98, Weekly Entry

I'm afraid Lor isn't going to get a Guild. He made it sound like he was okay with that. He always wanted to be a roundsman and was only doing this for his dad, so I get it. If he ends up marrying Damaetra, she could earn a lot for them, even if he decides not to go into Law. I don't know how that would work with Guild Central, though. As far as I know, you have to live there to work there, and if Lor doesn't have a Guild, I can't see him living away from her. That would be too hard. I think they have a couple's quarter at Guild

Central. I think. In Formulator news, Horace told us today that because Formulators rely on taste to create and reverse-engineer draughts, we are immune to all kinds of poisons. That's pretty cool, but I would be nervous to test that.

Nico Dicus: 2/2585/108, Weekly Entry

There's only a little over a week left, so this is going to be my last entry. We're not turning these in anyway, so it doesn't matter. I may never look back at this again.

I found out something today that blew my mind. Horace is a Weggevens. I overheard him talking to the Foscan, Valge'jor (I think that's how you spell it). It was a kind I've heard of but don't know much about because most of them are runners, strongmen, and skin walkers. Horace is a two-mind. I'm going to have to look that up sometime—I think it has something to do with having another internal voice that knows things? Sounds horrible. He mentioned something about needing to meet someone for more syringes. My guess is that's how he deals with it. Maybe that was his dealer we met after Tad's funeral... the weird-looking dude named Jack. I haven't decided whether to tell anyone in the circle about it. Horace keeps it hidden for a reason, and what kind of person would I be to spill someone else's secret?

In other news, Lor has given up trying to find his Guild. I think we all feel it won't happen—except Dill. He's ever the optimist! Even so, Lor's in good company because over half the class is Guildless.

Chapter 15

Seized

Loren

"I WOULD NEVER DATE HER in a million standard years," Nico said when pressed by Dill about Nariah.

"Why not? She's pretty hot... Dumb, but hot. And she's a Shepherd."

"You forgot narcissistic," Nico reminded him.

"Oh, yeah. There's that... Can I ask her out?"

"Didn't she set a bunch of waterbirds on you?"

"Maybe. But that's beside the point."

Nico laughed at the thought but gave him his blessing, which he regretted later when he and Lor spent an afternoon mending Dill's ego after she laughed him from the water.

"She would be blessed by the Maker for someone like me," Dill whined.

"Of course she would, but I told you already that Nariah is obsessed with Nico. Why don't you try asking out Emilia?" Lor said.

Nico made a killing motion around his neck.

"You think?" Dill perked up.

"Ah, uh, well, maybe not. She seems... high-maintenance."

"I'm done with girls. I want a *woman*." Dill sighed.

"That's a good plan, Dill." Nico clapped him on the back. "Once we get to Guild Central, you'll be like, 'Nariah and Emilia who?'"

Dill tittered.

"Ah, when *you* guys will be at Guild Central," Lor said. "While I'm all alone..." he sang out.

"You and Damaetra could have conjugal visits." Dill smirked.

Nico popped his hand on Dill's shoulder.

"That reminds me, Damaetra and Paerli should be done with their girl's dinner soon." Lor looked up at the sky, seeing the sun directly overhead.

"Speaking of which." Nico pointed toward the cafeteria, where the two girls strolled up to the three of them lounging on the beach.

Damaetra wore her purple dress that day. It always reminded Lor of the day he tried to ask her out, but she beat him to it. He lounged in the sand, pants rolled up to his knees at the cuff with a breezy long-sleeved shirt. She sat next to him in the wet sand, sliding one leg over his and leaning back, touching a pinky to his hand.

"What'd you eat?" Nico asked the girls.

"Nothing good," Paerli said, squeezing between him and Lor. She kept her hands to herself while Damaetra was around.

"It's cafeteria food, so just rations," Damaetra said. "But there was a really good, steamed meat bun that I'd never had before."

"I'll have to try that sometime," Lor said, kissing her forehead.

"So, what *is* the plan?" Dill asked.

"What plan?" Lor said.

"You know, Guild Central. What are you going to do?"

"Oh, I don't know." Lor looked over at Damaetra. "We'll figure it out, I'm sure. Maybe I shouldn't have taken out the implant."

"Shh, not so loud." Dill looked around. "I don't want to get in trouble."

Nico bopped Lor on the shoulder. "We've already proven the implant doesn't do shit."

"Yeah, you're right. There are only a few days left, so if it hasn't happened by now, it's not going to happen. Gale's going to kill me."

"What can he expect? He forced you to come here... that's on him," Nico said.

"Yeah... still sucks, though."

A warm breeze washed over Lor. It was thick and sticky, smelling of dust and rot.

"Did you all feel that?" Lor asked. He wrinkled his nose.

"Feel what?" Nico said.

"That hot stinky air."

"No. The air is nice." Nico shrugged and held a hand out.

"Well, I think there's still time for you, Lor," Dill said. "Horace *said* that once you are murphamurmafur..."

Dill's voice faded fast. Lor felt cotton in his ears and winced at a high-pitched wail.

"Wait... w-what?" he asked, rotating a finger in his ear.

"I *said* mahrphamurphamolor..."

Lor shook his head. He didn't even close his eyes, and the colors splashed into his vision. The sea was coated in painted hues, jittering like gee flies swarming over the water, and the sky was a spread of purples and sparks.

It's not the second sun yet.

He squinted.

"Are you okay, Loren?" Damaetra's voice cut through the foam in his ear. She squeezed his hand, and for a split moment, the white gold fractal flashed.

"I-I don't know. My colors are glitching." He only heard his voice echo inside his head.

"Colors?" Nico said.

Damaetra helped him stand, but the blood crashed into his legs, making him wobble. Paerli grabbed his other arm.

Lor felt every hair of Paerli's arm scratching his and the heat of her skin melting his pores.

"Lor... Hey Loren..." Nico snapped in front of him, but all he saw were ghostly traces swimming in the white static of multiple colors.

"Get him to the dorm," Nico said, pushing Paerli to the side and drawing Lor's arm around his neck. Dill moved to the other side to help hold him up.

Sweat popped over Lor's temples and dribbled down his face. The double heartbeat kicked in, pushing the back of his as if trying to take over completely.

He reached up to touch his face as his friends dragged him toward the dorm. Cold, slimy sweat clung to his hand like glue.

"I-I don't feel so good," Lor mumbled. He pulled his hand from his forehead and looked at his fingers. He wasn't sure if it was just his colors when the light from the sun glimmered translucent gold over the wet fingertips.

He was struck by an unfamiliar sense of grief, and the phantom heartbeat pounded slow and hard into the arpeggio of his own.

Am I dying?

More sweat trickled down to his chin, where the drop dangled and jittered with each footfall. His knees shook, and his thighs turned into jelly.

"Help me," Nico said. He grabbed Lor's armpits, and Dill grabbed his ankles. They took stuttering steps through the thatched hallway. The girls followed close behind as their male classmates gawked at them in the hall.

They burst into the room, and Dill swung Lor's legs onto the bed. His touch burned Lor's ankles, sending pulses of fear and loneliness over the second heart. The colors splashed everywhere in the room, coating the walls like paint tossed everywhere. Electricity shimmied through his muscles, then his limbs started to twitch.

"Oh hell," Nico said. He ripped off his belt and folded it in half, shoving it between Lor's teeth.

Please, Maker, don't turn me into a Weggevens!

Lor thought of Tad. His bright eyes descended into the earth, forever gone from this world. So young.

The belt squeaked under Lor's teeth as he ground down into the leather.

Every muscle tightened, and limbs shook out of control, beating the mattress in staccato vibrations.

Please don't explode.

Nico and Dill's faces blurred and focused in quick succession as Lor's neck tightened and foam dribbled from the corner of his mouth. He threw his head back.

"I think he's having a seizure." Nico pulled Dill's pillow from his bed and cradled it next to Lor's head, trying to cup his face inside the barrier of pillows.

A deep groan bubbled from Lor's throat.

"Horace! Help us!" Dill shouted out the window.

Damaetra sat on the bed next to Lor. She put a small hand on his cheek. Her purple dress smeared all over his vision, but her face was clear. He tried to focus on her, but his eyes twitched side to side.

The double heartbeat slowed, pulling his own heartbeat down in tempo until they pumped in tandem. She pressed her lips on his sweat-slicked forehead and left them there, waiting for the seizure to stop. Damaetra's hand felt cool on his temple, and she rubbed her thumb across his brow. As her thumb massaged his head, his heart slowed, and his vision went black.

Lor knew he wasn't awake, but something told him he wasn't sleeping. Was he dead? Flashes of color and twisting memories flickered in rapid succession without time enough to fully decipher what he saw.

An ancient wasteland, blood scattered on the sand.

A young boy in tears pressed a button on a stone funeral plinth. The glossy wooden casket descended into the ground, no bigger than a child.

Another boy sat crouched in the corner of a dark closet, pressing his ears with a lone tear crawling down his cheek.

An image of Dag watching him.

The final flash was a stream of multicolored wildflowers bursting through the room.

"Mister Turtingas?" the deep voice cut into the flowers as light filtered through Lor's eyelashes.

"I think he's waking up," a low whisper sent the message to others, and a murmur traveled through the room, down the hall.

"Mister Turtingas?" the deep voice repeated, and Lor felt a light push on his shoulder. Ash-colored hair bobbed in front of him, with readers buried deep in the strands.

"H-Horace?" Lor croaked.

"Oh, thank the Maker," Nico said, blowing out a hard breath and raking fingers through thick curls.

"We were afraid you were going to end up like our friend Tad, Mr. Turtingas," Horace said, his rheumy eyes peering directly into Lor's.

Was he about to cry?

He looked beyond Horace to see the silhouette of the familiar Foscan standing behind him, presumably waiting for the moment he needed to pull out Lor's silvery life force.

"I guess I was lucky..." Lor cleared his throat. "That it was just a seizure."

Damaetra had her hand in his, squeezing hard enough to whiten her already white knuckles.

"And you peed," Dill said. Nico pushed his shoulder.

"Alright, the show's over, everyone." Horace waved at the group of students standing behind Valge'jor.

They craned their necks, trying to gawk at Lor lying there, vulnerable, covered in pee. Leaving the dorm, they whispered to each other through the hall. He heard a distant squeal of laughter.

"You can go too, my friend." Horace nodded at Valge'jor. The Foscan bowed and followed the train of nosy students.

"I'm sorry, I didn't mean to cause a scene." Lor propped himself up on an elbow and rubbed his eyes. He glanced down and saw a dark, wet circle on his pants. He tried to cover it with a hand but didn't want to touch it.

"Don't be ashamed of that." Horace nodded at the circle. "You certainly gave us a scare, though. That's for sure."

The guide looked around for any stray students lingering for more drama. When he was satisfied no one was nearby, his gaze bored into Lor's eyes. "I had full faith that you weren't suffering from the implant."

"What do you mean?" Lor asked.

"I won't tell your families, but I know all of you except Miss Praes cut your implants out."

Lor hiccupped. "H-how did you find out?"

He pointed at his head and grinned. "A guide knows his students. Just like I know about all the times you and Miss Praes snuck out after dark."

Lor flushed a deep crimson, and Damaetra twisted her hair in front of her, looking down with a small smirk.

Nico put his fist out, and Lor bumped it.

"I'm sorry about the implant," Lor said, "a-about all of it. We were scared after Tad, and we just—"

"It's fine. I'm not worried about it, and neither should you be. Although it might be a little more difficult for you to get a Guild job."

Lor shot Horace a look. "What do you mean by that?"

Horace chuffed. "Well, I guess I should go ahead and congratulate you."

"Congratulate me?"

"Yes." Horace lowered his voice and examined Lor's face. "You, sir, are a Reaper."

CHAPTER 16

Yaslecha
LOREN

DILL BOUNCED LIKE A WELL-LUBED piston, shouting, "I knew it! I knew you'd get one! And a Reaper? You are one lucky son of a—"

"Relax, dude." Nico put a hand on Dill's shoulder.

Horace stood up and brushed off his trousers. "I must say, it doesn't happen very often that we get one Reaper in a class, let alone *two*."

Lor cleared his throat and sat up straight, swinging his legs over the side of the bed. "Is what happened to me normal?" he said.

Horace pursed his lips and scratched his nose. The silence was thick as everyone waited for his answer. He shook his head and sighed.

"Well, I can't say *I've* ever seen that."

Lor looked around the room. No one said anything, not even Dill. Horace cleared his throat.

"Well, Mister Turtingas, I'm glad you are not dead," he said. "Please do get some rest, and I will bid you adieu for now. We can talk more tomorrow about your new gift."

He bowed at the group and slipped through the door. Several voices chattered in the hallway, no doubt trying to ask Horace questions.

Lor heard him in the distance tell them, "Let him have his peace, go on back to your rooms! That's an order, or I will fail you all!"

Harried feet shuffled through the thatch, scuttling away, making Lor chuckle to himself. Several doors slammed shut. He put a hand to his greasy forehead. Pulling away his fingers revealed nothing—just thick sweat, no gold.

"I need a shower bad," he said, "but I need to catch Horace real quick."

Lor stood up, and his knees wavered.

"Whoa, now. He *said* you needed to get some rest," Nico said, putting a hand on his shoulder.

"No, really, I need to follow him. I'll be right back, I promise. Stay here."

Nico loosened his grip as Lor bolted from the door.

The hallway was dark, and several students stood at their doors, watching him go and whispering to each other. It made him uncomfortable to be the center of attention, especially after pissing himself. He never wanted to cause a stir in the program—just stay in the background, learn his "gift," and go. Now, he was some sort of statistic that would be written in a textbook that he would definitely buy.

He burst through the front door and saw a distant silhouette of Horace tromping through the sand with his puffy hair bobbing in the wind. He ran to catch up.

"Horace?" Lor jogged up to him. His legs still felt weak and rubbery while he dodged the dead tech poking out from the sand.

Horace turned and smiled at Lor. "I thought I told you to rest?"

"Yes, I'm sorry." Lor bent over and took in a deep breath. Weakness wracked his bones.

"How can I help you, friend?" Horace put a hand on his shoulder. It felt strange, yet familial—and heavy.

"I, uh... I don't know if I should even ask, but..." The feeling of Horace's hand on his shoulder nagged at him.

"Don't be afraid to ask," Horace interrupted, taking his hand away. "If I can't answer, I'm sure Valge'jor would be happy to tell you as much as he can about being a Reaper in the next day or so."

Lor raised an eyebrow. "Does he speak Northern Common?"

Horace barked out a laugh, causing Lor to take a sharp step back.

"Valge'jor speaks many languages. He just prefers his own," he said, lowering his eyes. "He doesn't want it to die out with the dwindling number of Foscans. I took the liberty to learn it as well, as a good guide would."

Dwindling numbers?

Lor hadn't thought about Foscans too much before coming to the program. The only one he really knew was Dag, and she never said much.

"O-okay. Um, I just wanted to ask about some... 'visions' I had during my episode."

"Yes, yes," Horace interrupted. "You see, reaping is a unique and powerful ability. You are aware that it is extremely rare, aren't you?"

Lor bit his lip. The Law books he buried his face in did not help his knowledge of reaping. Even Eva's engineering held no interest. He had a whole fat, dusty tome about Guilds at home that languished in his bookshelf, spine uncracked.

"No, sir. I didn't know."

"I'm going to say this once, so listen well." Horace peered around for signs of eavesdroppers, then whispered, "You are in a unique position right now. You are free of the implant, and you have a rare ability. Take that for what it's worth." Horace spun around on his heel to leave.

"Oh, and do talk with Valge'jor!" he shouted, spinning a finger above his head and walking away.

Lor didn't want to talk to Valge'jor. The man was eerie and had waited there to "pull" him, as Paerli had said.

He glanced north. The black mountain of Gehenna stood in the distance. A dense haze rose from the water, obscuring the bottom half of it. It was mystical.

As he stared off at it, he smelled apples and violets.

"Hey," Paerli said. "How are you feeling now?"

Damaetra slid her hand into his.

He sighed. "I've been better."

"Seems like we're both Reapers now."

"Which leaves me as the lone Engineer!" Dill jumped and slapped Lor's shoulder.

Lor spun around and saw Nico coming up to them also.

"I told you guys to stay in the room."

"We wanted to check on you," Nico said.

"What did ole Horace tell you?" Dill asked.

Lor shrugged. "He told me to talk to Valge'jor."

"That Foscan *devil?*" Dill spat.

Lor laughed. "The very same."

"That guy is creepy," Paerli said, shuddering.

Damaetra squeezed Lor's hand, gazing up at him. "He's just a Foscan. Nothing scary." She smiled.

He stroked her face, and the memory of her calm covered him in a warm blanket.

He turned to Paerli. "Maybe you should come with me too? Since you're a Reaper and all."

She cupped her hands behind her back, pushing out the black-stoned pendant in the crook of her neck. "No, *thank* you."

She wore short sleeves that day with the ratty strip of shirt knotted around her arm. It tugged downward a little, revealing a touch of smooth skin underneath. Lor raised an eyebrow.

"Don't let his hands near your neck!" Dill said, making a choking motion around his throat.

Lor tittered and rolled his eyes. "He wouldn't dare pull another Reaper."

"He can't," Paerli interjected.

"Nah, we're too valuable," Lor said, smiling. "I'll visit him at his hut at second sunrise. For now... I need a shower."

The second sun swelled over the horizon, casting its purple light over the sea. The color it made over the deep blue water reminded him of Damaetra. He sighed, wanting nothing more than to just turn around and find her, rather than spend an evening with Valge'jor.

He jogged across the sand, feeling stronger than earlier, and lithe enough to dodge sharp ancient debris. A single-person straw hut was where the man lived, right next to the school.

Like every other building on campus, the entry steps were wooden and rickety. An oval window set into the door was at Lor's eye-height. His feet creaked over the aged planks, and he rapped sharply on the equally aged wooden door.

A shadow in the far room perked up, then hurried to the door.

Valge'jor was shorter than Lor thought—but then he remembered the only times he had been close to the man was either when he was sitting or lying on his back, waiting to be reaped by him. The door creaked open.

"Good evening. How can I help you?" His white eyes scanned Lor's face in a way that exposed him.

His Northern Common was a forced labor on his tongue. Even the small sentence had a few throat clicks that Lor wouldn't know how to replicate if he tried. He was surprised that despite Valge'jor's struggle with the language, his voice was still ethereal, like his appearance. Since Dag never spoke a word at home, hearing the accent was a pleasant surprise.

"Um, hello, Mister... Va-Valgay..hor."

The Foscan chuckled. "No, no, it's VAL-geh-yore. Please call me Val."

Lor felt his cheeks go pink. "I'm sorry... Val. I've never spoken a word of Foscan."

"No problem, don't worry about it. You are Loren, yes?"

Lor nodded and swallowed the scant slick of moisture in his dry mouth.

"You are Reaper?" Val ushered him deeper into the small hut.

"A-ah, yes, sir. That's what I've been told."

Word traveled fast. I guess he was there...

Inside the dirt cottage, the air was warm and smelled of freshly baked hearty red rolls. Lor's stomach gurgled. He hadn't eaten most of the day. Now that he was feeling stronger, his appetite woke up.

"You want?" Val asked, pointing at a tray in the kitchen with the meaty bread buns. He must have heard Lor's gut.

Lor bit his lip. "You don't mind?"

"No, no, please! I love to cook. I am alone here, and cooking is... too much." Lor could listen to the man talk all day. Val hurried toward the counter, pulling a plate out, and dropped three of the red buns on it. Then, he slid it across the crooked kitchen table, motioning for Lor to sit, and Lor obeyed.

He tore the bun in half, revealing the steaming meat inside, and took a long, deep inhale. The aroma was savory and absolutely divine.

"Wow, this is amazing. Did you make these for the cafeteria?" Lor said.

"Ah, yes! I love to help. Did you try them there?"

"No, my girlfriend was talking about them earlier, saying how great they were. Back at home, we're given rations from Audun. Gale doesn't cook."

"Gale?" Val raised an eyebrow and sat across from Lor, tearing into his bun with slender, bony fingers.

"Sorry. My stepfather. He's a medic. He's good at stitching people up, but not so good with cooking tools."

"Oh, medic is good job. He is smart?"

Was that a question? Gale is terribly smart.

Lor pinched at a fold in the bun, thinking about his chilly stepfather. "Yeah, I guess so. But he doesn't think he's good enough. He thinks Guilds are the best future for me and my sister."

Val nodded pensively. "Sadly, he is not wrong."

Lor took a bite of the red bun and muffled, "I wanted to be a roundsman." He forgot his manners already. Val didn't seem to care.

"Roundsman? Oh no, Guild is much better. *Medic* is better than roundsman."

Val had a lot of similar qualities as Dag—slim and petite, with odd pallid skin that was borderline gray. They both had stick-straight black hair they gathered into a low tail. Sitting next to a Foscan was normal for Lor—*talking* to one was unusual.

Watching Val pick apart his food and talk so freely made Lor regret not trying to get to know Dag better.

Did Val have a servant's name at one point? What was Dag's real name?

"You want to know more about reaping, yes?" Val's throat clicked even through the food in his mouth.

"Honestly? No." Lor didn't know why that came out.

Val laughed at that. He nodded his head, smiling and chewing. He was not the kind of person Lor thought he was. This man had a kindness about him.

"You are not wrong for *that*"—Val pointed a finger in the air, still smiling—"but you must know some things before leaving this place. I can try to help."

Lor stared off, beyond Val. He was in his golden bedroom, reading a guide on Law, marked at the section on advanced partitioning and zone control by a crinkled brochure for the program. It felt so stupid now. He wasted opportunities to learn more about Guilds. His own Guild. And Roseaarde.

"Y-yes. I could use a little help."

Val put his hands down on the table, peering at Lor with those strange eyes.

"You are sad?"

Nothing gets past this man.

"It's nothing. I'm just... going through a lot right now."

"I understand. You are full adult now. It is scary, yes."

Full adult.

Lor had never heard it referred to like that before. It made sense, even in a choppy Northern Common phrasing. Lor wondered what that meant for him. Val wasn't a Foscan devil at all. He would be sure to let Dill know as much.

"Val," Lor started to say. He chewed his lip again, looking directly at those white eyes. Val pushed his plate aside, folding his hands in front of him. He didn't move a muscle. His full attention was on Lor.

What can I say? I saw what reaping looked like.

Lor sighed. "I'm terrified."

That was all he knew to say. If he was forced to tell a stranger about his inner struggles with this new ability, he would tell *this* stranger. The one who almost reaped him.

"Is understandable, yes. To reap is a strong gift. To reap is a an even stronger burden."

"Do you have the implant?" Lor blurted.

"Implant? No. Those are Guild property only."

Guild property?

The old shirt banded across his forearm scratched at him. The sound it made *schluping* from his flesh and the blinking light stirred in memory.

"How did you become a Reaper then?"

Val clicked his tongue and eyed Lor. "Is Foscan way."

"I'm sorry, what?"

"Well, not *all* Foscan become Reaper..."

"Why would they tell us the implant brings out our gift?"

Val shrugged. "I didn't know they told you that."

"I cut mine out."

Val's eyes widened. "Cut?"

Lor tugged at the shirt band. He hadn't washed it in days, and it was crusted with salt and sand. Underneath was the puckered, pink crescent scar. He poked at it, then held his arm out for Val to examine. He grabbed

Lor's arm and pulled it toward him. His grip was warm and eerie with those skinny fingers.

Val opened and closed his mouth, tracing the curve of the scar. "Lan guae'alja onaecha'te? When you do this thing?"

"A-ah, after Tad's funeral. Not long after the program started."

Val relaxed and let go of Lor's arm. He sank back into his chair while continuing to eye Lor.

"Did I do a bad thing?" Lor tied the band back around his arm.

"Hard to say."

Lor sighed and thought about Damaetra. Her implant was still firmly stuck under her skin, with the black needle buried deep into her muscle.

"So, they're Guild property?"

Val nodded. "Nothing for you to worry about now."

Lor didn't want to push it any more. He was free of the thing.

"So!" Val stood up. "Reaping, yes?"

Lor reached for another bun but realized he had devoured them all when all he grabbed was air. He tried to pass off the swipe as pushing the plate forward.

"Horace said you could tell me some things. I don't think he meant for you to train me or anything."

"Oh, no, I can't train. I am only Reaper allowed to practice on Heart Island. You need to travel to Secas and find a... what is the word... professor? No... mentor. Yes, I think that is the one."

"Secas?"

"Yes, that is it. Or any other Guild city. But there are other things you must know. Your journey will be hard."

Everything seemed so easy for Paerli. She wasn't running to Val or Horace for advice. He envied that about her—to be tough in the face of this challenge was a trait Lor wondered if he even had.

"How so?"

"I can only tell you things. You must experience to understand. Tell me, what did you see this afternoon?"

Afternoon was eons ago.

"You mean during... you know...."

"During your sleep. Wait, no... during your... coma?"

"*Coma?*" Lor reared back. "Was I in a coma?"

"No, hold on..." Val slumped his shoulders. The unknown weights he carried were etched in his forehead, and it took a toll on his state of wakefulness. He let out a long yawn.

"You're tired," Lor said.

Val ignored him. "Your... let's say you blacked out. What did you see?"

"I don't know if I can describe it."

"Please try."

"Okay, well, the first thing was sand. Lots of it. I didn't know where I was, but it must have been in the Span or something... but not. It was scarier. The last thing I saw was blood spraying on the sand. Like someone had flung a bucket of it."

Val studied him. As interesting as the man's eyes were, Lor still felt exposed under his watch.

"And then what did you see?"

"Um, let me see... there was a boy. He was crying at a funeral. It looked like Tad's funeral, except the boy was the one pushing the trigger to lower the casket."

"That one is more clear, you think?"

Lor nodded, trying to remember the vision in greater detail, but the memory was moving further away into a blurred haze. It was almost as if mentioning the vision as being clear made it flee at the words.

"I-I'm struggling to remember any more."

"Did you see anything else?" Val took several small yawns in between stories. Lor felt bad for keeping him awake.

"I think I did, but I only remember another sad boy and some... flowers. I-I can't seem to picture them in my head anymore."

"No worries, it happens. Did you touch anyone?"

Lor cocked his head to the side and furrowed his brow. "My friends carried me up to my room, if that's what you mean. A lot of people touched me. I'm kinda embarrassed about it."

Val chuckled a little, yawning again and slumping lower.

"Val, I can find you tomorrow. You are very tired."

The next yawn was hearty and wide, squeezing a little water at the corners of his eyes.

"Yes, I apologize. My journey was also hard and remembers me even as I age."

"How... how old *are* you?" Lor didn't know why he asked that question. Once again, Gale would not be impressed by his manners.

Val tittered and the corner of his mouth turned up. "The truth, friend, is stranger still. In time, you will learn more. In time, you will not recognize yourself today."

"Thank you so much for dinner, Val. That was just... amazing." Lor stood up, pushing the rotting wooden chair back to the table.

"My pleasure. I am sorry to be so tired. There is a Foscan word for that... we call it yaslecha. It is more than sleepy—it is... a draining of energy from the weariness of life, you see?"

"Yas-LEH-kka." Lor carefully repeated the word.

"That is right. As you travel this path after years and years, you will remember yaslecha."

Yaslecha.

"Thank you, Val. I hope to talk to you again tomorrow."

Dear Loren,

I am sorry about last night and yaslecha.
I wanted to tell you more, but I was overcome
by the sleep. I write because I did not know it
was my last night on the island before returning
home. Please forgive me, there is much left unsaid.
It is good for you to go to Guild Central. You are
Reaper, they might beg you to stay, but I don't
know about your friends. Keep them close, do
not let them go. You need friends for your journey.
I told you it would be hard.

I am glad to talk with you. I return to
Heart Island at the cap end of this year,
after storm. I do hope we meet again.
If you are ever in Pohay'an, I live there.
Is small town, but cold.

Take care,

Val..

CHAPTER 17

The Chroma Night
LOREN

LOR FOLDED VAL'S LETTER AND tucked it carefully between the socks in his duffel.

They left in the morning to get back to Secas and mark the official end of their time in the program. Gale would be meeting Lor once the ferry dropped him off. Nico's parents lived in town and would be there, while Damaetra's family was traveling all the way from Audun to celebrate with her. Dill said his aunt would be there, but he didn't want to introduce her to anyone, and Paerli said she only had her grandmother. Lor didn't remember her ever telling him about family.

Lor wrote to Gale a handful of times during the program, only because he didn't have access to his e-disk to message him more often. The callus on his middle finger was swollen and hard, the way he remembered in grade school. To Lor's surprise, Gale was supportive of his intention to move to Guild Central if he found his ability. He would be that much more surprised to know that he was a Reaper. For once, Lor was excited to talk to Gale.

He stared out at the ocean, watching Mount Gehenna shrink from view through the small porthole of the ferry. Damaetra held on to him. She held on to him with a greater intensity since the afternoon of his seizure. She had the right side of her face buried in his chest and her eyes closed. He wondered if she could smell the ocean and hyacinth in his armpit.

"Am I going to meet your parents?" Lor asked.

She hummed. "And my twin sisters."

"Do you think they'll like me?"

"They'll love you."

The ferry ride was short like always. Once docked and the gangway dropped, Lor led Damaetra to the exit. Paerli didn't say much to anyone on the trip but followed close behind, while Nico and Dill buzzed in the background, arguing about something. Lor made out the words "bouncy" and "motor." He wasn't sure what Dill meant by that, and knowing him, he didn't want to ask.

As they walked the passage to the dock, several families gathered at the end, holding colorful balloons, banners, and laser pops that projected holoconfetti. Gale was in between two larger boys, and he jumped to wave at Lor. Damaetra's family stuck out like a beacon. All Anglia—paper-white skin and white gold hair. She got her looks from her mother.

"Let's meet at the visitor center in a little bit," a breathy voice whispered behind them, accompanied by the scent of apples.

"Did you want to meet my dad?" Lor spun around to Paerli.

"I'm sure we'll meet sometime. My grandma is waiting for me, so I need to get to her."

"Fair enough, we'll get the word to Dill and Nico," Lor said, nodding over to the pair, already joined with their families. They squeezed hands, then Paerli strolled away.

"Go to your family, and I'll grab Gale and find you." Lor ran his thumb across Damaetra's mouth. Her cheeks flushed and she squeezed his other hand, turning toward her family.

Gale still stood between the two burly boys, waving Lor over.

"I didn't get a letter from you in a while," he said, grabbing the duffel. He held up Lor's e-disk with a grin and slipped it into a side pocket.

"Yeah, sorry... Manual writing is harder than I remember."

"So, what did you get? You never told me—you did *get* something, didn't you?"

"I did, actually. It didn't come until almost the last day, so I don't really know what I'm doing, but... I'm a Reaper now."

Gale jumped back. "You don't say? Wow, that's great, son. A *Reaper*." He shook his head in disbelief.

Lor smiled. He knew Gale would be happy with anything, but a Reaper was the best... and most lucrative.

"Can I introduce you to someone?" Lor asked.

He led Gale to Damaetra's family. When she spotted him, her face lit up and she waved him over.

Her dad wore a pressed navy blue shirt and silvery tie with smart tan pants. With his white gold hair cut neat and without a strand out of place, Lor pictured him as a member of non-Guild finance. His sharp green eyes were nothing like Damaetra's. Her mother looked like an older version of her, with the same style of clothing. A pale lavender dress with yellow trim, the crystal lavender-blue eyes his girlfriend wore so well, and a long braided updo gave her mother the look of a demure queen. The twins appeared to be around Eva's age with short white bobs, big blue eyes, and matching breezy pants with green polka-dotted shirts, barely containing their curves. Dill would be very pleased to meet them.

"Loren, this is my mom Thea, my dad Aedras, and my sisters, Eloria and Caella."

"Good to meet you, Loren. Dame wrote to us about you. Aren't you just a handsome lad?" Thea took Lor's hand, and he blushed, never knowing a compliment like that. It was always Nico being ogled over.

Aedras squeezed his palm with a strength that belied his Anglia features. While Thea's hand was soft, Aedras had the prickly hard hands of a laborer.

Maybe not finance after all…

Lor introduced them to Gale, who whispered to him out of the corner of his mouth, "You didn't tell me you had a *girlfriend*."

"I meant to tell you, I'm sorry." Lor grimaced.

"So *hot*," Dill whispered in Lor's other ear. He spun around.

"Oh shi—" Lor swallowed. "I mean oh, Dill, you scared me."

Damaetra giggled and introduced Dill to her family, taking special care to highlight her sisters.

Eloria and Caella were so different than Damaetra. They had a boyish demeanor but the voluptuous curves of the cafeteria girl. Eloria chewed on a wad of herbal gumtree, smacking it behind a set of thick juicy lips, while Caella whacked Dill's hand with hers, sending him a fluttery wink.

He leaned over to Lor and whispered, "*Nariah and Emilia who*, am I right?"

"You're good to our baby sis, I hope?" Caella addressed Lor, cracking her knuckles. He'd never seen a girl crack her knuckles so gruffly with appeal, yet here she was.

"Yes, ma'am." His voice cracked and he raised his hands. Damaetra giggled again, clearly entertained by her sisters.

"So, Thea tells me you plan to work at Guild Central. Is that right, Dame?" Aedras spoke for the first time, and his voice was even deeper than Nico's, sending fresh fear under Lor's skin.

"Yes, everyone is going to go," Damaetra said in her soft twinkling voice.

"Very well, if that is what you wish. You'll always have our support and can come back to Audun anytime."

"Thanks, Aedras." Damaetra hugged him, setting wrinkles into his sleek blue shirt. He kissed the top of her head.

Aedras?

Maybe it was an Anglia thing. Gale was his stepfather, but he still called him "Dad."

Gale pulled Lor aside. "While it would be nice to have you closer to home, I'm glad that you are settling somewhere with friends. This is a great town."

"Thanks… I hope so."

"Eva's going to miss you."

"She can visit," Lor said, smiling.

Gale squeezed Lor's shoulder. *Maybe I've been wrong about him.*

"We booked an inn for a couple days while you figure out your situation here," Aedras said, glancing down at his daughter still holding on to him.

"Oh? Which inn? I'm booked in town too," Gale asked, raising a hand.

Aedras told him about the small inn called The Chroma Night, which wasn't the one Gale had reserved, but they were close by. Lor didn't know how much he wanted to weave their families together so soon, afraid he would scare Damaetra off with his somewhat unpredictable stepdad.

When asked about his aunt, Dill just said he sent her away. The shock in Gale's face at the comment was a sight to behold. Lor never pressed Dill about his aunt because he never wanted to talk about her.

Nico eventually wandered to the group, introducing his parents to everyone. While Damaetra favored her mother, Nico very much favored his father. He didn't think a man could get any more handsome, but there he stood, radiating in the sun in all his chiseled glory, mister Stephan Dicus.

"Damn, dude," Dill whispered, "put *that* guy's picture by 'handsome' in the definition tome."

"I heard that," Nico whispered back while his parents were distracted talking with Aedras and Gale.

"Oh, he was just joking," Lor said. "We all know you're the cutest of all time." He pinched Nico's cheek, and Nico shook his head, slapping at the air in front of him while flashing those dimples.

Thea asked the group if they wanted to grab lunch, which the twins heartily agreed to. As they walked toward the visitor center where Lor told Paerli they'd meet her, a familiar voice crept up behind him.

"Well, if it isn't Loren and Gale from the train." Fowler strode up to the group, wearing a black coat and white undershirt. His black hair was slicked back, pulling at his hairline, and accentuated his pointed nose.

"Oh, hey, Fowler, fancy meeting you here! It's good to see you." Lor put a palm in his and shook the skinny twig fingers.

"I got your letter, so I thought I would come find you at the end of the program," Fowler said.

Lor shrugged. "Did it make sense to you? I don't know how things work at Guild Central."

Fowler laughed. "Of course it did. In fact, I've already drafted a notice of intent for you and your friends to the board."

Gale stepped in and clapped a hand on Fowler. "Thank you for taking care of him. It's kind for you to help Loren."

Gale's shift in friendliness shook Lor, but he was glad to see the man in a light mood for once.

"I'm happy to help, of course." He smiled at Gale, stretching his odd features. It made Dill chuckle under his breath, and Nico bumped him in the shoulder in response.

"Now Lor, in your letter you hadn't gotten your ability yet. But I do hope you have it now. That way, I can fill in the rest of the request," Fowler asked.

Lor told Fowler about how he just barely got his Guild, but Fowler was more interested in the fact that it was as a Reaper. He didn't feel it was important to mention the seizure. To Fowler *or* to Gale.

"Come have lunch with us!" Thea said to Fowler, who agreed, mentioning that it was his day off and "why not?"

Lor craned his neck, trying to find Paerli at the orange building, but she was nowhere to be found. She would certainly stand out in this crowd.

After waiting for several minutes, the twins started to grumble, so Lor apologized and they left. Earlier, Paerli had scribbled her number down for him on a scrap of parchment from her program journal, and it was folded neatly in his back pocket. He told himself to send her a QuickChat when they got to the restaurant and apologize profusely.

Lor: Hey, Par, we're at the restaurant next to Chroma Night inn. We waited for you, but Damaetra's sisters were getting cranky. The location is 725002.

Paerli: Sorry, Lor, I didn't mean to ditch you. Grandma has been having troubles, so I'm going to stay with her today.

Lor: Take care of Grandma. We miss you!

Paerli: I miss you too.

Lor clicked his e-disk on the table, letting his friends know she wasn't coming.

"Gee, what a bummer," Nico said with a sarcastic slant.

Dill wasn't paying attention, fully wrapped up in conversation with Caella.

"Hey, look, Dill met the female version of himself," Damaetra whispered to Lor, making him chuckle.

"You aren't worried about that?" He smiled at her.

"Caella is tough, and Eloria is tougher. They can handle Dilly."

Lor clicked his tongue. "That's pretty tough. Even I can't handle him half the time."

Lor learned that Thea was a guide like Horace, but for secondary kids wanting to go into arts, and Aedras was in construction. Eloria and Caella both went into arts after their mother, leaving Damaetra to be the lone Guild member.

"Aedras took a loan out against the house to help pay for sissy's program," Eloria mentioned to Lor.

He didn't know where Gale got the plats, but he wondered if he had done the same.

"You didn't want to go?" Lor asked.

"Nah, that would've been too much money for both me and Cae." She stabbed the meat on her plate, jamming the chunk in her mouth. Lor noticed she talked with her mouth full too, but Aedras never got on her about it.

Fowler left lunch earlier than the rest, telling the group he had errands to run but that he would meet Lor and his friends back at the visitor center in two days to take them to Guild Central. It wasn't long after that the rest of them made moves to leave.

Aedras assured Damaetra they would stay in town with her until she was safely in Guild Central. Nico's parents told him to come home when he was done hanging out with his friends. They didn't live far from the market, and he could just walk home before second sun.

Gale gave Lor the location of his hotel, which was only a few blocks from the Chroma Night.

"Please come to the room before the second sun," he said, glancing up at the sky and then checking his e-disk. Lor agreed, watching Gale go.

Caella and Eloria strolled toward the main building of the inn with Thea and Aedras. As they walked away, Dill leaned over and whispered, "Do you think the carpet matches the drapes?"

"Oh *Gehenna*, Dill..." Nico rolled his eyes and shoved him.

Damaetra giggled, and Lor shrugged. "I dare you to ask," he said.

"Ha! I'm not that dumb. But a man can dream..."

"It does," Damaetra said, grinning.

"Oh ho! Listen to this one here," Dill said, jabbing a thumb at Damaetra.

Lor shot her a look with his mouth open. He went scarlet, having never known his own girlfriend in that way. It immediately struck a mental image.

She sniggered again, and the peach flush crawled up her cheeks. "What?"

He leaned down to kiss her and said, "Send me a QuickChat later, okay?"

"I'll send you two." She grinned, running her hand down his side and squeezing the little bit of skinny fat over his belt. He jerked away and chuckled.

Dill had no snide comment about Lor and Damaetra's goodbye. He was too busy ogling her sisters as they sauntered toward the inn, no doubt imagining the shiny twin carpets. Damaetra turned to catch up at a trot, her long hair bouncing behind her and twinkling in the sun.

"Well, it's just us guys now. What do you wanna do for the next... two hours?" Nico asked.

Twinsies
LOREN

THEY DECIDED NOT TO DO anything too crazy and settled down in a local park just outside the open market to rest and digest.

"I think I'm in love," Dill said, falling back on a bench.

"That's not love making your pants tight," Nico said, laughing.

"You guys don't understand... Cae *gets* me."

"Oh, we're on a nickname basis already?" Lor chuckled.

Dill swung his legs at the bench, staring at the multicolored trees swaying in the breeze. "It's beautiful, isn't it?" he said with a sigh.

Nico pressed the back of his hand on Dill's forehead. "Uh-oh, the boy has fallen ill. We must get him to Gale, *stat*."

Lor laughed, nudging his small friend. "Come back to us, Dill."

"You just wait, Cae is going to be my wife, and Lor and I are going to be *real* brothers when he marries Damaetra." Dill smirked.

"Ten plat says you won't even know which one's which tomorrow," Nico said.

Dill clicked his tongue. "Yes, I would. Cae has bigger boobs."

"Of *course* she does." Lor rolled his eyes and laughed.

Nico sat up and rubbed at his forehead. "Hey, guys, I never told you this, but... I used to have a twin too."

Dill spun toward Nico. "What? No way! What is it with twins in the atmosphere?" he said, gazing back off again.

"Yeah. We were *almost* identical. Not quite like Eloria and Caella."

"*Were?*" Lor asked, raising an eyebrow.

Nico bobbed his head. "I didn't tell you because it's a weird story. And sad. No one wants to hear sad stories."

Lor knocked his shoulder into Nico's and smiled.

"You're our best friend... You can tell us anything."

"No matter how weird," Dill added.

Nico tittered.

"Tell us about him," Lor said.

Nico smiled. "Just promise not to get sad about it. I've already made my peace," he said.

Lor crossed over his heart and stuck a palm forward.

"His name was Niklaus."

"Wait a second," Dill interrupted. "Your parents named you two Nico and Ni*klaus*?" He clutched his belly and laughed into the breezy trees.

Nico couldn't help but chuckle. "They weren't the most original, that's for sure. Everywhere we went, it was Niki Ni-*koh*!" He cupped his hand around his mouth to shout out the call.

Lor tittered. "Did they yell it out like that too?" he asked.

"Oh yeah, it was our calling card. That is, until he decided he wanted to be called 'Klaus.' He thought he was getting 'too mature' for games like that. We were like... eleven."

"What a *grown-up*," Dill said, rolling his eyes.

"He was always Niki to me." Nico gazed off into the market entrance. "But he... had somewhat of an accident."

"An accident?" Lor asked.

"Well, I mean, obviously he's not here anymore," Nico said, "but what happened to him... I was reminded of it the night you became a Reaper."

"So, Niki had a seizure?"

"Well, yes, kind of. It was more violent than yours but similar in a lot of ways. When you went into it, I was terrified... having kind of seen that before."

"So is that what, you know, took Niki?" Dill asked.

"At the time, I believed so. I didn't know what to do for him, I felt so helpless. My dad threw me from the bedroom while it was happening, and all I could do was pound and pound on the door until I bruised my fists and busted my knuckles."

"How *old* were you?" Lor asked.

"It wasn't long after he started going by Klaus. We were thirteen, I think." The friends sat in silence for a minute, listening to the wind.

Nico took in a sharp breath. "Want to know what I think?" he said. "I think Niki got Guilded early."

Lor raised an eyebrow. "What makes you say that?"

"Well, I got to thinking..." Nico paused, tapping a finger over his chin. "All of us—we took our implants out, and it still didn't make a difference— we still got our Guilds. Who's to say Niki didn't just go through second puberty early?"

"*Puberty*?" Dill said. "And you guys call me twisted." He laughed so hard he snorted, making Lor and Nico belly laugh. A couple of girls nearby saw Nico laughing and blushed, whispering to each other.

"Well, that's what it's like, isn't it?" Nico wiped away a tear.

"Alright, in all seriousness." Lor straightened his face, stifling a grin and choking the laughter. "You think Niki got a Guild ability? At *thirteen*?"

"I know it sounds crazy, but hear me out. Remember Tad? Didn't Horace say something about his system being overwhelmed? By like, a Weggevens ability?"

"Oh yeah, a strongman."

"I never actually *saw* Niki's body. What if he became a Weg, and my parents were so ashamed they sent him away? Remember, my dad put me out of the room."

"Wait, but didn't you lower his casket into the ground?" Lor didn't know why he said that. It came out so naturally, as if he had heard the story several times before—a distant memory, hiding in the corner of his mind that bubbled to the surface with a triggering story.

The color left Nico's face. "H-how did you know *that*?" He was still handsome with his mouth gaping open. Dill had turned his full attention to Lor, tilting his head so far over that he thought the guy's neck might snap. Lor's throat clacked from a dry swallow.

"I-I, um... I..." He tried to remember where that came from. The image tickled the edge of his memory.

Nico glared at Lor. "I don't remember ever telling you this story," he said. *Your journey will be hard. Keep your friends close.*

Val's words echoed in his head. Then it hit him like an out-of-control jumper.

"The seizure," Lor muttered.

"What about it?" Nico asked.

"I had visions during it... and right after I passed out."

"What did you see about me?" Dill asked.

"I-I don't—" Lor strained to think about that day of his seizure. It happened not long ago, but felt like ages ago. "I remember the casket. I didn't know it was you at the time... *or* Niki."

Nico sat back, folding his arms across his stomach. "Yeah, I lowered his casket," he said.

"What'd you see about *me*, Lor?" Dill asked again, but his voice sounded panicked.

"I honestly don't remember. I saw random things, and it's all jumbled together. I think I only remembered this one thing just now because you were telling me about it."

Yaslecha.

"I still think he's out there somewhere," Nico said after a long pause.
"Niki?" Lor asked. "Where do you think he is?"
Nico shrugged, peering off in the distance. "Somewhere," he said.

CHAPTER 19

The Eastern Branch
LOREN

AFTER AN UNEVENTFUL COUPLE OF days with family, the day arrived when they were to meet Fowler at the orange visitor center. Lor hoped Paerli would show, as he hadn't heard from her at all during that time. Nico didn't seem to mind and actually opened up a bit more without her there.

Dill spent every moment he could chatting up Caella. Lor thought he saw real tears in his friend's eyes when they had to say their goodbyes. Cae slipped him her number, and he made sure to tuck his into her cleavage. She giggled at that and winked at him.

When Lor turned from the jumper taxi circle, he spotted Paerli leaning against the orange building. She waved at him. Fowler came out of the building and motioned the group over to a different type of taxi. It was a long cruiser, with the words "Guild Central" in fancy script across the side.

Guild Central was on the far outskirts of town, up the stretch of forest, north of everything. It was also much closer to Mount Gehenna.

Fowler pulled the cruiser up to a copse of dense trees in purples, pinks, and yellows, with a small guard at a security booth. He rolled down the window and flashed a translucent card with credentials etched in light within the material. The guard nodded and let Fowler through.

They drove for several yards through a corridor of trees. It reminded Lor of his first trip to Secas in the jumper with Gale, but he wasn't prepared for what he saw once inside the Guild hub.

Arranged similarly to the Seven Cities, Guild Central had clusters of buildings surrounding a core hub with a fountain in front. Each cluster represented one of the "cities," resembling the Guilds for which they were built.

Sleek industrial buildings with tasteful strips of neon lights accented the exterior of the engineering cluster, with holopics of trinkets encircling the top floors. In contrast, the formulations cluster had traditional wooden buildings held together by chunky metal brackets and rivets that honked out billows of different colored smoke from its multi-layered sets of chimneys.

"That's your complex," Lor whispered to Damaetra.

Opposite to the engineering cluster was the strange Reader complex. Plain, black glass buildings stood slender and tall, with residents wandering around wearing hues of gray and black. Next to that were more wooden buildings decorated with curling ivy weaving throughout cracks in the planks. Land animals trotted along by their owners, and flocks of birds circled and perched on the buildings' rooftops.

Mismatched materials crafted the Weggevens cluster. Buildings cobbled together by recycled material scraps gave the buildings a chaotic, dirty appeal. Statues surrounded the cluster, made of smooth stone that stuck out by their cleanliness. A foot with wings, a woman mid-transformation into a doe, and a man with oversized biceps holding a boulder above his head stood stark against their background.

"Hey, there's our cluster." Paerli tugged at Lor's sleeve.

It was a gleaming beacon. Regal, castle-like black stone with gold inlay in fascinating patterns dotted the surface. It was like nothing he'd ever seen. Marvelous. Hypnotic.

"Okay, here we are," Fowler announced. "This is the Eastern connection to the Seven Cities. Don't ask me why they call themselves 'Central,' but they're very proud of their station, so keep that in mind."

Busybodies crawled all over the central hub, flowing around the fountain to different buildings to work and cabs for leave. A small blond woman carried a large stack of ordinary papers toward the main building, and a tall, slender man heading for a cruiser cab held a clear box of phials full of all different colors of eneris.

Lor was responsible for gathering that from now on, and he had no clue what he was doing. Piney sap smells wafted through as the phial-carrying man passed. The smell reminded him of home in cold Peakwood. He even missed Gale in a weird way.

A pure white and towering stone building curved around the central fountain. They strolled through the front double glass doors and stepped onto the hard white marble tile. A cool breeze glided over Lor's arms, making the hairs stand up. Violet and apple scents were strong in the sterile building. He gazed at Damaetra, who clutched his hand. Paerli had his other elbow, just barely fingering his shirt, but enough for Lor to notice.

A circular welcome desk sat in the center of the atrium, and a squat Mesaman girl with thick glasses and drab frizzy brown hair was parked in the middle of it.

"Welcome to Guild Central, the Eastern Branch of the Seven Cities! I am the appointed guide here, Livia Bookerly. How can I help you today?"

Her voice was a cheerful mask. Lor sensed the discontent behind the bottle-thick lenses.

"Yes, hello, Miss Livia. I am Fowler, and these newly fledged Guild members are my charges." He waved a hand across the five of them.

"Oh yes, Mister Fowler, I received your notice of intent just this morning." She swiped over her tablet. I see we have an Engineer, two Formulators, and... oh my, two Reapers. How fantastic! That's just so unbelievable. GC will be so pleased." She grinned at the group and glanced back down at her tablet.

Livia paused for a moment, then sucked her teeth. "Oh, but I'm sorry, Mister Fowler, we only received approval for *one* Formulator..." She made several more swipes over her tablet. "For a Mister Nico Dicus."

Damaetra squeezed Lor's hand again, and his heart quickened. There was no way he would stay here without her.

Paerli strode up next to Fowler and leaned over the counter. "I see," she said, tapping her lip. "Well, if you can't seem to find room for just one more Formulator, I guess you are going to have to lose two Reapers."

Livia shot Paerli a glance. "I u-uh, yes, ma'am. Let me check with floor three to see... if I can make it happen." She hurried toward a small hallway, disappearing through a set of double doors.

"Way to go, Par!" Dill put his hand up for a high five. She rolled her eyes and smiled, slapping his hand.

Damaetra had a hand on her chest, breathing heavily and gripping Lor's palm with all of her strength.

"It's not a sure thing yet," Paerli said, "but I guarantee they wouldn't want to lose *us*." She pointed between her and Lor.

Lor noticed a foul look on Fowler's already ugly face. He was being upscaled by a newbie and it didn't sit well with him.

"I wonder why they only accepted Nico?" Dill said.

Damaetra flushed, clearing her throat. "Ah, well, Nico had a higher score than me by the end. That would be my guess."

"Well, that's stupid. Formulator's a Formulator... who cares about scores?" Dill crossed his arms.

Harried footsteps crossed the marble floors as Livia returned to the desk. She smiled up at Paerli with those over-large eyes under the lenses. "Good news, miss. They decided it would be good to accept an Anglia, regardless of score."

Damaetra breathed out a long sigh.

"Give me just a moment to gather your IDs, and we'll get you all set up. Feel free to browse the guest center right over there." She pointed toward a nook just inside the entrance lined with couches and a holoprojector flashing scenes from the different clusters. Actors posed in front of buildings, speaking through their lines about how great life was at Guild Central. It was uncanny.

More brochures?

Lor swiped one from the rack. It was entirely black with gold letters that said: *Reaping and You, What Comes Next?*

He glanced around to see if anyone was watching him, but everyone else had scattered, thumbing through the other brochures. Fowler stayed at the counter, tapping his claws over the surface. Lor folded the brochure and crammed it into his back pocket.

"I saw that," Paerli whispered. She touched his elbow.

"You saw nothing," Lor said with a nervous laugh.

"We're in this *together*. Don't worry... before long, you'll have this whole reaping business mastered. Just wait."

"I don't know about all that. But... I'm glad you're here. At least someone understands. And you got Damaetra in."

"Of course I understand you. Even if we didn't have the same Guild, I'd understand."

Lor nodded, biting his lip and shrugging. Feeling the scar on his arm, he found it curious that Livia didn't ask about the implants. Horace made it seem like it would be hard for them to find a job without them.

At that moment, Fowler called out to them, and they reconvened at the desk where the stubby attendant flipped through a series of cards. She pulled a silver one from the stack, lined with softly glowing blue strips around the edge.

"Ah, this one is for our Engineer... Dill Storgut?" She raised her eyebrows to scan the group. Dill stumbled over himself to get to the counter, barely able to see over it.

"That's me!" He grabbed the card, flipping it back and forth.

"Just so you know," Livia continued, pulling out two more cards, "these will work in Audun, as well as any other Guild hub in the country. You're members now, and wherever you decide to visit, these will take you there... but your home is here."

She examined the top card of the two she held. "This is our first Formulator, Nico Dicus."

Nico raised a hand, taking the white card with a smart multi-colored trim glowing around the edges.

"Damaetra?" She butchered the name, but Damaetra didn't fuss, grabbing the fancy ID.

"And you must be Paerli Harea and Loren Turtingas…" She flipped both cards out to them. They were similar to the other ones, but black and lined with strips of golden light.

Loren ran his finger over his name. It was embossed metallic gold, and the only thing on the card.

Livia cleared her throat and peered up at Paerli. "This building is your social meeting place. There's food, entertainment, a gym… if you ever want to meet up with your friends that aren't in your Guild, this is the best place to come. Otherwise, your individual apartments only allow non-family guests once during a quintet. If you are in the same Guild, it obviously doesn't matter. Any questions for me?"

Damaetra is in the same complex as Nico…

"No, miss. Thank you for your help," Fowler said, putting a hand on Lor's shoulder.

They filtered from the building, back to the fountain courtyard.

"This thing is neat," Dill said, holding his card up to the light and turning it in his hand.

"Don't lose that," Fowler warned. "They'll fine you if they have to make a new one."

Dill jumped and fumbled the card, dropping it to the hard pavement. He swiped it from the ground and gave Fowler a nervous smile as he stuffed it into his pocket.

"I'll escort everyone to your clusters, then you might want to spend the evening learning more about what's expected of you tomorrow." He led them back to the cruiser still parked in the circle drive.

Fowler's bird-like features were enhanced in the stark sunlight. His black eyes had a subtle clarity, where Lor could see the pupils within the black, making him appear that much more inhuman. The bird man circled to the driver's seat as everyone settled in.

The first stop was Formulator Hall. Fowler slowed to a stop, opening the door for Damaetra.

Lor leaned over and kissed her goodbye, his hand lingering in her hair.

"Aww, I just might *die*," Dill moaned, cupping his hands together at his cheek.

Nico bumped Dill's arm. "Shut up, Dilly. We'll catch up later," he said, sliding out behind her.

Dill whined about being alone when it was time to drop him off, and Fowler told him to wait for him while he dropped off Lor and Paerli.

Reapers Apartment Hall was a gaping mansion, with a ceiling extending the full height of the building, arcing around a scrolled open staircase. Encircled by tiers of landings and decorated by dark wood posts inlaid with gold, a scant few future colleagues leaned on balconies overlooking the atrium. An enormous skylight, decorated with chiseled glass, threw rainbows into the hall. The front stairwell curled toward them, inviting them upward and deeper inside.

Their footsteps tipped through the cavernous hall and bounced off the gold trimmed mahogany walls. Strange and beautiful, it was like a choir of bells.

A black counter stretched in the center of the hall, where a stocky man flipped through an e-disk, projecting a puzzle game. He yawned and tapped at the black disk. Catching Lor and Paerli out of the corner of his eye wandering to the counter, he flicked the screen where it went dead, and he skidded the disk across the desk, annoyed.

"Hello..." he groaned with another yawn. "Are you the new charges?"

"Yes, we are under Fowler the skin walker."

The man clucked. "Oh, *that* guy."

Lor didn't want to ask what he meant by that. He was really starting to like Fowler.

"Do you need these?" Lor said, ignoring the comment and flashing the sleek black ID.

The man snatched it from his fingers and waved it over a reader. "Looks good. Room two-eighteen," he said, holding out a hand to Paerli.

She huffed and stuck her card in his hand.

"Peer-lee. Room two-oh-nine." He flicked the card up between two fingers. She snatched it back, matching his attitude.

"It's PAR-lee," she said.

"Lift is that way, or you can take the big roll of stairs that way. Bye bye now. Stay colorful." The guy picked up his e-disk again and resumed his puzzle game.

They hoisted their bags and opted for the lift while carrying bags.

"Well, that was rude," Paerli said. She flicked her hair to the side.

"Maybe he's just jealous," Lor said, "being an assistant to greatness." He cracked a smile and nudged her. She reluctantly smiled back.

Their rooms were on the second floor, with Paerli's being the closest to the elevator, while Lor had to travel a little farther for his room. The lock clicked open with a swipe of her ID.

"Give me a minute to shower, and I'll come to you," she said, peeking through the crack in the door as she closed it.

No one was in the hall, leaving space for Lor's footsteps to echo through it. He found room 218 on the opposite side of the hall, after a few twists and turns. He wondered what his pay would look like, based on the opulence of the hall alone.

I might be able to pay Gale back sooner rather than later.

Gale never asked him for money.

Opening the door, a cool breeze flushed over him, smelling of nothing. He missed Damaetra—her white gold hair, the smell of violets on her neck as he would press his mouth over it.

She's with Nico now.

A sharp pang of jealousy hit him. Nico was his best friend, and he could tell he was interested in Eva considering how much he asked about her. He snuffed out the thought and strode into the wide-open apartment.

The room loomed, much like the atrium, with tall walls and an arced ceiling lined with the same gold-lined mahogany supports. A large dresser stood against the wall with an intricate mirrored tray covered in various sizes of empty phials. Made of glass, some phials were square, some had a wide round bottom, and some were in the shape of teardrops. He examined one of the teardrop bottles. A slight hazy residue smeared the inside of the glass, reflecting a small rainbow in one of the facets. He wondered if they were cleaned and then reused. Glass designed like this was hard to come by. Only a skilled non-Guild artisan could create it.

The bed stood in the far corner, the mattress thick and fluffy. The headboard beamed golden etchings around the trim. The only window in the room was high up on the ceiling, but there was a sliding door he could step out to lean on the balcony rail like he saw in the atrium earlier. He sighed, knowing the light peeking in from the window was only coming from the atrium's techlight mingled with a touch of sun from the skylight.

He plopped his bag on the floor and sank into the bed. A healthy-sized magazine sat neatly on the nightstand. He swiped it from the table. The cover resembled the brochure he took from the hub—it was black with gold lettering that said: *What to Expect in Reaper's Hall, the Handbook.* He flipped through it, seeing colorful pages covered in images of all races of people smiling and holding phials, or animated with colored liquids hovering over their palms. Lor knew Reapers favored the Foscans, but the images were Mesamen, Danashi, and Anglia.

Propaganda against Foscans, it seems...

He flipped to the Hall's advertisement:

Here at the Reaper's Hall, we welcome you! Reaping is a glorious ability, and you can now call yourself among the rare elite of the Guild classes! While you could have chosen to stay at West Bank of the Seven Cities, we are glad you chose the Eastern Branch of Guild Central right here, in beautiful Secas!

The best thing about your stay here is that it is completely complimentary, as a thank you for your service at the branch. You will have all you need here at Guild Central, so there is no need to travel for food, clothing, or anything else other than work. Our in-house Foscan staff will deliver three meals each day to your room, with your stipend for the day's activities.

We here at Reaper's Hall start fresh at the rise of the first sun and complete the day with plenty of time for personal activities and relaxation!

The lower level below the atrium has our massive, three-screen holofilm projector so you can watch the latest popular story with your Reaper friends and family. Or, burn off some energy in the rich gaming gym right on the first floor! Join in on a game of shots or win big in a round of Gehenna's Pass.

If that's not enough, Guild Central core hub hosts social events daily, so you can mingle with other Guild members and get to know your peers. Whatever you choose, there will always be an activity available to entertain you!*

*Terms and conditions apply. Neither the Eastern Branch, nor the Seven Cities will be held liable for personal injury or disability. In the event of fatality, the Hall will take care of grievance costs at a rate of 15%, or 350 pL, whichever is lowest.

Lor recoiled at the small print.

Grievance costs? What kind of place is this?

Lor put down the manual and turned toward the rest of the room. He felt a strong pull in his chest—the second heartbeat knocked at his in a mismatched rhythm, making him woozy.

There was a light rap on the door.

Lor squinted through the visitor glass to see a turquoise eye staring right back at him. He swung open the door.

"That was freaky," Lor said, laughing. Paerli stepped through the doorway and took in a deep inhale.

"Your room smells nice. Mine smells like dirt."

"Dirt? I don't think my room smells like anything."

"Well, here we are, at Guild Central. Did you read your manual?" she asked, helping herself to his bed. She flopped down on it and swung her legs.

"I skimmed it. We're supposed to meet our new mentors downstairs right around first dawn, right?"

"That's what I hear."

"We should try to find the others... at least before second sun." Lor flipped out his e-disk and swiped a pattern over the surface. The holopic flashed the time: 22:44:58. "We've got a little over a standard hour."

"Yeah, let's get out of here. It's stuffy." Paerli sprang from the mattress and strolled to him, grabbing his sleeve. She led him to the door while he patted his pocket to make sure his ID was there.

They chose the stairs this time to get down to the atrium.

"Have you ever played Gehenna's Pass, or shots?" Lor asked Paerli. He had never heard of either game.

Paerli tittered. "No, those are dumb. Why?"

"I just read about it in the manual. Apparently, we have everything we need here. No need to go anywhere... not even Secas."

"They can't keep us prisoner here," she said.

They hit the marble tile, making the choir bell echo through the atrium as they made their way to the front doors. Two burly Mesaman roundsmen stood at the entrance.

The man on the right put out a hand to stop them. "I'm sorry, sir, miss... but since you are new to the Hall, we've been instructed to inform you that you must return to your room for the evening and read your manuals in preparation for tomorrow."

"*Excuse* me?" Paerli put a hand on her hip.

"I'm sorry, but this is the way. After you become familiar with the job, you will gain more freedoms."

Freedoms?

"Alright, thank you," Lor said, nudging Paerli back to where they came from. She glared at the men, turning slowly with him.

"How *dare* they!" Paerli hissed as they made their way to the stairwell.

"It's fine, Par. He said things would change as we worked, so we can wait until tomorrow. Besides, I'm sure the others are on lockdown too."

They found their rooms again, and Paerli grumbled the whole way.

"Good night, Lor," she said through the crack in her door, pouting her lips.

Lor returned to his beautiful, sterile apartment. He kicked a toe at his duffel, sick of the same clothes he had for the last six months. Gale promised to ship him some more supplies, along with a few of the books from his shelf on Guild life that he never opened. He rifled through the duffel for night clothes when Val's letter tumbled onto the floor. He remembered he had told himself he'd look into Pohay'an.

Digging the e-disk from his pocket, he swiped in a search for the town. The holopic told him that it was north of Audun, where the ice met the plains. One article he found was a travel rating that described at length the beauty of all the natural hot springs. He wanted to take his friends there sometime. *Pohay'an.* He hoped he wouldn't forget.

Swiping over the e-disk, he flicked in the message, "I miss you," to Damaetra's number.

The e-disk wobbled on the nightstand as he stared at it, waiting for her reply. It came quickly.

DAMAETRA: I miss you more.

LOR: Never.

DAMAETRA: Dream about the carpet tonight. It's soft... My salty flower ;)

Lor's heart fluttered, and he adjusted himself in thin bed shorts. This time, he was glad not to have a room mate.

LOR: Every night until I die.

A WORD FROM YOUR FRIENDLY ETHICS COUNSEL

Thank you for being a part of Guild Central, the Eastern hub of the Seven Cities! We're glad you're here!

As always, we greatly appreciate it when our citizens abide by the very important rules put in place by our esteemed panel, the most egregious of which are listed below:

First and foremost, it is every member's responsibility to report stray Yeunish vagabonds to your local roundsman.

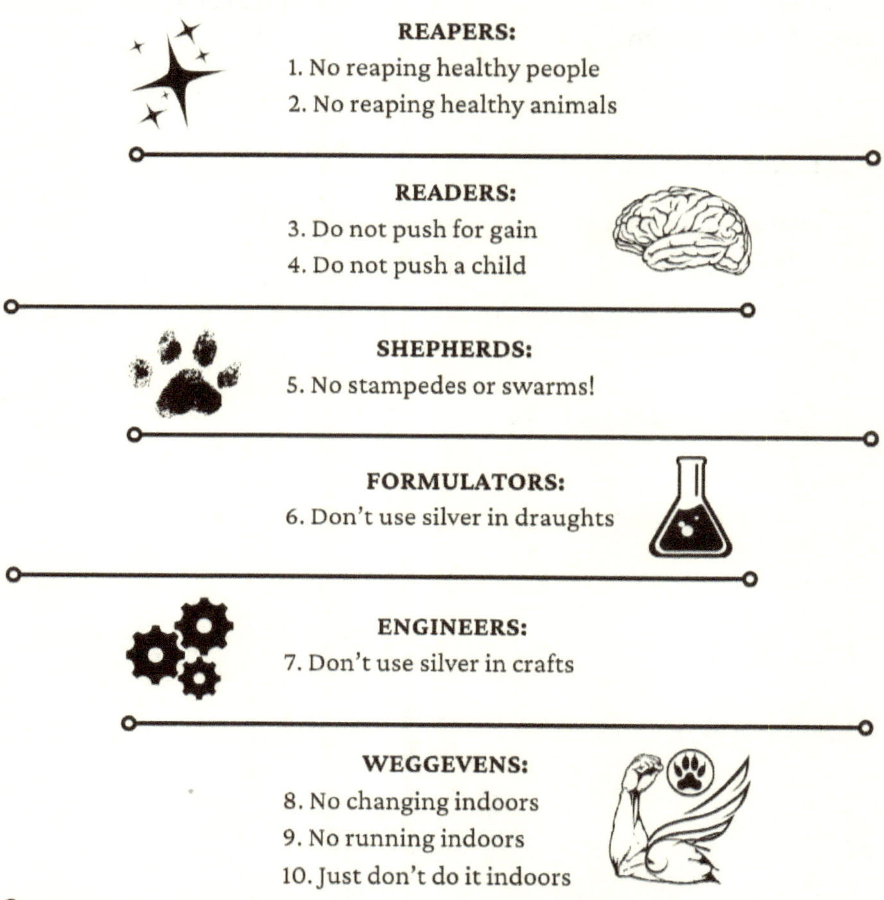

REAPERS:

1. No reaping healthy people
2. No reaping healthy animals

READERS:

3. Do not push for gain
4. Do not push a child

SHEPHERDS:

5. No stampedes or swarms!

FORMULATORS:

6. Don't use silver in draughts

ENGINEERS:

7. Don't use silver in crafts

WEGGEVENS:

8. No changing indoors
9. No running indoors
10. Just don't do it indoors

Breaking any of these laws, and any other laws as dictated by the Ethics Counsel Rules for Guilds is punishable by a fine of *pL* 100 - 5,000, or up to 7 years imprisonment. Other crimes not listed above that could raise ethical questions for use not listed in the rules for Guilds, can be raised to the panel for scrutiny with a determination of punishment to be assigned forthwith.

For any questions or grievances, please petition your local roundsman. Thank you for your support and have a colorful day!

CHAPTER 20

Beachy Dead Things
LOREN

THE FIRST SUN WAS CLOSE to rising, and Lor paced the apartment. He was nervous to go downstairs and start doing actual work with an ability he was wholly unfamiliar with. As he paced, a sharp rap knocked at his door.

"Par?" He went to look through the visitor glass, expecting to see that blue-green eye staring back at him, but all he saw was the top of a Foscan head. Cracking the door open, he mumbled, "Hello?"

"Good morning, Master Loren."

"Don't call me master. You can call me Lor," he said back, opening the door wider.

"Apologies, Lor, I am assigned to you by Master Fowler to help with your duties." His Northern Common was a touch more refined than Val's but with a similar accent. The small man wore a black eye patch, with one white eye scanning Lor's face. He shivered.

"Are you helping Paerli too?" he asked.

"I am here for you both, yes. My name is Krik'tha," he said, "or, if you prefer, I am also called Spurn the Blind."

Lor thought about Dag. He resolved to ask Gale what her real name was.

"I prefer to call you Krik'tha, thanks."

"Very good, Lor." The man bowed, as if unbothered either way.

"So, do we go now?" Lor wiped sweaty palms down the sides of his plain green shirt. It had a stain near the hem where Dill had tripped and spilled some sort of oily sauce from his lunch tray. Gale's shipment of extra supplies couldn't come fast enough.

"Yes, but"—Krik'tha eyed Lor's clothes—"this might get you strange looks."

Lor glanced back down at the stain. "I'm sorry I don't have any nicer clothes. Gale said he'd ship me some of my other stuff, but it's not here yet."

"Don't worry, I will order you a few things while you wait. They come tomorrow, okay?"

"Sure, thanks," Lor said.

They made their way to Paerli's room. She was already ready, leaping from the apartment and eager to leave. Her wavy black hair swished in the hall, wafting that sweet apple fragrance over the two men so strongly that even Krik'tha noticed. His eye fluttered, and he smiled.

They stuttered down the scrolling stairwell, where Krik'tha led them to the front desk where the same bored man sat, studying the game on his e-disk.

Krik'tha cleared his throat, and the guy looked up, annoyed.

"Hello, sir," the Foscan said. "I am checking in with Mister Fowler's two charges. Please send word to him for me." Krik'tha handed him his card, which he swiped quickly and flicked back.

"Yeah, yeah, whatever, Spurn. Kindly screw off." The man waved Krik'tha off like last week's leftovers.

Lor's jaw dropped. "Wow. I think I hate that guy," Lor whispered.

"Is nothing. There's been worse." Krik'tha shrugged.

Paerli eyed Krik'tha, then the man, who resumed burying himself in his e-disk.

A handful of others waited at the entrance. A few Mesamen, two Danashi, and one Anglia circled around a disheveled middle-aged Mesaman woman with a tablet.

Lor swallowed and licked at his cracked lip, while observing his new peers. They were mostly older, gruff, and didn't look too friendly.

Lor missed Nico, Dill, and Damaetra. He wanted the day to hurry up so he could use his evening for his friends. He was dying to hear about Damaetra's first day.

"Hurry now, or our day will go too long," the woman with the tablet said and gestured them over. She held the tablet with a stylus. Her graying hair was pulled back into a tight bun, tugging at her loose aging skin, reminding him of Fowler's hairline. She wiggled the stylus between her index and middle finger as it rapped against the edge of the tablet. Lor glanced at his e-disk to see that they still had five standard minutes before taking off.

She stopped tapping for a moment to stick out a hand to greet them. "My name is Janice. Nice to have some new members among the group. I am your foreman for the day." She peered at her screen. "Loren and Paerli, I presume?"

"Yes, that's right." Paerli rounded in front of Lor and Krik'tha.

Janice didn't give Paerli time to say anything else. "Very good. Alright, time to head out!" she shouted and gestured to the front door.

The others shuffled forward as they had so many times before. The Anglia girl gave Lor a long, hardened look and popped gum between her teeth before turning around and sauntering toward the door.

Lor watched her go. She was nothing like Damaetra. That Anglia didn't even hold a flame to his girlfriend—in personality or looks.

The work group took another long cruiser ride to a nearby beach. Stuffy air hit Lor the moment they opened the cabin door. It was salty, sticky, and warm. Lor could barely breathe. Waves of heat brushed over his face, mingled with the soft cool breeze from the tide pushing up on the shore.

Janice cupped her hands over her mouth and shouted to the group, "Okay, clean-up crew!"

Everyone shuffled toward Janice, lining up around her in a semi-circle.

"Clean-up crew?" Paerli whispered to Lor. He shrugged.

Janice continued, "We had quite the rains in the middle of the night, and now we need to take care of all the blues washed ashore."

She pulled a sack from the boot of the cruiser and opened it up, revealing several empty glass phials that had been poorly cleaned.

So they do reuse them after all...

"Come get a handful of phials, please." Janice opened the bag wider, pulling out a few of the bottles.

Before Lor could take one step toward Janice's stash, Krik'tha ran forward to grab enough for both Lor and Paerli. Something about watching him hurry like that made Lor feel sorry for the Foscans. He didn't ask for their servitude; it was just something they did. Even Dag was always compliant, putting up with him and Gale.

"Here you are, sir... miss..." Krik'tha handed them three phials each. They were all different shapes and sat funny in Lor's hand. He put the neck of each phial between his fingers to carry them.

Janice shouted again, "Alright, everyone, the beach is yours!"

Krik'tha motioned toward the water. "I will show you how, yes?"

"Let me try on my own," Paerli said, marching toward the water. Krik'tha shrugged and put his attention toward Lor.

There weren't many people at the beach at this hour. Only a few mothers and their young children were there, spending their mornings at the empty beach before it became crowded. It wasn't long before the smell hit Lor.

"What in Gehenna is that smell?" Lor pinched his nose, scanning the shore.

"We gather blue today," Krik'tha said matter-of-factly, pointing at the waterline.

Lor wandered up to Paerli, who was examining the ground. Several silvery spears lay at the water's edge, shimmering and still. He realized what Janice meant by "blues"... blue eneris from beached fish.

"Not exactly what I thought this job would be." Lor wriggled his nose, attempting to purge the smell.

Several waterbirds circled above, cawing and nipping at each other. They dipped down every few seconds as if trying to get a better look at the carcasses.

A different circle of waterbirds hung above Lor and Paerli. This flock was different. They had a smooth flight pattern as they circled, not stopping to dip or check out the fish. Lor raised an arm over his head in hopes of not becoming a target for bird crap.

"Over here, yes?" Krik'tha motioned Lor to a cluster of shimmering pucks.

Puck fish were common smaller lures for bigger fish. Lor knew this from one of his many non-Guild study tomes for gatherers. He glanced down at the pile, with their glassy eyes staring into oblivion.

"Grab fish, and hold." Krik'tha picked one of them up and held it toward Lor. Paerli picked up her own puck, letting it rest in her hands like a hammock. Lor took the fish from Krik'tha and stared at it. He felt bad, knowing what he would be forced to do. Fish or not, it had been alive at one point.

"Focus on fish," Krik'tha said, closing his one eye. Lor wondered if he could close the eye that sat under the patch. Or if he even had an eye. Obeying, Lor closed his eyes too.

"Think about the eneris in the flesh," Krik'tha said. His voice was like a guide through meditation. "Think about how it flows under skin. Think about how water gives fish life..." He continued to talk about eneris, life, and water. Lor thought he heard Paerli giggle under her breath.

Lor sighed. He didn't know how to picture what Krik'tha was saying. All he knew were the colors under his eyelids. This time was no different—swirls of all hues spun around and bobbed, with sparks here and there. He watched them for a moment before taking a deep breath and focusing his efforts on the Foscan's guidance. Krik'tha's voice droned on, and the colors obeyed. They pulsed and hummed to the tune of the man's voice until the sparks became blue. Then more blue washed over the rest until his whole vision was coated in blue under blue sparks.

His chest struggled to rise and fall. The air in his lungs felt heavy. It began as stinging prickles deep into the flesh of his lungs. As he took in more labored breaths, the air became a salty fire, and he gasped for fresh air—not the rotting stink of dead beach. The pain was agony, and the meditation chant became a mocking verse in his ears. He felt like he was drowning, and rather than a calm meditation, his anger broiled.

Calm now, calm... was the sardonic chant of the one-eyed bastard. He restrained the urge to slap him for being so relaxed.

Lor tried to speak but he only gurgled. When he opened his eyes, all he saw was blue. His fingertips tingled with the same strange numbness he felt when sleeping wrong on one of his limbs. As the cold traveled up his arm, the blue drained from his sight. His eyes searched for Paerli, and she stood in front of him, with her eyes rolled back. The expression she made on her face was a twisted version of her beauty. He didn't like it.

Is that how I look?

"Good job, you got some!" Krik'tha clapped his hands and pulled one of the phials from between Lor's fingers, scooping up the blue liquid puddled under the fish in his palm.

Fried puck rested in his palm. It had dried up in his grasp, with a thin layer of scales draped over tiny fish ribs. He didn't know why, but he wanted to cry. Triumph? Sorrow?

Paerli's eyes came back, and she sighed, collecting the blue liquid on her own before Krik'tha could help her.

"That's it?" Lor asked. He held up the phial. It contained a scant puddle in the bottom that barely filled a tenth of the volume.

"It's not quick work, no," Krik'tha said. "I can guide you for all day if you need?"

Lor thought about it. He wasn't sure if he could actually do this on his own.

How could Paerli do it?

"Yes, I probably do need you to guide me. Thank you."

"My pleasure, sir."

"Don't call me sir. Just call me Lor."

"Yes, Lor."

"Can I ask you something, Krik'tha?"

"Of course, anything." The man was examining Lor's phial, swishing it about and watching the traces of thick liquid drip back down the sides.

"Why did it feel like I was dying? I mean, I felt like I couldn't breathe."

Krik'tha clicked his tongue made a grin that crept up to his eye. "You are new, I know. It takes practice. To become Reaper, you must let go of your humanity."

Yaslecha?

Lor's arm hairs prickled. "What do you mean by that?"

Krik'tha placed another fish in Lor's palm and closed his fingers over it. "Fish is not like you. They swim and breathe salty sea. You live and breathe fresh air. When you take from fish, you see through fish's eyes—just for a moment. You must become fish to make comfort of this thing we do."

Lor stared at the little puck in his palm, and he wondered how long it had been dead.

We are monsters.

In Krik'tha's broken Northern Common, Lor understood that he felt like he was drowning because he was actually drowning. He was trying to use Mesaman lungs to breathe salt water. He glanced up at Paerli, who was calmly scooping up another dollop of blue eneris. She caught his confused look and shrugged, mouthing "*what?*"

"Try again, I am here to guide you." The Foscan stared at him with one milky white eye. He couldn't look anymore, so he closed his.

Krik'tha guided him again, with a low, soothing voice. He told him to focus on the eneris first, then switched to guiding him through breaths. He went back and forth between them until Lor saw the blue sparks over indigo wash under his lids once again.

As before, his lungs heated to a burn.

"Remember, you are fish. Fish have gills. Fish use gills. *You* have gills. *You* have gills..." The Foscan's voice faded until Lor felt the burning scroll back. He cleared his throat, and the same numbness squeezed at his fingertips. Once the cycle was complete, he saw the little blue puddle in his palm under a bone-dry fish.

"You are healthy, yes?" Lor's hand trembled as Krik'tha gathered the eneris.

"A-ah, yes, I'm good, uh, *healthy*. I think."

Yaslecha.

"Good! We have big beach with many dead fish..."

"Hey, Krik'tha?" Lor cleared his throat again, and the Foscan perked up his head. "What can you tell me about yaslecha?"

The man took a staccato step back and grinned. "Ah, yaslecha! Yes, yes, it is... good word for Reaper." He bent down to grab another fish. Paerli was almost done filling her phial.

"What I can say to you about yaslecha is this: life... it is a gift! What *we* do as Reapers is taking back gift to transform into new thing. It is not easy to do, and to fail is common. It makes Reaper... a little sleepy."

Lor thought about Valge'jor and his drooping eyelids as they talked. Glancing up, he saw the same gliding circle of waterbirds overhead. They were calm and quiet, just circling... circling. He flinched at a speck of sand that struck his brow, thinking it might be shit.

Yaslecha explained why Foscan Reapers didn't mount an assault on their enslavers.

Lor stared Krik'tha directly in his one eye. "Is there a Foscan word for what we do? For, you know... losing your humanity?" Lor chewed the inside of his cheek.

Krik'tha studied him for a moment with a raised eyebrow. He opened and closed his mouth a couple times before uttering, "Yes, we have that word... You said the thing. It is yaslecha."

Chapter 21

A Flock of Waterbirds
Loren

Lor's heart skipped a beat. Maybe he had it wrong when Val explained it to him. Losing his humanity added a whole new layer to the concept of just "being tired" from the job. He glanced at Paerli, who had finished her first phial and was staring back at him. Her lip curled in a small grin, then quickly frowned when Lor didn't return the look.

"You okay?" she asked.

He didn't know why, but he suddenly became angry. "How are you already done with a whole phial?"

"It's not that hard, Lor. You just focus and pull."

Lor chuffed. "I don't understand you," he said. "Ever since we got here, you've been strutting around like you own the place, practicing your *gift* without Krik'tha, as if you've done it a million times before and it bores you. Do you not feel anything when you suck the life from something?"

Paerli peered at Krik'tha. The man put his hands up to shield himself from the conversation.

"Lor..." she said, staring at her feet, "I get it. I do. But this is our lot in life. This is our calling, and I don't want to suffer *more* by beating myself up over it... and neither should you."

Lor huffed and toed a bit of the sand. It wasn't the nice pink of Heart Island, but a dirty mustard color.

"Hey, let's talk about it later, okay?" she said, running her hand down his arm and squeezing his wrist. She uncorked her second phial and strolled closer to the waterline for more pucks. He watched her go, feeling a twinge of guilt for snapping at her. He would have to apologize to her later.

Most of the waterbirds had flown away once the group had begun collecting eneris. Except the one group—still circling overhead.

"Hey, Krik'tha," Lor said, "have you ever seen waterbirds act like that?"

Krik'tha looked up at the slow circling birds and cocked his head to the side. "No, that is strange. It is good omen maybe?"

"Or bad."

Krik'tha chuckled at that. "Nothing about waterbirds is bad omen."

Fowler could transform into a bird. Lor wondered what type of bird he became. All he knew about skin walkers was what the bird man told him. Was he one of these?

Was he up there watching them?

They looked like ordinary birds.

He jogged toward Paerli at the shore, with Krik'tha following. There were still several small families laughing and playing in the water.

An older woman sat on a nearby bench. She was hunched over, with her legs together and a cloak wrapped around her shoulders. She looked lonely. The woman shot a glance up at Lor, catching him as he watched her, and it made her grin. Several of her teeth were missing, and a deep scar traveled from the middle of her forehead to her hairy upper lip.

He curled his mouth in a fake smile and nodded before spinning around to turn his attention back toward Krik'tha.

This has been the strangest day of my life.

After spending a long, grueling day at the beach, Lor still hadn't gotten used to feeling like he was drowning. He managed to squeeze out all three phials, despite the agony of each pull. The small group of Reapers made their way back to the cruiser, and he couldn't help but clear his throat every few minutes to rid himself of the feeling of salt scratching it. Paerli sat in the cruiser, unbothered by the whole situation. She gazed out the window with a small smile planted on her lips.

The look made him uneasy. He wanted to talk to Krik'tha, but he was sitting closer to the front of the cruiser. As he craned his neck to find him, he caught the Anglia girl glaring at him and smacking that gum between her teeth. Rolling his eyes, he looked out the window to watch Guild Central come into view, eager to learn how the others did on their first day.

As the cruiser came to a stop, Janice popped out from the front passenger side and opened the slider for the rest of the group.

"Alright, everyone," she said as the door slapped open, "be back at the hall by the setting of the second sun. If you're not back by then, your pass won't work, the roundsman will be called to help you, and you will receive a dock in your pay."

"Yikes," Lor hissed. He glanced at his e-disk. Second sun would rise in a standard hour. Then, he would only have another standard hour to do anything.

"What kind of labor camp did we get ourselves into?" Paerli whispered to him.

Everyone filed out of the cruiser, and Lor was happy to see Nico and Damaetra standing at the center square. Nico laughed loudly, waving arms around while talking to her. The serious, smart, and good-looking friend never usually animated himself in such a way.

"Hey, how was your first day?" Lor said, sliding his arm around Damaetra, pulling her closer.

Nico laughed. "It was actually pretty fun. You should have seen Dame create some wild catastrophes!" he said.

Dame?

Jealousy brewed in his gut.

"I'm glad I caught you!" Dill came running up to the center square, bending over to catch his breath.

Paerli stepped toward the group, with the same dreamy smile on her face.

"Did you make anything good?" Lor asked.

"Not me," Damaetra said, giggling. "Maybe tomorrow, though."

"I was able to make a blast core and bandage," Nico said. He grinned wide, shoving those dimples deep into his cheeks.

"Whoa, what's a *blast* core?" Dill said, still breathing heavily.

"It's just like it sounds—it's an explosive phial." Nico made a sweeping gesture with his hands.

"I didn't know you could make stuff like *that*," Lor said. Something about spending a day on a stinky beach feeling like he was drowning didn't seem to compare to the day his friends had.

"We're learning about all kinds of phials to make... nothing we could do during the program," Damaetra said, gazing up at Lor with a smile.

"I wish I made something cool! I have a prototype, though... *might* end up as something cool," Dill said.

"We only have until second sundown before we have to be back," Paerli cut in. "Is anyone hungry?"

"I could eat," Damaetra said.

They made their way to the main unit to find a bland cafeteria that reminded Lor of the program. He was pleased to find sarga fruit there.

Two hours wasn't long enough to spend with Damaetra at night. He craved his alone time with her, but every minute was spent either eating or talking with everyone else. He swore to take advantage of every day off and every moment the Hall allowed cross-Guild visits. Soon, she'd be spending more time with Nico than with him.

I hope I don't have to worry about Nico...

There was a light tap at his door. Paerli was in the hall with her hands behind her back, not peeping through the glass but looking the other direction.

"Hey," he said, cracking the door open.

She strode inside as if she lived there. Her apple aroma wafted through the room.

"Hey," she replied.

"I'm sorry about earlier," he mumbled, taking her hand and squeezing it.

She shrugged. "Don't worry about it. It's not easy work, and I understand."

"I just don't get it, Par. How is it that you just took to this job so easily? Val told me it slowly takes your own life."

"Val?" She tilted her head. The techlight illuminated her face in an ominous mask.

"Yeah, you know. Valge'jor from the program."

She huffed. "Oh, him. Didn't know he had a little nickname."

"He's actually a pretty nice guy. Very knowledgeable. In fact, he's from Pohay'an, a little town up North of—"

"Lor... I haven't been entirely honest with you," she interrupted, striding over to the small nightstand, running her finger across his mattress. When she stopped, she tugged at her sleeve.

"What have you not been honest about?"

She fussed with the cuff of her light blue linen long-sleeve, rolling it over her dark skin. The spot on her forearm, where Lor had his crescent scar, was a smooth canvas on her—unmarked and unblemished. He glanced down at his own forearm at the pink scar there. In the techlight, it cast a shadow into the depression.

"I never gave myself the implant," she said.

"But you were bleeding."

"It was *your* blood."

Lor tilted his head. "Mine?"

"I smeared it on my arm from the knife."

Lor suspected that she might not have taken the implant. The whole time everyone was distracted by the implanting process, she was nowhere to be found. When they removed them together in the dark, she conveniently dropped hers and couldn't find it. He never did see her wound, and never thought to ask.

"Why?" was all he could muster.

She bit her lip and paced slowly in front of him, making the floorboards squeal in protest. She halted and turned on her toes to face him. It was an oddly graceful movement. He knew she was this way, but it was almost as if she was dancing for him.

"Because I didn't need it. At least, not for the reasons they *lied* about." She looked up at him with round eyes under those curling thick lashes. The turquoise color shimmered in the techlight. They were beautiful... scary.

"I don't understand."

She hesitated again, locking eyes with him and saying nothing for a while. It could have been a few seconds, or an hour.

"I didn't need the implant because..." She continued to pace. "I didn't need it because I was already a Reaper."

Lor's body turned cold.

"I'm confused. You were *already* a Reaper? Why were you in the program? Wouldn't that have been expensive?" As well-read as he was about non-Guild factions, he knew nothing about the actual Guilds other than very scant knowledge of reaping, formulation, and engineering.

Paerli chuckled to herself and shook her head. "You wouldn't believe me..." She peered up at him as if to say: *ask me, ask me.*

"Of course I would believe you. Please tell me—I'll believe you, I promise."

She grinned, making her lovely features twist in the techlight. "I went to the program to find *you.*"

Lor's heart thumped. The curious double heartbeat undulated behind his. That was not the answer he was expecting. "You came to find me?" He cocked his head to the side with a thumb at his chest.

"Yeah, you. See? I knew you wouldn't believe me..." She gave Lor that same look that begged him to ask her for more.

"Par, I'm really confused." He put a hand on the side of his head and shook it. "What do I have to do with anything?"

"You have everything to do with everything. To me."

He closed his eyes, and the colors whipped in a frenzy—sharp bloody reds washing over frigid gold.

"Can you please just explain more? You're not giving me much." He opened his eyes again, seeing nothing but the red-gold draping every curve and feature of her body. She had gripped his wrist.

"In some circles, I am known by another name. I am a leader. I am a follower. There is a job that needs to be done, and I am the Locksmith."

Lor ripped his wrist away from her, and the red-gold in his sight melted away, revealing the mahogany posts and decorative filigree of the room once again.

"What in Gehenna is a Locksmith for?" He swallowed.

Paerli folded her arms and clicked her tongue at him. "I should have been more honest with you in the beginning, when we first met. You were so naive and *pure* back then."

"I can tell you now that if you had, I wouldn't have believed you at all then."

"Don't you *feel* it, Lor? Don't you feel the connection?" She strode back up to him and twined her hands in his.

The double heart punched his chest and he looked down at his hands to see not the white fingers of his love, but the dark ones of a stranger.

"It's that inexplicable bond that beats in our chests, tears at us, and molds us all the same!"

His chest thrummed. There was excitement and an emotional surge that nudged his heart over and over and over again.

"I was so drawn to you on the shore that day," she continued. "You were standing there, all shy and sweaty. Look at you now—so much more sure of yourself and walking the path to your future... *our* future."

"Par, what in Gehenna are you talking about?" He knew. He knew in that moment that the heart was hers all along, nagging at him every moment she felt a strong emotion.

"I knew when you became a Reaper that all of my feelings toward you made sense." She held his hands up to her mouth, rubbing her lips into his palm. "The Locksmith needs a tool... a *key*, if you will. You are that key—you are my match." She breathed into his hand, planting a kiss in the grooves.

Lor yanked his hands from her mouth, sliding them down his sides. "Par, don't. You're still not making sense. Are you asking me to do something for you?"

Damaetra is not going to like this. She will hate it.

"You are my *match*, Lor. Do you know what that means?"

"No."

She tittered and grabbed his arm again. His neck was hot, and he tried to imagine pushing away the throbbing organ squeezing against his, but the resistance made it stronger. It poked at him, pierced his ribs, and wrapped its sticky fingers around his mind.

Where did this rage come from?

Her fingers coiled around his wrist and squeezed. It reminded him of a snake suffocating its prey before swallowing it whole.

"You and I are meant to *bind*. We can be even more powerful as one."

"I don't want to get married to you..." He wanted to throw up. He imagined the hurt in Damaetra's violet eyes, and it squeezed his real heart.

"It's not marriage, silly. It's an eternal bond that would give us unimaginable power. Don't you think that would be cool?"

"I... no... I don't know. What?" His knees turned to jelly, forcing him to flop down into the hard chair behind him.

"All you would have to do is take my eneris, and I would take yours."

"Par, this is getting weird."

She let go of his wrist. "I told you I have a job to do. It would be much easier to do the job if I had *you*."

"What am I supposed to do?"

"Remember? Unimaginable power? That's what."

Lor sighed and sank deeper into the chair. He didn't like this conversation, and he felt like he had stepped into someone else's world, listening to someone else's story. He opened his mouth to say something but thought better of it and shut it again.

"Hey, I have an idea!" she said, grinning. "Remember when we made that bet at the beginning of the program?" He didn't like where this was going.

"I'll give you my first paycheck," he blurted out.

Her laugh was maniacal. "I don't want your plats. It was a *favor*, remember?"

His reservation about making that agreement with her as a stranger back then was coming around in a way he never imagined.

"Par, this is making me so uncomfortable. I don't even know what you are asking me."

She huffed. "I *told* you! We just need to exchange eneris, that's all."

"That's *all*? It sounds like some wicked blood ritual to me."

"It's not blood, it's eneris. And only you can pull your own... I can't do it for you."

"What does that mean?"

She clicked her tongue again. "Lor, haven't you learned anything yet? A Reaper can't pull another Reaper."

He furrowed his brow and flexed his jaw.

"So, let me get this straight," he said, "you need me to agree to this... 'plan.' I need to *suck* my own eneris out and just *give* it to you... Wouldn't that kill me?"

Paerli backed up a few paces, then resumed her graceful steps around the room. "What if I told you..." She paused and studied him. "What if you knew that by swapping eneris with me, then performing my favor, it would create a seal that would never let you die? Ever."

"What are you trying to say?"

"What I'm saying is, we could be immortal... you and me against the world. Always."

The thought of immortality had never crossed Lor's mind. What would he do with that life, if it never ended? How would he handle constantly seeing others live and die? Watching Damaetra die? What was living a life without the threat of death? Of love? He stood up to his full physical height, for the first time towering over her.

"What is your game?"

"I told you, I have a job to—"

"*What* is your *game*, Par? And don't *lie* to me."

She stepped back, scrunching her face together in a look that Lor might interpret as mild disgust. "Match with me, and I'll tell you."

"No. Tell me now, or get *out*."

She crossed her arms and licked her lips. How naive had he been this whole time? The regret he felt for ignoring Gale's nagging was bubbling to the surface. He wanted to scream at himself.

How could I be so ignorant?

They stared each other down, his gray eyes into her aqua. The moment lasted an eternity as he watched her throat rise and fall with that black gem cradled there. She fluttered her lids and broke the spell.

"It's Mount Gehenna," she said at last, in a deep sultry voice. She turned her back to him.

"What about it?" He softened his pitch, hoping to avoid a wicked argument.

She spun back to him and raised an eyebrow. "You know all the stories, right? The rumors about the place?"

"No, I don't know them all. I've only heard what Dill said about it, and you know him—he tends to exaggerate."

"There's a hole," she continued. "It's deep in the center of the mountain. Some say it goes down to the core of Roseaarde." She resumed pacing in her dance-like grace. "I know better than that... because I've seen it."

"I said don't lie to me. How would you have seen it? That place has been heavily guarded by roundsmen for centuries. That I *do* know."

"You don't know anything!" she shot back.

He swallowed. "Fine. Continue your story."

"It's called the umbilicus. It leads to a cavern deep under the mountain where its roots used to be."

"Hold on," Lor interrupted. "What do you mean by roots?"

"I'm not here to give you a history lesson, Lor. I'm telling you what my job is."

He sighed and made air circles for her to continue.

"Look, there is a seal down there. A seal that only a Reaper can open. It's a strong one, and I can only do it with my match. With you."

"How do you expect me to help you with that? What's behind it?"

"Match with me and I'll tell you."

"Par, no. I can't just go down into a zone sealed for hundreds of years to open some secret seal just on your word."

"Think about Damaetra. Think about how strong and powerful you could be for her."

"By making what seems like an intimate pact with *you*? That would *destroy* her. Are you insane?"

She strode up to him and did something he didn't expect. She pressed her body against his and ran her hand down his chest. Fingers played over all the sensitive nerves, pumping the double heartbeat—a strong, lusty throbbing. Her hair smelled like sweet apples under the heat of her scalp. She smirked, staring up at him with those blue-green eyes. He felt the desert heat crawl through his veins, sprouting fresh sweat drops over his brow. She stood on the tips of her toes, parting her lips and matching them to his. She was exquisitely warm, and her soft mouth kept coming back for more of him.

"Par," he breathed out, barely above a whisper. She went back in, touching her tongue to his.

"Par..." He didn't know what was happening. The double heartbeat quickened, pushing and pumping against his own. His weak whispers made her more aggressive, going in for more and more.

"Par, wait..."

Damaetra forgive her.

"Par... stop." The word came out as a gust of breath.

She pulled him in, crushing her lips against his and feeling his teeth with her strong tongue. He couldn't stop her. The sweet apple smell he had come to adore about her turned to acid in his mouth as he thought about Damaetra. She cradled his neck, pulling him closer to her.

"Par, *stop* it," he managed. She forced her mouth to his again, choking his words with that rigid pink tongue. He wanted to bite it off. She tugged at his belt. It was like a rat digging at his waist, trying to get a taste of his flesh. She loosed the buckle as if she had done it a thousand times before, thumbing at the button of his pants. Lor squirmed, trying to force out the twisted desire of his rotten human instinct that desperately wanted to comply with the terrible beauty wrapping herself around him. The rat burrowed its way down to his pulsing energy core, latching on with its cold teeth, giving it a squeeze and causing the double heart to flutter.

"Par, stop!" He pushed her away. "Damaetra is your *friend!*" He didn't care what she did to him, only what her actions did to the love of his life.

Paerli stumbled back, her mouth wet and bleeding.

Did I actually bite her?

She stared at him, breathing heavily and running the back of her hand across her lip, seeing the red stain across her thumb. Lament etched into her features. She wiped the blood across her billowy pants while Lor fumbled with his own as if forgetting how to latch a buckle.

"You're not so complex, Loren," she whispered in a heady candor.

"Oh yeah? There was a time—*long* ago—I would have easily done all of those things with you, and more. *Easily.*" He latched the buckle at last, brushing his shirt, then running his fingers through sweaty hair. "But I chose her. I chose Damaetra, and now I'm going to have to explain this to her."

"And you call *me* insane." Paerli stood upright, sucking at the wound on her bottom lip.

"Look, I didn't mean that, I just don't know what it is you truly want from me. Other than *that.*"

The chill in the air returned, causing him to shiver under all the sweat and stink of sour apples.

"Match with me."

"No."

"I'm sorry I threw myself at you. Match with me."

"No."

"I need you, Lor. You don't understand—a match like ours comes once every thousandth turn of the moon."

"You should have thought about that before violating me."

"*Violating* you? Is that what you call the raging hard-on I felt in your pants?"

"That's enough, Par. My answer is no." Lor belched and felt sick in the cold, sterile air. His feelings about Paerli and her friendship had been a ruse all along—a play from the "thousandth moon" to create a monstrous amalgam of power and immortality. He ran past Paerli to the bathroom, squeezing his guts into the toilet.

"Well, I'm glad I'm so disgusting to make you puke," he heard Paerli mumble from the other room.

"You're not disgusting," he managed to squeak before hurling again.

"Right, okay." He imagined she rolled her eyes. "I'm going to go, Lor. Sleep on it and we'll talk in the morning."

She didn't wait for a response, as the door clicked shut seconds after her last word.

CHAPTER 22

Going at it Alone
LOREN

THE PURPLE SUN CAST COLD shadows over the black rock of Mount Gehenna. Lor stood in the middle of the charred sands, staring at its peak and wondering at its history.

"Why did you bring me here?" Damaetra asked, sliding her small hand into his.

He gazed down at her petite frame. She stood stark white and clean against the shadows, with her pale feet almost glowing in the sand. She wore the lavender dress from Tad's funeral, except the hem had a loose thread that flapped in the breeze.

"There's something I need to do here," he said. The words didn't sound like his own, but he knew he was needed at this place.

Paerli.

He shot a look forward at the mountain. She stood at the base of it, beckoning him forward. He glanced at Damaetra again, and she only peered at him with her gentle smile and lavender eyes.

"We have to go now," Lor said. He tried to take a step forward, but his foot was stuck. The black grains tumbled across his feet and stacked higher and higher over his ankles.

"W-what's going on?" he said, watching his calves get swallowed by the blackness. He was almost eye to eye with Damaetra, and she looked terrified. She squeezed his hand and tried to pull him, but the sand had him and wasn't letting go. It was swallowing him.

"Loren, you're sinking!" Damaetra cried out. He let go of her hand and tried to push himself from the sinkhole, but it sucked at his waist, hissing grains into a void below.

"Don't leave me, Damaetra!"

Tears swelled at the base of her eyes, and she whispered to him, "I can't leave you... and I won't! But Loren... You have to wake up!"

Paerli appeared in front of him like a whip-crack. Her black hair flapped in *the wind as the black sand swallowed his neck. With a swift slap to the face, she screamed, "Wake up!"*

Lor fell from his bed, hitting the marble floor with his shoulder.

"Ow, damnit!"

The feeling of sand clinging to his arms and neck persisted, and he slapped the imaginary grains to dust them off. He rolled to his back and stared at the intricate ceiling. For some reason, he pulled Damaetra into his weird dream, and she didn't belong there. They agreed to meet for some alone time after the job today, but he dreaded having the conversation with her about Paerli from the night before. No one had ever known him like that, and he was ashamed that his body reacted in that way. A fresh wave of nausea washed over him. Nico was right all along—he needed to stay away from Paerli.

Pondering how he would do that, he thought Krik'tha might be able to help. At least for a while.

As he lay there, he rolled his head to the side, catching a glimpse of a few small boxes that someone had slid through his mail door in the night. He turned over, rubbing his sore arm, and rose up to patter to them. One was wrapped in slick black paper with a gold note fixed to the top. As he got closer, he noticed a small white box behind it, and a plain brown box. He swiped them off the floor and brought them to the table.

Plopping down in the chair, he scanned the golden note.

THE DAY'S WAGES. THANK YOU FOR YOUR SERVICE. - JANICE

He smiled at the note, not realizing he would be paid so quickly, and daily. Opening the lid, the shock of stacks of plats slapped him like Paerli in his dream. There were thousands there—more plats than he ever imagined for months, let alone one single day. The number for each slip glowed green under the translucent surface. Twenty-five...fifty...one hundred plat tickets illuminated the inside of the black box.

Maybe I can pay Gale back this year.

Still smiling, he closed the lid on his earnings and reached for the plain brown box. Inside was a neatly folded new outfit from Krik'tha. He unfolded the set, and the black collared button-up still had the creases folded into it. How the man knew his size was a mystery, as Lor always struggled to find shirts that would cover his long torso. It was a perfect fit.

Sitting back down again, he spotted the small white box. It was too small to contain any type of funds, and he wondered if it was some token for being a Reaper. Something about it bothered him. He stared at it for a long time before tracing a finger over the lid.

Lifting the top revealed a delicate phial, pointed at the end and capped with a glass stopper. Inside the glass was a bright golden liquid the thickness of pine sap. The phial rested on a bed of what appeared to be coiled blanched fibers, making the gold inside appear even brighter. He pinched the fibers between his fingers, wondering where it came from. Tucked underneath was a note.

Dear Lor,

If you don't know what this is, you should. But since I'm pretty sure you don't know what it is, I will tell you. This is my eneris. Please reconsider my request to become my match. Understand that refusing could have considerable consequences. All you have to do is drink it, and I will find you.

With love,

Par

With love? Consequences?
He glanced at the vial and shuddered. How did she extract her own life force? The note mentioned she would find him, but Lor didn't know what that meant. She was just down the hall and working by him that day. Hopefully not *with* him.

The phial felt heavy in his palm. For such a small volume, the liquid had a heft to it. The thought sickened him. Wrapping his fingers around the glass, he felt the lingering warmth from the liquid.

Gross.
He placed it back onto the fibers and closed the lid. There would be a long conversation about this.

The black box grabbed his attention, and he opened it once again to see all the green numbers flickering on each sheet. Checking the time on his e-disk, he still had a standard hour before shift, so he thought he'd start to work on depositing the plats. He noticed a missed QuickChat.

Damaetra: I miss you

Damaetra: Good night, Loren ;)

His heart sank.
Was she thinking of me while Paerli had her tongue in my mouth like a parasite?
He made a few quick swipes to message her back.

Lor: You are my everything.

He watched the e-disk, waiting for any sign that she read his message. It hovered there, unopened. He sighed and put the disk down to start depositing his pay.

Gale never allowed him to get an upgraded e-disk, so he would have to make the deposit one ticket at a time. He made gestures over the surface of the black disk, opening a sensor at the bottom. Running the sensor over the first slip, the green number disappeared, only to reappear as a continuous ticker hovering above the e-disk, underneath the title: *Fifth Treasury of Audun*. He scanned each ticket until he was left with a pile of empty dead slips that he put back into the box for reloading.

Three thousand fifty-two plats. Just for a day.

The holopic above the disk projected the number. While he was in shock at the amount, he was annoyed at the large Guild tithe that came out of it. The total should have been five thousand. He wondered what the Guild did with that tithe. He pocketed Paerli's strange box, intending to draw answers from her about it.

After locking up, Lor headed down the hall to Paerli's apartment. The hallway wasn't a straight line; it twisted like a snake, and he felt like a morsel being digested as he walked through it. He didn't know what to say to her after last night, or if he would even try. He lingered at her door, weighing in his mind whether to knock.

Why couldn't we just go back to who we were?

If he knocked, would she expect his eneris in return? He thumbed the box's corner under his pocket. Each individual thread woven into his pants thumped over the ridges of his thumbprint.

What would it taste like?

Lor softly rapped on the thick wood to her room, barely hitting the surface. He waited. Flipping out his e-disk, the time hovered over the gadget. They only had ten standard minutes to meet their foreman for the day. Lor wondered if it would always be Janice.

He knocked again, a little harder. Pressing his lips to the crack in her door, he called out, "Par?"

No answer.

Knocking even harder, he tried peering through the visitor glass, waiting to see the eye looking back at him. The glass distorted everything, and he didn't see even a shadow inside.

What if she was dead in there?

"Par, we have to get going." He banged on the door again, pressing an ear against it. He didn't hear anything.

She's downstairs already waiting for you. Go down there and check.

Lor didn't want to make a scene, so he relented and made his way to the atrium.

The same group waited at the bottom of the stairs, with the same Anglia girl staring him down. He rolled his eyes at her and scanned the room for Paerli. Krik'tha stood at the back of the group, waving at Lor.

"Good morning, crew! I'm Oran, your foreman for the day." A younger man only a few years older than Lor held the same tablet and pen that Janice had while addressing the group.

Paerli was nowhere to be found among the handful of Reapers. That sat funny in Lor's stomach. He threw up twice after she tried to sleep with him… he feared he had embarrassed her enough that she ran off. Krik'tha approached him.

"Good morning, Lor—I see Paerli is not with you today?"

Lor's gut flip-flopped. Images of her ravaging his face with her lips flashed in his mind. "N-no… she didn't talk to you, did she?"

"Afraid not. This will not be a good thing for her if she does not show on second day."

"Will she be kicked out?"

"Perhaps. But I can do her a favor for today only. I will check her in." Krik'tha jogged to the desk to send the message to Fowler that they were together. The desk attendant waved Krik'tha away, most likely mouthing off in some way that made Lor want to sock him in the throat.

The group left the building and filed back into the cruiser. "It's just me and you today then," Krik'tha said, smiling.

Lor nodded and stared out the window. Large paycheck or not, he wasn't up for reaping more fish. Instead, the cruiser drove them to the border of Secas and the hazy desert known as the Span. Lor was uncomfortable here, knowing the desert bred desperate renegades… and it reminded him of Paerli. He checked his disk again to see his message to Damaetra still unopened.

Oran cupped his hands over his mouth and shouted to the group, "Your goal today is a phial of white, green, and red. Not having a full phial will be a deduction in pay. Alright, get to it!"

Lor looked at Krik'tha, who pointed up north, near the tree line. "Let's start up there, yes?"

They wandered up to a cluster of plump cacti, to which Krik'tha motioned. "Green is easiest. Let's start with this." He plucked one of the succulents from the sand and placed it in Lor's palm. The prickles stabbed the meat of his hand, but thick green liquid almost immediately dripped into it, running into the wrinkles of his palm where Paerli had only the night before pressed her mouth.

"Oh, a ripe one!" Krik'tha's one eye showed excitement, and he grappled for one of the phials.

If reaping green was this easy, Lor didn't mind only pulling plants. As he pondered the thought, micro jolts of electricity ran up his fingers, reaching up to his elbow and numbing his forearm.

"Uh, is it supposed to make my arm go numb?" Lor asked, as Krik'tha scooped up the green syrup from under the cactus.

The man bobbed his head. "If you have reaction with venom of plant, then yes."

"Venom?" Lor didn't know of any plant that held venom in its reserves.

"This one is poison, yes. But not to worry, is mild. You should feel better soon."

The feeling dissipated, but it didn't prevent Lor from being unnerved by it.

Do all reaped things involve pain? Did Paerli feel it too?

He pulled more of the little pain pods until the numbness lingered longer and longer and he couldn't do it anymore. Krik'tha relieved his anguish by flashing a full phial of green and grinning.

"Oh good," Lor said, wiping his brow.

"The other two are red and white—or, land and air creatures."

Lor glanced up, hoping to see the eerie circle of waterbirds to reap—nothing but clear blue sky.

"Where will we find the red and white?"

"There is farm nearby—come. Many will be there already, but is where we should go."

The pair wandered farther into a line of colorful trees. True to his word, there was a small farm about three hundred feet deeper in. The owner was talking to two other Reapers, one of whom was the rude Anglia girl.

The owner's voice became clearer the closer they got. "I don't have a whole lot of orders today, but I'll give you what I got." Lor was not looking forward to this task.

Animals were always his soft spot. He reasoned that they were humanity's first friend after creation and always found it odd that anyone would ever want to hurt them. While their meat was necessary for food, he didn't really want to see behind the scenes. He wondered if he was the only one who felt this way. If he knew where Paerli was, he'd ask her too. A piece of him felt guilt for being there without her, but then he imagined her grabbing him where no one had ever before and it turned his stomach. He looked over at

Krik'tha to see if he saw any trace of the shame Lor felt written on his face. The man was preoccupied with getting Lor to the farm.

The farm owner waved him and Krik'tha over to the conversation and repeated himself while jogging into his cabin to retrieve a few slabs of meat.

The nasty Anglia girl grabbed a hunk and pulled the red from it. Lor was relieved to see that he wouldn't have to kill anything. Krik'tha handed him a thick cut of dripping red meat.

"What did this come from?" Lor asked.

Krik'tha shrugged. "It looks like maybe something big... like eletonk? Just do same thing on meat and you will get red."

Lor concentrated on the meat until red dominated the color show under his eyelids. His lip twitched and he scrunched his nose.

"Why would it show me that?" He recoiled and held the piece of meat away from him. Krik'tha chuckled and collected the thick red liquid pooled in Lor's palm.

"Yes, is not pleasant. You see last moment of eletonk."

"I'm not doing that again. I'll take the pay cut."

Krik'tha capped the phial, wagging it at Lor to show half a bottle. "You might avoid yaslecha yet, my friend!"

The Anglia girl pocketed a full phial of red and white and left the owner's bench. She smacked her shoulder into Lor while making her way back to the foreman. Lor frowned, not knowing what he ever did to the girl to make her so hostile. Damaetra was nothing like her—she was beautiful, calm, and witty. He wanted to call her so bad, just to hear her musical voice and tell her how much he adored her. The more he pictured his white-haired beauty, and the events that unfolded the night before, the more he wanted to let her know how he felt about her.

"Some Reapers suffer yaslecha sooner than others," Krik'tha said as his eye followed the girl walking away. Lor huffed and agreed to that assessment.

"Humanity flees from them like a roach in the light." The Foscan pulled out another phial.

Lor couldn't argue with that sentiment. He understood what Val meant by keeping his friends close. They would help him maintain his good nature.

"Let's try white, yes?"

"Sure," Lor mumbled. He didn't want to watch another animal die in his mind. The farm owner handed Krik'tha some bird meat.

"Is big bird!" He smiled, plopping the slippery pink piece of flesh into Lor's arms.

"Ugh, this is messy, Krik'tha!" He fumbled with the bird chunk. "There's no way this is just a waterbird."

The little Foscan giggled like a boy. "Just do same thing as red."

As Lor cradled the meat, he thought about Fowler. Was he as big as this when he turned? Was he actually holding a Weggevens skin changer?

He concentrated on the meditation with closed eyes until the colors morphed into a bright white.

"This one broke his neck on the side of a tree," Lor said as he handed the meat back to the owner.

The owner clapped his hands and grabbed the bird. "Very good, son!" He plopped the withered meat back onto its wrapping and brought it inside.

White liquid filled Lor's palms. Krik'tha scooped it up, waving a phial not quite full, but very close. He raised an eyebrow at Lor.

"Yeah, I'm still not going to do that again," Lor said, holding his arms in front of him as far as he could muster. "Does Reaper Hall offer a laundry service?"

Krik'tha laughed and nodded. "I will help you with that."

"I'm glad *you* find this funny," Lor said with a smirk.

"You are fun, I like you!" Krik'tha said.

Satisfied with his pullings of the day, Lor asked if he could stop.

"Is up to you." Krik'tha placed the phials into a custom box made for exactly three of the bottles. Their round bottoms clanked against each other as their necks wiggled in the holder. Lor held his breath, hoping they wouldn't break, knowing that he was already taking a hit in pay for incomplete phials.

He frowned, remembering Paerli again. He hoped she at least told someone where she was. He hated her for last night, but he didn't want her hurt... or dead. The thought of her lying on the floor of her apartment lying in a pool of red and gold flashed through his mind.

I got her letter, though...

"Hey, Krik'tha," he said as the Foscan finished sealing the box of phials, "before we go back to the cruiser, can I ask you a few things... in private?"

"Yes, of course—anything."

They moved away from the farm and walked along the forest edge. Lor fidgeted with his fingers, kicking at the dirty sand woven among blades of grass.

"You said you had questions?" Krik'tha broke the silence.

"Yes, I... well, I'm not really sure how to ask, but I'll try. Have you ever... or, have you ever known anyone who has... reaped their own eneris?"

Krik'tha came to a halt, his feet planted firmly in the grass as if he could drill a hole in the ground with the friction. He spat on the ground and made a motion over his chest with his hands, then pointed to the ground after raising them to the sky. He stared up at Lor. "Who tells you this thing?"

Lor opened his mouth, then shut it tight, afraid he said too much. Paerli was already in trouble for not being there. What more trouble would he bring her by talking about this? Krik'tha continued to stare at him with his glowing white eye.

"I-I read about it... in one of my books at home."

The Foscan was unconvinced. "There are *no* books about this thing. Who tells you?"

Lor swallowed and ran a dry tongue over a cracked lower lip. He knew the law would protect him if he backhanded the man for talking to him in this way, but he wouldn't... he couldn't. Knowing Krik'tha wasn't letting it go, he suppressed the thought and sighed. "Paerli. She told me about it."

Krik'tha spat on the ground again, making the same odd gesture. "Valoa'brenga!" he hissed.

"I'm sorry?" Lor knew the name. He had heard it from Dill on the first day of the program. Dill gave him that old history book to borrow, and he never opened it but brought it with him in his duffel. Dill never asked about it.

I need to read that soon.

"Do not worry about that. How does she know?"

Lor shrugged. "That, I really *don't* know. She came to my room last night asking me about it."

"She is Valoan?"

Lor tilted his head. "What is Valoan?"

"Valoan is cursed worshiper of the breach."

Lor furrowed his brow, setting deep wrinkles into his forehead. In all the books he had read, there was no mention of Valoans and what they were. Nor was there any mention of a breach. The most he knew about any of that came from Par, and she didn't tell him much. The longer he sat in silence, the more suspicious Krik'tha became.

"I don't know what the breach is, I'm sorry. She didn't say anything about that. She mentioned a *seal.*" Lor pursed his lips and looked away. He was too embarrassed to say any more.

"If you are done, we must go." Krik'tha bristled and barged forward, stiff-limbed as the trees that poked from the ground. Lor raised a foot to follow but stubbed his toe on a piece of tech peeking out from the sand. It tore through the sole of his boot and let sand rush in under his sock.

"Son of a—"

Why is there tech in every inch *of sand?*

He watched the silhouette of Krik'tha disappear toward the cruiser as he plunked down on a nearby boulder to take off the boot.

CHAPTER 23

Ritual of Self
LOREN

THE RIDE BACK WAS QUIET and awkward. Krik'tha sat near the front, leaving Lor at the back, alone with his thoughts. His e-disk buzzed, and a QuikChat from Gale scrolled across the screen.

GALE: How are things at Guild Central?

Disappointed to see Gale's name instead of Damaetra's, he thought about how his stepfather's questions always started innocuously. It wouldn't be long before the probing began and Lor would say something to piss him off. Of all days to reach out, he chose this one.

LOR: Oh, same stuff, just learning.

GALE: Oh, good. How are your friends?

LOR: I don't get to see them much.

He didn't want to talk about it. It was bad enough that Damaetra's message still flashed "unread" at the end of the day. Sweat prickled at his forehead.

What if Paerli told her? What if she decided she would rather be with Nico? He's smart, amazingly attractive...

GALE: I'm sorry to hear that.

Lor shut off his e-disk. If the messages weren't from Damaetra, he didn't want to see them at all, even if Gale was being nice. He felt guilty for shutting him out.

The cruiser pulled around the central hub, and Lor was the last to get out. Krik'tha didn't wait for him. His shiny tail of black hair bounced as he stomped toward Reaper's Hall.

Nico stood at the fountain, talking with Dill. Lor jogged up to them.

"Where's Damaetra?" he said, blowing out a puff of air.

"Hey, she slipped me a note this morning that said she wasn't feeling well, so she stayed in her room today," Nico said.

Lor eyed him. "Why would she write a note? To *you*? Why wouldn't she just QuickChat?"

Nico raised his hands. "Whoa, I don't know." He dug through his back pocket and pulled out a slip of paper. "I knew you'd ask about her, so I brought the note."

"Why didn't *you* send me a message this morning to let me know?" Lor furrowed his brow, peering up at Nico.

"Lor, are you okay?" Nico put his hands down and glanced over at Dill, who shrugged.

Lor snatched the note from Nico and read it:

Nico,

Hey, I'm not feeling so well. I think I'll tell Fowler that I'm not going to make it today. Please don't bother Loren about it.

See you later.

Damaetra

Lor rubbed his face like Gale. "That doesn't make a lick of sense," he said. "She sent me a QuickChat last night telling me she missed me. Why did she say not to bother me in this bogus letter?"

Both Nico and Dill shrugged at each other.

Nico cleared his throat. "Where's Paerli?" he asked.

Thick heat rose in Lor's black collar, and he felt the pulsing warmth wave over his face.

"We, a-ah"—Lor swallowed—"we had an argument last night."

Nico perked up and cracked a small smile. "An argument?"

If he knew the real content of the argument, he wouldn't be smiling.

The note. Lor examined it again, seeing the curling letters dancing on the parchment. His hand ran over the small box in his pocket, feeling the sharp corners. When Nico and Dill saw the box bulging from the fabric, they tilted their heads.

"Par gave this to me this morning," Lor croaked, pulling it out and handing it to Nico.

Inside was the small phial shimmering with its internal brilliance. A similar note perched on top of the phial in the same curling handwriting. Nico pulled out the note. He furrowed his brow, then turned his attention back to the box.

"I don't get it. What is that?" he asked, stabbing the phial with a finger.

"Wait, what is *that?*" Dill asked with a finger hooking around in the box. Nico bent forward and traced around inside too, periodically rubbing his thumb and forefinger together.

"Oh, that's just a cluster of threads or something that Paerli stuffed the box—" He stopped talking and swiped the circle of hair. It was thinner than the mane of any creature he knew. Sunlight shimmered through the gossamer threads, revealing under the white the faintest shade of yellow that the techlight of his room wouldn't detect. Golden core, aroma of violets. "Oh God..." Lor whispered.

Dill cocked an eyebrow, tilting his head and pulling the hank of hair from Lor.

"Oh no... oh no, no, no, no..." Lor repeated.

"What? What is it, Lor?" Nico stood by Dill to look at the hair. Dill shot a look back to him.

For the first time, Lor noticed real dread carved into his Danashi friend's features.

Lor's hand shook, threatening to drop the box and splatter the phial all over the courtyard. Nico grabbed it from him and led him to sit down.

"This..." Lor grabbed the hair back from Dill and pressed it to his nose. He closed his eyes, feeling the sting of a tear at the corner of his eye as he smelled the scent of his sweet Anglia. "This is Damaetra's *hair.*"

His stomach curdled. Everything hit him at once. Paerli had him by his balls, and he had to go through with the eneris swap, or she would do something to his girlfriend.

"What? That's crazy, why would Par cut off Dame's hair?" Nico asked.

"I know why," Lor moaned.

"Is this about your argument last night?" Nico held Lor's arm as he swayed. Lor leaned forward and put his head in his hand.

"Is everything alright? I hope the illness is not spreading between you all." The deep voice approached the fountain. Lor glanced up to see Fowler standing there; his arms were crossed, but he smiled.

"Fowler, thank the Maker, we need your help," Lor said, grabbing on to the bird man's jacket. Fowler took a step back and glanced around.

"What seems to be the problem?" he asked, prying Lor's fingers from the jacket.

"Paerli has Damaetra," Lor said.

"What does that mean? She has her?"

"Par kidnapped my girlfriend because I wouldn't make a binding pact with her last night to drink her eneris."

Dill jumped from the bench, away from the box. "Is *that* what that is? Sick!"

Nico took the phial out and held it in the sun. Gold dripped in thick swollen slogs into the liquid below.

"This... this is bad news," Fowler grumbled.

"You don't say," Dill said, crossing his arms.

Nico's whole face wrinkled inward. "I don't know what it means to drink a living person's eneris, but if what you're saying about Dame is true, and Par's note says that she will find you, maybe you should drink it."

Everyone stared at Nico like he was insane.

"But I don't know what this will do to me." Lor snatched the phial from Nico. "She says it will give me eternal life, but what if she lied? Or what if it kills me first in order to give me this new life? What if this eternal life is less than alive and more than dead? What torture that could be!"

"Like a zombie?" Dill asked.

"Worse than a damn zombie."

"Eternal life?" Nico asked.

Lor bit his lip and stared at the phial. "If I drink this, then perform her favor, then we would be bound and live forever. That's what she said."

He turned the phial around in his hand, watching the golden liquid slither over the sides. His dream flashed in his mind—it was the moment he started sinking when he tried leading Damaetra to Gehenna.

Was the Maker trying to tell me something?

"Who would even want that?" Nico asked.

"That is some dark, foul magic." Fowler lowered his voice to keep out any eavesdroppers.

Lor clicked his tongue. "This... this can't be right. Paerli must be in some kind of trouble. Yeah," he said. He didn't recognize his own voice. "This isn't like her at all. She's smart, funny, and cares about her friends. Why would she hurt her friend?"

"Dude, are you in denial? Listen to yourself, man!" Dill shook Lor's shoulder.

Fowler stepped forward. "Maybe Nico is correct. Maybe you should drink it."

"Not you too..." Lor groaned.

"Paerli is a Reaper, and apparently, she's two pricks shy of a full cactus right now. If we don't get Dame back, what do you think she will do to her?" Nico asked.

Fowler frowned. "How well do you know your abilities?"

Nico grimaced, and Dill shrugged. Lor continued to stare at the phial in his palm.

"I've only been able to successfully make blast cores, bandage, and fever drip," Nico said.

Dill stubbed a toe into the concrete. "I haven't made anything cool yet. I've only learned about wiring and mountain ores. Haven't crafted anything but prototypes for amputees."

Everyone glanced at Lor. "Don't look at *me*," he said. "I've only reaped green, blue, red, and white. My *gift* actually sucks."

"There is still a lot left for you all to learn," Fowler said, sighing, "but time for your girlfriend seems to be running out. If it comes to it, I can take flight and get help."

"She's going to expect my eneris in return," Lor said.

"Can you get it to her?" Fowler asked.

"I don't know how. But I know someone who does. I have to make amends with him first."

"Can you get it by early morning?"

"I'm going to do my damnedest."

Lor sat at his table, checking his e-disk every minute for a message from Damaetra... or Paerli. Nothing. The disk wobbled around as he spun it over the glossy surface of the table. The message he sent to Krik'tha went unread. He tried finding him in the Hall, but he was a ghost. Thumbing through Dill's old history book did nothing to help. There was nothing in there about reaping his own eneris.

Did she do this on purpose?

He closed his eyes, watching the colors swarm like gee flies in disorder. It was just the way his mind felt. His e-disk buzzed, sending his heart into his throat, when he saw it was from Nico, asking if he'd heard anything yet. Not *yet*.

Lor closed his eyes again, watching for the white gold fractals. Anything to get him closer to her. Anything.

Maker, what do I do?

There was a faint knock at the door.

He stood up so fast that he knocked over his chair.

"Damaetra?" he said, jogging to the door, knowing it wasn't her. He peered through the visitor glass and saw the slicked-back black hair of a Foscan head.

He opened the door. "Hey, I'm so glad you're here," he said, letting Krik'tha inside.

"I am sorry to come late, but... I thought about our talk earlier. May I sit?"

"Yes, of course, please." Lor led him to the single table in the middle of the apartment. Krik'tha had a dumpy tan bag that hung across his body and rested on his hip. He looked around for a little while, mouth open, smiling.

"Is cozy, yes?" he said.

Lor took a seat across from him, pulling out the small box Paerli gave him. He tapped it with a shaking index finger. Running it across the edge, he pictured the thick golden liquid inside.

"It's nice here, but I miss home. I miss my girlfriend."

"I was disturbed by your question, friend, but I did much thinking about it. I know sometimes a thought can make the mind sick, so I decide to show you what it means to do this thing before you learn on your own."

Lor shifted in his seat, no longer preoccupying himself with the box. He didn't ask Krik'tha *how* to do it, but he was thankful he didn't have to. The last thing he wanted was for the man to leave.

"It is important," Krik'tha continued, "that you keep this between you and me."

"Will it kill me?" Lor blurted. An image of the little puck fish resting in his palm, all bones with paper-thin flesh clinging to them, flashed in his mind. He imagined his face caved in, with razor-sharp cheekbones cutting through dried skin.

Krik'tha sighed. The lines in his face grew as he sat in the dim room. It reminded Lor of the conversation he had with Val, and the first thing to come to his mind was a dousing of cold water to keep the man awake.

"It might."

Lor swallowed.

"There is Foscan story," Krik'tha continued. His low voice drawled, "I learn story as a child—all Foscan learn as a child. It is what you call a *fairy tale*. But we all know is a real history. Not like books capitol gives.

"There was... first Reapers. A bargain was made with Igni leader—"

"Wait, I'm sorry to interrupt, but what is Igni?"

"Igni is people... well, Igni is gone, but once were keeper of Great Tree."

"I'm sorry again, Krik'tha. What is Great Tree?"

He sighed and looked up, as if trying to fish words from inside his skull.

"It is what you now call... what is word..."

As Krik'tha sat there, tapping his chin trying to come up with the Northern Common words for his story, Lor felt a stirring in his chest, as if he already knew the answer. Par's cryptic ramblings began to make more sense, and waiting for the man to confirm his thought was a fire in his belly.

"Great Tree was source of life and abundance in country... no, *world*... many, many years ago. A rot took hold of root and needed closing by Igni. Time forgot Great Tree when tragedy burned it away, making unusable the thing. It is now what you call..."

Krik'tha stared up at the ceiling. "You call it... Mount Gehenna."

Where the roots used to be.

Paerli's words rang in his skull, just before she touched him. She practically bit his head off when he asked about it, but now it made sense. The knot forming in Lor's throat stifled any spit he wanted to swallow, causing him to choke.

"Mou-nt Gehe-nna?" He gagged the words out.

"Yes, that is it. But it happened so long ago, is now fairy tale to all but Foscan child."

Once Lor was able to talk again, he folded his hands on the table and grunted out the rest of his spit. "So you're saying Mount Gehenna used to be a giant tree that burned up... why, because of a bargain made with an Igni? A race of people that no longer exists?"

"Is hard to understand, yes. But I must tell you about Reaper essence, yes?"

"Yes, I'm sorry, go on." Lor had much to think about. Was any of this captured in writing? Could he borrow it?

"Bargain was like eneris trade. It was as you ask today when I spit on your shoe."

"You spit on my shoe?"

Krik'tha glared at Lor. His white eye was eerie in the dimly lit room. "I show you how to do this thing, but I do not like it."

"I understand," Lor said. His skin rippled into goosebumps as the cold sweat formed a film on his forehead.

Krik'tha reached around at the tan sack on his hip. After digging around and cursing at himself in the Foscan tongue, he pulled out a small engineering switch. Its edge gleamed in the bright techlight, and he could see his perfectly sweaty reflection in it.

"W-hat's that for, eh?" Lor chuckled and swallowed, but his throat was dry and scratchy.

"This is part that might kill you..." Krik'tha turned the blade back and forth, passing a reflected orb over Lor's cheek. Lor flinched, anticipating the tip plunging between his ribs. "...but don't worry. I am here."

The man held the switch with the pointed end toward Lor. "I need to open you a little. It is to help with energy flow."

"I, uh..."

Sensing Lor's hesitation, Krik'tha folded the blade back into the sheath. "How important is this to you?"

Lor opened his mouth and gazed down at the white box sitting on the table.

Paerli did this alone? Is she crazy? This is for Damaetra. You need to get her safely back with you.

"It's very important. Just... let's just do it."

The Foscan studied Lor. His eye wandered around his face like a miniature spotlight. He wondered if his ignorance was etched into each crinkle in his flesh. Krik'tha flipped the blade out once again and it cried out a *shink!* causing Lor to jump.

"I need your arm," he said. His eerily slender fingers waved to beckon him to hold his arm out. Lor obeyed, stretching his arm across the table. "Close eyes if you must."

Lor didn't close them. He didn't want to fall into a color trance while someone he just met cut into him.

"How deep?" was all he could say before the tip broke his skin and jabbed downward. Lor sucked in a breath so hard the chill of the air bit his teeth.

"How deep?" he said again, feeling the worms in his belly.

"I must prick the bone. Just a little."

Lor's shoulder jerked out of his control as red welled up around the silvery switch and dribbled down his forearm. He felt bile in his throat and a cold sweat on his neck. It wasn't *his* arm with a switch sticking out of it... it wasn't *his* flesh foaming out his life force... it was only a holofilm. Just a story.

A slight pinch of pressure shot fiery bolts of electricity up his arm.

"Got it," Krik'tha said, holding the switch in place.

Lor let out a loud breath. "Okay, pull it out, pull it out!"

The Foscan clicked his tongue and turned his eye toward the blade. "That is not how it works. I must leave it in. Please... try not to think about it."

Lor let out a half gasp-laugh. "It's all I *can* think about!"

"Try not to."

Lor wanted to sock him in the mouth. Each quiver of the man's wrist twisted the edge ever so slightly to send another jolt through his arm.

"Then hold the fuck still!" Lor spat. Cold fingers of nausea slid across his brow.

Krik'tha tightened his grip, resting his elbows on the table and attempting to hold the blade still.

All Lor could think about was Paerli sitting alone at her own table, one hand holding a switch deep in her lovely dark flesh, with her turquoise eyes glassing over with tears. *Did she even know how to cry?* A trickle ran down his cheek.

I'm definitely crying.

"Let us hurry... you will lose much blood this way." Krik'tha gripped his blade wrist to hold it steadier.

Lor nodded and licked his lips, attempting to blink the wetness from his eyes.

"First, you close eyes."

Lor obeyed, seeing his old friends, the swirling colors. This time, there was something new—black crackles webbing through them.

"Now you focus. Focus on you, on your future..."

His voice droned with that alluring Foscan accent. The colors bounced to the tempo, cracks and all.

Only think of yourself. No one else, just you.

Lor's mind went straight to his golden bedroom, his sanctuary. His bastion of solitude, where he sat many evenings reading his tome on Law and the roundsman. He thought of his future in Law, and how it was taken from him. Another jolt shot through his arm. All the reading and learning about a field he would never know. No one existed outside his space—he was in a bubble surrounded by blackness... and Eva's blanket.

A sharp pain rocketed up through his left temple.

"Ow, shit!" Lor said, opening his eyes, expecting to see the little servant holding the switch deep into his skull. He was watching him from across the table, still holding on to the blade hidden in Lor's forearm, nothing more.

"You thought of someone else?"

"I guess I thought of my sister... It was just for a split second! Damn, this hurts!" He cupped his forehead, attempting to stanch the pain.

"My friend." Krik'tha tried not to jiggle the switch. "To draw own life force is selfish act. You must only think of yourself. To think of any other will bring pain, and maybe more."

"Maybe *more*?" Lor still rubbed his head.

"We must hurry... This is why I came to you—to learn on your own this thing may bring you death only. Do you want to try again?"

"Yes, okay, okay. Just give me a second to purge my mind of everyone."

He closed his eyes and tried to think of everyone he knew before trying the ritual again. Images of Gale, Paerli, Nico, Dill, Eva, Val, Fowler, and even Horace passed over his mind until he found himself sitting in his golden room again, with Damaetra sitting on the bed. His mouth was on her, and she held him close, smelling of violets.

"Ow! What in Gehenna!" Lor felt the stab across his entire head and into his temples.

"You went back into ritual." Krik'tha gripped the handle with both hands and his arms trembled.

"Okay, okay. I won't close my eyes, but I have to think about everyone I know and get it out of my system so they don't invade my brain when I do this..." The sides of his face were pink from rubbing.

"We must hurry." Krik'tha glanced at the growing pool of red under Lor's arm. Red bubbles collected around the switch.

Lor scanned the room. Krik'tha's grace at holding the blade wavered, and multiple jolts stung his arm to where he started to get used to it. He embraced it.

As he examined the room, he pictured it as his new home without anyone in it. It was a new, cold room all his own. Nothing on these walls belonged to him, and everything was on loan. Metallic traces lined the design of the ornate decorative pillars, radiating a chill. No evidence of friendship, love, or family hung in the air, and he took in a deep breath, smelling only the sharp buzz of sterility.

"Okay, let me try it again."

"Think only of yourself. Think of your goals, future... just only concentrate on you. Alone."

Lor closed his eyes once again, watching the dance of colors. He focused on the gold swipes, willing it to come into focus when the matching sparks made their appearance and vibrated in place. Visions of his life in the Reaper Hall flashed day after day as boxes of plats skittered through his mail door, one after the other. He could buy anything, be anyone, and do anything with that money. He dressed himself in finery and bought himself his own personal size cruiser. He closed himself inside his apartment, leaving the world to count the plat boxes. While he sat on the floor counting hundreds of thousands of glowing green plats, a golden liquid slithered over every surface. It was a living thing, crawling and eking a home within each crack and detail. His golden hands closed the lid on his last golden box, and he made his way to the golden bed. He lay under the golden sheets, reflecting on tomorrow's plats, and fell asleep.

"Master Loren! Please open your eyes!" Krik'tha shouted. A small hand gripped his shoulder, jerking it back and forth, and Lor could feel his neck wobble like a spring with his sleep-heavy head bobbing. The fuzzy world came back into focus, and he could count the stitches in Krik'tha's eye patch with as close as the man was to his face.

"I'm up, I'm up!" He reared back. Still sitting at the table, he glanced over at the bed, seeing his ordinary sheets and no piles of plats at the door.

"I need your help now," Krik'tha said. His fingers waved over the switch handle as it pointed erect from Lor's forearm.

"What do you need me to do?" Lor said. He ran a finger across his upper lip, feeling beads of sweat. When he saw his finger, his eyes widened. "Do you have a phial?"

"Yes, of course, all Reaper has phial. Hold still!"

With a sharp yank, Krik'tha pulled out the blade. The hole in Lor's arm was a bloody toothless mouth. Krik'tha covered it with a wad of bandage.

"We must hurry before you dry up," the man said, producing a phial from his bag and running the opening across Lor's lip and neck. He tilted it toward Lor's wet finger.

Lor sat in a daze while letting Krik'tha tend to him. He no longer felt pain in his arm. The ritual memory lingered in his mind as he tried to remember his friends. He knew their names... but what did they look like? All he saw were the plats and the rolling increase in his account.

Damaetra. Remember Damaetra.

"Go look in mirror."

"Did it work?"

"Go look in mirror."

It must have worked.

He jogged to the bathroom, holding the bandage tight, and the techlight popped on as he crossed the threshold. There in the mirror was his own messy blond hair, with smears of gold swiping out from his hairline. The pores on his nose had tiny flecks of dried eneris, and his lip was a smeary, shimmering mustache.

He uncapped the phial, running the mouth of the bottle across his lip and nose, then attempting to gather the drops at his hairline. A slick of gold squished in the fold of his neck. Everywhere he could sweat, there was gold.

CHAPTER 24

Golden Opportunity
LOREN

KRIK'THA TOOK CARE TO LET the foreman know that Lor was going to be out that day, and he was grateful for it. He fingered the bandage wrapped around his forearm, which was officially collecting scars—first the crescent from the implant, then the gouge from the switch. He thought about poking a hole under the switch scar to make it look like a question mark on his arm... fitting for how his life was unfolding.

The plat box sat just inside the door, and he sighed, remembering the visions from the night before. He never wanted to forget his friends' faces in exchange for *that.*

He opened the box, and the deduction was there, just as he expected. Two thousand, seven hundred forty-seven. It was still a hell of a wage for one day. Something about the glowing slips made Lor frown. A QuickChat from Nico popped up on his screen.

NICO: Hey, did you get it?

LOR: Yeah. It was not fun.

NICO: Meet us at the fountain immediately.

The first sun hadn't risen yet. It was perfect for him to slip out without notice. He threw on some day clothes to bolt out the door. He paused before closing the door to step back inside and swipe Paerli's box and gather a few phials.

Reaper always carries phial.

The atrium was empty except for the plump jerk at the visitor's desk. He was nose-deep into his e-disk and didn't even notice Lor leave.

The courtyard was also silent and still—the only noise came from water splashing in the stone basin of the fountain. Its white noise beat over his ears in a tumult.

Paerli's box nudged his thigh with every step he took, as if constantly reminding him she was there. Similar to the way she always had to hold on to him during the program, the biting box corner swelled into a nuisance. He had to get it out of his pocket.

"Here," Nico said, walking up to Lor and holding out a utility pouch. He didn't know where Nico got it from, but he didn't care. Lor was able to fit both the box and phials inside, relieving himself of their burden.

"You need to start carrying a bag or something," Dill said. He had a new gadget in his hand that he flipped between his fingers absentmindedly.

Lor nodded, as there were still some things he could be better about. He scanned the area for Fowler.

"Dude, what happened to your arm?" Dill asked.

Lor held up the bandaged arm. Tiny specks of blood dotted the slash where Krik'tha sewed his skin back together, tainting the gauzy wrapping.

"That's how I got my eneris," he said. Krik'tha asked him to keep it between them, and he prayed his friends wouldn't rat him out. "Please don't tell anyone about it. Apparently, it's a very old and dark ritual."

Nico zipped his lips.

Fowler strolled up to the group shortly after.

He drove them to the beach where Lor had his first day reaping blues, reasoning that they couldn't do something like this in the middle of the square.

He parked the cruiser by a strip of trees lining the edge of the beach. Lor stood on the edge of the dank shore that smelled of spoiled crab and death.

"You all really think I'll be okay?" he asked.

Fowler nodded his head. "We're here for you."

Lor stared at the phial. In truth, he was curious about it. Here he was, at Guild Central, about to do something that no seasoned Guild member knew about, when not a standard year ago, he studied Law ignorantly in his room. Paerli's immediate friendship gave him the drive to stay in the program and be near her... and then he met Damaetra.

Par wasn't thinking right, bringing Damaetra into her quagmire, and it was up to him to pull them both out of it. Before realizing it, the thick golden liquid dripped down his throat.

It was warm and sweet—with the flavor of apples. As it trickled down to his belly, a curling rot set in. A bitter aftertaste stung his tongue, like acid and blood. His stomach turned, and he felt the familiar electricity buzzing through his muscles.

"This... does not feel... good." Lor belched and swayed on the spot. He felt Fowler's bony fingers wrap around his shoulders, guiding him to sit in the sand. He obliged, feeling the sand's dampness soak through his pants, chilling his butt.

Foam dribbled from his lip as the electricity pulsed along his limbs. He didn't know why he jerked his head, but the last thing he saw was Nico's belt sliding between his teeth.

The air stunk of sulfur and decay. Great trees dripped with slimy vines, and there was a persistent fog that hung in the air. A thick man sat on a log by one of these trees fashioned with a hole in the center.

"There's an old Foscan saying..." the man said as Lor approached—but his voice cut off and his image dissolved into the mist. He reached out to grab him, seeing dark-skinned hands rather than his own. He looked at the delicate fingers, destroyed by the filth of labor. He found a bag on the ground, with the name "Karl" stitched into the side.

I'm coming for you, Lor... a voice echoed on the wind.

The bag dissolved with the man, leaving behind a blanket of mustard-colored hot sand. Glancing to his left, his surroundings had morphed. There was the familiar town of Secas, but it was different. It was wild and uninhabited. In the distance was a great tree, taller than any mountain. It was only a swim away.

"You look lost," a man said, smiling as he approached. He was unlike anyone Lor had ever seen. He was rugged and tall, with the best parts of Anglia and Foscan features. Was he Yeunish? Lor opened his mouth to speak, but the man dissipated into the swirling dust.

I'm not far now... the same disembodied voice called on the breeze.

Lor's surroundings dripped down, revealing a thick wall in front of him. Gazing upward, there was a tremendous canopy of leaves and branches, stretching for miles. Thousands of many-colored birds twittered among the branches, singing songs and filling the air with a twinkling melody. He was at the tree. He placed a hand over the wall, feeling the trunk's life.

"I can't stay with you." The same man from the desert stood next to him, putting a hand on the bark next to his. It was much larger than his, and pale. He stretched his little finger out to touch Lor's hand, but it merged with the bark, leaving him alone again.

That's enough, wake up, Lor... the atmospheric voice sounded perturbed.

He backed away from the tree, feeling a pit of rage forming in his heart. As he scanned upward at the tree, it burst into an inferno, forcing the birds to flee. Paper-thin wisps of embers floated aimlessly, landing in the water and tainting it black. Screams and siren wails blared just before he was dragged away, watching the blaze become a cloud on the horizon.

I said that's ENOUGH!

Lor's eyes shot open. A cool breeze brushed through his hair, followed by stagnant heat and the smell of dead things. Nico and Dill stood over him while Fowler's claws were wrapped around the sides of his head. The man slowly loosed his grip, and Lor felt the sticky sweat he left behind.

"This is bad," Lor croaked. That final voice thrummed in his chest. It was a beautiful and terrifying, dual-layered sound that stuck needles into his soul.

"What did you see?" Nico asked.

"She's coming," Lor said, fighting to get up. His head wobbled forward as lingering dizziness wracked his skull.

"Who, Paerli?" Dill said, glancing around for signs of her.

"I think she's planning on doing something bad." Lor propped himself up on one hand and pulled out his e-disk. He didn't know why, but he felt a strong need to reach out to Gale.

LOR: Hey, sorry to bother you, but I think I'm in trouble.

He waited for an answer, but it didn't come.

"Loren, tell us what you saw," Fowler said, putting a hand on his shoulder.

Lor tried to shake the fuzziness out of his head. He opened his mouth to say something, but a strange feeling covered his chest. He couldn't tell what it was—it didn't feel bad, but it didn't feel great either. He felt connected to a machine.

"I knew you'd do the right thing... but why did you have to involve *them*?" Paerli stepped through the trees.

CHAPTER 25

Long Lost Rabbit
LOREN

"WHERE'S DAMAETRA?" DILL STOOD DEFIANT, fists clenched by his sides. Nico scowled next to him, and Lor wobbled to his feet.

"Whoa now, Dill, you weren't supposed to be here. I'd go back to Engineer Hall if I were you. Same to you, Nico," Paerli said.

"Well, you're *not* me, and I'll do what I want! And I want to know what you did with our friend!"

Paerli cracked a grin. Lor's heart vibrated as two beats out of sync, making him dizzy. He took in slow, deep breaths and focused on Paerli. Her outer appearance betrayed her inner turmoil—Dill was pissing her off.

"Oh, Dame? She's hanging out with my team right now. In fact, I'd like to introduce you to them."

"Your *team*?" Lor's voice was scratchy and weak.

Paerli smiled and strolled toward Lor. As she did, his dual heartbeat synced in time, creating a long, hard thrum. She slid her arm through his like she had done thousands of times before, holding him up like a puppet.

"What's that in your pocket?" She snaked her hand down his leg like she had the other day, feeling the lump where his phial pressed against his thigh. She knew it was there after he drank her gold. She knew everything. "Is that for me?"

Fowler glared at her.

Lor hung his head and wanted to weep. The force of her rage filled him—it was a new feeling that had total hold within. His own heart was at war with hers, and he knew it would only get better if he gave her the phial. He slid his hand into his pocket, and it had never felt so tight around his fist. Curling the phial under his fingers, he drew it out and presented it to her.

Paerli snatched the phial and smirked. "Thank you for that. Let's go meet my team and I will make the match permanent. After all, it would be nice to have so many witnesses."

"Why, Par? W-hat happened to you?" Lor gurgled, his head still hanging low and bobbing. Weakness wrapped its numbing coils around his limbs.

"Meet me at the northwest tip, where the forest meets the Span. We'll talk there." Paerli unwrapped herself from his arm, jangling his phial toward the group as she backed up. "Of course, I expect you not to back out... just the four of you. No roundsmen. Oh, and Lor..." She paused, smiling sweetly at him. "Dame depends on you."

Dill tried to chase after her as she disappeared into the trees, but Fowler grabbed his arm, shaking his head. "I don't like the idea of her having a team," Fowler grumbled.

"I always thought *we* were her team," Dill said.

Lor stood upright and gazed upward. The waterbirds had returned, circling. They flew around Lor only, creating a moving halo.

"She is watching you," Fowler said, pointing at the birds.

"But she left, how is she *watching* him?" Nico asked.

"The birds... she has a Shepherd on her 'team.'"

Once Fowler said it out loud, Lor knew it. He had so many warring thoughts in his head that he couldn't organize them, but the seed sparked the memory—it was her memory. He hoped this feeling was temporary.

"No roundsmen," Fowler said. "I don't like where this is going."

Nico reached over to steady Lor as he wobbled on the spot. "Well, we know where she has Damaetra at least," he said. "Did drinking her goop do *anything* for you?"

Lor shook his head, "Not yet, but I'm still trying to figure out how to manage her rage inside me."

"Rage?" Dill asked. He returned to flipping the gadget between his knuckles. "How much rage are we talking?"

Lor swallowed, biting at a loose piece of skin on his lower lip. "Tons."

"Who would have ever guessed that?" Nico said.

"There was something about her," Fowler said, "when we first came to Guild Central. I couldn't put my finger on it, but she seemed out of place with all of you."

"The longer we stay here, the more time she has to hurt Damaetra. We have to go." Lor steadied himself and smoothed his hands down his pants. He threw the box and empty gold phial into his utility sac. "How are we going to get there?"

The group went back to Guild Central to rent a jumper. Lor was hesitant about cramming his long limbs in with three other people, but Fowler was smart enough to rent a roomier one.

"I owe you for the ride," Lor said, making swiping gestures over the surface of his e-disk.

Fowler put his hand over Lor's, pressing them down. "Don't worry about it."

The driver was another Danashi, and it made Lor wonder if all jumper drivers were Danashi. The man turned his head back to Fowler. "I can only go as far as the sand strip. Company rules."

"No problem," Fowler replied. He turned the rest of them and whispered, "It will be good if he doesn't take us right to them, so we can quietly sneak up and see how many people she has with her."

"We have nothing to fight her with," Dill whispered.

Nico perked up. "Are we planning to fight?"

"Let's hope it doesn't come to that," Fowler said, staring out the window and holding his head.

Lor flipped out his e-disk, hoping to see something from Gale for once. Nothing. Instead, he felt the urge to reach out to him.

Lor: Hey, I'm going to be at the northwest edge of where Secas hits the Span. If anything happens to me, I want you to know that I'm sorry. For everything.

He didn't know why he said that. Maybe it was the fact that Gale took care of him and didn't send him to foster care when his mom died. Maybe he felt bad for all the plat he spent on the program, just for Lor to die a few months later. Maybe he was just scared.

He didn't know what he could do as a Reaper if he had to defend himself. Reaping anything was as hard on him as it would be on any attacker, taking him out of a fight at the start.

"We're approaching the strip." The driver's voice had a deep drip to it.

Lor wasn't ready for the ride to be over yet. What would he say to Paerli? How could he save Damaetra? A malformed plan sat like a fleshy lump in his brain.

The Danashi opened the door for them, and they all slid from the tall jumper cab using the telescopic ladder. The jumper skidded away, barely breaking the air with sound.

The sand strip wasn't far from the edge of Secas. Lor ducked behind a boulder when he saw slight movement beyond the tree trunks. Everyone followed Lor behind the boulder, but Dill tripped on a piece of old tech poking out from the sand, sending him face-first into the grains.

"Shhh!" Nico said, pulling Dill up.

Lor closed his eyes and focused on Paerli. The colors behind his eyes swirled until there was nothing but gold. He didn't see the group; he sensed them.

"She has five people with her."

"Five?" Nico hissed.

Fowler groaned. "This is not good."

"Two of them are harmless," Lor continued. "And two are very dangerous."

"We outnumber two, so that's good," Fowler interjected. "What about the other one?"

"Come on out, Lor!" Paerli shouted in their direction.

"Damn," Nico spit.

Lor looked up to see the lazy circling waterbirds. He stood slowly, hands high in surrender as if Paerli was a roundsman ready to make an arrest. The others followed, and they shuffled toward the edge of the tree line.

Lor stepped onto the mustard yellow sand, and Paerli stood several yards away with two burly men behind her. One of the men was heavily altered with engineering implants. The other man had Damaetra's delicate white throat under his piggish arm. Her hair had been butchered into a short hack job, and it stuck out at odd angles. She was quiet and calm, with her eyes closed, holding on to the man's arms with her petite hands. They were so white against his tanned flesh. She almost stood on her toes as the brute held her.

"Let *go* of her, you asshole!" Lor's vision splashed in crimson, ready to pounce at the group if it weren't for Nico holding him in a vice grip.

"Come closer!" Paerli shouted back, ignoring his comment and beckoning him forward. Lor peered at his friends, and they nodded at him. He strode toward her with his group trailing behind. The waterbirds flew toward Paerli and landed near an old woman sitting on a rock.

As Lor got closer, he saw more of the team. The woman on the rock was the same one he had seen on his first day of work—the rough-looking older woman with a scar across her face wearing the cloak. She grinned at him with only a few teeth. *A harmless one.*

The girl from the Guild Central hub administration desk was there with her thick-lensed glasses enlarging her already round hazel eyes. *Harmless.*

He didn't recognize the two burly men, but he knew they were the highly dangerous ones. He was almost there when a slender man stepped out from behind Damaetra's captor. It was Jack, Horace's acquaintance from Tad's funeral. Lor stared at the odd crew, wondering how all the threads tied between them.

"This is Cricket," Paerli said, pointing at Jack. "And this is Book, Crow, and Hammer." She pointed to the assistant, the bio-hacked engineer, and the man squeezing Damaetra's neck. "This is Grandma." She pointed at the older woman. "Or, that's what I call her. We're not actually related. My other assistant is running late, which you'd think would be unusual for a Weggie runner, but here we are. Ah, I spoke too soon. There he is!"

A puff of dust ballooned from the ground, and a familiar face stood in the middle of it. As the dust dissipated, his features chiseled into view. He looked oddly familiar, but Lor couldn't place why. As he stood there staring at the newcomer, Nico stepped forward, moving his limbs like water. He stopped next to Lor, putting a hand on his chest.

"N-Niki?"

Chapter 26

Eyes and Legs
Loren

"It's Klaus now. Or the Hare. I kinda like Hare. What do you think?" He smiled at Nico.

"I-I thought you were *dead*!"

"Yeah, I thought you were dead too. So let's get on with the show!" Hare sat on the rock next to Pigeon, bouncing his knee.

Nico frowned, and his lip quivered. Lor could tell they weren't identical but very close. All of Nico's suspicions were true—he never distrusted his instinct that his brother was still alive, only to be met with a complete stranger.

"A touching reunion," Paerli drawled. "At any rate, now that you've met my team, you know who's going to help us with the task."

Lor put a hand on Nico's shoulder, squeezing and tugging him back. He obeyed with little resistance while his twin swung his legs like the thirteen-year-old he was when he turned.

"Let Damaetra go," Lor demanded. He stepped forward again, blocking Nico and the rest.

"Just hold on a minute, let me do this, then I'll let her go, cool?" Paerli stepped forward, pulling out the phial she took from Lor.

"Why did you need an audience for this?"

Paerli clicked her tongue and grinned. "Well, once it's done, we can go straight to Mount Gehenna. You know that place is crawling with roundsmen, and I need my team—*our* team—to help us get through."

Fowler's long fingers wrapped around Lor's shoulder. He whispered, "Mount Gehenna is forbidden, you know that."

Lor nodded, knowing the truth of what he said, but what could he do? Dill and Nico were just amateur Guild members, and he himself couldn't get through a simple reaping without feeling like he was going to die. He was also in a deep state of anguish, seeing his girlfriend suffocating under some hairy ape of a man.

"Get on with it then," Lor said.

"I knew you'd see it my way. You won't regret this, I promise." Paerli flicked the top of the phial with her thumb, tilting the bottle back and sucking it down like a thirsty animal. Knowing what he knew about drinking the stuff and where it came from made him nauseated.

After finishing the phial, her face went slack as her eyes rolled back. She froze on the spot, not one muscle moving or twitching. Lor thought it odd to see this from the other side. While he couldn't stop twitching during his vision, she couldn't move. Hare continued to swing his legs as if he were at a playground, while Hammer squeezed Damaetra. Lor focused on the man, imagining tearing his throat out, letting the brute's blood trickle down his arm into the sand as he held a severed tongue in his fist.

Damaetra closed her eyes, with her pale hands still trying to hold on to the meaty tanned arm. Her short strands brushed against her delicate, peach, flushed cheeks. Lor glanced back at Paerli and took a short step backward when he noticed her glaring at him.

"You're *Yeunish*? Are you actually *kidding* me?" She spat.

"I'm sorry?" Lor's confusion eclipsed everything he knew about himself. His physical features were simplistic—all the way down to his bone structure. He didn't move with grace like the Foscans, he didn't have the beauty of the Anglia, and he definitely didn't have their distinguishing eyes or hair. Yet, she had to have been telling the truth. After all, he experienced his own visions when drinking her phial. He turned to his friends, who looked at him with fresh curiosity.

"After all this time," Paerli continued, "you've been wandering around, hiding the fact that you're a bastard blend of Foscan? No wonder you get along so well with those slaves. What an absolute *let*-down!"

Lor swallowed. He was now a marked man.

Paerli paced back and forth, shooting glances at Damaetra. She flashed a wicked grin toward Lor. "And to think..." she said.

Don't say it, Par. Don't you dare say it.

"...I almost let you have your way with me the other night. A Yeuni... great Gehenna, what a bullet dodged!"

Damaetra squeezed her eyes. Wet tracks carved over the dust on her face, plunking down on Hammer's thick hairy arm.

"Don't listen to her, Damaetra, she's *lying*," Lor called out, shooting a glare at Paerli so fierce he saw a red ring around his vision. "I love *you*. I love you so much!" Why didn't he tell her that forever ago?

"Oi, you almost made it wif *'im*?" Crow jabbed a finger at Lor. Then he bellowed out the loudest guffaw.

Hammer punched him in the arm, rocking Damaetra on her toes as she continued to sob through the dirt on her face. "Shut up, *Crow*," he growled.

Fowler stepped forward. "I'm sorry, miss, you must have it wrong. Lor is a Mesaman, it's clear to everyone."

"Be quiet!" she barked. "I know what I saw."

Lor wrung his hands and his heart pounded for his sweet Anglia. The only thing he could think of was to try to reason with Paerli. He held his hands out to her. "I-I didn't know. I really didn't know, I'm sorry."

Hammer squeezed Damaetra harder.

The rage-filled heartbeat punched his ribs again, beating out of rhythm with his own and making him feel faint.

"Oh, you didn't know? You. Didn't. *Know*. That's a terrible lie. You should be banished, you know. How they ever let you into the program is a crime in itself!"

"Now hold on just a minute," Fowler cut in as her team stirred.

"I *said* shut *up*." If a look could slit a throat, hers would have beheaded Fowler.

Crow chuckled, flinching at Hammer, which made Hare laugh.

She tapped her finger on her chin. "I should give you a slave name..." She paced and spun on her heel like a dancer. "How about, Stig the Stupid, or Gurn the Ignorant?"

Crow laughed again, triggering a chuckle from both Hare and Hammer. The strange man, "Jack" stood in the back, still as a block of wood. He was frowning.

"Oh, I have an idea." She stopped, raising a finger in the air with a lighthearted smile on her face. For a moment, it looked as though she was the happiest she had been in a long time. "How about... Lor the *Bastard*."

Lor felt hands on his back. All of his friends held on to him as he wobbled. Paerli's rage beating in his chest threatened to knock him over. He *was* a bastard. He knew it. Gale wasn't his real dad. He didn't even know who his real dad was.

While Hammer, Crow, and Hare laughed, "Jack" stepped forward, rounding in front of Paerli. She stumbled back and parted her lips. He was significantly taller than her, looking out of place in the desert sands with his stained white coat and black goggles. He raised a hand and it made her flinch—something Lor had never seen her do. Rather than strike her, he gripped the side of his goggles, moving them to the top of his head. When he did this, she swallowed and licked dry lips.

"I'm sorry, Cricket. I didn't mean it," she murmured.

Cricket, as she called him, turned to face Lor. His eyes were the same type of lit from within that belonged on Dag, Val, and Krik'tha, except they were a brilliant shade of yellow. Without a word, he marched into the trees, with his slender frame disappearing among the weeds.

"Cricket, I'm sorry!" Paerli shouted after him.

"Yeh din' know?" Crow asked her. His voice was low and gravelly.

"Of course I didn't know, you *idiot*." She stormed up to Lor and poked a finger into his chest. "It's too late now, we're matched and there's nothing I can do unless you *die*."

"I don't think so, miss. You're going to be locked up for all you've done here today," Fowler said. His nose and lips elongated, causing Lor to recoil in disgust. "I'm turning you in."

It was the final thing he uttered before his nose merged with his lips to form a slick beak. His shoulders dislocated backward, and his arms curled into magnificent black wings. The movement was too quick for Lor to truly understand what was happening before Fowler jumped into the air and took flight as a raven.

"Oh no, ye' don'." Crow pulled out a tube with multiple switches and dials. He placed the tube over an eye and hit one of the triggers, sending some kind of splinter-like projectile at Fowler.

A sharp squawk rang out as he dropped like a stone into the sand. Lor gasped.

"Ironic... a Crow for a crow," Paerli said, flicking her hair back.

"You killed him! You killed Fowler!" Dill screamed. He turned to run toward the dying man, but Hare bolted forward, gripping his arm.

A melancholic wail echoed from the bird man, setting Lor's teeth to chatter. He stood there in shock as Nico spun toward his twin brother, grabbing the arm that held Dill.

The three of them were locked in place, gripping arms in a twisted triad.

"Let go, Nico," Hare said, holding on to Dill.

"No." Nico's voice was dry but firm as he squeezed Hare's wrist.

"I said let go!"

"No."

"Fine." Hare whipped out a switch faster than anyone could breathe and slashed it across Dill's eyes.

The scream he made was inhuman—Lor felt it in his bones. Hare let go of Dill, yanking his arm from Nico's grip, and ran back to the old woman sitting on the rock.

"My eyes! I can't see, I can't *see*!" Dill wailed, arching his back on the sand as blood spurted in an arc around him. Lor rushed to his friend, kneeling down and pulling off his outer shirt to press onto Dill's face. Dill took the shirt and whimpered in between jittery screams.

"Nico, you said you know how to make bandage, right?" Lor said.

"Well, y-yes, but I need some reaper material," he stuttered at the sight of Dill. Lor stood up to face him and grabbed his arms.

"I'll get you what you need, but—" Lor stopped, tilting his head to the side when color drained from Nico's face. His handsome features dulled, and he started to fall forward. Lor caught his friend. Nico grasped at Lor's undershirt as he continued to fall. Lor helped him down in the sand, confused. Two pillars stood behind Nico for a moment before Lor noticed dripping redness. The pillars flopped over, bouncing over each other like jumper tires before finally resting on the ground. Nico's face was green, and he croaked out a small groan while still gripping Lor's undershirt. He was a torso.

"Oopsie!" Hare said. He put on an innocent veneer and placed a finger over his upper lip. He held a different blade in his other hand, crusted with Nico's blood—it was longer and double-sided.

Lor's friends were dying around him. It wouldn't be long before it was his head that tumbled in the sand. His mouth hung open, and he fought for the saliva to lube his vocal chords.

"That's your brother, you *dick*!" Lor found his voice. It sounded pathetic.

Paerli chuffed and spun around, strutting back toward her group. Damaetra still had her eyes closed, growing even paler than she usually was. Lor bolted up and marched toward Paerli as she walked away. While reaching out for the hood of her cloak, he felt a sharp pang in his left side. Red liquid spread over his shirt. The sweet, musical voice he had known for the past several months screeched in a terrible howl as Damaetra screamed his name in anguish.

"You idiot!" Paerli spat.

"Wha'? I thou' yeh wanned 'im dead?" Crow stashed his smoking tube weapon.

"Not yet, you great buffoon! Do you know how much longer we'll have to wait for me to get another match? It will be decades, and you and your merry band of Valoan assholes will be dead!" Paerli huffed and stormed away, glancing over her shoulder at Lor. He fell to his knees with a hand over his side. He wanted to throw up.

"What should I do with this one?" Hammer asked, holding Damaetra up in his grip. Her toes brushed against the sand and she hugged her eyes shut. A small cry uttered from her lips, barely heard over the agitated breeze as Hammer squeezed her.

"Bring her with," Paerli said. "Maybe she can be our Formulator now that Cricket's gone."

She whirled around, taking backwards steps away from Lor. She cupped her hands over her mouth and shouted, "If you survive, come find me in five standard days and we'll finish this... Lor the Bastard!"

She spun back around, and he heard her say, "Hammer, when we get back to base, you need to take care of me *immediately*."

"Yes, ma'am!" he bellowed like a panting animal.

They disappeared in the dust. Dill continued to groan and sob behind Lor. His noises reassured him that he was still alive. Nico's silence worried him. His hands shook as he tried to hold his side. Thick red seeped between his fingers. He felt so unprepared, so stupid, and so naive. Gale was a medic. How did he not learn anything from him? Now, Fowler was dead, Nico was probably dead, and Dill was forever marred.

"Lor! Nico! Where are you?" Dill moaned. Lor opened his mouth, but his throat was too dry to respond.

He felt a raw chill. The sun flickered overhead, blazing yellow light over him. The warmth should have baked his skin, but it was ice on his flesh. He fell back into the sand as red oozed from the wound. Sluggish leaden blood slogged through his veins, losing pressure as it poured from his side. Strength left his grip, and his hand plopped in the sand next to him. He turned his head toward the Span. Never before did he look at a scene in such a way. The dunes undulated and blew magnificent puffs of yellow dust from their tips, whirling and whirling in the breeze with a glittering magic. All the stout cacti dotted the terrain, showing off their resilience in the waterless heat. Lor swallowed, wishing he had some water.

The sunlight was turning dark.

Was it the second sun already? Lor faced the sky, feeling as though he was sinking into the sand away from life. The sun moved farther away as he sank deeper into the darkness. Is this what it felt like to die?

I'm sorry, Damaetra. Maker, will you save her?

A brilliant cloud of dust burst next to him. A man's face appeared through the dust, and Lor reached out to him. He couldn't quite make out who it was with the sand's yellow powder coating the darkness of death, but his features felt familiar and safe.

Gale?

CHAPTER 27

Nico's Vitality Stew
LOREN

YOU'RE SINKING, LOREN! DAMAETRA'S VOICE called out to him. He tried to tell her it would be okay, but the black sand filled his mouth and spilled down his throat.

Am I still dying? When will it end?

Dark clouds passed over the sky, casting long shadows over his head, barely poking from the sand.

He heard Damaetra's faint cry: Loren Turtingas, wake up right now!

"You scared me," a deep voice came from his left side.

Lor cracked his eyelids to see his stepfather sitting in a chair next to him.

"S-he…" Lor croaked.

"Don't talk. Thank the Maker you're going to be okay. I'm glad I got here when I did. And your friend here has been more than helpful."

"F-friend?" Lor's blood chilled. *Was Paerli back?*

"Yeah, your friend, Jack. He made a lot of healing draughts for all of you."

Lor opened his eyes a little wider to see the spindly man Paerli called Cricket tending to the bandage on Lor's side. Lor's shirt was gone, and he was only covered by a thin sheet barely capable of blocking any drafts. He shivered in the warm breeze.

No longer in the desert, he lay on a small bed in a rustic wooden house. The surroundings looked familiar—it was the farm he visited with Krik'tha when he was assigned to pull red and white eneris.

"Close your eyes for a little while. We'll talk when you get up." Gale rose from his chair and left the room.

Jack removed the gauze from Lor's wound. He pulled out a square-bottomed phial and shook out some light green tincture onto a cloth.

"Your father is a smart man," Jack said. The black goggles were pressed over his eyes, with the strap digging into his temples. Underneath, Lor knew, were the yellow eyes of the Yeunish. He seemed to always hide himself in this way, even from Paerli. Jack dabbed at the hole in Lor's side. "And you are a very lucky man."

Lor tried to clear his throat. "Where's Dill? Nico?" His voice was hoarse.

"They'll be alright. Your little friend lost his eyes. Your other friend will never walk again."

Lor grunted as Jack stuffed the wound with more green liquid-soaked material. "Do I call you Cricket, or Jack?"

"Only Par calls me Cricket. I am done with her, so call me Jack." He turned back to a table covered in phials of all shapes and sizes, filled with a variety of colors that matched the dirty smears all over his coat.

"Is that actually your name?" Lor asked.

"It is now."

"What were you doing with her anyway? What were you planning?" Lor hissed through his teeth as he tried to prop himself on an elbow.

"No, lie down," Jack said, turning to push Lor's shoulder back into the mattress. "We can talk later."

"Where's Fowler?" Lor groaned again.

Jack turned to busy himself at the table again with the phials, not answering. The glass bottles clinked over each other as he moved them around.

"Jack, where's Fowler?"

His lanky body froze, and he dragged his hands across the sides of his coat, leaving fresh green stains in their wake.

"Fowler is... not well."

"But he's alive?"

Jack sighed, refusing to turn around. "Only just." He strode from the room, taking with him any answers. A throbbing ache swelled at his temples, so he closed his eyes. The swirling colors returned, but it was chaos. His head spun circles, making him queasy while lying like that. Gale was right—he needed rest.

The hearty aroma of stew was tantalizing enough to rouse Lor from sleep. He opened his eyes and scanned the room. No one was with him, but the sounds of muffled talking came from the next room.

Thankfully, he had no cryptic dreams to torment him this time, but he wondered if Jack's healing salve had the benefit of knocking him out completely as well. He glanced down at his left side, where a white bandage with a spot of blood in the middle clung to it.

The tape was lifted at a corner, so he used a nubby fingernail to poke at it. Peeling it back, the white bandage came free. The patch where Jack had packed the wound was healed over, leaving a jagged, bruised indentation in its place. Lor heard of such draughts capable of working this way during his time in the program, but Horace mentioned only top tier Formulators knew the proper mixtures. Jack was literally a humble professional.

He lifted himself up at last, sitting upright and stretching. He swung his legs from the bed, sitting at the edge for a moment. The room was cozy. Framed tech images on a rustic shelf were out of place in the quaint room, and they cycled their holopics just like the ones on his wall in Peakwood. There was an image of the farmer with his son. The frames were programmed to cycle from when his son was young, all the way to a single image of him at Lor's age, stoically gazing back while dressed in sharp roundsman gear. Lor chuffed, cracking a smile at the image. His false dream seemed so long ago.

Small trinkets also peppered the shelf. Draped beads hung over the side of a couple tech frames, surrounded by carved wooden creatures and little vases with single flowers plunked inside. A few of the flowers drooped to the side, threatening to drop their petals onto the floor.

"You're up." Gale stood in the doorway.

"Yeah, I am now. Who's cooking?"

"Your friend, Nico. He's quite the cook."

"Nico?" The last he had seen of his friend was him tipping over into his arms and into the sand. A little spark of hope flickered in his heart.

"Come get some food. The farmer here is very generous."

Lor couldn't refuse a meal. He slid from the bed, loose socks hitting the wooden floor. For being shot in the side, he felt pretty good. He saw his bloody shirt wadded up on the table with Jack's phials, so he swiped it and brushed it out to cover himself. It wasn't clean or pretty, with his swollen spread of blood on the side, but he'd rather the world didn't see his bare, skinny chest.

I should work out or something. If I were stronger, Damaetra would be here with me.

He followed Gale to the next room, conjuring all the questions he was going to ask. A part of him wondered if he was still dreaming... or dead and in Maker's Limbo.

"Hey," Lor said as he strolled into the kitchen.

Dill's head perked up at the sound of his voice. He had bandages circling his head to cover his eyes. "Lor! You are so, so lucky!"

Lor chuckled. "Me? I think I got the least of the attack."

"Nuh-uh, that little thingy that Engineer shot at you sliced right through your stomach. You were bleeding out so fast."

"Who told you that?" Lor took a chair across from his spritely friend.

"Gale did!" He grinned and tried to point at Lor's stepfather leaning against a support beam but ended up pointing at the air between him and Jack. "He did emergency surgery on you *in the desert*!"

Dill's reverence for Lor's stepfather was plain. It sounded as if he wished Gale was his father.

"Well, I *am* a medic," Gale mumbled, turning a little pink from the praise. He tried to deflect the attention to someone else. "But if Jack hadn't come through with these draughts, I just don't know if I could have done it..."

Lor raised an eyebrow at Gale's deflection. Normally, he basked in the praise... why he acted like it was embarrassing was a sight Lor didn't expect.

"Know what else? That projectile that went through you was designed to split into ten splinters when connecting with its target." Dill pulled out a thin silvery toothpick, the length of his hand. It still had a little of Lor's blood on it. "It malfunctioned and stayed this way, making a clean entry!"

"Augh, put that away, Dill!" Nico turned from the stove.

Lor hadn't noticed Nico at the counter. He was ducked down so low that Gale and Jack's bodies blocked his view. Nico wheeled himself to the table.

"Nico..." Lor gasped.

"Please don't." He waved his hand in front of his face. "This is just my reality now."

"Dude, Nico was pretty lucky too, really." Dill said as Nico slid a bowl of the stew in front of his friend. "We've got his legs on ice until we can figure out what to do with 'em." He pawed around the surface of table, attempting to find the bowl.

Lor grimaced at the memory of the bloody pillars tipping over in the sand. The residual image haunted him. He glanced over at Nico, picturing the disembodied legs of his handsome best friend sticking out of a barrel of ice like two cocktail shrimp.

Jack stood next to Gale, slurping up spoonfuls of stew while watching the group at the table with those buggy black goggles. The front door slapped open, and the farmer came through, holding armfuls of desert carrots and stacks of big yellow leaves Lor had seen on the forest floor.

"Oh, you're up! How wonderful!" He strolled to the counter by the stew and let plants roll out onto the surface.

"Yeah, thank you for letting us stay here to heal," Lor croaked, clearing his throat. Gale skidded a can of water to him.

"It's not every day you see something like *that*," the farmer said. "Gale and Jack were champs, just hauling the two of you while the little one was holding a pair of severed legs following close behind. Boy, there was no way I couldn't help! And, well, I was happy to at least have some company for a little while."

"*Little*?" Dill grumbled, sipping from the rim of his stew bowl.

Lor scanned the room. Gale, Jack, Dill, Nico...

"Where's Fowler?" he asked.

The room went silent. Even Dill couldn't see fit to open his smart mouth. They all looked around at each other.

"So, he's dead then?" Lor slumped back into his chair.

"N-no... but he probably *should* be," Gale mumbled. His expression of guilt painted him as a man who had done all he could to save another and failed. It made sense then why he didn't bask in the praise Dill gave him.

"Well, can I see him?"

"Actually, yes. We wanted you to wake up and get your strength first. Please eat something," Jack said, placing a bowl in front of Lor. The steam rose from it, and the fragrance didn't seem quite as nice as it had before.

"Well, *I'm* going to meditate on this," Dill said, scratching his chair from the table. "Maybe I can repurpose it into something cool!" He jumped up too quickly, almost knocking himself over. Following the warm breeze from the open door, he skated his feet across the floor holding the silver projectile that almost killed Lor in one hand and feeling the air with the other.

Lor felt the warmth this time, taking in a deep breath. He spooned stew into his mouth, surprised at how magnificent it was. "Wow, Nico, this is probably the best thing I've ever tasted!"

Nico chuckled. "Apparently Formulators make pretty good cooks too. I was able to recreate that stew from the hole in the wall in Secas market."

"I can teach you much more," Jack said low.

Lor stopped his spoon halfway to his mouth at the comment, then clanked it back into the bowl. "That reminds me... Why did *you* come back to us?" He jabbed a finger at Jack, surprised at his own anger. Gaining his strength back stirred all the memories back into focus.

Gale raised an eyebrow, unfolding his arms from his chest. Lor owed his life to a man who ran in Paerli's circle of fiends.

Jack listed his head toward Lor, and he could see his reflection in those goggles. "You were in trouble."

"That can't be the only reason. Is that all?"

"No." He lowered his shoulders and stretched out his neck. It was an odd gesture that made the man resemble a spider.

The haze of the desert in the air and the piercing yellow eyes that stared back at him suggested more than just good will to help a group of complete strangers.

"Why don't you take off those goggles?" Lor said, then resumed eating. Everyone turned their heads to Jack—even the farmer, who had been busy trimming the desert carrots. Nico jerked his head to the side, eyes wide, and mouthed "don't" to Jack.

"Alright." Jack used his bony fingers to claw at the strap around his head. He slid them from his face, and they slapped against his hands as the elastic recoiled.

The farmer gasped. "You're Yeunish..."

Gale opened his mouth and his forehead wrinkled.

Jack zeroed in on Lor, ignoring all the other eyes on him. "To her, I was just her Foscan servant."

His features really did favor the Foscan.

"But she was *scared* of you." Lor spoke with his mouth full—something Gale had always asked him not to do.

Jack shrugged. "Because I know who she really is. I know her better than Hammer, Crow, or even that jumpy Weggevens, Hare."

Nico flinched at the mention of Hare and frowned.

"But," Jack continued, "she also knows I can kill her."

"What?" Lor about dribbled broth from his cheek.

Jack nodded. "She's too far gone that she thinks I wouldn't use that against her."

"Okay, so what is her deal? What does she really want?"

Jack glared at him with those yellow eyes, eerie and lovely. "Justice."

"Justice? For what? She's, what, twenty...five? What justice does someone like her need?"

"The Locksmith is not twenty-five."

The Locksmith. Paerli had referred to herself by that name in his room the night she violated him. His heart pounded for Damaetra.

"The Locksmith" clung to him throughout the program because she felt the connection before it became real. She touched him that night to coerce his compliance. She didn't care about him at all; she only wanted someone to make her more powerful. When Lor realized this, Jack was already talking again.

"She found me when I was just an orphan in Kanckette. They called me Cricket there, and she never stopped calling me that. She thought it was cute." Jack folded his arms across his dirty coat. Lor swore he saw blood on it—either from him, Nico, Dill, or Fowler. There was no telling whose it was.

"When you were an orphan? A *kid?*" Nico spoke up. His fingers were steepled under his chin with mouth open, ready to catch stray gee flies in the room.

"That's right. She's immortal," Jack said.

She was already immortal when we met.

Jack looked directly at Lor. "And you drank her phial. If you choose to give her what she wants, the curse will be yours also."

"You drank her *what?*" Gale interrupted.

Lor swallowed, remembering the taste of the thick gold in his throat and the feeling as it plunked into his gut, turning his insides sour.

"I drank her... eneris."

"Please explain." Gale folded his arms.

"You don't understand, I had to do it." *Damaetra needed me.*

"I *said* explain."

Lor promised Krik'tha to keep the ritual between them. He hoped if the man knew Lor was faced with this dilemma, he wouldn't be upset with him. So, Lor told what he felt he could. Without too much detail, he glossed over the ritual of self he had to perform to get his own eneris.

"Good Maker, Loren! So that's what happened to your arm?" Gale pointed at the bandage still tied around his forearm, covered in yellow stains from the sand.

"It was the worst thing I've ever done, and it won't ever happen again." Lor said, cupping his palm across the bandage. Tenderness zinged across his arm, and he was curious if Jack already took care of the wound underneath, as he took care of the hole in his side.

He didn't want to talk about the ritual. When Par tried to convince him to do it that night in his room, he knew it was wrong. Bringing it up now felt obscene to his ears. What choice did he have? She had Damaetra and wouldn't take no for an answer. She knew how to play him. She knew how to put her hands on him even if he wouldn't let her. He wanted the questions to stop, and more than anything, he wanted to forget about the whole exchange entirely.

"Can I please see Fowler now?"

Gale led Lor to a guest area in another part of the house that was cordoned off by a digital lock. The room was a personalized den—cozy and full of character. The farmer had a projecting holofilm setup with surround sound speakers in the ceiling and walls. There were game tables and lights strung around the room. It was an interesting choice for his ailing mentor to be locked inside.

They moved to the far end of the room where a wide gray couch was pushed into a nook. Lor saw fresh scratches in the wood floor from the legs being scraped across it. They moved this couch into the nook special for Fowler. On the couch itself was a covered lump.

The malformed bird man resembled his old friend, but there wasn't much left to recognize. His lips were twisted to the side, unnaturally positioned under his right earlobe. The skin stretched from the left side of his face, dotted with specks of glossy black beak material. Lor thought the human mouth used to sit under the beak and someone twisted it violently to the side, causing the hardened beak to fragment.

He was in a deep sleep. One eye was open and fixed to the side of his face like a bird, but the flesh around it was lobed and wet. It was wrenched opposite the beak lips, causing his face to resemble a half-twisted cloth. The bird eye was glassy, covered in film, and staring at the wall. The other eye was in the human position, closed.

The man's head was stabilized to face upward, but there were wrinkles in his neck as if the act of positioning his head this way was the wrong way to do it. His slender, pointed fingers rested over his chest. They rose and fell with his heavy drugged breathing. Black feathers stuck out of his flesh in jellied red patches, and one shoulder was still dislocated backwards the way it had been seconds before he took flight.

"That projectile did *not* malfunction in this one..." Gale said in a low voice as to not wake him. "My guess is some, if not all, the splinters pierced special transformation muscle and nerve bundles while in his bird form, forcing him to turn back into a man after being shot. Kind of."

Fowler's face twitched, twisting the flesh tight briefly, then releasing it.

"Can you fix him?" Lor whispered.

Gale shrugged. "I've never treated anyone like this, so I don't know. Those bundles may be irreparable because he was small when he was shot. They may have torn clean through them—and I just don't have the knowledge to repair them."

"The man will die." Jack strolled into the room. "As a Weggevens that is stuck like this, his hours are already numbered."

Jack's voice roused the human eye, which slowly blinked open. There were nodules of crust at the corners, and the bird eye didn't blink with the human one. It remained staring at the wall. The lips that were pulled to the side moved, perpetually pursed and taut. He mumbled something inaudible, and it was strange to see such a malformation move like a kissing fish.

"Lor?" His black eye rolled over to see him. Flecks of blood decorated the white of the human eye.

"I'm here," Lor said.

"Good. Good." The noise he made sounded like he was chewing on a wad of meat too big for his mouth. The human eye blinked, and a tear swelled in the corner of it.

"I'm so sorry, Fowler." Lor didn't know what to say. The silence of Gale and Jack didn't help, and he was alone in this conversation.

Fowler smiled with the eye. If he could have done it with the lips, he would, but they were frozen in place. "I'm... going to... die." He drew out the words as he was able. Lor wanted to put a reassuring hand on his shoulder, but his body was so broken that he was afraid he would make it worse.

"Remember... what I... said to you... when we...met?" A spot of drool trickled at the corner of the puckered lips.

"Yes, I remember. You said the Guild is a gift, I have to work to make it a skill."

"Work... is not... for the... lazy."

Lor felt the sting of his words. He had been lazy. He had been ungrateful. He positioned himself into a path that he would never take and, like a true lazy person, never tried to learn another way. The Maker had other plans for him, and now he must work harder to undo what he had already done.

"I will work for it, I promise."

Fowler's contorted neck twitched as if he was trying to nod. "Start... now. Take... my... eneris."

The more he spoke, the weaker he got. Lor looked at Gale, who had scrunched his face into the concentrated look Lor knew so well when he was studying a new gadget or working on med charts at the table. Gale's eyes were fixed on Fowler. Lor glanced at Jack, who nodded his head in agreement.

"Fowler, I..." Lor stuttered.

"Take it... Before it's... too late."

Lor's eyes burned, and water swelled onto his bottom eyelids. Fowler was the first Weggevens he ever met. He was brilliant and knew how to work his skill to benefit himself. He had connections that helped him get into Guild Central. He took care of Lor even when he was still a stranger. Lor reached his hands out, fingers twitching with hesitation before placing the tips on a featherless spot on the man's arm.

Lor closed his eyes and concentrated on the man while using Krik'tha's soothing voice. The colors didn't come this time, and he saw himself seeing the world through the bird eye. He moved backwards in time, moving out of the room, being carried by Gale and Jack. He was in the sand, crying out as best he could, but words wouldn't form. He was in pain, feeling every muscle contract and squeeze him into unnatural positions. He was in the air, determined to find help.

His life was moving backwards for the past day, until a dilation of time put him back on the train, meeting the young recruit waiting to go to the program, unsure of himself and worried. He tapped his foot, waiting for the train to take him back to Secas for a mentorship assignment with a young Weggevens that skin changed into a wild dog.

Another dilation, and he was back at Heart Island, just before his Guild gift. His hair was sharp black and cut short. He was surrounded by young women, trying to talk to him, get his attention. Tall and muscular, with large blue eyes, the Danashi's charm fueled his allure. He was never ugly, not then. Not now. He was telling a raunchy joke when his whole vision exploded into an iridescent rainbow splashing over the scene, melting it away like warm cream until there was nothing but black.

"Hold out your hand," Jack ordered. Lor obeyed without question, feeling the smooth phial lip scrape over his palm.

The blackness wouldn't shake, and Lor was left wondering whether he went blind with Dill. As the scraping continued, light began to filter into his eyes, and a blurry room surrounded him with shapes moving about frantically beyond the film.

He saw a blob on the couch, details to be left to the imagination until his vision returned.

Why did I see everything? Why was it more than just his last moments?

"His name was Jacob," Lor croaked. Saying his name out loud reassured him he would never forget it. Gale grunted as the phial continued its journey over his palm.

"How long was I out?" The shapes of his father and Jack sharpened into focus.

Jack bottled up a fourth phial of the most fascinating eneris Lor could have conjured in his imagination. "Not even a standard minute," he said.

Lor glanced at the couch. The corpse lay there, dry and sunken like he remembered Tad lying in the sand the day Val took his eneris. The tightened joints and muscles were in the same position, but slack. Lor nudged the skin suit's shoulder, feeling nothing but sharp bone underneath wafer-thin skin. His eyes stung again, and he felt like the monster he knew he was becoming.

"Jacob Fowler," he mumbled.

"This is incredibly rare eneris," Jack said, ignoring Lor. "You captured it while he was halfway between, so it came out... different."

Lor held out a hand, and Jack gave him one of the phials. They were round-bottomed phials with ground glass stoppers. Decorative chiseling on the surface of each phial formed a diamond pattern over the surface, and each diamond had a spectrum of pastel colors swirling in their facets. It looked like several opals set into the glass.

"It's called chromatis. Very rare indeed." Jack poked at the phial in Lor's hand.

Lor wasn't thinking about the rarity of the life force he just pulled from his friend. He peered at the figure on the couch again. If he weren't dried like meat crackers, Lor could have sworn Fowler would sit up and ask him for a glass of water or a bowl of Nico's vitality stew.

Gale noticed Lor staring at the man, and he slowly pulled the covering up over Fowler's head.

CHAPTER 28

Gale and His Son
Loren

THE SECOND SUN WAS NEARLY gone, casting a mix of gray and purple shadows through the window of Lor's eclectic room. He wondered if Krik'tha was worried about him. One more night with the farmer, then it was back to Guild Central. He didn't have time. Damaetra didn't have time.

"I brought you more water to help with your blood loss." Gale strode into the room, handing Lor a few cans.

"Thanks." Lor cracked open a can and chugged half of it.

"Fowler has been taken care of, just so you know. The farmer has a nice spot he dedicated to him out in the fields."

"Hopefully his body isn't feeding the desert carrots or sweet cane."

"No, nothing like that." Gale frowned.

Lor chugged more of the water. No revelation tonight had quelled his fear over Damaetra's capture. He swallowed hard, licking a rogue drop from his lip as he imagined that strongman brute with her tiny neck in his fat arm. There was no time to waste, but as Val had told him what felt like ages ago, his journey would be hard. At that moment, he wrestled with true rage. Paerli's angry second heart felt like gentle tapping compared to the unbridled murder on his mind.

Gale took a seat in the same chair Lor found him in when he first woke up. Looking at the man now, his presence in the room was uncanny and unusual. Gale's face was relaxed, but wary. Years of secrets were etched in the lines of his brow, not so unlike the ones he saw on Val.

"I've been meaning to ask you..." Lor took another swig of the water. "How did you get to me so fast?"

Gale stared at his feet. His hands were in his lap properly, which was not like him. Normal Gale rubbed his face in stress or frustration or fidgeted with some med trinket. Normal Gale would have dismissed Lor's question. "You sent me a message, and I was worried."

"And? The train takes longer than that."

That burst of sand, just like Hare, as I was bleeding out...

Gale let out a sharp exhale. "I'm glad I got here when I did."

Lor studied him for a moment. The man he'd always known as a cantankerous, easily angered and jealous man, sat before him holding an old secret. To Lor, it was obvious.

"You're a Weggevens, aren't you?"

Gale stopped looking at his shoes, and his dark eyes met Lor's. "It's been a while, but... yes. I'm a runner."

Lor didn't say anything; he knew and wanted to hear it from his stepfather.

"I never told you because I didn't want you to get discouraged while in the program. I... I also am not happy about it."

"You're not happy about super speed? I would much rather be that than this." Lor lifted his hands up, knowing they were stained with the death of his friend and future countless others... maybe even more of his friends.

"You don't understand."

"Explain it to me."

"Didn't your instructor tell you anything about what life is like for a Weggevens?"

"I saw one die on the island," Lor cut in.

"I see. What type was he?"

"Strongman. It was a really nasty death."

Gale nodded and chewed on his cheek. "That's not the only thing that can happen to a Weggevens. Every time I use my ability, it saps my life force. My eneris."

Lor had a suspicion, but he didn't know for sure. Most of his class dreaded the Weggevens call, but no one voiced why. He could have been a strongman, a runner, a skin changer, and maybe something else that he didn't know about. He didn't know that it slowly killed them, until Jack said it about Fowler.

"So... did coming to me take a bit of your life from you?"

Gale rubbed his face like normal, making Lor feel more relaxed that he was being himself. "Jack is a talented man."

"Yes. And?"

"He makes a special"—Gale glanced around the room and put a hand next to his mouth to whisper—"drug."

"What kind of"—Lor bent down to whisper like Gale—"drug?"

"It's unconventional and would be very frowned upon if the Seven Cities knew about it. But it works. It gives me that chunk of eneris back. I don't know how it works, but it does."

When Lor saw Horace with Jack in Secas, he wondered if they were associated for the same reasons.

"So, you're doing okay right now? I mean, he gave you this special forbidden drug?"

"I'm glad he was here... otherwise, I'd be a little worse for wear." Gale glanced away to change the subject.

"What's in it?"

"In the drug? I don't think you want to know."

"I definitely do now." Lor grinned and took a seat on the bed.

Gale sighed and locked eyes with Lor. He stared at him for a good moment with dark brown eyes obscured by the thick frame of his glasses. Brown stubble covered his scalp in the areas where he still had hair. He must not have been able to shave it off in a while.

"You know when you pull the essence out of a specific thing either living or dead? It has a color to it, right? Aquatic creatures give you blue, land animals give you red..."

"Yes, I know all these things. And?" Lor was impatient. He had other questions and not enough time to ask.

"Well, there's a special one. It comes from..." Gale looked around the room again, as if searching for eavesdroppers, or hidden listeners in the walls. "It comes from people. It's silver."

Lor saw this. He saw Tad's silver. The thought of his eneris being used to be shot into someone else's vein was a cruel joke.

"So you inject *people* into you?"

Gale huffed. "Well, a mixture of silver, green, and white. I told you it would be frowned on." He rubbed his head again.

"Could you... could Jack be *taken away* for that?"

"Possibly. But if I need to be there to help you stand off against those that hurt you, I'll take the risk."

Lor didn't know what to say. This man was never his real father but raised him as his own and protected him, even if he was grumpy while doing it. Did Gale know he already knew he was Yeunish?

"Who is my real father?" Lor blurted.

Gale flinched at the question, then cleared his throat. "I-I, um, well... He was an Anglia that your mother knew from grade school."

Lor bit a lip and furrowed his brow while nodding his head and taking in the information. "Except, by '*mother*,' you mean someone else. Not the woman who died when I was young. Right?"

Gale raised an eyebrow, wringing his hands. His skin was dry, making loud *shuff, shuff, shuff* sounds as he rubbed them together. "That's right."

"Well, who is she? Is she alive? Is my real father alive? Where are they now?" Lor's questions shot from his mouth in a stream. If they were upsetting to Gale, the man didn't show it. It was as if he expected this conversation sooner or later.

"Your mother... she's alive, yes. Your father is not."

His mother had to be Foscan. It was the only way he could be who he was with an Anglia father. The image on the wall before he left for the program flashed in his mind. It was the look on her face as she held him, and the tenderness in her touch as she fed him.

He thought about her. His real mother, Dag the Small. She watched him at night, that was clear now. She loved him in secret, enduring Gale's anger to stay close to her son. If he ever got another day on Roseaarde, he would love her back so fiercely.

"Is my mother... is she Dag?"

Gale swallowed, examining the floor again. His shoulders drooped and he rubbed his already pink scalp with the brown stubble. "Yes. It is her."

"Why are you so mean to her?"

"I'm sorry, Lor. It's the way it has been."

"Could you stop? Please?"

"For you I will."

For me? Why is he suddenly treating me as special? More special than Eva?

"Why do I look the way I do?"

"I don't know. I think your father may have had some Mesaman in him from far down his ancestry."

"Did you know him?"

"A little."

"Why did you want me in the program if you knew what I was?"

"Slow down."

Lor took another long swig of the water. He reached down and played his fingers over the dent in his side, wondering how he got here in life. Had he been granted permission to stow away in his basement bedroom, he wouldn't be here, and life would carry on. He wouldn't have Damaetra.

The two sat in silence for some amount of time. Lor tugged at the band across his arm, pulling the knot and letting it slide off onto the floor. Beneath the bandage was a matching puckered pink scar, underneath his implant scar. Jack healed it after all. Gale peered at them.

"I've been meaning to ask you about *that*," he said, pointing at the crescent where the implant used to be.

Lor ran his thumb over the lumpy flesh. It pulled in odd angles, typical for the back-alley surgery he performed on it. "I cut it out."

"Why?"

"It was after the strongman died. We were scared. We thought it was the implant."

Gale sighed. "Well, at least you know now."

"Know what?"

"That the implant doesn't give you your ability."

Lor huffed. "Is this some kind of weird conspiracy? Why are we told we have to get this thing in our arms to make our ability come to us? I feel like I'm being left out of some secret conversation at the expense of my soul."

That thing is still in Damaetra's arm. Damaetra is with that group of animals.

Lor's brow prickled with new sweat, courtesy of the water he was putting into his body.

Gale rolled up his sleeve and held out the underside of his smooth arm— no evidence of implantation or removal. "It *is* some kind of weird conspiracy. You see that I don't have one, yet... here we are."

"So, what is the conspiracy?"

Gale folded his shirt back over his arm and shrugged. "It's different for everyone."

"What is it to *you*?"

Gale studied his son. "To me... well, I think it's simple. I just think it's how the Seven Cities spy on us. Control us. Others have their own opinions."

"So why in Gehenna would you want to send me there? Let Eva live there?"

"Watch your language."

"I mean it, though. Why?"

"Loren... your heritage puts a huge target on your head. If the farmer knew you were *Yeunish*, he might turn you in for a hefty sum." He whispered the word, regretting speaking it out loud.

Lor clicked his tongue. "He wouldn't do that. Would he?"

"You never know. He may already have told them about Jack. Look at this place. You don't think a good seventy-five thousand plat payday wouldn't be on his mind?"

"It's *that* much?"

"Last I checked, it was."

"Well, Paerli and her goons know. What's to keep them from turning me or Jack in?"

"Something tells me they're up to something greater than plats. Otherwise, the roundsmen would be here by now."

Lor opened the next can of water and glanced up at the farmer's framed photo sequence of his own son. It happened to be sitting on the image of the young man in uniform, staring back at Lor, as if letting him know he knew his secret.

Gale put a hand on Lor's arm. "Everything I have done has been to protect you from them. When you were born, I was shocked at how... *normal* you looked. Nothing like Yeunish at all. Dag begged us... begged me to raise you as my son so that you could live a normal life. By living in the Seven Cities with the way you look and holding a Guild certificate... I was sure you'd just fly under their radar."

"Why do they hate the Yeunish?"

Why do they hate me? And who are they?

Lor couldn't specifically relate to the plight of his kind. Gale was right: he had given him a normal life, and he had a lot left to learn.

"It's another conspiracy, I'm afraid."

Lor rolled his eyes. "And everyone has a different theory. How convenient."

"This conspiracy goes back hundreds of years. To be honest, I think people just forgot the reason and continued hating the Yeunish, business as usual."

Lor pictured his golden room, with the large bookcase spanning his wall. He saw it clearly, *The History and Annals of Guild Abilities and Memberships: Formative Years, Tome 1*. The letters were scripted on the side in an embossed shimmering black over green binding. His lack of interest allowed the book to sit on the shelf, unperturbed and in pristine condition. He wondered if there was a clue in that book about why his kind was hated so much.

"I wouldn't trust history books," Gale blurted out as if reading Lor's mind. "At least, not any of the more recent ones. The Seven Cities control that, too."

Lor sighed. Dill's book had a few things in there. There was a reason his fellow recruits called them fairy tales, but he wanted to look into them further. Perhaps this book was yet uncorrupted by the influences of the cities. If he survived Mount Gehenna, he would study it.

The thought of the mountain chilled his spine. He had to save the love of his life. He had to save Damaetra. What could they possibly be putting her through?

"So you're going to help us? Fight back, that is?" Lor asked.

Gale's face lit up at the change in subject.

"Of course I will. Your girlfriend is still captive, right? Damaetra, is it?"

"She isn't just my girlfriend. I *love* her. They took her from me, and I need to get her back." Lor's voice shook.

Gale's expression melted. He pulled his son into an embrace Lor had never experienced with him. If he had, it was ages ago and lost in the catalogue of his memories. Everything in the past week came rushing at him, and his weak vessel of human flesh was bursting at the seams. Before he realized it, he wept into Gale's shirt.

"How did we get here, Dad? *How?*" His voice came out muffled in Gale's arm as he shook.

"We'll get through this, I promise."

PART 3

CHAPTER 29

Brotherly Love
LOREN

THE NEXT MORNING HAD A certain smell in the air, like sharp electricity and minerals. The farm wasn't far from the edge of the Span, and the Desert Maelstrom would be there soon. Lor woke up from a dreamless sleep, thanks to one of Jack's concoctions. He swung his legs around from the edge of the bed, and a neatly folded note slapped the floor.

> *Loren, I'm sorry about what happened. I take responsibility for not doing something sooner. I left you a few phials of the stuff I gave you last night. I also left your friend Nico some recipes and instructions to help him learn in the next few days. There's not much time. I believe the farmer made a call to the roundsmen because of me. So, I had to leave prematurely. Don't worry, I will meet you near Gehenna, where you need to go. Check code 732441 on your e-disk for the location. It's very important that you meet me there in three days. If not, the storm will come, and they will have already broken your girl to take my place. It is her plan.*
>
> *Hurry,*
>
> *Jack*

Lor glanced at the side table to see exactly three phials of bluish eneris. *Jack must have slid this note under my ass.*

Gale had told him about his fear that the farmer might try to turn Jack into a payday. He thanked the Maker that he didn't know about him too. Despite all that, the farmer didn't seem like a bad guy—just someone trying to make their way in this twisted world.

Lor hopped from the bed and threw on the same bloody t-shirt, anxious to get back to Guild Central for a real shower and a talk with Krik'tha. He gathered up the phials, sliding them into the utility pouch Nico gave him, careful not to break the glass and make a further mess of things. Feeling the cold glass reminded him of the chromatis he pulled from Fowler the night before. Did Jack leave it with Nico?

A muffled radio chatter resonated from the kitchen. Sweat prickled at Lor's brow as he spun to watch the door. He had to get out of there.

Stuffing Jack's note in the side of his boot, he put an ear to the door, trying to make out the conversation.

"I don't know, I'm sorry. He was here last night... slippery bastard," the farmer pleaded.

Bastard?

Lor crinkled his nose. Maybe he was a bad guy after all. He turned to the mantle to see the same image of his son in roundsman gear was frozen on the picture frame.

Damn.

Lor creaked open the door, triggering glances from the farmer and two roundsmen. One of them was the farmer's son. Dill sat at the table with the same wrapping around his head, listening to the room.

"Oh, you're up!" the farmer said. "Sorry you had to wake up to this." He leaned on the counter, in front of several foods half-chopped and dripping their juices.

"Where's Gale and Nico?" Lor ruffled his hand through his hair, trying to appear as casual as he could for the surprise visit.

"What happened to *you*?" the partner roundsman asked, pointing to the bloody splotch on his side.

Lor swallowed. "Oh, uh, that? Just an accident with some, a-ah, red eneris. My friend is... learning."

The roundsman peered at Lor. "I hear there was a Yeunish Formulator here yesterday. You wouldn't happen to know anything about that, would you?"

"A-ah Yeunish Formulator? Can't say that I do." He hoped his lie was believable enough to get him out of there with his friends and Gale.

The farmer didn't move. He stared at the ground, trying not to make eye contact with Lor.

"I see," the farmer's son said. "Well, there is clearly no Yeuni here, so we will be on our way." He nodded at his father.

"Adam, please come visit sometim—" The door slammed shut as the farmer called out to his son.

Did he report Jack just to see his son?

Lor wondered what kind of roundsman he would have made. Would he have gotten that far? Would he cast off Gale so easily?

Nico wheeled into the room shortly after, sensing the change in the air. "What did I miss?" he asked.

The farmer just turned back to the counter, busying himself with the half-prepared foods.

"Thank you, sir, for helping us out. If there is anything we can do for you, please let us know," Lor interrupted, making a chopping motion at his neck toward Nico.

Gale emerged from the locked den. He carried a heavy light blue oblong case about the right size for a pair of human legs in one hand and a black Formulator's chest with his med bag hooked around his other arm. Nico reached out for the Formulator chest, and Gale set it onto his thighs. He moved to Dill and tugged at his sleeve. Dill stood silently and held Gale's elbow. Gale strode up to the farmer, shook his hand, and slipped him a modest stack of plats, then waved everyone out the door. It was a strange and silent goodbye, but their risk was clear.

As they left the cabin, a large jumper idled in the sand just beyond the patch of sweet cane, summoned there by Gale early enough to make their escape. Lor pushed Nico's chair through the soft blend of grass and sand as Dill hung on Gale's arm. They folded Nico's chair and stashed it in the compartment below, along with the set of cases and bags.

Once settled in the cabin, Gale ordered the Danashi driver back to Guild Central, along with a short lecture to the rest of them about the importance of secrets. Lor's secret.

Lor felt guilty for egging Jack on. Curiouser still was the fact that Jack let him. He blew out a sigh, thankful he was smart enough to leave in the middle of the night.

The jumper ride was smooth and painless, pulling up around the courtyard fountain, where Lor caught a Foscan standing nearby, craning his neck every which way, wearing a lone eye patch.

"Krik'tha!" Lor ran up to the man and hugged him. The little servant returned the embrace in shock. He offered to help carry bags, making a move for the blue oblong case, but Gale stopped him and told him he'd handle it.

"I was worried for you," Krik'tha told Lor.

"I'm okay."

"You're bleeding..." Krik'tha pointed at Lor's shirt. He forgot how unkempt he must look.

"It's nothing, I'm fine. Is the Hall mad at me for missing days?"

"No, no, nothing like that. I told them you fell ill with parasite. You were 'throwing up' all day and night. As gift, they left for you soup and salt packet rations."

Lor laughed, patting him on the shoulder.

Ironic... I do have a parasite... its name is Paerli Harea.

Lor introduced Krik'tha to Nico, Dill, and Gale. "Can Gale come with me to Reaper's Hall as a guest? He's my dad."

"Oh! Yes, of course. Halls allow family unlimited times."

"Perfect."

Krik'tha told Lor he would lead Dill to Engineer Hall and would be back at his room soon.

"Servant can go to any Hall," Krik'tha said, leading Dill along. Even when blind, Dill knew he was at the mercy of a Foscan, and he wore a deep scowl.

They planned to meet again at noon to begin preparations for Damaetra's rescue mission. As they started their paths toward each respective hall, Lor stopped and called out to both Dill and Nico. Dill turned toward his voice and grinned. Nico spun around in his chair and tilted his head. Jogging up to the wheelchair, he bent over and hugged his friend. Nico squeezed him back, and they stayed there for a moment.

"You were right, and I'm sorry," Lor said.

"You have nothing to be sorry for," Nico responded.

"You're my best friend and I should have listened to your warnings. Now we're here, mangled to hell with Damaetra in Par's clutches." Lor raised himself to look at his two friends.

"Consider it a *very* hard lesson learned. But we're going to fix it. We'll get Dame back." Nico grinned, making Lor appreciate the man's handsome features. The tanned skin and ruddy blushed dimples meant he was alive.

"You don't know how much I appreciate both of you."

"Aw, you're going to make me leak water from my eye sockets. If I can even do that anymore." Dill smiled while pressing the bandage over his eyes.

Lor chuckled. "I especially appreciate my horny comedian."

Dill and Nico laughed while Krik'tha grinned with pink in his pale cheeks.

Lor cleared his throat. "I mean it though. I love you guys."

He ruffled Nico's curly hair. Nico smiled, slapping at the air in front of him.

"We love you too," Nico said.

Grabbing Dill, Lor pulled his little friend in for a hug.

"Yeah, yeah, you're my boy..." Dill said, grinning. He slapped Lor's back. "We've got work to do."

The first thing Lor planned to do was shower, ridding himself of the desert funk and that stare-inducing bloody shirt. He was consumed by the contents of the Formulator's chest. Was Fowler in there?

No one gave Lor and Gale a second glance when they made their way past the front desk with the same ornery attendant nose-deep in his e-disk puzzles. The man never moved.

Winding through the second floor, he couldn't help but glance at room 209... Paerli's apartment. The door was wide open, and a few Foscans were inside cleaning.

She must have put in her "notice."

His heart weighed heavy at the sight, and the parasite squirmed inside of him as the memories of their world together for nearly the past standard year had come to a brutal end.

They stepped inside Lor's apartment, untouched and clean. No plat boxes, or any other boxes, waited at the door. No letters, no nothing. It was a cold, empty room. The salt and broth ration packets sat at his tiny kitchen counter, piled up where Krik'tha must have left them.

"I'll be out in a minute," Lor called to Gale, closing himself inside the sleek black bathroom lined with strips of gold. Several frosted white techlights flickered on at his presence, and for the first time, he noticed they were all in the shape of birds.

Fowler.

He stared at them for a moment. The memory of the man transforming to get help stuck in his mind. "Thank you, Jacob," he said to no one.

When activating the shower, the water couldn't have come out of the tap more perfect—temperature, pressure... standard of living for Guild members. Something as simple as water spared no expense for the elite, while his own kind was practically hunted to extinction.

If Maker willing we can save her, would Damaetra still even want me, knowing now that I'm Yeunish?

He let the water trickle over him. It moved in slow waves over skinny shoulders and legs, pooling in the basin in a mixture of yellow dust and residual blood. The wound in his side had already gone yellow-green, with a shallow fleshy crater at the center. He poked it with a finger, and it no longer felt tender as it had. The light green tincture-soaked patch was a work of genius. Did Jack use the same patch on Dill's eyes? Nico's leg stumps?

He traced a finger down his scarred arm. The thin purplish switch wound running vertical from the ritual had closed. Jack did patch it after all, and the scar was healing.

He would have to learn a lot in the next days before meeting Jack at Gehenna. If the past few days taught him anything, it was that he really didn't know anything at all.

Satisfied with his shower, he stepped out to grab another t-shirt from the wardrobe. It was a black one this time—good for hiding stains. He took a sniff of the armpit, and it had a freshly laundered aroma. He wondered if Krik'tha ordered laundry service while he was gone. The Foscan was turning out to be quite the helpful companion. He paired the shirt with a loose pair of tan pants with roomier pockets. As he got dressed, he heard Gale and Krik'tha laughing through the partition.

The men stopped talking when Lor came into the room. The Foscan watched him with that single white eye.

"Krik'tha, I'm going to need your help," Lor said.

"Anything, what is it you need?"

Making Connections
LOREN

"THERE IS A SPECIAL, HOW you say, practice area for all Guild members. Is mostly empty," Krik'tha said, leading the group to a circular outdoor area behind the main white hub building.

"Why's that?" Dill asked, holding on to Gale. He still wore the bandage over his eyes. Lor had a morbid curiosity to flick off the bandage to see the shallow wells where his eyes used to be.

"Most people like to stay alone, or be with their own," Krik'tha said. He pointed an arc around the courtyard to various booths set up with attendants lounging at them, bored. "Many good resources for practice."

"What about me?" Lor asked. "Surely they don't just have dead stuff lying around in there."

"No, not dead stuff, but other good stuff for use. I show you."

Decorative ivy wound around finely chiseled statues in the courtyard. Between statues the booths were spread out, with their bored attendants and specialized workbenches. A few people meandered around the courtyard, but mainly to sit at a bench and eat rations. Krik'tha was right—there weren't many people around. It was a sore waste of amazing resources.

"Each booth has material. But I warn you, it is not free, so decide wisely."

Nico had that same square black bag hooked on his wheelchair. It swayed as he wriggled in the chair. Lor had no doubt Jack left him with recipes and materials beyond their skill. Nico was smart. Lor had faith in his friend.

"I can help too, in whatever way you need me." Gale led Dill to a nearby table to sit down. "I know a lot about the different Guilds. Plus, Loren's sister is an Engineer."

"I plan on making something with this," Dill announced, pulling out the projectile.

Lor made a face. "Did you have that in your pocket? Or did you have it up your hole?"

Dill's face puckered, then he grinned. "Guess."

"Really?" Lor sighed.

"What? It's good material, right? Waste not..."

Nico plopped the bag on the table, and it opened up in a trifold. Parchment cards were neatly banded together in the lower corner, with several empty phials, mixing vessels, a small hot plate, and bits of material on one side. The remaining two sections were full of different colored solutions. Some appeared already formulated, while others were raw.

Lor found the four hanging phials of chromatis. They dangled and shimmered in the light.

"That's Fowler," he said. He poked one with his finger and their bottoms clinked against each other.

Nico reared back, swallowing without a word.

"I'm sorry, was that weird?"

"No, no. It's okay. It's just... you know. It's Fowler."

Lor picked up the stack of cards. They were handwritten in a slanted, elegant script, with each card having the instructions for some recipe.

"Looks like Jack did things the old-fashioned way," Nico said, taking one of the cards and running a finger over the script. "Nice handwriting."

"Here, this one is very valuable." Lor flicked a card from the stack, one with the words, *Verdigris Mend*. "I think this is the one he used on the hole in my side."

Nico flipped through the stack of cards, reading off a bunch of names:

Red mash, ivory saltpeter, lapis evening, verdigris biosore, wittis rejuvenate, jaune spirit...

He flipped to the back of the stack to find a card not in the usual script, but in bold letters: *Last Grudge*.

Lor swiped the card, turning it over in his hand, seeing a distinct ingredient in the recipe... chromatis.

"He must have just written this recipe last night before bolting," Lor said.

"He had to taste it, you know." Nico scrunched his nose.

"It's a dirty job, but someone's gotta do it."

Nico took the card back, examining it. "I've got to make it. I wonder what it'll do?" He turned the card over again. "The use says, 'Toss with extreme prejudice.'"

"*Definitely* make some of those. Oh, and ask Gale which one of these other ones he needs." Lor ran a finger over the edge of the cards in Nico's hand.

Nico bobbed his head, sorting through them.

Dill sat still across from them quietly with the projectile lying across his palms. Gale nudged at him, trying to instruct him better on how to hear its potential and send influential messages back.

"Shhh, I'm channeling my *inner eye*," Dill mocked, stroking the projectile like a pet.

Nico frowned. "I don't know how much help I'm going to be in this chair." He flicked the wheel, and the flexible material squeaked.

"*Actually*," Dill drew out the word, eyes still closed, "I might be able to help with that."

Lor leaned over to Nico and whispered, "If we ever need Dill to calm down, we could always chuck him a piece of metal." Nico chuckled.

"I heard that." Dill grinned, then gasped. "I think I've got it!" He hopped up from the table, nearly falling back on his butt. "I need a workbench now, before I lose it!"

"There's that energy again," Lor said.

Krik'tha ushered him to a workstation nestled between two booths, equipped with standard shaping tools. He guided Dill's hands over the various pieces, explaining what they were.

"Gale"—Krik'tha motioned—"do you mind, ah, supervising? Some of these tools make fire."

Gale jogged to the table, where Dill was already twisting and pulling apart the projectile. Several splinters clattered to the table, as he began assembling them in a line.

The tool bench had a coolant line spanning its length, giving it an interesting design. The Danashi's lithe hands moved over different objects on the table as he poked, pinched, and prodded. He stuck his tongue from the corner of his mouth.

Nico shrugged and rolled to a different workbench. Before long, his upper half swayed back and forth as he mixed various concoctions from the cards. Lor could hear him mumbling to himself in fits and revelations. Occasionally, he saw Nico drop a little of the raw eneris on his finger for a taste.

"I'm practically useless here," Lor said to Krik'tha.

"No, no, you are not useless at all. Trust me, when time comes, you will know the depth of your gift."

A pop sound came from Dill's bench, and several booth operators peered around their windows.

"Sorry!" he shouted, continuing his work.

Krik'tha tugged Lor's arm. "Here, let us gather green eneris. Is easy."

They wandered toward one of the booths with a sign above that said: SOURCE. Lor paid for a box of the same cacti he saw in the desert, as well as several bundles of round vegetables. The total came to only ten plat, which he thought was a reasonable price to pay for more practice.

"Okay, now remember from before, yes? Cactus might sting, but vegetable is harmless."

"I remember the cacti…" Lor held the plump succulent in his palm. He remembered the buzz in his flesh from the poison. After nearly dying in the desert, the stubborn little plant took on a new meaning for him. It meant to survive, no matter what—and Lor intended to do the same.

Green juice dripped into his palm before Krik'tha gathered a phial for him.

"Oh! Oh!" the man said, fumbling around with a bottle from the dumpy brown satchel he always carried.

Krik'tha scooped the neck of a squat triangular phial right as a drop wiggled at the edge of Lor's palm. As green fluid dribbled into his palm, the cacti wrinkled inward, resembling a wad of crumpled parchment, drained of its color.

Lor picked up the next cactus, feeling the tingle in his fingertips from the obstinate fruit as more liquid poured into his palm.

"Slow down." Krik'tha bottled the first phial, to work another one from the satchel.

He couldn't slow down. Paerli was a skilled Reaper, and he was determined to be her true match. He had to beat her at her own game and save Damaetra. If it meant squeezing the life out of some prickly cacti and tubers, he would do it. Krik'tha's hands moved quickly from one phial to the next as Lor dumped crumpled wad after crumbled wad onto the table.

"Master Loren, you must slow down," the man warned again, gathering another phial.

Ire burned in his gut the more he thought about lying in the hot sand, feeling nothing but cold, hearing Paerli's distant cackle while taking his love away. The tingling in his fingertips raged and his cheeks flushed. The cacti pulsed green from its pores, squirting ribbons over his hand onto the ground, shrinking and shrinking. The crumpled wad frayed at the edges, curling and darkening into char.

"Lor, slow down!" Krik'tha stopped collecting the eneris as a black tar oozed from the dried ball. The tingling scorched his fingers as his hand and arm went numb. It was at that point he realized he wasn't focused on the plants *or* the eneris.

"Drop it, drop it now." Krik'tha slapped at Lor's arm, causing the ball to fall from his grip and land on the ground. It continued to wither and blacken until it became a puddle of tar.

Residue clung to his palm, seeping into the cracks of his hand. A few booth operators glared at Krik'tha for slapping at Lor.

"What happened?" Lor said as he stared at the filth. Krik'tha took a cloth from his satchel and wiped the black stain.

"You go too far. This is fastest way to yaslecha."

"What? You're joking, right?"

"Is no joke." He scrubbed at the ooze while Lor stood there letting him. "Do not let your emotions guide you in this."

"I-I'm sorry, I got carried away."

Krik'tha clicked his tongue and opened his mouth to say something when Dill called out from his bench.

"Hey guys, come here! Check it out!"

As they gathered at Dill's workstation, he held out the projectile. The metal had been worked into a thin rectangle with hammer divots pounded in an irregular pattern along the surface. It was curved into an arc, with sharp needles protruding on the inner side, right at the center.

"What is it?" Nico asked.

"You'll see, hold on..." Dill placed the object on the table, reaching up to fumble with the bandage over his eyes.

Lor took in a deep breath, curious about the mess underneath, but mortified all the same. When the wrappings fell to the table, Dill felt around to find the object once again. He still had eyes, though covered in a hazy white film with speckles of blood at the corners. A swift horizontal slash extended beyond the sockets toward his ears. Gale had stitched the wounds closed, with evidence of Jack's patch coloring the scar into a purple mouth.

"This is going to suck but be totally worth it," Dill said as his fingers found purchase on the new object. He brought it to his face, pinching around at the sharpened spikes in the center.

Lor swallowed. "Ah, Dill, are you sure about—"

Dill ignored him and slid the spikes around his eyes, pushing hard and gritting his teeth. Grunting, the grating sound of his teeth scratched Lor's ears. Nico held his breath.

A small button in the center lit up green once the device was fully in place. Dill moved his finger across the device like an inch worm to find the button. When he pressed down, it lit up purple. A trickle of blood dribbled down his cheek, and he dabbed it with a sleeve. He looked around at the group.

"Aw, don't look at me like that!" Dill said. "Now I can see all your ugly mugs again. Isn't that cool?"

"You can see with that thing?" Lor asked, trying to touch it but getting a swat from Dill.

"Yeah! It knew what I needed, and I knew what it could do. Which reminds me..." He pulled out a set of empty cylindrical tubes that had smaller, flexible tubes coiling out from them. "While I was at it, I made these for you, too, Nico."

Nico poked at one of the cylinders. "What are they?"

"They're coolant tubes."

"Coolant tubes? For what?"

"I'm glad you asked! For that, we're going to need your frosty legs." Dill grinned. His goofy smile curved parallel with the gadget on his face, making him look like a frog. "The best part is, I finally figured out plastic."

"I don't know, Dill." Nico grimaced.

"No, for real! It'll be awesome, I promise!"

"Dill, I have those, ah, stashed away in Lor's apartment. It may have to wait until tomorrow," Gale said, rubbing his cheek.

"No problem, no problem, we'll get it tomorrow!"

"Let us call it a day," Krik'tha said, pointing at the sky. "It will not be long before second sun, and this courtyard will close."

There wasn't much time. Jack's letter emphasized the point. Damaetra was a prisoner, soon to be formulations slave. He clenched his fists. "Okay, we'll wait until tomorrow. But we need to work hard and fast tomorrow. For Damaetra."

The angrier Paerli got, the more agitated Lor became. He lay in bed in the pitch black, staring at the blue phials on his nightstand casting glinting sparkles from the high window. Gale slept on a small couch. Not a tall man, his legs still draped over the arm of the sofa with a thin, spare sheet draped over his torso.

Lor debated using a drug phial to get him through the night unperturbed, but a thought occurred to him during the short meal he shared with Gale in his room. Being connected to Paerli, he thought he might be able to track her in some way. He reasoned that by leaving his mind open during the night, he could find her and learn what she was up to. It was a shot in the dark, but one he was willing to take if it meant gaining any sort of upper hand and getting Damaetra back. In this way, he felt a little less useless again.

Now if I can just close my eyes...

The day was long and difficult, but the creeping fear that it would only get worse kept his heart pounding and mind racing. He tried meditating on his colors, but they were buzzing with irritation and not helping.

Damaetra.

She was small for an Anglia. Lor could cup her wrist with a thumb and forefinger. The thought of that dirty Weg dragging her around shifted the colors under his lids to scarlet. He imagined Paerli luring her out of her apartment, pretending to be her friend, only to whack off her long shimmering hair, then kidnap her to be a part of that cursed "team."

If that strongman animal even tried to touch her...

Lor felt the heat pulse his eyes hard enough to imagine they dripped with blood. Murder was on his heart.

Go to sleep go to sleep go to sleep!

Lor opened his eyes to glare at the bottles of drug on the nightstand. If he glared at them long enough, maybe his eyes would tire and make him sleep.

Just a little. To take the edge off.

Jack instructed him to take an entire phial for a night. If he just took a sip...

Down the hatch.

It tasted just as awful as the first time he had it—like sour oil and burnt wood. He successfully gulped just enough from the skinny neck of the phial, no more than that. It was enough to knock him out.

Wind gusts played his ears like a drum. Wave after wave of torrent as if he were in the eye of a storm. Black grains whorled around, looking for purchase on something... anything. They carried with them the guttural wail of the air, a sound like bass trumpets out of sync.

Lor stepped forward through the black earth, aware that eventually he would come across the platoon of roundsmen guarding the sacred zone, but they never showed. His toe caught something protruding from the sand—a burnt husk, black as pitch, snaking from the ground in a writhing coil. He followed the thick charred rope as it multiplied into many, with crusted surfaces of skin that peeled off and drifted through the vortex with the rest of the sand. Or was it ash?

The air was thick here, and he suppressed the urge to gag, despite feeling the itch deep in his lungs. He wanted to call out to Damaetra. This was where he saw her in his last dream. She was here, somewhere.

The thought stirred the vortex into violence. It pelted his face with the tiny grains, clinging to his skin in smudgy patches and collecting on his eyelashes. He ran, following the snaking coil as it grew to a size he couldn't measure. Where it ended, it gathered into one—a tall, jagged peak. Gehenna. The storm subsided, dumping its whirling payload back to the earth, leaving behind a purplish haze that hung in the air. In the depths ahead, he saw her white form, and she wasn't alone.

She cast a ghostly aura around her as the team led her into the groin of the mountain. Lor tried to call again, feeling the scratch of dust on his palate. So he ran to her—her skin was a beacon and her short, whipping white hair a flag to follow. They disappeared into the void.

Lor managed to reach the entrance—a nondescript hole in the side of the mountain, only large enough to crawl through. It was surrounded by the ashy corpse of winding ivy. He squeezed inside, bearing lashes from the petrified edges of burnt ivy. Once inside, he straightened himself into what was a large chamber, echoing the tirade of one, Paerli Harea.

"I told you assholes not to hurt him!" she bellowed.

Mutters from the team undulated through the cavern.

"Now how am I going to get him down?" A slap rang out, followed by the scurrying of boots across the ground.

"Oi! I ken craft ye somethin' ta help—"

"Shut your mouth! Shut your rotten, bio-failure, implant-ridden mouth!"

Lor crept forward. In the dark he saw her—Damaetra sat on the ground, her knees pulled to her chest in a self-hug. Even from the distance he saw the grief in her eyes. He wanted to run and grab her. Why shouldn't he? This was just a dream, nothing more. If he wished hard enough, he could pull her through the dream into his bedroom where she would be safe. He jogged to the next outcropping and watched from behind it.

"No, Pigeon, I'm not going to pull your stupid ignorant son."

Lor moved to the next rock, locking eyes with Damaetra. She wore her lavender dress, with a loose thread hanging from the hem. Her crystal eyes found his face, but she looked right through him like a ghost, then cast her eyes back to the ground and laced her fingers together in a prayer.

She was surrounded by patches of glowing blue algae. It lit up the cavern, showcasing the dripping wet walls and scores of mushrooms sprouting from different crevices. He reached for her, just to touch her, to feel her soft skin under his fingers once again… but the moment never came. His heart squeezed hard and his vision turned red.

"You'd better get on your knees and be thankful that Yeunish bastard survived!"

Damaetra perked up ever so slightly, then closed her eyes with the tiniest hint of a smile.

"'Smith, I thought you hated his kind."

"Shut your hole, Hammer! It doesn't change the fact I need him to scrape Maron from the breach."

Maron?

"He ain't gonna agree to it, ma'am. The Desert Maelstrom is 'bout here, and you've got his girl."

"Didn't I tell you to shut your damn hole?"

"I love it when you talk dirty to me, 'Smith." The brute cracked his knuckles loud enough to echo in the cavern.

"What are you doing here? Get out!" Paerli stormed up to Lor and shoved his chest hard. The unusual power propelled him backward.

"Come back when you're not hiding behind your pathetic dream!" she called out as he fell forever, trying to right himself and get to Damaetra. He could only drift back, helpless like a bug on its back. He braced for impact on the sand, but instead he plunked through the earth.

"Augh, shit!" Lor hit the hard wood floor on his shoulder, hearing the ligament groan.

"You okay?" Gale sat at the table, scrolling through his e-disk and sipping on something hot.

Lor squeezed his shoulder, nodding with a scrunched grimace.

With as much as I fall from my bed, I probably need to start sleeping in a crib.

"Bad dream?" Gale sipped the hot stuff.

"I think I connected with her. With Paerli." Lor rubbed his forehead. His hair was shaggier than normal, and the strands flopped over his eyes.

"Do you know for sure?"

Lor pulled up a chair, holding his shoulder. "I'm not positive, but what I saw couldn't have been just a bad dream. What time is it?"

Gale flicked to the time hovering over his e-disk. "It's still dark."

"Why were you up?" Lor took a seat across from him.

Gale shrugged. "Couldn't sleep. What did you see?"

Lor told him about the cavern, the arguments, and how she knew he was there.

"That certainly sounds like more than a dream," Gale said, taking another sip of the hot drink. "You said you were connected to her now. You've got to think about how that will affect you after all this... and how it will affect your relationship with Damaetra."

"Yes, I know, Dad. I didn't know how else to get Damaetra back."

"Fair enough. Do you know how you are going to take care of this mess?"

Lor sat back, running fingers through his hair and chewing on his cheek.

"I have to figure out a way to kill Paerli."

CHAPTER 31

The Engineer's Lab Notebook
DILL

LAB NOTES: DILLY DOG

Since that projectile spoke to me and I was able to make new eyes, I'm pretty confident that I will get Nico some legs. Side note—this one girl at booth 3 is kinda hot. Not Cae hot, but hot.

My thought is that I can attach these coolant tubes to his new legs and give him super speed to match that no-good twin of his. Except, he'd be better because he's no damn Weggevens.

<u>**TRIAL 1:**</u>

Gale helped get me some ancient tech from the beach to repurpose into attachment stumps. I tried to listen to the material, but when they say "dead tech," they mean it. And by "they," I mean, the dudes in charge. Instead of hearing its potential, it didn't talk at all, so I just went at it with the tools.

The material shaped pretty nicely with lathes and raw hammering power, but working it too hard makes it brittle, and unsuitable for attaching to human flesh. Sorry, Nico.

<u>**TRIAL 2:**</u>

Should I dare use living flesh? I dare say I do! I still want to try making attachments, just in case Nico is feeling spiffy and wants to switch to his date night legs. Maybe the thing he needs is an infusion... but an infusion of what? What can Lor give me? Gale says to try the ancient tech again. I can't argue with the smartest man in the world.

So, that Foscan demon, Krik'tha, somehow found some eletonk legs. I was like, "These are too fat for Nico!" But I wanted to try real muscle and bone, so eletonk it was. How he got them is anyone's guess... but he is a *Foscan devil*. Lor told me to stop doing that. Maybe I will, maybe I won't!

Back to the trial. Eletonk legs seem to respond well to electrical spasms. Not sure what to do with that information, but in the notes it goes!

TRIAL 3:

I'm not giving up on you, living flesh! Gale said I really need to relax and focus. It's hard when we don't have much time! I think there is something to that ancient tech. I may try it again, but there's got to be something I can use to make it less brittle... I asked Krik'tha for more legs, but in that broken language, he was all like, "No, no more legs here."

Okay, back to the trial. I bet if I get some eneris from Lor, I can reinforce the ancient tech. Oh, I have an idea!

TRIAL 4:

My idea *kind of* worked? And it was so simple! Those little plump cacti that litter the beaches and fields are full of juicy green juice. It has just the right type of living essence that straddles the plains of humanity and machine. I don't know, I think I made that up. BUT it made the ancient tech a little more workable. Nico says to stop bothering with it all, but I'm here for you, buddy!

TRIAL 5:

By Gehenna, I think I got it...

CHAPTER 32

The Formulator's Lab Notebook
Nico

LAB NOTES: DAY 2

Objective: Utilize the forward notes from Jack to create new formulations and discover others.

Purpose: Duh.

MATERIALS AND EQUIPMENT:

Red Eneris (*roujis emporum*
White Eneris (*witis volatus*
Green Eneris (*verdigris plantum*)
Blue Eneris (*lapis piscus*)
Fowler (*chromatis hominum*)
Silver Eneris (*argenis hominum*)
Black Eneris (*obsenis forturum*)
Assorted crystal phials and stoppers
Assorted crystal mixing vessels and pitchers
Tasting droppers
Hot plate
Chill bath
Fuel torch and flint

BEGINNING NOTES:

Jack only left a small amount each of yellow eneris (*jaunis rancum*), orange eneris (*naranis corpum*), and violet eneris (*purpuris porum*). In an effort to preserve Fowler's eneris, I will be creating other phials as practice first.

EXPERIMENT:

1. LAPIS EVENING

Measure 2 drams *lapis piscus* into a crystal mixing vessel. Heat gently with mixing, and add four drops *witis volatus*, taking care to not add the fourth drop until adding a single drop of *verdigris plantum* at the same time. Cool, taste test, bottle.

Taste test—as expected.
Use: for dreamless nights. Drink or inject.

2. IVORY SALTPETER

Measure 1 dram *witis volatus*, 2.5 drams *obsenis forturum*, and one-half dram *roujis emporum*. Add half the *witis* to a crystal vessel over a chill bath. Dropwise, add the *roujis*. The mixture will get hot, so take care to maintain chill bath. Quench with remaining *witis*. Bring to room temperature and mix well with *obsenis*. Taste test, then bottle.

Taste test—as expected.
Use: effective weakness poison, and potential explosive.

3. WITIS REJUVENATE

Measure 3 drams *witis volatus*, 1.5 drams *verdigris plantum*, and 0.5 dram *argenis hominum*. First, purify *argenis* over flame. Do this by adding to a crystal vessel, then applying flame directly to liquid until bubbly and glowing orange. Allow to cool.

Add *witis* to crystal vessel over heat. With stirring, add *verdigris* in three portions, allowing mixture to reheat after each addition. Stir for at least ten minutes. In the meantime, remove *argenis* pellet from vessel and rinse with clean water or alcohol. Dry thoroughly. Once mixture has completed mixing, add hot liquid to phial. Drop in *argenis* pellet and swirl. Taste test.

Taste test—not sure. Gale says it looks good.
Use: Weggevens helper injection.

4. LAST GRUDGE

Measure 2 drams of the *chromatis hominum* first and add to large crystal vessel over a chill bath. Add the following in order: 1 dram *roujis*, 1 dram *naranis*, 1 dram *jaune*, 1 dram *verdigris*, 1 dram *lapis*, and 1 dram *purpura*. After each addition, the mixture will chill to a solid. Wait for the solution to return to liquid before adding the next dram.

Once the final dram is added, warm to bench temperature, and add exactly seven drops of *obsenis*. Take care to only add seven drops. Mix well, taste test, and bottle.

Taste test—this will be interesting.
Use: Toss with extreme prejudice.

DISCUSSION:

Jack left some pre-made formulations, namely, a few phials of red mash, four phials of verdigris biosore, and two phials of jaune spirit. One thing I've noted is that the more complex the recipe, the more involved the result.

CHAPTER 33

Special Access Pass
LOREN

THE SUN WAS A SLIVER over the distant horizon, casting threads of light over the courtyard.

Lor sat with Gale at a table. They were the first to arrive, and he passed the time by focusing his thoughts on the colors under his lids, hoping to see white gold fractals or signs from the Maker. All he saw was black whirling dust and Paerli's hand shoving him through the nether.

Krik'tha wandered toward the table, wringing his hands. His eye shone in the blue of the dawn as it scanned Lor's face. "I am sorry," he said. "I must stay behind. I am servant."

Lor nodded. "That's good. Stay here and stay safe," he said.

Krik'tha nodded and gave Lor a long, final stare. "Remember to slow down. Here, I have gifts for all of you." He pulled four hand-sewn leather belts from his satchel. They were strung across with pouches and clasps. Loops decorated the sides for holding accessories or tools.

"What are these?" Lor asked, turning the belt around in his hand.

"They hold phials and other tools. Good for easy access." Krik'tha took one of the belts and unclasped it. He draped the contraption around Lor's shoulders and under his ribs, cinching it closed like a light harness. The leather packs rested on his waist, with the easy access loops lining the straps across his chest. "Maybe they help. For later."

Lor adjusted the belt, fingering the sturdy stitch work across the harness. "Thank you, Krik'tha. You're a great friend."

He smiled, patting Lor's shoulder, then turned away.

Lor closed his eyes again, feeling the smooth leather cross strap. Finishing the task for Paerli would seal the bond and make him immortal like her.

How do I kill someone who is immortal?

The black spot on the ground still burned into the grass. Krik'tha had warned him the fastest path to yaslecha was using emotion to drive his gift.

How far gone was Par already?

Dill skipped up to the table, wheeling Nico in with him. His new visor cast a purple light over the bridge of his nose. The button in the center looked like a singular alien eye.

"Did you bring 'em?" he asked Gale.

Gale nodded and pulled out the blue oblong case holding Nico's legs.

"Oh, this is going to be fun... This will just take me a few minutes." He cradled the case, trotting it to the same bench he worked from the past two days.

"What're these?" Nico prodded the extra belts sitting on the table.

"Krik'tha brought these. They're utility harnesses like this one." Lor looped his thumbs under his two chest straps like suspenders.

Nico looked down and frowned. "If I'm unable to walk after..."

"Just give Dill some time. If it doesn't work, it doesn't work, and you'll stay here safely in Guild Central, okay?"

"Alright, but I'm not happy about that."

"Were you able to make a good amount of draughts? Namely, the special one for me?" Gale asked.

Nico hoisted the black bag on the table, flicking it open. The side that used to contain empty phials was lined with several rows of concoctions from blue, to red, and even dark black. Lor spied Fowler's eneris dangling in one partition, with a row of iridescent phials of different shapes underneath, even more vibrant than the raw material.

"Is that what I think it is?" Lor poked at one and it swayed, reflecting a spectrum of color against the black case.

"It is... and I need you to be careful if you use it."

"What does it do?"

"I have no idea, but I can tell you it's no healing pot."

"Be ready to be amazed!" Dill shouted from the table. He grabbed the case by the handle and held two disks in the other hand. He set the disks on the table, and Nico picked one up.

"What's this for?" he asked, turning it around. It had the distinct markings of the ancient tech Lor repeatedly caught his toes on in the sand.

"Here, watch." Dill wheeled Nico from the table and turned him face out. Nico had a dark blue blanket with the roundsman academy logo stitched into it draped across the stumps of his thighs. Dill yanked the blanket off, exposing frayed bandage caps and rounded flesh.

"Dill, hold on." Nico splayed his fingers out to cover them.

"Don't be ashamed of that," Lor said. "Remember when I pissed myself in the program?"

"You did?" Gale asked.

I never told Gale.

"I-I just didn't make it in time."

Gale hummed, eyeing Lor, making Dill laugh.

Pulling off Nico's bandage caps, Dill threw them to the side and went for the ancient tech rings on the table. Nico too, had two purple-colored stitched mouths grinning over each leg. It was the first time Lor had really looked at his friend's legs after that day in the desert. The image of the blood-slicked pillars wobbling over to rest in the yellow grains flashed in his mind. He never registered how much Hare had sliced off his brother.

They stopped halfway up the thigh. Gale mentioned earlier it was a miracle Nico survived. Evidence of cauterization decorated the flesh, sealing vital arteries and veins. The skin had been folded over and stitched in place, with Jack's trademark healing draught leaving nothing but those fading purple scars.

"These'll be better under the caps. Less chafing," Dill said, holding up a pair of black socks made of some soft material. He stretched one over each one of Nico's thighs before holding out one of the ancient tech caps like a steering wheel. Blunt needles lined the center of it.

"U-uh, Dill..." Nico turned pink, with a slick of sweat forming on his upper lip.

"Don't worry, this won't hurt at all." Dill shoved Nico's hands away from the stumps, jamming the ring around his thigh. Nico flinched and went rigid. Dill twisted the other cap on. The ivory-colored adapters fixed to his legs gave them an unusual mechanical look. Old symbols encircled the rings, lighting up purple like Dill's visor.

"Woo hoo! They're live!" Dill jumped up and down. "Now this is the best part."

"Dill this feels weird," Nico said, poking at the ring.

Dill ignored him, flinging open the blue case. Inside were a pair of human legs unlike anything Lor had ever seen. The coolant cylinders Dill made the other day were surgically implanted along major joints and connections. Flexible tubes filled with a thick green liquid ran from one cylinder to the next. The end of each leg had a matching ancient tech cap that lined up with the other two.

"Gale helped me with the implants yesterday," Dill announced, grinning. He picked up one of the legs, and it wobbled in his grip. It was a bizarre sight.

"Here, let me..." Lor bent down and helped guide the end into the cap. There was something odd and chilling about handling the severed leg. The flesh was cool to the touch, and pliable. Dill twisted the leg until it clicked into place, illuminating the coolant tubes into the same purple glow.

"This is *so* weird," Nico repeated himself, gripping the sides of his wheelchair. The right foot twitched, followed by the left.

"Can you feel them again?" Dill asked.

"Sorta." Nico stared at them, transfixed.

"Well, it won't be exactly the same"—Dill paced around to the back of Nico's chair, then ran a finger down the attachment—"but those pins inside the cap touch muscle fibers and nerves under your skin, sending impulses through your body to help your brain know there is a leg there. Kinda like it was before, but since this is a mod, it's not as good as the way you were made. Try standing up."

"What's keeping the legs from rotting?" Nico gripped the bars of his chair, trembling.

"The coolant. It's actually a mixture of grease and green."

Lor remembered the copious phials of squeezings he gave Dill the day before. "Oh, that's what that was for?"

"That's not even the best part—these tubes give you super speed. Just like Gale."

"And my no-good brother," Nico grumbled.

"Get up, try them! Don't think about it too hard. Let the pins do the work."

Nico scooted forward, and the knees bent in response. Bubbles in the green liquid squeezed and squirted through the tubes, causing more twitches in the feet.

Nico grunted. "We don't have time," he said, pushing himself from the chair. The legs straightened and his upper half wobbled.

"Cool, huh? I based them off all the prototypes I made while at work." Dill was pleased with himself, looking over to Gale for confirmation, and he received a hearty smile and nod in return from Gale. Dill flicked one of the tubes filled with liquid. "Lor should be able to help you with refills."

"They'll do, Dill, thanks." Nico grinned.

"Come on, try the speed! Just picture being over there." Dill pointed to the far end of the courtyard.

Nico hummed. "I'll try," he said, swaying over stock-still robot human legs. He stared at the far end, focusing on a trail of ivy curling up the side of a statue. It was dotted with small yellow flowers. He stared at the flower, imagining it in his hand.

A gust of air blew through the courtyard, flattening the grass. Nico stood at the chair, wobbling on the legs. Sticking out a fist, he unfurled his fingers to show them a little yellow flower.

Dill clapped while Gale examined the coolant tubes. "You *are* a prodigy! I have faith that you'll master those in no time." Dill smacked Nico on the shoulder. "Oh, by the way, I made some weapons for us too."

He dug out a handful of hollowed needles and four simple slings. "It's not much, but these pins will go great with these tech-less shooters. Using basic physics, they'll shoot the pins straight into those goons—and they're hollow, so if you wanna fill 'em with any special pots..." Dill wagged his eyebrows.

Lor plucked one from Dill's hand, examining the little thorn. Its core was perfect for stuffing with one of Nico's concoctions.

"You've done so well and worked so hard, Dill." Gale wrapped his arm around Dill's shoulder and squeezed. "You did great."

Their small friend beamed at the compliment from the man he adored, practically splitting his face in two.

Lor checked his e-disk. It was officially morning, and it wouldn't be long before the Guilds would begin their workday. Packing up their things, they left the courtyard and Nico's chair behind.

Getting to Gehenna was not easy. The zone was highly protected, without any sort of commuter station nearby. Gale rented a jumper for the bulk of the ride, then they would have to walk deep into the black sands to meet up with the forbidden wall and the squad of roundsmen there to keep them out.

"You ain't goin' to Gehenna, are yeh? They don' let visitors," the Danashi driver asked, chewing on a slimy wad of tobacco.

Gale told him they had field research to do at the edge of the Secas forest. His professionalism made it sound real enough that the driver wasn't interested probing further into their research but dutifully drove them to the tip.

The smell of electricity buzzed in the air. Lor checked his e-disk. The time hovered, glitching every few seconds.

"Look." Gale pointed west into the Span. Dusty bursts of sand randomly rocketed into the air. "It won't be long before the Desert Maelstrom gets here."

"Let's pray we can get in and out," Lor said, tucking away his e-disk and tightening his harness. He touched the bottoms of several offensive phials that hung from the loops. Krik'tha took great care to add supports for the bottom of each phial, to keep them from swinging around and breaking.

The more they walked, the more natural Nico's new legs carried him.

"Why are there gates around the mountain anyway?" Dill asked.

Nico shrugged. "My guess is that someone has to go there every now and then to check on things."

"Check on what, though? Isn't it a dead zone?"

Another conspiracy.

When Lor asked Krik'tha about it, he didn't seem to know any more than anyone else in the group. Based on his dream the night before, he had an idea of what they would find—and who.

Gale planked a hand over his brow to shield his eyes. "There it is," he said.

In the distance, a stone wall stood twenty feet tall with six silhouettes pacing in front of it. The four of them stopped, taking cover near a cluster of boulders. Lor pulled out his e-disk. Jack's coordinates swam in static, but they were on top of their meeting point.

"We're still a little early," Lor said, stashing the disk and looking around for any sign of the Yeunish Formulator.

"See that up ahead?" Nico said, pointing up, beyond the wall.

Lor stared forward, seeing a semi-transparent gray veil shooting up behind the wall. "Yeah, what's that?"

"That's where the black sand starts. The wall closes it in... and if we somehow make it past the wall, we won't be able to see very well, which is why we need to wear goggles."

Nico pulled out the pair he bought from a stall in the courtyard. They were meant for Engineers but would protect his eyes from sand either way. They were black and mirrored, like Jack's. Lor saw his reflection in them, wearing his own blue mirrored ones.

"Honestly, I'm a little nervous." Lor said.

"As you should be," a deep voice slithered from behind them. Dill squealed and jumped. Lor spun around to see the lanky mad Formulator stroll up to the group. He ditched the dirty lab coat for more desert-appropriate gear. If not for the black hair, goggles, and pallor, he would blend into the sand.

"Jack, you scared the crap out of us." Lor let out a sharp exhale. "Were you following us?"

Jack's thin lips spread into a wide grin, with his buggy goggles staring at them.

"Of course you were." Lor sighed. "Now that you're here, how are we going to get past them?" He pointed at the row of tiny guards at the base of the wall.

Jack glared at the silhouettes. Not one muscle twitched. He opened his mouth for a moment before any sound pushed out. "Par... she has the Reader with her. The small one with thick glasses."

"You mean Livia? The Guild Central attendant?" Lor squinted toward the wall to find her.

"She was ordered to allow your girl to join Formulator Hall. Along with the rest of you."

"Ordered? How could she do that?"

"It was a push. She pushed the committee at Par's command."

"I'm sorry, I don't know what that means."

Jack sighed, pinching the bridge of his nose just under the goggles. "If Par wants you here, there is nothing these guards can do to stop her."

"So what are you saying?"

"I'm saying that the guards will let us in."

CHAPTER 34

Cavern of Souls
LOREN

THEY CROSSED OVER INTO THE forbidden zone, weapons and all. Lor glanced behind his shoulder as the guards pushed the heavy door closed. A series of latches echoed in the hollow zone of ash.

The area was just like Lor's dream. With less turbulent winds, the ash hung in the air, sapping all color from everything. He gripped his harness, feeling the weight of the phials attached to it. Gale stood next to him with a scrap of cloth wrapped around his nose and mouth and his silver goggles reflecting the dark clouds.

Dill was silent, with the purple glow from his glasses tracing a line across his nose. It was all Lor could see of him in the dusty air.

A lump in the sand pressed against Lor's foot. It didn't feel like a stone. While hard, there was a fragility to it. Lor peered down at it—a burnt husk, coiling forward like an arrow in the sand.

"This way," Lor said, grabbing Gale's arm. They followed Lor in a train, gripping arms to stay together in the haze. Lor knew this path—he had taken it before.

He followed the coil. It was the blind leading the blind through a veil of ash, until the haze thinned to a muted lavender hue. Just like the dream, the object in the sand connected to the base of Gehenna.

"Whoa." Dill sighed, craning his neck upward.

Lor trudged forward, looking for the small opening he would know by the covering of petrified ivy.

"Do you know what you're doing?" Jack asked.

Lor grunted, continuing forward, dragging Gale along, followed by Dill, Nico, then Jack.

"It's just up ahead," Lor said, finally feeling sure of himself.

Chained to each other as they felt their way through the haze, the great stone behemoth loomed ever closer. Lor squinted through smudgy lenses to search for the elusive ivy-decorated hole.

"I need you to know that I can't fight with you," Jack said.

"Why not?" Dill asked.

Jack stared toward the mountain. "I am... not equipped to handle her."

Lor chuffed. "And you think we are?"

"You are bound to her. You all are—through each other."

"What does that mean?"

Jack stared off again, walking forward with everyone through the haze. Lavender shadows criss-crossed over his buggy goggles. "All I had was her. And now she is yours."

"Ew, no she's not." Dill spat on the ground.

"What I mean is, I no longer mean anything to her. I need you to get her pendant."

Lor remembered seeing the strange black jewel reflecting red that she wore around her neck.

"What is it?"

"Just find a way to get it," Jack said as they reached the ivy-laced opening.

"Guys," Nico said stopping in the dirt. Black swirls danced around his tech legs, strobing the purple glow from the cylinders. "Even after he did this to us, can we try to save him? Save Niki?"

Lor clapped him on the shoulder. "We'll try," he said.

Everyone ducked inside, careful not to scratch themselves on the hardened fossils. Once inside, the cavern opened up into an endless maw, just as Lor remembered in his dream.

The walls dripped in moisture and blue light—not from tech but a film of life clinging to them. The light brightened the cave almost as well as the second sun.

"What *is* this stuff?" Dill whispered, touching it with a fingertip.

"I would guess that it's luminescence from cave algae," Gale murmured, looking around. The sharp blue light flickered in spots like pixels on holofilms.

Outside was a dead wasteland. The inside of the cavern teemed with life. Plants of many colors littered the ground, with large mushrooms poking from the walls and peppered with the same twinkling algae. A damp mist hung in the air, with the pleasant aroma of fruit, unlike the expected smell of rot and mold. The cavern went on for a great distance, harboring several fully grown trees of types Lor had never seen before. This area was a budding paradise, and something worth protecting.

A squeeze gripped Lor's stomach, and he had a thought that he might vomit. Curled over, he wrapped his arms around his midsection.

"Hey, are you okay?" Gale put a hand on his back.

Laughter echoed through the cave, with the thick accent of the man who shot him and killed Fowler—the man Lor only knew as the Crow. Dill and Nico spun toward the sound, while feet shuffled and stomped through the fields of life. Lor clutched his stomach.

Why isn't she affected by this connection like I am?

His connection with Paerli grew as the foreign noises got closer.

"Cutting it close, aren't we now?" A breathy voice cut through the damp air.

Lor coughed and stood upright, steeling himself against her emotions inside his gut. "I'm here now. Where's Damaetra?"

Nico guarded Lor's right, and Dill his left, while Gale stood behind him. Jack stood next to Gale, arms crossed and glaring.

Paerli ignored him. "Well, well, good to see you, Cricket. Even if you are a Yeuni." She stepped into view, with her team following behind. Hammer lugged forward, with Damaetra's arm in his grip, dragging her with him. Lor wanted to kill him. Damaetra's pale face glowed under blue light. In the days of her captivity, she had grown gaunt. Her eyes were swollen and pink, with no more tears to give, but they reflected new life when she saw him.

"Loren!" Damaetra called out to him. She tried to step forward, but the brute held her in place.

"Hold tight, baby, I'm here." Lor called back.

Jack said nothing, backing into the shadow. Paerli scanned the group, smiling at Lor. "I'm going to have to apologize on behalf of my oaf of a colleague. See, he wasn't thinking when he shot you."

"Let Damaetra go, Par," Lor demanded.

She clicked her tongue. "My, my, are we in a place where you think you can make demands of me?"

"Let her go, and I won't kill your men."

"Oh, that's funny. You're a funny guy. Tell you what, I'll let her go once we're done with your favor to me."

"You know, Par," Lor said, watching her team, "I've been doing a lot of thinking, and I think I'd rather not live forever with *you*."

Paerli hummed. "I can still torment you until the day you die."

"Not if I kill you first."

"Loren, Loren, Loren. Did you not listen to me when you were all over me the other night? I can't die."

"She lies, Damaetra," he called to her. He touched one of Fowler's phials fixed on the utility strap.

"Well, this has been a fun chat, but we've got a job to do. I'm sorry, Dill, Nico, and whoever you are back there, but we don't really need you." Paerli waved her hand, summoning Hammer and Crow.

Hammer handed Damaetra to Paerli as he took his place next to Crow in front of her. The focus of Lor's wrath was on the big strongman, Hammer. For the first time, the rage bubbling inside of him was his own. He pointed directly at Hammer, and the man laughed at him.

Nico braced himself, gripping the harness belt. Dill hovered a hand over his waistband, where he had tucked his tech-less shooter.

"Now wait just a second," Gale growled.

"Come along with me to the umbilicus, Loren. Or… should I pull her dry?" Paerli wrapped her fingers around Damaetra's throat.

"Don't you even *think* about it." Lor gritted his teeth. The Reader, Livia, stood nearby. Her eyes were downcast and wet.

"You still haven't learned, have you, Lor the Bastard?"

"Stop calling me that."

"I'll call you whatever I please, *bastard*."

Lor turned to his friends and his dad. Gale nodded at him and mouthed "go."

"Hey, Nico," Lor shouted to his friend, who glanced back at him. "Toss with extreme prejudice. *Extreme*."

Nico smiled. Lor descended deeper into the cavern with Paerli, Livia, and Damaetra.

"Why are you guys just going along with whatever she says?" Dill said to Hammer and Crow. "Can't you think with your own tiny brains instead of your tiny dingers?"

Hammer chuckled. "None a your business, chump."

"Actually, I'd like to know," Nico interrupted, "what is it we're missing? Should we follow her too?"

He glanced down at Dill and half winked.

"We go' our orders teh kill yeh, so don' think that'll do yeh well."

"Shut your stupid face," Dill blurted.

"Oi, did yeh make all a these gadges?" Crow pointed to Dill's visor and Nico's legs. He stroked the tube with dials and knobs responsible for slicing through Fowler and Lor.

"What, you jealous that I'm better than you already?"

Crow laughed. "Ain' no one better than me."

Dill scoffed. "Well, all I see is a pair of no-brained jerk-offs," he said.

Crow laughed, scrunching up his nose to speak in a high-pitched mocking voice. "You 'ear tha, 'Ammer? The little boy jus' called us jerk-offs. Why don' we go ahead an' finish off ole Hare's job 'ere." He grinned, showing off the shiny black modified teeth.

"Like hell you are," Nico spat. A breeze punched the air, and Nico flew backwards from the impact. Laughter echoed in the cavern behind them. Nico jumped up and took off, chasing after his brother.

"O-oh, look at you two all '*geared*' up." Hammer flexed an arm, showing a bulging muscle.

Dill cracked a smile, flipping out his shooter.

"Oi, look, 'Ammer, 'es got a li'l squirt gun!" Crow chortled.

Dill pulled the trigger and it *thwanged*, sending a needle hurtling toward Hammer. It plunged into the man's flexed bicep, nearly burying itself wholly in his flesh.

"Ow! You little sh—" Hammer drew the needle from his arm, staring stupidly at it.

"Have a little ivory saltpeter, bitch!" Dill laughed and dipped behind a cluster of trees, running farther into the cavern. His purple light bounced away. Hammer stumbled forward a step, then over-corrected and fell backward, shaking his head.

"Wha'd you stick me with, you little prick?" he slurred. He rolled on the ground, trying to get back to his feet.

Crow stuck his dart scope over his eye, aiming for Dill. He shot the projectile at his back, but it missed when Nico sprinted through and pushed Dill into soft grass. The projectile stuck the wall and activated, spraying small splinters through the air. They clanked against the floor and thunked into mushrooms.

As the two tumbled on the ground, Hare sprinted forward, leaping into the air to tackle them. Nico spun around and shot a needle full of lapis evening into Hare's cheek.

The wild runner dropped like a stone on the floor, skidding to a stop at the base of a small tree. A gust of air brought Gale with it. He held a length of thick ivy the strength of steel cable. He tied Hare's arms and legs together in front of him, then sat on the ground to keep watch.

"I'll keep an eye on him, I've got more needles," Gale said.

Dill jumped up. "Ha! You missed! Did you need to go cry to your *mommy?*" Dill shouted at Crow.

"Shut up, shrimp!"

The old woman known as Pigeon leaned against a wall, watching everything unfold.

Paerli led Damaetra by the neck as Lor and Livia followed close behind. The passage curved and snaked with a barely noticeable downward slope.

"Boy, I'm just so excited, you have no idea," Paerli said in a fake positive lilt.

"Shut up, Par."

"Ohhh, so feisty!"

"You know what?" Lor said. "This is not the person I knew in the program. This is not the person Nico knew, Dill knew, or Damaetra. Who *is* this person?"

Paerli chuffed. "Well, my name is Paerli Harea, and I come from the Span," she said in the same lilt. They turned a corner where the algae was thicker, shining a more vibrant blue over her form. "Or at least I *did*... over fifteen hundred years ago."

"Fifteen hundred years..." Lor whispered.

Paerli clicked her tongue. "You see, Loren"—she turned Damaetra down another curve, and they followed—"you aren't my first."

"Stop lying about us to hurt Damaetra. You know I never tried to sleep with you."

Paerli giggled. "Well, isn't your mind just in the gutter? I was talking about you not being my first match, silly."

"How many have you had?" Lor grumbled.

"Don't be so jealous. I've only ever had one other." She laughed. "He is special—there's no one on Roseaarde that is anything like him. He is... *was* an Igni." She tossed her hair to the side and pressed her chin to her shoulder, making kissing lips at him. "But I don't expect you to know what that is, considering how little you know about anything."

"I know who the Igni are," Lor shot back.

"Oh, he *knows* something! That makes me so hot." She turned Damaetra's neck again down the next corridor.

"Would you shut the hell up about that?"

"Fine. We're here now anyway." Paerli tossed Damaetra to Livia, who delicately held his girlfriend's arm.

The corridor opened up to a small chamber. The far wall was coated with ash and death. Tendrils of black rot coiled over the surface, and in the center of it all was a man. His flesh merged with the wall, discoloring his body entirely in blacks and deep crusted crimson. Lor couldn't tell where the wall ended and the man's body began. A tiny sliver of gold clung to an elbow, hanging by a thread of sticky sap.

"Lor, this is Maron Valoa'brenga, my beautiful Igni match, and the last of his kind."

The wall groaned.

CHAPTER 35

By Reaps and Bounds
Loren

PAERLI STROLLED UP TO THE withered corpse spread like dried jam across the wall.

"Oh Maron, my love. Where did we go wrong?" Paerli said. She reached a hand out to stroke the sunken cheek.

Valoa'brenga. The Valoan cult worships this thing.

"Maron, meet my *new* match. He's young and supple, unlike you."

"What... *is* this place?" Lor couldn't keep his eyes off the withered flesh attached to the cave.

"This is the breach." Paerli paced in front of the man, occasionally running her fingers over the rotting wall.

"Is that man"—Lor swallowed—"alive?"

Paerli chuckled. "Oh yes, very much so." She cupped her hand on Maron's cheek. "But sadly, his time has come to an end."

"Par, tell me what the breach is. Please," Lor asked.

"We'll find out soon enough." She put a hand on a blackened trunk that could have been the man's arm. "I need you to go to the other side." She nodded to the other arm trunk. Lor stood defiant, glaring between the wall and Damaetra.

The chamber shook.

Paerli scanned the room, watching black dust shake loose from a network of crevices. "Maelstrom is here. We've got to hurry."

Hammer wobbled and put up his fists. He swung at Nico, missing and striking a tree, flinging bark through the air. The punch broke open the skin on his knuckles and he roared.

"What did you inject me with, you little asshole!" he shouted into the void. Blood spurted from one of the wounds.

"I told you already," Dill said, fisting a phial of red liquid, "it's ivory saltpeter. Basically poison." He laughed and flung the red phial toward Hammer.

The Red Mash exploded in front of him, spraying acrid smoke into his face.

"It burns!" he cried, throwing his head back and rolling to the floor.

Crow pulled out a tooth, loading it into a different weapon, pointing it at Nico.

He pulled the trigger, but Nico dodged the arcing projectile as it zipped past and pinged against a rock.

"Are those actually bullets you're keeping in your dirty mouth?" Dill said.

"Nah, they ain't. But when the situation calls an' all." Crow broke off another tooth, loading the weapon.

Hammer writhed on the ground, clutching his face and neck as flesh bubbled and burst. Boils spilled yellow liquid onto the ground.

Another shot rang out, grazing Dill's ear.

Nico loaded a needle full of more lapis evening, sticking Hammer with it. The man howled, pulling out the needle and cursing. His squirming limbs slowed when Nico stuck him with another. Then another.

Crow broke off another tooth, aiming his weapon at Dill again, coming to peace with his colleague losing the battle next to him. Dill gulped a swig of a yellow phial Nico had called jaune spirit. He buzzed on the spot, with more energy jolting through his veins.

"Loren, this is where you come in," Paerli cooed. She stroked Maron's face again. "My favor to ask is for you to help me pry these dusty bones from the breach."

That moment at Heart Island when they made that stupid bet came to the front of Lor's mind. If he had guessed the favor to be anything but rousing a corpse from an underground tomb, he would have lost that bet too.

Lor glanced over at Damaetra. She watched him with wide eyes shining bright blue under the luminescent algae, shaking her head no. Paerli saw the exchange, and the second heartbeat raged in Lor's chest.

"This is not your call, *Dame*." Paerli marched over to her, grabbing her neck again, shaking it.

The second heart had no effect on him. His rage met Paerli's.

"Get your hands off her!" Lor shouted. The red rings of anger circled his vision as he felt flames licking his arterial walls.

Paerli put a hand over her chest and gasped. Lor had fought back. Now the second beat in her chest took *her* breath away.

"How does it feel, you spiteful *bitch*?"

She leaned over, a thin trail of drool oozing from her lip. Breathing heavily, she hissed, "You will do this with me... or I will suck every drop of silver... from her *organs*."

"One drop and you die," Lor spat.

Paerli smirked, then grabbed Damaetra's wrist and squeezed. His sweet Anglia cried out, clawing at the dark hand holding on to her. Lor stormed up to the pair, closed his fist, and socked Paerli square in the mouth. He felt her teeth scrape his knuckle as she fell backward into the dirt. Covering her face, she giggled and rolled around in the ashy rot.

The chamber quaked again.

Lor wobbled, then examined Damaetra's tiny wrist to see smudges of silver there and swollen tears running down her dusty cheeks. He wrapped his arms around her, and she sobbed into his shirt.

Paerli cackled even louder. "I will never stop, Loren. Never," she said, licking a split bloody lip. "As long as we're connected, I will always find you, and your precious Dame will *never* be safe."

Lor let Damaetra go. Cupping her heart-shaped face in his hands, he kissed her.

"I love you," he whispered. The water shimmered in her big crystalline eyes. She pressed her lids shut, letting the fat drops fall to the ground.

"I love you more," she whispered.

His heart trilled.

"Oh how *precious*." Paerli clucked, still sitting on the ground, clutching her chest.

Lor glared at Paerli, bending down and grabbing her arm, yanking her from the ground. Damaetra's silver still clung to her palm, mingled with dirt and ash. He flung her toward the wall, where she stopped short of slamming into Maron.

"What do I need to do?" he growled, marching to the other side of Valoa'brenga's grotesque display. Livia watched him through thick lenses, and he saw she had a hand out, gently holding on to Damaetra's fingers.

Maron groaned again, and the smell of dust and decay filled the room. The withered face peered down at Lor through tired yellow slits.

"I'm sorry," he whispered.

Paerli took in heavy breaths as she attempted to recover from Lor's emotions pounding in her body. "We have to... reverse the eneris... flow," she said.

"And how exactly do I do that?"

"Don't be stupid, Lor. Grab on to him...and focus like you always do." She regained her composure, back to the insults.

"Fine," he grumbled, tapping angry yet nervous fingers over the molten flesh of Maron's arm. He locked eyes with the man. "I thought we couldn't reap other Reapers."

"We're not reaping him. We're making him *stop* feeding the breach with his gold."

Lor sighed, taking a closer look at the sticky old liquid gluing the ancient man in place.

"Close your eyes and focus."

"Shut up," Lor spat.

He closed his eyes and saw the colors once again. They lazily listed in his vision, waiting for their instructions.

Fractals of all colors emerged and spun, coming together to form the pulsing aperture. He floated toward the hole, and it swallowed him, taking him into the mind of Valoa'brenga.

What he saw were hundreds of years of flashes, hardly making sense of any of them. The desolate landscape from his seizure popped up, with the same bucket of blood being tossed across it.

The tree loomed, glowing with life. Several tall men and women gathered at the base, talking and laughing with each other, golden eyes twinkling in the first sun piercing the leaves. Children ran through the image, giggling and chasing each other—Anglia and Foscan.

A deep root had been hollowed out, stinking of corruption. A tall man with yellow-gold eyes wrapped his arms around a dark woman swollen with child.

She slapped him, turning away as he wormed through an opening in the tree.

Anglia and Foscan touched fingers, drawn to each other, creating new life with each other, thriving in the wilds together. The tree flared, bursting in a cone of death. Charred corpses scattered the base of the tree. At the base of Gehenna.

Lor felt a tug at his waist as he was pulled from the aperture window. He traveled back to the multi-colored fractals that shattered into gee flies scattering over dark waters. He opened his eyes.

Maron peeled from the wall like a paper doll, falling face-first onto the ashy floor. The juicy scraping and sliding noises made Lor's stomach turn. Old tarnished gold liquid clung to the breach, running in sticky globs to the ground. A gaping maw was behind Maron's "seal," belching the aroma of funk and sulfurous fumes. No light escaped the void. Lor leaped backward, nearly knocking himself over.

"See? That wasn't so hard," Paerli said, brushing off her grimy linen pants and grinning.

Lor whipped out his tech-less shooter, preloaded with lapis evening, and shot her in the neck. She dropped like a stone.

"Let's get out of here," Lor said, running to Damaetra and lifting her into his arms.

"Whatever you stuck her with, she won't stay out long," Livia said, pushing Lor toward the path they came.

They jogged through the umbilicus. Damaetra was such a small thing, weightless in his hold.

"How did you get mixed up with her?" Lor shouted behind at Livia. The chamber shuddered.

Livia took several quick breaths as she ran, clearly not in any shape to be running through an ancient tunnel. "She needed a true Reader," she huffed, "I had no choice... I'm just as captive as her."

Another quake of the wormy tunnel and Lor sprinted back through the umbilicus with Livia following close behind.

Dill zipped through the cave, dodging Crow's toothy projectiles and returning needles filled with verdigris biosore back at him. Several needles missed, striking the ground and squirting green liquid payload into the dirt. He skipped around the trees when the cavern shook, causing him to catch his toe on a rock. The shooter discharged a needle, missing Crow's neck by a hair, and striking the back of Pigeon's hand as she lifted it to block her face.

"Ma!" Crow yelped, running to her.

The poison went to work immediately, opening her skin and turning it black. The woman couldn't scream, as her vocal cords had been destroyed ages ago. She could only wag her tongue in and out of a toothless mouth that now matched her son's.

The biosore crept up her arm, peeling back the flesh, exposing tender muscle and nerves underneath. Arteries snapped, shooting crimson over Crow as he held her and wept. The woman shuddered when her heart gave away.

Crow laid her on the ground gently, then stood, unfurling himself to full height. When he turned back to Dill, his eyes and face were wet and deep red.

"She did nothing to you! I'm going to kill *you both*!" He ripped out the last tooth, fist shaking as he loaded the weapon and aimed for Nico. Out of needles, Nico backed up, re-joined by Dill.

"I'm sorry, I didn't mean to hit her!" Dill shouted.

Nico caught his heel on a stone, falling backwards as his modified legs stiffened at the impact. Instinct caused him to reach out to steady himself, but he grabbed Dill's arm instead. They fell on their backs as the large, grief-stricken man advanced on them with his weapon.

The glowing walls rumbled, letting more sand puff through from the cracks. Lor ran through the umbilicus, cradling Damaetra and trailed by Livia. Damaetra gripped his neck, burying her face in his chest as he called out for Dill and Nico.

Once in the main cavern, he spotted them near a tree deep in the cave on the ground with Crow pointing a different weapon at them. Lor sprinted toward his friends, noticing other trees, mushrooms, and stones with several metal splinters sticking from them.

Nico pulled out a phial, rearing his arm back to throw. "This is for Fowler!" he shouted.

Crow wailed for a moment, then stopped to laugh. "Who?" he asked.

Nico chucked the phial containing Last Grudge and grabbed Dill's sleeve. They crab-walked away from Crow as the phial shattered in front of him. Lor's feet skidded on the ground once he saw the pearly mist rising from the man's feet. He gripped Damaetra close to him and turned to run the other way.

Bursts of artificial wind swirled around Crow. It was a miniature tornado, picking up speed and cavern debris. The man waved his hands around him, deflecting pieces of bark and mushrooms that broke and splattered over his muscled arms. Shimmering wind pulsed back and forth, turning into thin razors that see-sawed across his flesh while reflecting rainbows of color. It was a gorgeous and unfettered chaos. Crow roared, alternating between windmilling his arms and trying to cover his face. Silver splinters lifted from plants and stone, carried with the wind. His body became a pincushion of his own design, as splinters originally thought to be duds activated and sprayed their payloads into his limbs and face.

Crow's primal scream echoed in the cavern. Dill and Nico found their footing, bouncing up and running toward Lor.

"Where's Gale?" Lor shouted over Crow's screams.

"He's got Nico's brother tied up near the entrance," Dill shouted, huffing.

They spun around to watch the wind razor through Crow, as one final scream was silenced in a red mist.

Dill spat on the ground toward the puddle of scarlet running rivers through grass and stone. Fowler's wind slowed to a calm breeze, letting go of everything it held and leaving behind a hazy cloud of colors.

"What's *she* doing here?" Dill pointed at Livia.

The room quaked.

"No time, we've got to get out of here—the Maelstrom is coming." Lor squeezed Damaetra and turned toward the entrance.

"*Loren Benedict Turtingas!*" a voice bellowed from deep in the cavern.

Lor whipped around to see Paerli moving toward them in the cavern's blue glow.

"Nico, please take Damaetra to safety. Meet me at the entrance." Lor placed Damaetra in his friend's arms, kissing her cheek. Nico held her and nudged Dill.

"*Benedict?*" Dill asked, confused.

"Livia, go with them," Lor said.

Paerli shot her arms out to the side as she moved. Her hips swayed as spiraling ribbons of eneris pulsed from blue algae, mushrooms, and grass, splashing up to her palms and raining down to the dirt until thick and black. The force of pulling lifted her from the ground, and she hovered toward the group, darkening the cave behind her.

"Reapers *can* fly!" Dill said in awe.

The cavern shook again.

"Go, now!" Lor shooed them toward the entrance. They disappeared into the blackness, leaving Lor to face his match.

Paerli whipped the black ooze at Lor, missing his head and raining dark acid over twirling vines. Lor tumbled to the side, pulling out his shooter again. His fingers shook as he attempted to load a needle—any needle—into the weapon. She was strutting on the ground again, advancing toward him. Lor didn't know what needle he had, but he rolled to his back and pointed it at her. She threw her head back and laughed. Next to a dark blue dribble from a pinprick in her neck, the black stone in her pendant twinkled, rocking back and forth in the small dip.

I forgot about the pendant!

Paerli glared down at him, curling her upper lip. "You think you're special?" she shouted. "You think after fifteen hundred long years, you won't be exactly like me? You'll find out when your precious Anglia *whore* dies in your arms while you continue to live on and on... forever!"

Paerli raised her arms again to pull more eneris but froze in place with her hands above her head and face twisted into a look of disgust and fear. Tendrils of blackened bark twisted around her torso, gripping her tight. Her face went slack and she dropped her arms to her sides.

Lor lowered his shooter, confused. Behind her, the shadow of a man peered at him from above her shoulder in tired yellow slits.

"Valoa'brenga," Lor choked. The corpse of a man animated, reached up and plucked her pendant from her neck, tossing it to Lor. The tiny gem *piffed* in the grass between his legs, glinting in the blue cavern.

Lor clutched the necklace and glanced up to see Maron yank Paerli back through the darkness.

Lor emerged from the cavern into a chaotic wind swirl of black dust. He fixed the goggles over his eyes.

"About time," Jack said. "Did you get the pendant?"

Lor held up the gold necklace with the black stone dangling from it. It glittered red under the black haze.

"Protect that. Follow me."

"What is it?" Lor asked, stuffing the pendant in his pocket.

"It's leverage."

Leverage?

Jack didn't explain further and turned to jog along the base of the mountain.

Lor followed behind. "Is everyone safe?" he shouted through the wind.

Jack turned his head toward Lor as they ran. "As safe as they can be."

They rounded a corner where everyone waited for them next to a large jumper. Damaetra was standing on her own again, and Lor sprinted to her. When he got to her, he kissed every part of her face—cheeks, forehead, nose. She giggled, and it was the most wonderful music in Lor's ear. He held on to her as she gripped the skin of his back.

"I thought you were dead," she whimpered.

"I came back to life for you." Lor kissed her head and she sobbed into his chest.

Nico wrapped his arms around the two of them, and Dill came in and closed the circle. The four of them stood in their embrace as the wind stirred and churned around them.

Several geysers popped out of the sand beyond the wall.

"We have to get out of here before the storm gets too strong," Jack said, pointing at the jumper.

"Where did this come from?" Gale asked.

"It was Par's. For getting around the desert."

Lor took a deep breath, still holding on to Damaetra. "Dill, do you know how to drive this thing?"

Dill snorted. "Don't be racist. Just because I'm Danashi doesn't mean I know how to drive!"

"Well, what do we do?" Nico crossed his arms.

Damaetra's stained lavender dress flapped in the wind. That loose thread twined and swirled just like in one of Lor's dreams. Her bare feet stood stark white against the black sand as she took small steps toward the jumper. She turned around, her short white hair whipping around the crown of her head. She parted her lips and pointed at the cabin.

"Get in."

CHAPTER 36

Jumper Mach 10
LOREN

THEY CRAMMED THEMSELVES INTO THE cabin as Damaetra sat in the driver's seat, flipping several switches and turning knobs. The engine hummed to life.

"I didn't know you could drive," Lor said.

Damaetra pushed a lever and adjusted one of the mirrors. "Aedras insisted we learn." She turned and smiled at him in the back, bunched up with six others, including newcomer Livia and Hare, who was still bound and snoring.

"Ready?" she said, pulling the jumper away from Gehenna. The front sphere turned, drifting the vehicle to the side, and she directed it toward the gate.

The jumper soundlessly skittered over the sand as Damaetra kept watch on the small radar monitor for the wall. Their world was surrounded by black ash, with little visibility.

Once the image crept up on the screen, she called out to someone to open the gate.

"The jumper can't break through without falling apart," Damaetra said, shifting more levers and flipping a few switches before coming to a stop.

Jack and Livia hopped from the cabin to jog up to the gate. It was deserted of roundsmen who took shelter form the storm. The jumper barely made it through the width of the gate, but Damaetra sped off into the sand once clear.

The Desert Maelstrom picked up speed. Lor had never given it any thought in the past since he lived far out West. Before, it never affected him. Now, here he was in the middle of it with practically everyone who meant anything to him.

"Just head for Guild Central," Lor said. Damaetra obeyed with multiple switches and levers, banking a hard left.

A geyser burst before them, and she skittered the front jumper sphere to the right, drifting to the side and catching the left cabin panel on the down spurt. Grains rained on the overhead sky panel, bringing with it several small stones that plunked down on it. Everyone ducked instinctively, when the final pebble bounced and cracked the material.

Damaetra pulled a lever, shot-gunning the jumper forward. Wind whirled up mustard dust, coating visibility with thick haze and forcing her to rely on radar. Some objects weren't picked up, as buried stones hid themselves from her screen. They bumped and rocked over the secret boulders, just to dodge more cyclones sprouting from the earth.

"I'm going to puke." Dill swayed in his seat, turning a light shade of green.

"Don't you dare," Nico said, putting a hand over his friend's mouth.

One final dodge, and Damaetra drifted left, making a straight course for the tip of Guild Central's border, where Lor and his friends had almost died a few days before. Where Fowler died.

The haze lifted, showing off the colorful tree line and the edge of the storm. Lor glanced behind to see only yellow dust whipping through the air. They were lucky to only have traversed the outskirts of the storm, rather than be caught dead in the center of it.

The jumper slowed through the path in the trees, traveling over the sand strip, then farther down past the farmer's house until finally at the main road.

All of these locations zipping by held new meaning. Life was different. Lor glanced to Gale, who smiled back at him. He held the knot at Hare's arms and legs. Nico's brother looked like a slab of meat waiting to be stuck on a spit.

Damaetra pulled the jumper around the circle fountain. Second sun had risen, coloring everything purple. No one said anything. They slipped from the jumper and stood in the fountain yard. The small one-eyed Foscan sat on the bench, standing to attention when they arrived. It looked like he had been waiting there most of the day—after his duties were done. He ran up to the group and bowed, then nodded toward Reaper's Hall. Rather than follow the rest of the group, Livia turned to go back to the central building.

"Will you be okay?" Lor called after her.

She turned back around to look at the group of friends, smeared in black soot, ragged, and tired. She adjusted her thick glasses and shrugged. "Don't know." Lor watched her disappear toward the central building.

Krik'tha led them through the double doors at Reaper's Hall. The atrium was silent, with their footfalls echoing off the walls. Lor wrapped his fingers through Damaetra's, while Gale had Hare slung across a shoulder, and the strange Yeuni trailed behind. Next to him were the heavily modified Nico and Dill. The rude attendant sat at the desk, buried in his e-disk games. Only, this time he noticed the sound of their footsteps in the atrium.

"Excuse me, you can't..." he croaked, opening and closing his mouth at the sight of the group, coal black and trudging through the pristine hall. Lor glared at him, with a crazed look in his eyes and hair whipped to a frenzy around his head. It was a look that could have gouged out the guy's eyes and fed them to the worms. The attendant bit his tongue and sat back down, looking the other way.

Once inside the apartment, Gale set Hare on the couch, still knocked out and drained from not having his dose of Jack's miracle drug made with people.

Krik'tha left the room, promising to get fresh clothes and food for everyone. Dill crawled over Lor's mattress and curled up in the corner, turning off his eyes. Nico sat by his brother, while Jack opted to brood at the table.

Lor examined Damaetra's face and arms, seeing small cuts and bruises all over her ash-covered porcelain skin. He picked her up again, squeezing her into himself, then carried her into the bathroom and drew her a bath with piles of bubbles. Her delicate white strands were muddied and marred, so he ran the standard issue Reaper Hall shampoo through them. She closed her eyes as he massaged her head and watched streams of soot trickle over her shoulders.

Once her hair was clean, Lor fetched a can of water for her to have while she soaked in a batch of fresh water. He took care to hand-wash her clothes as she did so and trimmed off the loose thread at the hem. All this he did under the bird-shaped techlights reminding him of Fowler.

"Jack, I need some answers," Lor said, coming back into the main area while Damaetra dressed in the bathroom.

The man lifted his goggles, setting them on the table. No one there was interested in turning him in for being what he was. His yellow eyes scanned Lor, with black dust circling his sockets. Jack crossed his spindly fingers over the table.

"What happened in there?" Lor asked.

Jack smacked his lip, then pressed them together, watching Lor. "You helped Par unseal the breach."

"Yes, and?"

"I know that once you performed the act, you became immortal. Like her... and like Maron."

"So you knew who was down there?"

"We only knew what she let us know."

"Are you Valoan then? A worshiper of the breach?"

"Never."

"Then why go along with it?"

"She is all I know."

"I see." Lor bit his lip. The man had been orphaned as a young child and found by a strange, beautiful woman.

Of course he'd follow her.

"So why now? Why leave her now?"

Jack leaned back in the chair, looking the most relaxed Lor had seen him since they met.

"It was time," he said.

"What is the breach?"

Jack looked over at Gale, who shrugged. Jack shook his head. "I don't really know."

Nico stood up and rubbed his mouth. "Hey, guys?" he said. "What are we going to do about him?"

Pointing at Hare, the wild runner lay tied up on the couch, eyes open and sneering.

<h1 style="text-align:center">Epilogue</h1>

Blue light twinkled over damp walls of the vast cavern. Old blood snaked through the grass, congealing into red-brown goop and sprouting new mushrooms. A set of green tinted bones lay blanketed in a cloak nearby with a mostly toothless screaming mouth that grew another large white mushroom from its throat.

The far side of the cavern darkened into pitch, covering once healthy ivy and grass into black tar. Beyond the darkness was the glint of blue leading into a network of tunnels.

A stench of decay rolled in waves from the tunnel, pulsing with wet heat through the cavern. The acrid tendrils curled out through the petrified ivy and into the atmosphere. Carried by the wind, the rot traveled over the gate and into the Span.

"You can't hold me here, Maron!" a voice shouted from deep within. "I demand you let me go!"

"Your children cry out in sadness and pain."

"I don't care. I don't *care!*"

"Yes, you do. The tiniest morsel of your soul cares. You locked that piece away, and now it is in the boy's hands."

"Why, Maron? Why did you do this to me?"

"It is what you have become that is blasphemy. You know what you've done, don't you, wife?"

The noon sun blazed overhead, heating the sand to temperatures daring anyone to walk shoeless over it. Young Danashi children played mech hunt, calling out to each other in code behind rocks, brush, and squat desert palms. New dunes rippled through the fields, carved by the Desert Maelstrom the week before.

The train rushed overhead, whomping its breeze over the campsite, sending ration wrappers blowing through the terrain and forcing yellowed sand over clothes in the middle of a beam dry. A young, single mother cursed and pulled a shirt down to flap away rogue grains, leaving ochre smudges across the white linen tunic.

"Gehenna..." she muttered, licking a thumb and attempting to wipe them away. After failing, she flopped the shirt back into the basket for another wash.

"You kids don't get off too far!" she shouted toward the children playing hunt. The young girl with braided buns and hazel eyes belonged to her, but the others were orphans who hung around the track camp. She felt protective of them all and called them her own. "Did you hear me, Ayala?" the woman's voice called on the wind.

"Yes, Mommy!" the girl shouted back. She gave herself away from behind a tall patch of brush, making all the kids rush her spot, screaming and laughing.

She squealed and giggled as she ran while they chased her through the dunes.

The boy known as Zane caught up to her and tagged her shoulder. She screamed and spun around, falling in the sand. "Owie!" She shot back up, brushing the sand from her dress. "The sand's hot! I burned my booty!" She giggled.

"I got you, Ayala, now you're the mech!"

"No fair!" Ayala stuck out her lower lip and blew a raspberry.

Zane chuckled as the others caught up, circling around and gasping for breath.

While the children laughed and argued over how fair or unfair Ayala's capture was, the aroma of bitter sulfur crawled through the group.

"Ew, Zane, did you fart?" A boy called Quint held his nose and glared at Zane.

"Zane farted! Zane farted!" the children cheered.

"I did *not*!"

Ayala giggled and pushed his shoulder. "Everybody farts."

"You know what I think?" Zane started to say, but the words caught in his throat.

"*What* do you think?" Ayala said, flicking at her dress again.

The boy stiffened and fell over, twitching in the hot sand.

"Zane?" A girl with short black hair and blue eyes knelt down and poked him.

Zane continued to twitch, loosing a groan and dribbles of foam from his mouth.

"Mommy! Mommy!" Ayala screamed. "Come quick! Mommy!"

The young mother dropped her laundry into the sand, running toward the children. Another train raced overhead, blowing waves of sand into her mouth and nose. When she got to the boy, he was rigid, all muscles tensed and jaw clenched, with a drop of blood pooling at the corner of his eye.

"Back up now!" she yelled to the children. "Zane, baby, can you hear me?"

A jittered moan came from his throat as he shook. She cradled his neck, and his eyes rolled back.

"Zane, Zane, please try to calm down," she pleaded with the boy.

As he lay shaking in the hot sand, his dark skin blackened and cracked into channels of lava. The children screamed and scattered. Mother recoiled at the heat of his skin and crawled away when he burst into flames. He flapped on the ground, screaming fiery curls from his throat. She stared, mouth open and helplessly watching the boy scream as he turned to ash.

SEVEN CITIES UNION

BREAKING NEWS

Princeps Renae, Audun, 7C

The capital, and Princeps Renae have issued new decrees in response to the alarming increase in the use of unwarranted materials...

Continued on page 6

Strange reports have surfaced out of the desert zone known as The Span. Citizens of Kanckette are concerned over growing incidents of deaths caused by the sudden onset of a Weggevens malady.

If you or a loved one suspects you have fallen ill with such a disease, please dial 01-7C-0077 for your local medic to receive emergency care.

Once recovered, make sure to register your affliction with Audun within 30 standard hours (one day) or risk increasing fines for each day unregistered.

Thank you for your cooperation.

Author's Ramblings

THE WORLD OF NORTHERN ROSEAARDE came out of a nightmare I had a long time ago... probably sometime in the early 2000s, I can't really remember. In the dream journal in which I wrote up the thing, I'm sure there's a date in there, but time, and about a dozen moves have most likely lost that journal to the depths of a mouse-dropping infested cardboard box. Or, it may be in my parent's basement. I have no clue where that might be.

Anyway, in the dream, there was a man being held to a wall and he was in distress, moaning low and eerie. In the haze of waking where the dream is still a fog in the front of my mind, but quickly fading like cigarette smoke sucking into a ventilator, I scribbled a bunch of nonsense about what I saw. However, it was the image itself that was most captivating and macabre, so I drew him. I drew the macabre man tacked to the wall in a mess of gore and jelly because why wouldn't I? I'm a twisted little bean after all.

And then Maron was conceived. Except his name was Maeron. And he was an elf or something. What do I know, I was like... 17 when I dreamed about him.

I wrote some preliminary chapters to get a feel for this world forming in my art major mind with Maeron the immortal elf guy who has magic and stuff, and I remember showing some of that work to a boyfriend at the time. Very vividly I remember this: he scoffed at me. He told me I couldn't just make up words like that (it was the beginnings of the "nudge" implant—I named it something weird like siek or something. I was a weird kid). Well, I don't know about that boyfriend, but I'd be habbity if I didn't scumboo that bish (see that? I made up some words. And don't tell me you don't know what it means).

Here's where I say that I wasn't deterred, and I forged ahead with sheer will and gumption.

Except...

I *was* deterred, and felt stupid for even thinking about creating this world.

I put it aside for the time being, but I thought it about it a lot. I dreamed about it. I wrote a language for it. Over the next twenty years, I shaped this world, coming up with characters and abilities, and a few other things that either made it, or didn't make it into the final story. I sketched maps, created family trees... I was in over my head. As I stopped to actually write some random chapters of scenes in my head, I realized that I wasn't quite satisfied with certain aspects of the world itself, as well as my writing in general. I had a lot of polishing to do. I continued to write chapters in fits and stops, only to re-read them and cringe.

By the time I hit my 40s, and after publishing Metaxysm, I revisited this world. I thumbed through the pages of random world building I did years ago that I kept in a 3-inch 3-ring binder, seeing all the family trees, preliminary map, and the center of the whole story: the forbidden zone. I didn't have a name for the black sands, just that I knew it was forbidden and it was black.

I liked the concept of a forbidden zone, so after thoroughly raking my previous work over the coals, I ditched the language (wrote a different one), made everyone human versions of different races, kept the map, ditched the family tree, and renamed everyone except one person—Paerli. Except in my old version, she was the love interest. And she had coily blonde hair. I kept all the abilities and refined them, but de-Mary-Sue'd them.

Then I thought about Maron and his imprisonment for the supposed treachery he committed from when I first created him.

Then I thought about him a little more... what if he wasn't imprisoned there for some evil he did, but he was there to hold back some unknown evil? And from there, Maron as the last Igni survivor became a concept that bloomed.

I kept about 10% of what I originally created and tossed the rest, while teaching myself Scrivener, Autocrit, Atticus, Photoshop, Canva, and InDesign.

Oh, and Damaetra? I came up with her a week before my manuscript was due to the editor. How's that for eleventh-hour writing?

Special Thanks

So THIS IS THE PART where I thank everyone involved in my writing endeavor. It's easy to extend a thanks to someone, but the reality is, books aren't possible without the efforts of everyone in an author's bubble. I'm not just talking about the technical aspects of editing or design, but the people that have sat around and listened to me when I was at my lowest, those who read the book with a critical eye, and those who showed up for me regardless.

First, my husband. While he doesn't read hardly anything I write (I think he's read one short story), he's been one of the greatest cheerleaders when I wanted to give up, allowed me to pursue self publishing despite the financial burden, and continued to just be the person I cleaved to when we took those vows.

Second, my family. I've been blessed to have a close relationship with extended family, and my two nieces, Cailey and Lana have been amazing to talk to about the story and bounce ideas off their different view points. My mom and sister, who've always shown their support and have been integral in just listening to me, have taken time out of their schedules to have in-depth conversations about the more sensitive parts of the story.

Third, my beta readers, Mark and Holyoak (stage names, of course), who have been nothing short of amazing when it comes to the male perspective of what some women would call a young adult novel.

A general thanks for my excellent editor, Sara Kelly, who has now edited 4 of my novels! I also want to send a shout out to those who created an advanced review through Netgalley for Reaper's Gamble (the original title of this book).

Initial reviews of Reaper's Gamble reached an astounding 4.55 out of 5, and I'm so thankful for those readers! So why did I change the title? Well, my original thinking for the title, is that by now you know, Loren is a Reaper. He had a stupid little bet with Paerli when they met that came to fruition at the end with him helping her pull Maron down. So, it made sense to me at the time.

HOWEVER, also at the time, I really didn't have much in-depth knowledge of contemporary fantasy (being more connected to older fantasy), and didn't realize that there was a book out there already called *Reaper's Gale*, which is part of the Malazan series. If you're not aware, Malazan is huge in fantasy circles. When a different friend kept referring to my book as Reaper's Gale, I was so confused, and thought I'd look into it. Alas, there it was... and to top off the coincidental cake with the ironic cherry, I have a character named Gale. What are the odds?

The good news is, I'm much happier with the new title. I got a lot of feedback from some friends in Discord that *Nefarious Gift* is a lot more suitable for the dark, yet light-hearted story that I was trying to tell. It also really illustrates the consequences of having such an ability in a world like Roseaarde, while not just focusing on the main character, Loren, but all of the characters as a whole.

If you've been around for a while, you'll know that I had a completely different cover before. The previous cover is actually a re-stylized version of a commissioned work that I paid for 2 years ago where the artist flaked on me. It's re-stylized because they flaked in the middle of creating the book 2 cover, and I had no idea what to do. Either way, this cover is nice, but there has been feedback that it doesn't encapsulate the correct essence of the story. In their words, they thought it was a woman making a deal with the devil.

Anyway, this story has gone on a journey. I've improved some of the prose in this version (not a ton, don't get too excited), went through 2 editions, and completely changed its exterior for what I hope is a much better fit into the type of reader base that this series can find a home in.

Thank you for making it this far, and I want to cap this section to highlight my appreciation for YOU. Without your support, Loren and Damaetra would be living at the bottom of a void without a voice.

Thanks for reading!

If you liked this book, please consider writing a review! Reviews help indie authors like myself continue to grow and create more awesome stories for you!

www.ingramcontent.com/pod-product-compliance
Lightning Source LLC
Chambersburg PA
CBHW020141170726
47995CB00003BA/662